A CHRISTMAS KISS

Rachel couldn't prevent a surge of sheer joy as she finally gave herself permission to bring her hands to Reno's shoulders. Heat touched her as she trailed her fingertips over his naked chest. Wow. He felt even better than he looked.

The intense butterflies in her stomach didn't mean anything. She didn't have to be scared of this at all. Because this was really just quasi-vacation sex, Rachel assured herself—enjoyed beneath the multicolored glow of several strands of Christmas lights and sweetened with a little extra affection, sure, but straightforward vacation sex all the same. Everyone liked vacation sex. It was better than ordinary sex any day.

Which didn't fully explain why, when she cradled Reno's face in her hands and brought his mouth to hers, it seemed as if she'd waited years for them to come together . . . years to feel this way. So free and complete and perfect all at once.

But that was probably just leftover sentimentality, Rachel reasoned as she gazed in wonder at his face. A remnant of the holiday season. It didn't have to mean anything that she'd already confessed her love for him. In public. From a tabletop.

Even if—to her—it secretly did. . . .

Books by Lisa Plumley

Making Over Mike

Falling for April

Reconsidering Riley

Perfect Together

Perfect Switch

Josie Day Is Coming Home

Once Upon a Christmas

Mad About Max

Let's Misbehave

Home for the Holidays

Santa Baby
(anthology with Lisa Jackson,
Elaine Coffman, and Kylie Adams)

Published by Zebra Books

Home for the Holidays

Lisa Plumley

ZEBRA BOOKS
Kensington Publishing Corp.

www.kensingtonbooks.com

ZEBRA BOOKS are published by

Kensington Publishing Corp.
850 Third Avenue
New York, NY 10022

All Kensington titles, imprints, and distributed lines are available at special quantity discounts for bulk purchases for sales
promotion, premiums, fund-raising, educational, or institu-
tional use.

Special book excerpts or customized printings can also be created to fit specific needs. For details, write or phone the office
of the Kensington Special Sales Manager, Attn: Special Sales
Department, Kensington Publishing Corp., 850 Third Avenue,
New York, NY 10022. Phone: 1-800-221-2647.

Zebra and the Z logo Reg. U.S. Pat. & TM Off.

ISBN-13: 978-0-8217-8053-4
ISBN-10: 0-8217-8053-0

First Printing: October 2008

10 9 8 7 6 5 4 3 2 1

Printed in the United States of America

For John, with all my love.

Chapter One

The thing about her life, Rachel Porter realized as she scrambled out of her Malibu beach house with an armload of accessories, a collapsible rolling wardrobe rack, and a mouthful of chalky "French vanilla" protein bar at the unholy hour of 9:30 A.M. on a Saturday, was that it never stopped. Never. Ever.

Take now for instance. Most ordinary people would have been lolling in bed. Or making brunch plans. Or maybe—if they were really ultraambitious—hitting a local coffeehouse for a latte and a copy of the *Times*. But was she doing any of that? No.

Because she hadn't gotten to the top of her game by lolling, brunching, or reading the newspaper, Rachel reminded herself as she took a swig of Dayquil from the bottle she'd carried outside. She'd gotten there by busting her butt for her "team" (aka, her clients), and she wasn't about to stop now. Not even on a perfectly clear December day like today, when the sky soared overhead in pure Tiffany blue, and the sun sparkled off the Pacific, and even the seagulls sounded kind of nice.

Wintertime in L.A. You had to love it.

But if she didn't get a move on, she was going to lose it. A girl like her lived on borrowed time. In a borrowed house. With a borrowed car parked outside. Technically speaking, most of what she called her own was either on loan from a client or courtesy of a celebrity party goody bag. In fact, her whole life was kind of a loaner. Hers for now. But the way things looked, *now* was going to last a good, long, fantastic time.

After all, she loved her clients as much as they loved her. She made them look fabulous, and they made her look happy. Er, *successful*. There was no reason to believe their lovey-dovey relationship wouldn't continue. Besides, she'd earned all those freebies (in a way). Perks were part of the celebrity stylist package. She'd have been an idiot to turn them down (although, naïvely, she had at first). She might have been a Midwestern girl once, but she was a bona fide California girl now.

Clattering down the drive in her chicest sandals (to the dinging accompaniment of an incoming text message and her spare cell phone's ringtone), Rachel deftly rearranged two handbags and a tangle of silk scarves. She snared the wardrobe rack with her foot, then steered it toward her Tesla Roadster. The wheelie rack sailed to a tidy stop near the passenger side door, allowing her plenty of time to swallow her first bite of protein bar, glance at the text, then answer cell phone numero dos.

It was Jenn, her new assistant. Thank God. She was already on the job. It hadn't been easy to find Jenn—fourteen interviews later—but Rachel desperately needed the help. Ever since styling the cast of *Rendezvous* for the Emmys, she'd had more work than she could handle. It hadn't been easy to turn over the reins (even a few of them) to someone new, but Jenn's stellar résumé and outstanding references had helped make the process easier.

It was only smart, Rachel figured, to get solid verification before committing fully to anything. Or anyone.

"Hi, it's Jenn. I have Tiana on the line for you."

"No! I can't talk to Tiana right now." Rachel felt sure she'd made that clear to Jenn already. She propped the phone on her shoulder, added the scarves and accessories to the pile already on the convertible's passenger seat, then started folding up the wheelie rack. Stuffily and a little hoarsely, Rachel said, "Just tell her I'll call her later, okay? Because—"

"Oh, good. Here she is!" Jenn announced cheerfully.

Silence. Then a faint click. Damn it. Jenn had weaseled already! She'd sold her out. The sounds of surf came over the line, followed by the clink of cutlery and a strident voice.

"Rachel! I've been trying to reach you since Tuesday."

Uh-oh. Tiana Zane—with Alayna Panagakos and Melina Carras—was one-third of the superstar girl group, Goddess. Or at least she had been. When Alayna had gotten "discovered" by the film industry, she'd all but ditched the group to become the latest Hollywood "It" girl. Rachel respected Alayna's ambition—and was grateful that Alayna had brought her along for the ride—but her break with Goddess had left two very problematic side effects.

Namely, Melina and Tiana.

"I know, Tiana." Another shove brought the collapsible rack into the car, clothes and all. Rachel studied it, then redraped a few items. "I'm sorry. I've been absolutely swamped."

"Swamped working with Alayna?"

Guiltily, Rachel froze. She glanced at her brand-new car, a gift from . . . well, guess who? It was all electric, went zero to sixty in four seconds, and was rumored to cost over one hundred thousand dollars. There was a waiting list to get a Tesla Roadster, even for celebrities, but Alayna had had enough clout to snag two of them. Rachel's lit up her driveway in electric blue. Most people opted for fusion red, but not Alayna.

"Too midlife crisis," she'd said in dismissal. "Too predictable. We're anything but predictable, right, Rach?"

Shaking off the memory, Rachel wrenched open her door and got in. Ah. Luxury. "You know I do everything I can for my clients, Tiana. Did you get the dress I sent over?"

"That's why I'm calling. I'm not wearing this."

"It's from a new designer. A very talented man named—"

"It looks like gold Saran Wrap! You're kidding right?"

Inhale. Exhale. Neither was easy, given the head cold Rachel was currently battling. "Of course not. Loo is having a *Barbarella* moment right now, that's all. That dress is very inspired." Rachel had all but promised the designer that she'd get one of his creations on the red carpet. "It's avant-garde."

"It's tacky, and I hate it."

"Okay." Stealthily, Rachel slipped the key in the ignition. The car started in absolute silence. Thank you, electric engine! "I'll pull a few more things for you. You'll love them."

Tiana breathed a sigh of relief. "Yes. *Please*."

"No problem." Glancing over her shoulder, Rachel hovered at the edge of the PCH, waiting for a break in traffic. Who needed coffee, when L.A. rush hour could pump up your adrenaline instead? "I'll just have Jenn drop by to pick it up early. They're not doing the *Vogue* shoot with it until next week, but—"

"Wait a minute. This dress is going to be in *Vogue*?"

"Mmmm." Blithely, Rachel swallowed another bite of protein bar. She pushed up her sunglasses. "That's what I've heard."

A long silence. Then, "Maybe I'll try it on again."

"Are you sure? I've got a few other things here . . ."

"I'm sure. Actually, I mostly called to say thanks. For still being there for me. A lot of people in this town pretty much quit returning my calls, but you . . . Well, I appreciate it."

Ugh. Feeling twice as bad for trying to ditch Tiana's phone call earlier, Rachel let a perfectly good opening in traffic pass her by. She stared blindly at the Mercedes and Priuses whooshing past, her lungs filled with exhaust and sea air. Her other cell phone rang. Six text messages had come in, too.

"You're welcome. Anytime, Tiana. Gotta run."

She hung up and swerved into traffic. Because after all, sentimentality was a luxury she couldn't afford. She ran a serious business—in a very cutthroat town—and that was that.

Two and a half minutes later, Rachel pulled her carload of stuff into the busy driveway of the beach house next door—a house much bigger and more lavish than her own.

She sighed. Her commute wasn't bad, but the on-call hours were killers.

Time to go to work for real.

Alayna's house overflowed with people, from the gardeners laboring over the grass and flowering bougainvillea to the cleaners, caterers, and delivery personnel coming and going across the imported Italian stone floors. With her cell phone to her ear (and her other phone bleeping for attention in her tote bag), Rachel studied the scene as she popped her first Pepcid of the day. Chasing the antacid with a cough drop, she dodged a florist's van and two window cleaners, then briskly made her way up the steps and through the open front door.

As always, the interior of the place took her breath away. Starkly modern in design, it boasted an unmatched view of the ocean, expansive spaces, luxe furnishings, and a media room with an A/V system to rival any professional theater. The house also featured a chef-grade kitchen (Alayna used it to microwave Lean Pockets and store Diet Dr Pepper), a personal tan-by-mist salon, and two entire rooms that served as walk-in closets—one for shoes and accessories; one for clothing and jewelry.

Everywhere Rachel looked, things were expensively and expertly decorated. Although less than a month remained until Christmas, there was no sign of the holiday here.

There wouldn't be either—not until after Alayna's birthday today. The pop star refused to acknowledge anything mistletoe-and-holly related until *after* her big day. But with Christmas crowding into stores earlier every year, fulfilling Alayna's request to keep everything seasonal out of sight until . . . well, tomorrow—when she'd expect her home to be transformed into a winter wonderland—proved trickier for Rachel all the time.

In the end, she'd enacted her own Christmas boycott, just to keep herself on the straight and narrow. From Thanksgiving through early December, Rachel simply pretended the holidays didn't exist. She didn't wrap gifts, she didn't play her guilty-pleasure 'N Sync Christmas CD, and she absolutely didn't wander around with any delicious peppermint mochas in hand.

"Excuse us," someone said.

She turned. Two uniformed workers glided past her with a floral arrangement between them. It looked big enough to serve as a centerpiece at an Oscars after party. In a life this grand, the flowers simply had to keep up—and so did Rachel.

Rearranging the evening bags she'd brought, she charged past the foyer. Forty gazillion steps later (the house was just that big), she stopped to chat with Alayna's party planner, then with the charming French caterer, Henri. He insisted she try a bite of his *petite gateau*; it tasted orgasmic.

He winked. "I'll save a plate for you at the party."

"Thanks. I *never* get a chance to eat anything."

"You and me, too, *chérie*."

As though on cue, cell phone numero uno rang. With a smile and a wave to Henri, Rachel answered it. She talked Jenn through some paperwork and the day's call list as she navigated past a jumble of charity invitations, an array of busy decorators, and an extravagant pile of gifts. They'd been arriving for weeks, Rachel knew, from friends and fans and hangers-on alike.

She passed through the great room, looking for her client as she gave yeses or noes for Jenn to relay to the various designers, celebrities, and sponsors who wanted to meet with her. Alayna was nowhere in sight, but a nearly life-size rendition of the Acropolis—done in sweet red velvet cake and buttercream—stood in a place of prominence in the dining room.

Yum. People outside the industry probably wouldn't have understood making such a fuss over someone's birthday. After all, they'd have said, despite her Grammy and her acting roles and her number-one CDs, Alayna was just another girl, right?

But that wasn't right. Not at all. Alayna was special, and Rachel had dedicated three years of her life to making sure the whole world noticed that. Besides, it wasn't every day that a superstar turned twenty-five. Rachel had powered past that milestone herself just five years ago. Sadly, *she* hadn't had an enormous artisanal cake and a truckload of gifts to show for it.

In fact, if she remembered correctly, her twenty-fifth birthday had passed by mostly unnoticed, lost in a whirlwind of preparation for one of her clients' big events. Succeeding in her business required that kind of focus though. If Rachel didn't stay on her toes, another stylist would step in and steal the spotlight—along with her "team"—and then where would she be?

Off the A-list and out of a job, that's where.

Probably if she'd been with Tyson on her birthday, things would have been different, Rachel mused as she paused to check her bleary-eyed, red-nosed reflection in the mirror at the bottom of the staircase. Her new boyfriend was thoughtful. Loving. Fun. And drop-dead sexy, too. Tyson would have made sure she had a birthday to remember. He was just that kind of guy.

Which was why she hadn't mentioned that she had to work this morning. Why put the kibosh on their entire weekend?

Instead, Rachel had left just moments after Tyson had gone for his usual A.M. run on the beach. If she were lucky, she could finish early with Alayna, then sneak back home before Tyson even realized she'd gone. Before she knew it, she'd be kicking off her weekend the right way—with a steamy shower, a bunch of frothy, squeaky-clean bubbles, and a whole lot of hot, naked man—*her man*—to share them with.

Newly determined, Rachel hung up her phone, ignoring the ring of numero dos. She ascended the stairs as quickly as she could, rising above the commotion in the rest of the house and stopping twice to blow her nose. She probably should have brought in her Dayquil for another dose.

At the landing, she spotted Alayna's housekeeper trotting out of a nearby bathroom with an armful of towels.

"Carol! Hang on a sec."

The woman paused, then shook her head as she watched Rachel stuff tissues and cough drops in the pocket of her jeans.

"You don't look so good. Another cold?"

"Just a little one. It's almost gone." Shrugging, Rachel rummaged around in her tote bag—huge, handy, and Hermès. She found what she was looking for. Triumphantly, she pulled it out. "Here. For you."

Carol's eyes widened. "Is that a bottle of Femme Fatale?"

"The genuine article. You said you wanted to try it."

"Try it? I've been sneaking test strips out of Alayna's magazines for months now!" Carol hugged the bottle to her uniformed chest. "But it's not even in stores yet, is it?"

Rachel winked. "I've got connections."

She also had two good eyes. She'd seen Carol rapturously sniffing one of those strips instead of dusting a few weeks ago.

The housekeeper shook her head. "This is too much." She held the bottle at arm's length. "I can't keep this."

"Of course you can. You deserve it."

Carol eyed the bottle dubiously. "I can't pay you back."

"You're not supposed to! It's a gift."

"No." Eyes closed, Carol shoved it away. "Thank you."

Rachel exhaled. She'd hoped it wouldn't come to this. "It's a freebie. From a goody bag," she lied. "I got two."

"Oh." With a wide grin, Carol opened her eyes. "Hurray!"

"Don't use it all at once," Rachel warned with a faux-admonishing finger wag. "I've heard it's irresistible."

They laughed. After a few minutes of chitchat, Rachel headed for her client's apartment-size bedroom suite at the end of the expansive hall. She liked Carol—and most of the other employees she met on the job—but business was business.

She lowered her voice. "Alayna?"

No reply. Like Rachel, the pop star typically wasn't out of bed much before noon. But today, with so much going on for her birthday, Alayna had asked Rachel to be there early—to oversee the work of her hairstylist and makeup artist and to bring alternate evening bags to go with whichever dress (of four) she ultimately chose to wear to her party tonight.

As backup, Rachel had three more gowns on the rack in her car, along with the selection she'd brought for other clients she'd be seeing today. Over the years, she'd learned to expect the unexpected from her biggest client . . . like not being anywhere near ready at the time they'd agreed to meet today.

"Alayna? We've got to get busy—"

Putting on her most no-nonsense expression, Rachel nudged the door open, then entered Alayna's sitting room. She strode past a profusion of happy-birthday floral arrangements, a sleek settee, and a side table piled with well-thumbed tabloids.

Seeing them, Rachel shook her head. Alayna kept obsessive watch on her appearances in the media—a mistake, in Rachel's opinion. Stars might live and die by their press, but that was no reason to drive yourself crazy tracking every up, down, and makeup-free, poorly focused, paparazzi horror shot.

"Everyone's scheduled to be here at ten, so you'd better—"

Alayna was in bed, but she wasn't asleep.

"—Get a move on."

And she wasn't alone either.

Rachel glanced up from her watch, still hugging her armful of evening bags, and was confronted with the sight of a rumpled bed, a tangle of arms and legs, and a set of unmistakably hard-pumping naked male buttocks. During the millisecond that Rachel stood there, Alayna wrapped her lithe, famous arms around her partner and urged him on with both hands clamped on his rear.

"Yes, yes!" she cried in her unmistakably accented voice.

Oh, for Pete's sake. Not again.

Torn, Rachel hesitated. This wasn't the first occasion she'd stumbled upon Alayna in a private moment, but it was the most time-sensitive. And the most inconvenient. Uncharacteristically indecisive, she glanced at the tableau again, trying to gauge how much longer the twosome might be.

Hmmm. If she stayed much longer, her retinas might be permanently scarred. Also, lingering even this long was a pretty major (if accidental) invasion of privacy. On the other hand, if she bolted, Rachel knew, Alayna might be late for her own birthday party. Failure to prepare a client properly for an important (i.e., photographed) event was grounds for dismissal.

Losing her biggest client would be disastrous.

Making up her mind, Rachel averted her eyes. As quietly as she could, she headed back to the sitting room. She'd put the evening bags there, then zip down to the car for the other gowns she'd brought. By the time she hauled them upstairs, more than likely this *ménage à deux* would be complete, and she could get on with her day. She still had other clients to see, several shops and designers to visit, a lunch at The Ivy. . . .

Just as she reached the doorway, a huge masculine groan ripped through the air. *No. No. Tiptoe faster. Faster!*

"Yeah, oh yeah. You like that, don't you, Pookie?"

Instantly, Rachel froze. She craned her neck around.

She knew that butt! And, she realized all at once, she knew the man who went with it, too. She whirled around. *"Tyson?"*

Chapter Two

Honestly, she hadn't meant to blurt it aloud. But there was something about the shock of seeing your own boyfriend in bed with your biggest client that erased all the usual boundaries.

"Rachel!" With a gasp, Alayna wriggled partially sideways. She clawed up several yards of über-thread count Egyptian cotton, making it billow around her and an oblivious Tyson.

"Oh yeah, baby. Rachel, Rachel!" he mimicked in his deep voice, unaware of what had happened. "Whatever does it for you." He paused and looked down at her. "I always thought the two of you probably had a thing going on the side. That's hot."

Alayna smacked him. "No, you idiot. *Rachel*!"

"Yeah, yeah." Head back, Tyson kept pumping. "Oh *yeah*."

For the first time, Rachel realized exactly how dumb her boyfriend really was. Self-centered, too. Clearly, Alayna was no longer into the main event, but Tyson hadn't noticed. Suddenly, all those nights that Rachel had lain awake, frustrated beyond belief but thinking it was *her* fault, made a lot more sense.

She really should have seen this coming. She should have recognized Tyson sooner, too. But in her own defense, she had never actually witnessed him in action from this angle before.

With her gaze wide, Alayna pointed. "Rachel is *here*."

She squirmed harder, then tried to shove Tyson sideways.

"Ooh, you're a wild one, Pookie." He chuckled, sounding a little breathless. "Why don't you—" Abruptly, he broke off.

Guided by Alayna's pointing finger, Tyson glanced over his shoulder. He saw Rachel standing there. His eyes widened.

For a few heartbeats, everything stopped except Tyson. To her horror, Rachel watched as he gave another enormous groan of pleasure—one she recognized—then ground to a halt. A giddy grin slid onto his handsome face. Exhaling, he slumped atop Alayna.

Rachel could not believe it. She'd caught her own boyfriend doing the horizontal mambo with her most important client, and he hadn't even had the courtesy to skip the grand finale!

Impatiently, Alayna shoved him off her.

Tyson plopped on the pillow beside her, then shook his head. "You two planned this, didn't you?" he asked hoarsely, glancing between them. He held his thumb aloft. "Awesome."

Incredulous and unable to move, Rachel stared at Alayna across the length of that deluxe, treacherously outfitted bed. Her mind spun with questions, with decisions that needed to be made *right now* (because what she did *right now* would determine her life and career for the foreseeable future), but most of all, she couldn't help hearing, over and over again . . .

Pookie. Pookie. Pookie.

That was Tyson's pet name for *her*. The name he called her whenever he felt especially affectionate. The name he called her when he stroked her hair and listened to her career problems. The name he used when he promised they were made for each other.

"Rachel." Alayna spread her arms wide, palms facing. "This didn't mean a thing. It just happened. We didn't plan it. We're so, so sorry. Please, if you'll just forgive us—"

Nope. Sadly, that wasn't what the pop star actually said. That was what Rachel, in her distraught and disbelieving state, imagined she would say.

In reality, Alayna merely slid out of bed—naked, perfect, and utterly confident—then sauntered to the adjoining bathroom. She swished with some mouthwash, peed, then emerged.

"I'm so glad this is finally out in the open." With a yawn and a languorous movement, Alayna tied a silk robe around her waist. "This was inevitable, you know, Rach. Both of us living next door to each other. Tyson dropping by to visit . . ."

Incredulously, Rachel glanced at her boyfriend.

Her *former* boyfriend. He'd been dropping by to visit?

"We're both incredibly sexy people, Tyson and me." Alayna sat on the edge of the mattress, then gave Tyson a teasing squeeze on the biceps. "It was only a matter of time."

For an instant, watching them cuddle (and nearly get caught up in a kiss), all Rachel could feel was hurt. The long-suppressed, non-Hollywood, Midwestern girl inside her couldn't help it. Why, *why*? she wailed. Why were they being so *mean*?

Thankfully, she got a grip on herself. "What about me?"

"I've already thought about that." Alayna glanced up, a red carpet-worthy smile on her face. "I've got the perfect idea."

"I can't wait to hear it." Ooh, sarcasm now, too. That was better. More like herself. Rachel crossed her arms, waiting.

"Can you outfit Tyson with something for the party, too?"

Rachel frowned. She had to be hearing things.

But they both stared at her expectantly. Seriously.

"You want me to style Tyson?"

Alayna nodded. "Absolutely. Something to match me."

Briefly, Rachel entertained the idea of beating them both silly with her armload of evening bags. One was a Judith Leiber crystal-embedded clutch. It would probably make a dent in their stupid selfish heads. But she was a professional, she reminded herself. She could handle this.

Besides, she didn't have time for a personal life anyway, Rachel decided as her cell phone rang again. She was always too busy. And she'd been styling Alayna's steady dates for years. There was no other way to maintain a cohesive image.

She didn't want Alayna to go all Britney and K-Fed on her, did she?

"All right." Rachel faced them both, hoping to make it clear by her tone and her demeanor that she wasn't heartbroken by this. She refused to be. Besides, now this was business. "But you're paying the same rate as any other client."

Tyson gawked at her. "I don't want you to dress me!"

Alayna shushed him. "Of course you do, Pookie."

Ugh. There it was again. Rachel nearly lost her resolve.

"I want you to break up with me." Naked from the waist up, Tyson roused himself enough to sit up against the headboard. "Do you know how long I've been coming over here?"

"Shhh, Pookie. Let's not rub it in, okay?"

"Three months! And you never even noticed. Because all you ever do is work. You don't have time for real life. You don't have time for me!" Looking disgusted, he scanned her up and down, his gaze resting on her evening bags. "You're pathetic."

Rachel couldn't help but flinch. To her amazement though, she managed to hold her ground. She lifted her chin.

Then she raised her brow. "You'll be sorry," she said.

From the bed, Alayna and Tyson stared at her—probably envisioning her creating some kind of horrible, scandalous scene. Dimly, Rachel registered the hubbub still going on downstairs as the party planning, decorating, and cleaning crews labored to create the birthday of Alayna's dreams.

Rachel *could* create a scene if she wanted to—a scene that would filter into all the tabloids and press and expose Alayna for the man-stealing traitor she really was. It wouldn't be difficult. There were always spies among the service staff.

But all at once, Rachel had a better idea.

A more delicious, more public, more vengeful idea.

"Because I'm the best stylist in the business," she informed them both blithely. "I could make you look fabulous, Tyson. But . . . whatever. You can stick with your prefab, cookie-cutter, discount Abercrombie & Fitch style if you want to."

Alayna gasped. "You told me that was vintage Ralph Lauren!"

Caught, Tyson shrugged.

"In the meantime, Alayna, I've got some fantastic new dress options for you." Mentally, Rachel inventoried the selection in her car. None of those would do. Not for *this* special occasion. "I'll be back this afternoon to show you all five of them."

"Oh goody!" Alayna clapped. "I can't wait!"

Rachel only smiled. She'd just *bet* she couldn't. . . .

Chapter Three

By the time he found himself sidestepping his dad's dirty socks and underwear on the way to the coffeemaker in the morning, Reno Wright had had enough. There was only so much a grown man could be expected to take—and realizing that his own father had begun living like a teenager was the last straw.

Freshly showered and barefoot, dressed in a pair of low-slung jeans and his usual T-shirt, Reno dragged on a flannel shirt as he stared at his slumbering, pajama-clad father.

The sofa was too small for such a big man. Sleeping while clutching its cushions for dear life—even in his dreams—made Tom Wright seem unusually vulnerable somehow.

But "beggars can't be choosers," as his dad had said with a chuckle when he'd arrived on Reno's snowy doorstep a week and a half ago. And sons couldn't be the ones to refuse a safe winter harbor to their fathers. All of which explained why Reno had allowed his dad to crash on his sofa in the first place.

He glanced around, assessing the damage wrought by that decision with the same speed and certainty he'd once used to evaluate field conditions, wind speed, and potential kick rush as a kicker in the NFL. What he saw didn't encourage him.

Among the holiday decorations and the space Reno had

cleared for a Christmas tree, reading material littered the living room. Not his dad's usual fare—the *Kismet Comet* newspaper or even the Sunday *Free Press*—but a collection of *Men's Health* and soft-core girlie magazines. The kind that didn't boast about their centerfolds, but featured half-naked B-list starlets on the covers instead (this month wearing saucy Santa outfits), cavorting provocatively amid stories about imported beer, fast cars, and the latest video games. And speaking of video games . . .

Reno nudged aside football and flight simulator games, plus a system controller, shaking his head. His technophobic dad could barely manage Reno's complex A/V setup with its hoard of remotes and multitude of inputs and outputs connected to a big-screen HDTV. But his dad was immeasurably pleased with himself for getting high scores on the games he played. Reno didn't have the heart to tell his old man those games were over a decade old, brought out of storage for nostalgia's—and his dad's—sake.

"See? Finally played a few of these damn things with you," his dad had said with a knee slap and a grin. "I'm pretty good!"

Only in his dreams. But Reno wasn't going to be the one to say it. Especially not now that they were inadvertent roomies. The two of them had been living the bachelor life together ever since the day after Thanksgiving—that fateful day—and Reno was starting to believe he might be letting his dad have too much fun.

With a quick lean sideways, Reno scooped up a pair of grimy socks from his coffee table. He flung them at his dad's head.

"Rise and shine, sleepyhead!" He waggled the big toe of the foot his dad had stuck out of the covers—in direct defiance of the freezing Michigan winter weather outside. "Time to get up."

A moan. A grumble. A thunderous rollover on the sofa.

"Just ten more minutes," his dad muttered. Snore.

"You've got things to do. People to see."

"I'm retired. Buzz off."

Reno shook his head. Maybe his dad had developed amnesia about their lifetime together, but he hadn't. He still remembered the obnoxious ways his dad had woke him up years ago.

"Up and at 'em!" He clapped a few times. "Shower first."

"You're so damn bossy, Reno. Shut the hell up."

"Let's go. Chop-chop. Time's a wasting."

Reno grabbed the covers and yanked them off in a whoosh.

Oh man. *Mistake.* When the hell had his dad grown that much back hair? You could reupholster a water buffalo with all that.

Making a face, Reno dropped the covers. He clapped his hands, made a few more "go get 'em" comments, then bolted for his coffeemaker. The sooner he got to work today, the better.

Unfortunately, work had its own share of headaches. Not long after Reno unlocked the doors to The Wright Stuff, his sports equipment store in sleepy, snow-blanketed downtown Kismet, the damn Multicorp sales rep who'd been hounding him turned up with a pair of Dolphins tickets and a cheesy grin.

"Hey, I just thought you might like to get away for a while, Reno." The rep, Derek Detweiler, stamped snow from his boots. He shivered as he held the football tickets aloft in his gloved hand. "Catch a game, enjoy some sunshine—you know, get away from all this awful wintery weather."

"I like winter weather." Reno switched on the sound system, sending Christmas carols wafting through the store's chilly air.

"Beaches, sunshine, girls in bikinis—"

"You're wasting your breath." Reno crossed the store's equipment-packed floor, automatically adjusting price signs.

He stopped at a bin of baseball bats and deftly sorted through them, then moved on to a display of hockey sticks. "I'm not going to Florida, and I'm not franchising my store."

"Come on, Reno." Derek spread his arms in a jovial gesture. "Who said this has anything to do with franchising your store? Sure, you've got a great concept here. It's a big success. But it's a big fish in a little pond here in Kismet. I don't have to tell you, if you spread around the love a little more—"

Involuntarily, Reno shuddered. Derek made selling out sound like a hippie VD swap. He shouldered past the man, then went to the cash register. His part-time sales clerk had posted a sign warning not to take checks from Ernie Wexler. Frowning, Reno tore down the sign. It was Christmas, for Christ's sake.

"You'll be a shark in the ocean, Reno. A shark. They don't even stop swimming to sleep, you know. Don't you want that?"

"Sounds like hell with hot sauce to me."

Relentlessly, Derek pursued him all the way to the packed storeroom, his ninety-nine-cent smile fixed firmly in place. "If you're playing hardball to drive up the franchise price, it won't work, Reno. I'm prepared to offer you a generous deal. A very generous deal. I've got to be honest with you about that."

In Reno's experience, people who jabbered on about honesty were usually lying. Just like people who went on and on about how easy they were to work with—usually they weren't. And people who were "soooo busy?" They always had time to bitch about it.

"That said, it won't last forever," Derek warned. "We love your concept here, but if you're not interested in selling—"

"I'm not interested in selling." With a grunt, Reno liberated a box of holiday decorations from a storeroom shelf.

"—I'm going to have to move on to other prospects, Reno."

Pausing with the box in hand, Reno met Derek's gaze directly. The man was dense. "I'd suggest you do that. Here."

He handed over the box to the startled sales rep, then grabbed another carton of lights. He angled his head toward the front of the store. "Watch your step. These boxes are heavy."

Not waiting for a reply, Reno made his way past a rack of T-ball uniforms and a bin of basketballs, both wreathed—as were most areas of The Wright Stuff—in strands of plastic holly.

The bell over the door jangled, alerting him to a pair of customers. A gust of frostbitten air whooshed inside, too.

He'd spent the first part of his morning shoveling snow from the sidewalk abutting his store, and the second listening to a bunch of hot air. If Detweiler had arrived a little earlier, he might have proved useful in clearing the snow.

Reno nodded to his customers. He recognized them as "team mothers" for one of the local little leagues. "Morning."

Both women beamed back at him. One of them giggled.

Reno chatted a minute, made his standard offer to help them further if they needed it, then turned. Just as he'd expected, the sales rep had dogged his heels like a little yappy dog.

"I've put in a lot of time with you, Reno." Derek huffed under the burden of his box. "I wouldn't have done that if I didn't think it would pay off. If you franchised your store concept, you could become a millionaire practically overnight. So why don't you be straight with me?" Another ingratiating smile. "What do I have to do, right now, to get you to say yes?"

"Put on a skirt and dance a tango."

Detweiler stopped, a puzzled frown on his face.

Deadpan, Reno added, "With a rose in your teeth."

"Er . . ."

Trying not to crack a smile, Reno waited.

The sales rep swept his gaze over Reno's big boots, six-two flannel-and-denim-covered frame, and broad shoulders.

Nervously, he licked his lips. "You used to be a kicker for the Scorpions, Reno. You took hits in the NFL. You cracked ribs. You honestly want me to—"

"Shave your legs first." Reno winked. "Looks prettier."

With a gulp, Detweiler stared up at him. Then he shoved aside the box of C6 multicolored lights he'd been carrying and nodded decisively. "I'll be back. You just wait and see. These macho games of yours don't scare Derek Detweiler *or* Multicorp."

With a jerk of his head—a hasty good-bye, Reno assumed— the man all but galloped out of the store, tickets and all. Left standing there with the shop bell's jingle in his ears and his box of holiday light strings in his arms, Reno shrugged.

"You might not scare Detweiler," someone said from nearby with a thud of boots, "but you damn well scare me."

Nate Kelly stepped out from behind a floor-to-ceiling pegged display of football pads, wearing his usual good-natured grin plus a padded blue ski parka that made his six-five bulk look like the Michelin Man on steroids. He'd pulled a knit cap over his forehead, too. The look did nothing to dispel the overall impression that a jolly Cro-Magnon cave-woman and a shit-kicking jock had had a secret love child and named him Nate.

He arched a brow. "Am I supposed to wear a skirt now, too?"

"With your legs? Hell, no."

"Because if it would make me a millionaire—"

Unavoidably, Reno stiffened. He didn't want to talk about money. Especially with Nate.

"—like Derek the Dickless said, I'd do it. Right now."

"Hey. Be nice." Reno hauled his box of lights to the window, then took out a carton of clips. He shook out a handful. "Unless you've copped a feel lately, you can't say that."

"You're the one who wants to see him in a dress." Comfortably, Nate leaned against a display, watching Reno uncoil the first strand of lights. "I would have taken the freaking Florida vacation. I've got a school break coming up, you know."

Reno did know. Aside from being a former Scorpions left tackle and Reno's best friend since kindergarten, Nate was also Kismet High School's current shop teacher. And more.

"Seriously, dude." Nate eyed him with evident frustration. "When are you going to tell that chump to take a hike?"

"I already have. More than once."

"Maybe . . ." Baring his teeth, Nate smacked his fist in his palm. "Derek needs a more forceful no."

The two team moms skittered sideways, headed for a rack of peewee cheerleader outfits while keeping an eye on Nate.

"Easy, killer. You're scaring the customers," Reno warned.

He needn't have bothered. Two seconds later, Nate's mind was—typically—on something else. "Ooh! Christmas candy!"

The huge man wheeled sideways, making room in the doorway for a pair of preteen girls. They'd stopped outside the shop, spotted Reno, then beelined through the door.

"Hey, Mr. Wright! Want to buy some candy?" they chorused.

They held up their boxes of colorfully packaged ribbon candy, candy canes, and red-and-green-sprinkled chocolates.

Reno glanced down at them, clamped his light string under his elbow, then fished for his wallet. "Sure, girls. How much?"

"For how many?" one of the girls asked.

"The whole box." Reno nodded at it. "I'll take them all."

"Wow! Really?" Excitedly, they put their heads together. Whispered about the price. Counted on their fingers, flicking their pink-painted nails. Finally, they announced a total.

Nate almost choked on it. "For *candy*? Is it gold plated?"

"Doesn't matter." With a smile, Reno peeled off some bills. Within minutes, he was waving good-bye to the squealing girls.

"You're crazy, Daddy Warbucks." His buddy hooked his thumb toward the storeroom. "Or maybe you forgot that you've already got about six dozen boxes of that stuff back there?"

"It's for a good cause."

"Hmmph. Next you'll be adopting baby kittens."

"Or something even more unbelievable." Reno pegged up the first few Christmas lights. "Like watching you work."

Laughing, Nate started rummaging around the sales floor

near the window, sorting through baseball mitts and tennis rackets while Reno painstakingly strung lights.

Finally Nate emerged, a catcher's facemask in hand.

"Hey, can I borrow this? We're starting a unit on tuna melts this week. With the broilers running—and probably the kids running around, too—I don't want to take any chances."

Holding an extension cord, Reno stared at him blankly.

"My students aren't the most graceful." Nate tried on the facemask, punched his palm, then crouched in a ready position. "If I had one of these, I could deflect accidents."

In the most recent rash of school budget cutbacks, Kismet High had eliminated the home economics teacher. Theirs was a fairly rural area—a resort town of around a thousand residents when it wasn't tourist season—and a place steeped in tradition, from the buildings along the riverfront and marina to the restored railroad depot in old town. No one had felt right about eliminating home ec altogether.

Since home ec and shop were one-semester classes, Nate— burly, boisterous, and macho—had been elected to teach both.

His friend waited patiently. Reno's customers neared the cash register, and a few more wandered in from outside. They smiled as they caught the holiday tunes. Some waved at him.

"Take it," Reno said. But as Nate whipped off the facemask, preparing to carry it away in one huge gloved paw, Reno clamped his hand on it. "On one condition. This year, in Kayla's first-grade Christmas pageant, you're going to be—"

"Aww, hell, Reno. Don't say it."

"—an elf."

"Jesus. Not again. After showing up in public in that getup last year, I couldn't get a date until Valentine's Day."

"That had nothing to do with the curly elf shoes." Grinning, Reno dragged over a ladder, preparing to tackle the top of the store window with another row of lights. When it came to Christmas, there was no such thing as too much. "That had to do with *you* not asking anyone out for two months."

Tightening his mouth, Nate stared at the facemask.

"And I'd hardly call chaperoning the Valentine's Day dance with Glenda Nielson a 'date.'" Reno ascended the ladder. "You supervised a punch bowl together. If that qualifies as a date, I've probably been married once or twice and didn't know it."

Nate offered a middle-finger salute. "Ha-ha. Easy for you to say, big shot. Just for that, I'm putting leftover tuna melt in your Santa Claus suit."

"Hey, take a swing or step off the plate. That's all I'm saying." Reno couldn't stand it when people complained about things they were perfectly capable of doing something about. He spotted his team-mom customers still wandering around, their foreheads wrinkled in thought. "Back in a minute."

Both women glanced up as he neared them. One giggled, the other blushed, and they both shared a meaningful glance.

"I'll bet you're shopping for Christmas gifts for your sons." With a flourish, Reno brought two basketball jerseys from behind his back. "How about these? They're pretty popular."

With a squeal, the women grabbed the colorful jerseys.

"We've been looking all over for these!" one said.

"How did you know?" the other added.

Reno shrugged. "Making people happy is what I do."

Near the window, Nate made elaborate gagging noises.

Reno flipped him off behind his back. Grinning, he faced his customers again. "I've got gift boxes if you need them."

He led the women to the cash register, pausing only an instant on the way to offer another customer exactly the football he needed for his granddaughter's stocking stuffer.

Ringing up the sale was fast work. So was consulting with the other half dozen shoppers in his store, chatting with them long enough to figure out what they were looking for, then outfitting them with the perfect item. You didn't get that kind of service from a franchise store, Reno reminded himself as his last customer headed into the snowy Saturday with an overloaded shopping bag in hand. You only got it from guys like him. Independent guys with a commitment to the community.

Satisfied, he went to join Nate again.

By now, his buddy had probably finished the next couple of strands of lights and had started on the painted window decorations. Last year, Reno had hired a freelance Kismet company to do the job, but he hadn't been happy with the results. This year, he'd bought several holiday stencils and a huge pack of paint, and intended to tackle the job himself.

As he should have predicted, Nate was not working. Instead, the hefty man lolled beside an unopened carton of soccer balls, his hands full of the candy box Reno had bought. Nate popped another piece of peppermint bark as Reno approached, chewed happily, then licked his fingers. He went back for more.

Reno nudged a string of tinsel with his foot, then crossed his arms. He stared at Nate, one brow arched.

His friend glanced up. "What's the matter?"

"You're supposed to be hanging Christmas lights." This happened every year. "That's what you came down here for."

"I am hanging Christmas lights."

Reno gave the candy box a pointed look.

"Hey, a guy's gotta keep up his strength." With a blithe grin, Nate chose a candy cane next. He popped it in his mouth. "You can't help anyone else until you help yourself, right?"

God help him. Nate was a philosopher now.

"I wouldn't know." Reno wound up an extension cord, then shouldered it to climb the ladder. He added a loop of chaser light strands. "I'm usually busy helping somebody else."

Pretty much, that was his job. Go-to guy. Hometown hero.

Nate exhaled. Like a giant kid, he made a production of setting aside the candy, brushing candy cane dust off his shirt, then grabbing some lights. But his grin was cheery as he headed for the store's other window, and his hands were quick as he finally got serious about getting the job done. Too quick.

Reno glanced over. "Here. Let me help you straighten that."

"Yes, captain." Nate veered sideways to give Reno room. "More lights. You're putting on another strand, right?"

"Aye, aye, matie." Nate paused, then scrutinized the multiple strands of minilights in his hands. "Unless that's too many. I don't want to blow a fuse or something."

"Don't worry about it," Reno said. "Just keep stringing and leave the planning to me. I've got a date later, and I want this finished before I go." He peered closer. "Hang on, let me . . ."

He straightened the strand of lights Nate was clipping up, then surveyed the effect with approval. That was better.

"Don't worry about it, fancy pants. I'm on the job."

That's what Reno was afraid of. But with little choice in the matter if he wanted to finish decorating and help customers until his part-time clerk came in, he'd have to roll with it.

To tell the truth, he didn't mind. The view was pretty nice from up here. Kismet's main street rolled away from The Wright Stuff on both sides, hemming it in snugly between souvenir shops, cafés, and at least three Realtors who specialized in lakefront vacation homes. Most of the other shops were being decorated this weekend, too, in preparation for the annual Christmas parade and holiday light show—a Kismet specialty.

Already city workers had strung SEASON'S GREETINGS banners across the street and hung wreaths on the old-fashioned light poles at each corner. Even the fire hydrants were festooned with candy cane-style red and white stripes. The snowdrifts and foot traffic—busy, bundled-up local shoppers and a few stalwart out-of-towners—only added to the overall holiday ambiance.

His store, like his house, would outshine them all, Reno vowed as he added another extension cord and strung more lights. It would be the brightest, the most colorful, the biggest—

There was a subtle pop . . . then the whole place went dark.

Chapter Four

Reno strode into the kitchen at six-thirty that night, side-stepping several boxes of still-to-be-used Christmas decorations and passing his dad at the kitchen table.

He was meeting his date for dinner in less than half an hour. He'd worked overtime at the store today, dealing with those blown fuses and overloaded circuits—and buying more Christmas candy from neighborhood kids—and he didn't want to be late. But if he didn't pull himself together pretty quickly. . . .

"Where are my damn socks, Dad? I thought you were going to do some laundry today."

"Didn't have time." Casually, Tom Wright spooned up some chili—*hearty-man style*, the can read. "I was at the gym."

Reno scoffed. "The gym?"

"I'm getting buffed up." His dad offered a dignified lift of his chin. "If I could wedge a Bowflex or an Ab Roller into my new workout room"—when he'd moved in, his dad had decided the guest bedroom was a better place for getting "pumped up" than for sleeping in, and had moved out the bed in favor of a weight bench and elliptical trainer—"it would make things a lot easier. Doesn't matter though. I can get heavy-weight training at the gym and cardio here. The babes are going to go *crazy* for me."

"Dad . . ." Pulled out of his sock dilemma, Reno regarded his father squarely. "Cut it out. Mom is already crazy for you."

"Ha. Funny way she has of showing it. One simple gesture—"

Reno gave up. He couldn't listen to the rest of this rationale. Not again. His parents' argument had brought him nothing but trouble so far, and it wasn't even Christmas yet.

"I know. I sympathize, Dad. Hang in there." Giving up on his search, Reno put his hands on his hips. He faced his father. "And for the last time, stop wearing my socks."

An indignant look. "But I can't find mine!"

"They're all over the living room floor. Right next to your underwear." Exasperated, Reno shook his head. "When you're done wearing them, just put them in the hamper. That's all I ask."

"Fine."

"Fine."

Reno headed back to his bedroom. Today's leftover socks would have to do. He didn't plan on getting naked down to his toes with Sheila—one of those downtown Realtors—anyway.

"Just quit bugging me, Reno." His dad's voice trailed him down the hallway. "Geez. You're always on my case!"

"I am not!" Reno called back. He thought about it. "Don't forget to put your damn chili bowl in the dishwasher."

"Control freak," his dad muttered.

But Reno only grinned. If making life a little less cushy at their bachelor pad made his dad run back home to his mom . . . well, that would be the best Christmas present of all.

Reno had one hand on his doorknob, ready to leave, when he saw it—a folded slip of red paper, lying forlornly on the rug.

"Dad!"

Grumpily, his father emerged from the kitchen, holding a bottle of imported beer in his dubious grasp and wearing a pair of what appeared to be plastic pants. Across their high-waisted front, the words SWEATMASTER 2000 were emblazoned in macho type.

Reno waggled the red paper. "Where's the rule book?"

"Huh?"

"The rule book that goes with this slip of paper. This is the cover sheet, but there should be a rule book someplace, too."

A shrug. "Haven't seen it, son. Maybe it came while I was filling out my Match.com profile this afternoon."

Great. Now his dad was trolling for online dates.

Gritting his teeth for patience, Reno reviewed the paper again. Yep. There ought to be a rule book here someplace. They'd been delivered—oh hell. A week ago!

"I've been waiting for this," Reno said. "The rule book for the Glenrosen holiday lights competition. It changes every year, and it's not delivered until December so nobody can get a jump on the competition."

"Hmmph. Sounds pretty fussy to me."

"Dad—" About to impress upon his father the seriousness of this yuletide tradition, Reno took another look at the man in the plastic pants and gave up. "If you see it, let me know, okay? I've got to go."

"Okeydokey."

Hauling in a deep breath, Reno snatched his coat, then stepped onto his frosty front porch. He dug out his keys. No sooner had he fisted them than he caught sight of his neighbor, Mrs. Kowalczyk, standing in the light on her front porch, waving. Damn it. He was probably late to shovel her driveway.

Well, he'd just have to get to it later. Waving back, Reno headed for his truck. Halfway down the drive, he caught a glimpse of Mrs. Bender, who lived next door to Mrs. Kowalczyk. She was also waving. He usually kept her driveway clear, too, but this year he'd been particularly swamped at The Wright Stuff.

He hated letting people down. He did his best never to do it. But right now, he had a date to keep. And a pair of parents to reconcile. And a shop to run. Torn between his myriad obligations, Reno smiled and waved back to Mrs. Bender.

He also kept moving. But the moment he touched his truck's driver's side door handle, his phone rang. Now what?

His dad stuck his head out the door, holding a video game controller. "If that's your mother, tell her I'm not here!"

With a sigh, Reno waved him off. The front door slammed.

"Reno? It's Angela."

"Hey, Sis." Getting into his truck, Reno cradled the phone. His breath puffed into the dusky evening as he cranked the engine, letting his headlights illuminate the snowdrifts piled against his cottage-style house. Hoping Sheila wasn't the type of woman to expect five-star dining and a fancy wine list, he backed out of the drive. "How's it going? I'm on my way to a—"

"It's Kayla." His younger sister's voice sounded wobbly. "She had a bad day at school yesterday, and I'm not sure what to do." Angela sucked in a huge breath. "Do you think you could—"

"Come over and talk to her?" Peering down the curved residential street, Reno made a sliding U-turn beside a slushy snowbank. "Hang tight. I'm already on my way."

"Thanks. I'm sorry to bug you like this."

"No problem." Hey, it's what he did. For as long as he could remember, Reno had swung in to save the day—for the peewee soccer team he and Nate had once played on, for the Scorpions, and especially for his family. "I'll be there soon."

In the meantime, he had some bad news to break to Sheila. Ending his connection with Angela, Reno dialed up his date.

Getting together with her probably hadn't been meant to happen anyway, he consoled himself as he waited for Sheila to answer. She was nice. She was smart, too—exactly the kind of woman he liked. Unfortunately, for a woman like that, twice-worn socks were probably a deal-breaker no matter how you sliced it.

Chapter Five

"Ooh! Hang on. Here it is."

Rachel's closest friend, Mimi, smacked her arm to get her attention. The two of them were snuggled with a ridiculously calorific bowl of microwave popcorn on Mimi's sofa in her West Hollywood apartment, mainlining E! Entertainment television.

There weren't any signs of Christmas here either. Mimi was Jewish, so she was Rachel's go-to friend for the holiday season (thanks to Alayna's Grinchy no-Christmas ban). At Mimi's place, Rachel wouldn't feel tempted to, say, burst into a rousing chorus of Ricky Martin's "Ay, Ay, Ay, It's Christmas." Or dive headfirst into a batch of gingerbread cookies. Or chug delicious spicy eggnog straight from the carton.

Drowning your boyfriend sorrows at Christmastime, it occurred to her, could become a really yummy experience.

"Look!" With the remote, Mimi pointed at the TV.

Onscreen, one of E!'s on-air personalities posed at the end of a long driveway with a cordless mic pinned to a borrowed dress. Rachel recognized it as a creation from one of L.A.'s most up-and-coming designers. The color didn't exactly flatter her skin tone though.

"That shape is totally wrong for her body type," Rachel

pointed out to Mimi. "Maybe I should set up a meeting. I could do a lot for her image."

"Would you quit thinking about work for two seconds?" Impatiently, Mimi punched the volume button. "Listen."

The E! correspondent worked her way through a bunch of gushy scripted patter, punctuated with video of celebrities arriving at Alayna's birthday party. Actors, models, and music artists all flashed by onscreen. It was almost here. . . .

Helplessly, Rachel felt her stomach clench. The popcorn she'd already scarfed felt as leaden as the silver stuff they put on the top of MTV Movie Awards statuettes. Yesterday, this had felt like an amazing idea. Today—in the harsh light of an ordinary Sunday afternoon—it felt considerably riskier.

"Birthday girl Alayna stunned onlookers last night with her . . . fashion forward style." The E! correspondent paused almost imperceptibly but indisputably cattily. "With a new mystery man by her side, Alayna arrived at her gala birthday event—"

"Ohmigod!" Mimi choked on a mouthful of popcorn. Her eyes bugged. "Look at them! You styled Tyson, too?"

Transfixed, Rachel nodded.

"—sporting what style insiders are already calling the 'Bjork swan dress' of this year. It's an unusual move for the Greek goddess, whose latest CD, *Lipstick Anarchy*, achieved multiplatinum status all over the world. Now Alayna's star appears to be falling—and her unusual appearance is sending shock waves through Hollywood."

Mimi yelped, clutching Rachel's arm. An image of Alayna appeared on TV, with Tyson temporarily shunted to the side. The pop star turned this way and that, persuaded by Rachel— whom she trusted implicitly (kind of the way Rachel had once trusted *her*)—that her ensemble was both chic and trendsetting. Alayna struck a variety of poses, wearing a broad, practiced smile. She didn't even balk when the barrage of flashbulbs struck.

"Ohmigod." Mimi shook her head, looking awed. "I've never seen . . . I mean—*wow*. You did that? You really did that?"

Rachel nodded, her stomach somersaulting with a mixture of exhilaration and alarm. "I told Alayna no one would ever forget that dress. Especially if she wore it with that head-dress."

"No," Mimi breathed, mesmerized as she grabbed another handful of popcorn. "You wouldn't dare. It's too much!"

"I told her she'd leave J-Lo and that green Versace in the dust. I told her that when pictures of her in that dress hit the press, she'd be seen in a whole new way around the world."

"Well, you got that right." Mimi grinned as Tyson stepped forward in the shot, letting the cameras capture him in all his matchy-matchy glory. "Everyone thinks Alayna's off her rocker."

"Yeah, I . . ." A little appalled at herself, Rachel gazed un-blinkingly at the TV, which still showed images of her client and her ex. "I guess I was more upset than I realized. Alayna and Tyson look even worse on camera than they did in person."

On the TV screen, the E! correspondent arched her brow meaningfully. "Some are even suggesting there might be a stint in rehab ahead for Alayna. But will her new man join her?"

"That's still unknown, Dakota." Coverage switched to a pencil-thin blonde with a handheld mic, hair extensions, and a faux-somber expression. "But style insiders are already sug-gesting that this ensemble might actually be a cry for help."

To punctuate that, E! flashed a slo-mo shot of Alayna shak-ing out her hair, then running her hands seductively over her dress—a hideous mashup of feathers, sequins, plastic lace, and Naugahyde that had taken Rachel three hours to construct.

She'd had to sacrifice two other outfits and a variety of items from the nearest craft store—and her fashion-school sewing skills were pretty rusty at this point, too—but it had been worth it. There was no way anyone could look anything less than ridiculous in that getup. Especially if they were a no-good, man-stealing, double—

"Hey." Mimi pointed at the TV. "That's the lower half of a skirt from Loo's spring collection, isn't it?" She stared at Rachel. "You took apart other designers' pieces? Oh, Rachel . . ."

Mimi gazed at her as if she'd lost her mind.

"I bought them first!" Rachel said. "Besides, the pieces are deconstructed. The designers won't recognize them."

"Mmmm." Mimi pursed her lips. "I hope you're right."

Tyson, similarly outfitted in a lace-up pleather vest, culottes-style pleated man-capris, and four studded suede belts, joined Alayna onscreen again. Ultimately (and probably at Alayna's insistence), he'd decided to allow Rachel to style him.

At first she'd been worried he might blow her whole getting-even scheme. Tyson had spent a lot of time with her. She'd thought he might have absorbed some sense of fashion savvy; it only seemed reasonable. But looking at him now. . . .

Mimi hooted. "I can't believe he agreed to that!" She gawked at Rachel. "Obviously Alayna screwed his brains out."

Ouch. "Obviously," Rachel agreed.

Because in the end, Tyson had been just as gullible as his ultrafamous new girlfriend—and twice as susceptible to flattery. He and Alayna were both selfish, self-centered, and totally convinced that the universe found them irreplaceable.

As far as Rachel could tell, they didn't feel the least bit sorry for what they'd done to her—for the way they'd betrayed her *or* the way she'd found out about it. They didn't care that they'd hurt her. Alayna had even had the temerity to complain when Rachel had refused a piece of birthday cake last night.

She was lucky Rachel hadn't mashed it in her face.

"Ordinarily, Alayna is a major trendsetter," the E! correspondent continued, "outfitted in designer styles from Gucci, Versace, and more, all with the expert guidance of her jet-setting celebrity stylist, Rachel Porter."

Rachel's picture—a blurry but flattering paparazzi shot

from last year—appeared onscreen. Mimi and Rachel both squealed.

"Porter—almost as well-known as some of her clients—has created a number of iconic looks for Alayna and other stars in the music, television, and film worlds." A sequence of red-carpet images appeared, nearly making Rachel sigh with nostalgia and pride. She *really* did excellent work. "But tonight, friends and fans must be wondering . . . Exactly what was Rachel Porter thinking? And why didn't she save her ailing client from *this*?"

Onscreen, Alayna swiveled to show off the rear view of her ensemble. Mimi cringed. "A feather-covered bustle? Really?"

"With butt cleavage." Relishing her moment of revenge, Rachel nodded. "It's a minor abuse of trust, I'll admit. But what Alayna did to me is *so* much worse than feathery bubble butt. Granted, I didn't quite count on *this* reaction . . ."

She broke off, gazing in consternation at the TV.

"But I'm sure this will all blow over," Rachel finished.

"On day one of *Alayna Watch*, I'm Dakota Mitchell," the correspondent intoned somberly, "and this is E! Entertainment Television. Stay tuned for our latest special, *SOS: Alayna*."

A minor tickle of unease started in Rachel's midsection. Probably it was due to too much popcorn. She couldn't be sure.

The whole world couldn't possibly react in such an extreme way to Alayna's one night of fugliness . . . could it?

"She'll fire you after this," Mimi announced.

"No, she won't. Everybody makes fashion missteps. I'll just tell Alayna the world wasn't ready for that outfit, and we'll go on from there." With a shrug, Rachel unwound herself from the sofa. "Alayna and I have been together for three years. She's too wrapped up in herself to even think about me. Believe me, before you know it, this will be water under the bridge."

"I don't know . . ."

"Besides, who else is she going to work with? I'm the best stylist there is in this town. And Alayna *has* to have the best." Carrying the bowl of popcorn to the kitchen, Rachel felt newly energized. Now that all the brouhaha was over, she knew she'd done the right thing. "I merely sent a message—a clear message not to mess with me. That's what people do, right?"

Mimi looked dubious. "I don't know. This isn't exactly *The Sopranos*, sweetie. I work on *Sweetwater*, remember?" The hour-long drama was the latest squeaky-clean network teen sensation. "There's not a lot of bed-hopping or revenge going on over there." Sadly, she shook her head. "Mostly there's Clearasil. Buckets and buckets of Clearasil."

Rachel waved off her friend's concerns. "E! is kind of out-there sometimes anyway. This story probably didn't even register with the rest of the networks, much less the tabloids."

"I dunno." Mimi glanced up from her laptop, which she'd hauled onto the sofa. "It's already on a bunch of gossip blogs, complete with photos." Grabbing the remote again, Mimi flipped through channels. She went faster, then backtracked. "It's on the Style network, too. It's also on MSNBC."

Rachel swallowed hard. Maybe she hadn't thought this through. But she'd been a woman scorned! A woman dumped by her boyfriend for a client! Didn't that merit special consideration?

"It's coming up on *Access Hollywood*. There's a teaser." A pause. Then Mimi shouted, "It's on the crawl on CNN!"

Rachel met Mimi's panicked gaze. They'd been through a lot together. They'd met in design school and bonded over their mutual (if temporary) love of platform shoes. They'd come up in the styling world at the same time, working on editorials, music videos, and commercials, waiting for their big breaks. But neither of them, in their wildest dreams, had ever expected their work to wind up on the crawl. It was inconceivable.

But there it was. Pop star Alayna . . . Worst-dressed rehabee?

"Please." Disgusted, Rachel crossed her arms over her

chest. "They think the only reason for Alayna to be dressed that way is because she's on drugs? Didn't anyone *see* her sense of 'style' before I got a hold of her? There are pictures!"

"You have to admit, that's a pretty drastic change from how terrific she's been looking lately." Mimi frowned at another image of Alayna and Tyson. They looked like escapees from an arts-and-crafts fair. "If I didn't know better, I'd be wondering, too."

Rachel pooh-poohed the idea. "This'll blow over. You'll see." She hefted her Hermès, then smiled at Mimi. "In the meantime, I've got cocktails with a potential client to get to."

"Wait!" Mimi scrambled up from the sofa. She smiled. "Hang in there, okay? Breakups are hard."

"Yeah. Especially when you have to keep working with 'the other woman.' And seeing your ex in his underwear." Evidently, when in Alayna's company, Tyson was allergic to T-shirts and jeans. "I can do it though. Don't worry. I'm tough."

Mimi gave her a doubtful look, then squeezed her tight in a hug. "I'm here for you. Don't forget to turn on your phones."

"Oh yeah." In anticipation of seeing her payback realized, Rachel had turned off all her cell phones and her BlackBerry. With mighty willpower, she'd even resisted the urge to check them during commercial breaks. In a swift practiced move, she switched everything back on. "Okay. I'm off. See you next week!"

She only made it halfway to the door before the first phone rang. Within seconds, bedlam erupted. Ringtones blared.

"I've got fifty-two text messages." Rachel stared at cell phone number uno. "Nineteen voice mails, and it's still ringing." She glanced at cell phone numero dos. "This one's jammed, too."

"Maybe it's new clients?" Mimi suggested hopefully.

Rachel consulted the nearest screen. "It's Alayna."

Mimi bit her lip, looking concerned. "Umm . . . Maybe she's calling to have a laugh about this?"

"Maybe." A sensation of doom collided with Rachel's

giddy sense of revenge. Shaking it off, she answered. "Alayna! Hi!"

"You are fired."

For an instant, all Rachel could do was clutch her phone. She felt frozen all over, numb with disbelief.

Thankfully her business instincts kicked in.

"Alayna, come on. You don't mean that." Rachel made herself smile, knowing her positivity would come across in her tone. She was nothing if not persuasive. "If you're worried about damage control, it's no problem. I've got the skills to handle—"

A harsh laugh cut her off. "Skills? According to Tyson, you're like a dead trout in bed. No wonder he came to me."

Barely able to breathe, Rachel stuttered, "A-Alayna, everybody makes fashion missteps." Nervously, she met Mimi's worried expression. "You know that. The world wasn't ready for that outfit, that's all. Let's just regroup and—"

"Our association is over. Good-bye."

Click. Left with dead air, Rachel stared at her phone.

She glanced at a sympathetic-looking Mimi.

The situation was pretty clear. Revenge was one thing, but this . . . "I've made a huge mistake."

Chapter Six

"What do you think, Uncle Reno?"

Snapped out of the trancelike state he always fell into while stuck in a shopping situation, Reno glanced up. His six-year-old niece, Kayla, stood outside the fitting room at Tina's Togs, dressed in the new outfit he'd promised to help her find.

He examined her from the top of her dark-haired head to the tips of her small bare toes, only recently stripped of their Santa-and-holly patterned socks. He shook his head. "I think you look like a junior member of the Pussycat Dolls."

"Really?" Kayla's eyes lit up. She grinned hugely.

Uh-oh. When had six become the new sixteen? "I think we're going to try another store. Zip in there and get changed."

Kayla slumped in her favorite drama queen pose. "But I loooove this outfit! It's so pink and sparkly and cute. Those girls at school would *die* if I showed up looking like this."

Those girls at school. Those little hellions, she meant. They were the cause of Kayla's meltdown over the weekend, and the cause of Angela's phone call to him, too. Why couldn't he have gone down to Kismet Elementary and given those mean little girls a few choice words about hurting people's feelings? That would have worked. It would have been direct and effective.

But no. Angela had insisted that parents—not to mention doting uncles—should not get involved. Except in a purely bolstering capacity of course. Which was how Reno had found himself swearing to Kayla that they could go shopping together, just like she wanted, "all day Sunday."

"Well, that might be true." Reno studied the outfit—a pink miniskirt and sequined midriff-tied top—again. "But involuntary clothes-o-cide would be wrong. Very wrong. And if I buy that stuff for you, your mother will kill me."

"Nuh-uh. Mom lets me wear this stuff all the time."

"Oh yeah?" Reno arched his brow.

"Sure." Kayla gulped, fingering the fitting room curtain as she dreamed up a few details. "She lets me eat Ding Dongs, too. Packs and *packs* of Ding Dongs. With Diet Coke and Starbucks."

Reno grinned. "Your mom won't even let *me* have Ding Dongs, Diet Coke, and Starbucks at your house."

"Mmmm. You have to be special like me, I guess."

"I guess." With a waggle of his fingers, Reno shooed his niece toward the fitting room again. Kayla was a die-hard charmer, but he knew better than to take the bait. "Hurry up. We can hit one more store before lunch."

"And then can we go look at the puppies at the pet store?"

"Yes, we can go look at the puppies." Reno needed to find out which kind she liked most anyway. Angela had clued him in that "a cute puppy" was tops on Kayla's Christmas wish list this year. "But you can't take one home today."

"That's okay. I can wait for Santa to bring me one."

With evident confidence in Santa's puppy-finding abilities, Kayla disappeared. The fitting room curtain fluttered as she changed clothes, jabbering loudly (to be heard above the store's Christmas music) about Polly Pocket dolls and their accessories. For a girl who wanted to look like a four-foot burlesque dancer, Kayla had very girlish interests. Thank God.

She stuck out her head from behind the curtain. "What if we can't find anything at another store? At school tomorrow—"

"I promise we'll find something good."

"But Madison and Olivia said—"

"Forget what Madison and Olivia said. They're just mean girls with nothing better to do than pick on people."

"No, they're not! They're my friends!"

Looking at his niece's outraged expression and wobbly chin, Reno remembered that Kayla was almost as loyal as he was. Of course she didn't want him badmouthing Madison and Olivia. Which was probably why he felt, all of a sudden, as if *he* were the one who'd broken poor Kayla's heart at school Friday, not her lame-ass clique of backstabbing first-grade prima donnas.

They voted me off our lunch table, Kayla had sobbed to him on Saturday when he'd arrived at Angela's house. *I had to eat all alone. They said the tribe had spoken!*

Damn reality TV. It was showing people new ways to be buttheads to each other. Even when those people were only six.

Kayla seemed to believe that if she looked different, those same snotty little girls would magically want to be her friends again. Reno had his doubts. He couldn't help voicing them.

"Real friends make you feel happy to be around them."

Emerging from the fitting room, his niece jutted her chin as she pulled on her parka and mittens. "I'll feel *ecstatic* if I get these new clothes."

"Nice vocabulary." No doubt he had his brainiac sister— a teacher, like Nate—to thank for that. Reno handed over Kayla's scarf and hat. "And what you'll feel is *cold*. It's twenty-two degrees outside. Way too cold for miniskirts and skimpy tops."

Kayla rolled her eyes. "Fashion has no temperature."

Oh man. He was never going to survive her teen years. "Come on. We're going down the street to the sweatshirts-and-baggy-jeans-for-little-girls store." He held out his gloved hand.

Kayla took it, making his heart melt a little. He just couldn't help it. Despite his tough talk, Reno was a pushover when it came to his niece. There were no two ways about it.

"There's no store like that!" Laughing, she smacked him. "But I think *you* might need to go to the girlfriend store . . ."

Stretching her suggestion into six or seven extra syllables, Kayla waggled her eyebrows—an elaborate (and obvious signal) that she was done waiting for the new aunt she wanted.

"All I want for Christmas is a new girlfriend, huh?"

"Mmm-hmmm." Kayla nodded. "But she's got to be a good one."

"Of course." Leading his niece by the hand, Reno headed through the holiday-bedecked store outside to the street. The municipal system for broadcasting Christmas carols hadn't been turned on yet, but it was only a matter of days now. "I'll be sure to put *perfect girlfriend* on my wish list for Santa."

He laughed as they turned the corner. If only it were that easy. Even if the jolly big man were real, when fulfilling an outrageous wish like that—*perfect girlfriend*—there would definitely be a catch.

Okay. This was ridiculous.

After umpteen attempts to reach Alayna, Rachel still couldn't get through. Fisting her phone, she fought traffic to Malibu, feeling with every mile as though she were inching farther away from her dream life, rather than toward it.

She still couldn't believe Alayna had reacted this way.

Weren't all of her songs about woman power? About seizing the moment and making yourself heard (albeit with a good booty shake)? Her biggest hit from last year had been entitled, "You'll Be Sorry (Boy)," a blistering tirade against an imaginary cheating boyfriend. This was pretty hypocritical.

At first, Rachel hadn't even wanted to call Alayna back. Or to return any of the other client messages on her voice mail. Frankly, she'd wanted to bask in her betrayed-girl's triumph for a while. But then reality had snapped her back into play.

Of course she had to make amends with Alayna, Rachel had realized. Her whole livelihood depended on it.

Too bad she couldn't reach her now.

Impatiently, Rachel punched her speed dial again.

Suddenly cell phone numero uno went dark. So did her other ringing phone. Puzzled, she braked for a logjam and tried again.

Nada. She couldn't get a signal. Couldn't fire up a response from her BlackBerry either. That was weird.

Well, she was getting pretty close to Malibu anyway. In a few minutes, she'd be at Alayna's door. She could work her client-saving mojo in person as well as she could on the phone. Probably better. Heck, Rachel Porter was a legend in L.A. Hadn't they practically said as much on TV today?

Concentrating on traffic, Rachel felt both overheated and impossibly stuck. Roughly, she dragged off the lightweight scarf she'd put on, then grabbed the sunscreen she kept in her Tesla's console. She rubbed the lotion on her arms, squinting left toward the December sun sparkling off the Pacific.

A car slowed beside her, "Jingle Bells" blasting from its stereo. Perking up her ears, Rachel turned in her roadster's seat, suddenly alert to the holiday sights and sounds all around her. Another nearby driver enjoyed "Rudolph, the Red-Nosed Reindeer." Two cars ahead, someone had decorated their SUV with a gigantic red bow, a naughty-or-nice bumper sticker, and a Santa antenna topper. It was tacky, but undeniably cute.

She sighed, then resolutely faced frontward again.

Clearly, the stress was getting to her. Because going all mushy over a stupid holiday wouldn't help her now—but arriving at Alayna's might. Determinedly, Rachel zoomed a few miles farther, then veered up to the gate. Ordinarily, it swung open immediately. But today nothing happened.

She leaned out to hit the buzzer.

Nada. She pressed it again. Again again again.

"Go away, Rachel." Tyson's beleaguered voice came over

the intercom. "Alayna doesn't want to talk to you. You're through."

Incensed, Rachel leaned on the horn.

"Real mature, Rach." Tyson sighed. "Quit stalking us."

Incredulous, Rachel swiveled her gaze directly at the security camera affixed near the gate. "Stalking you? I'd have to care about you to stalk you!" From nowhere, a sob bubbled up. Staunchly, she tamped it down. "This is business. I have to—"

"Not anymore it's not." A buzzer sounded. "Security."

From nowhere, three guards emerged. They surrounded her car, wearing scary dark sunglasses and forbidding expressions.

She'd seen these guys in action against particularly aggressive paparazzi. She didn't want to be on their bad side.

"Hey, guys. What's up?" Rachel tried to appear as normal as she could while privately freaking out. This was much worse than Alayna's usual moodiness. "This is all just a misunderstanding."

"Please step out of the car, ma'am."

"'Ma'am?' Reggie, it's me. Rachel Porter." With a forced chuckle, she took off her sunglasses. "See? Alayna and I are—"

"Just get out of the car, ma'am."

Okay. Fine. Shaking with a combination of disbelief, anger, and carbohydrate overload (she really shouldn't have indulged in so much celebratory popcorn at Mimi's), Rachel opened the door.

The moment she stepped onto the pavement, two of the security guards descended on her roadster. They opened both doors and searched the vehicle. The third guard—the one who reeked of authority and belligerence—kept watch on her.

Well, this wouldn't be the first time she'd encountered hostility. Obviously, Mr. Grim Face had never witnessed Rachel during a dress fitting for a client whose "miracle diet" had backfired. These three were seriously underestimating her.

"Listen, Biggie," she said (because that was actually his name), "if you'll just tell me what you're looking for—"

A series of clothing items—things she'd pulled for her clients—hit the pavement. Next came Rachel's sunscreen, her empty Peppermint Mocha Ice Blended cup (okay, so she wasn't *actually* foolproof on the idiotic forced Christmas boycott), and her iPod, all dumped on the driveway in a crazy pileup. Then . . .

"Nooo! Not my Hermès!"

Ignobly, her favorite bag thudded to the ground. At the same time, Reggie pocketed both her cell phones. The other guard confiscated her BlackBerry. Then Reggie tossed her Tesla's keys to Biggie. He caught them . . . then frisked her.

Rachel was still sputtering when he released her.

"You're free to go, ma'am." He nodded to the street.

"Without my *car*? Reggie! This is ridiculous."

"We're under orders to impound Ms. Panagakos's car."

Oh. Great. "I know Alayna paid for it, but it was a gift. We bought matching cars together! I—" Rachel sighed, staring from one impassive face to another. She stalked to her Hermès, then lovingly picked it up. "You people are animals."

Biggie crossed his arms. "We're just doing our jobs."

"Yeah? That's nice. I'd like to do mine, too." Rachel nodded at her cell phones. "So could I have my phones back, please?"

"Sorry. We have orders to keep those, too, ma'am."

"What? That's outrageous!" Without those cell phones, she literally could not work. Everything in her life was in those cell phones—all her business contacts, all her sources. . . .

Utterly panicked now, Rachel put her hands on her hips. This time, Alayna was going too far.

"You cannot keep those phones. They're mine. I—" *I paid for them*, she was about to say, when she realized the truth. She hadn't paid for them—at least not for the latest must-have upgrade. Alayna had. Just like Alayna had paid for her car. Her currently *repossessed* car. "I've got to have them!"

Something tiny and red blinked in her peripheral vision.

The security camera. Alayna and Tyson were probably watching every minute of this! Ashamed and furious, Rachel retrieved her iPod and the designer clothing from the driveway. Then she slung her bag over her shoulder with as much gravitas as possible.

"When Alayna comes to her senses, tell her I'll be at home, waiting for her apology." Rachel held out her hand. "You can keep the car"—*for now*, she added under her breath, still unable to believe the depths of Alayna's childish temper tantrum—"but I'll need my house keys. They're on that ring."

For an instant, Reggie looked troubled. "No, you won't."

"What do you mean? I've got to go home. I have other clients to call, things to do. I'm an important person."

The security guards exchanged pained looks.

"I have to get inside my house," Rachel insisted.

She waited. The ocean roared in the distance. Traffic continued to whiz by on the PCH, just as though this were an ordinary Sunday afternoon. The security guards frowned.

"Do yourself a favor," Biggie said. "Just leave."

Rachel gawked at them. They stared back, stone-faced.

"Fine." She could hire a locksmith. She could walk home and crawl through a window. Whatever. She didn't go to the gym five times a week for nothing. "You'll be sorry for this."

To her left, the intercom crackled.

"That's what you told us!" Alayna said.

"And look who's sorry now!" Tyson added.

Peals of laughter came over the staticky line.

Unbelievable. They were just . . . so . . . mean.

Fighting back tears, Rachel shouldered her bag. She stomped down the driveway with her sandals clacking.

It was going to be okay, she reminded herself. She could handle this. After a day or two, things would blow over. It was impossible that life as she knew it was over, just like that.

She sucked in a huge, quavering gulp of air, then hobbled along the gravel beside the highway. All she had to do was get home. Regroup. Maybe cry a little in private.

A few unsteady and windblown minutes later, the roof of her beach house came into view, partially obscured by Alayna's ostentatious landscaping, but promising a haven all the same.

Rachel nearly bawled with relief.

Her eyes burned and her feet hurt, but Alayna and Tyson hadn't broken her. Everything she loved was still here, just a few steps away. Her amazing clothes—gifts from designers who'd hoped she'd use their garments for her clients. Her jewelry and handbags and shoes. Her CDs and photos and artwork.

She'd worked hard to accumulate all those things. Whenever Rachel wondered if all the effort, all the hassle, all the on-call hours were worth it, they were there to remind her it was.

Only now, she saw as she powered up the walk, every last item she loved was piled in boxes on the front walkway.

Stunned, she stared. Then she raced to the door.

The knob refused to turn. Irrationally, she pounded on the door. Stubbornly, she twisted the knob again, but it was no use.

Alayna and Tyson really *had* beaten her, it turned out.

And from where Rachel sat as she sank beside her boxes of carelessly packed belongings, it looked as if life as she knew it—life as she loved it and needed it—really *was* over with, too.

What on earth was she supposed to do now?

Chapter Seven

Wielding a pair of high-powered binoculars, Reno squinted across the snowy street through the window of his spare-bedroom-turned-workout-room. He spotted his neighbor and frowned. "That bastard is hiring a professional Christmas decorating service."

From the weight bench, his dad offered a careless grunt.

"He's hiring a decorating service, and he's trying to hide it!" Reno nudged aside a curtain that had partly obscured his view. He examined the scene more closely. "The side of the van says RIGHTY TIDY CARPET CLEANING, but I'm not falling for it."

Another grunt from the weight bench.

"I should have known. Hal does something like this every year." Reno shook his head. "But I'll be damned if I'll let him win the Bronze Extension Cord by cheating."

Another grunt, then a snort of disbelief. "The Bronze Extension Cord?" his dad asked in a breathless voice.

"It's the prize for the neighborhood holiday lights contest. It's new this year, to amp up the competition. You'll be seeing it firsthand as soon as I win it."

"Humph. We'll see. You always were a little overconfident."

Sure. And that "overconfidence" had sent him straight to the NFL. Tightening his mouth, Reno scanned the redbrick colonial across the street again. He was a man who knew how to get things done. But he couldn't stand shortcuts. Or cheating.

Behind him, Tom Wright clanked a couple of weight plates together. "Hey, I'm all done with crunches. Come spot me."

"Just a sec. The 'carpet cleaners' are going in the back of the van. I think they're about to pull something out—oh shit."

Hastily, Reno jerked backward. He yanked the curtain in place over the window. When he turned, his dad was poised on his new weight bench, giving him a puzzled look.

"It's Mrs. Kowalczyk." Reno frowned. "Again."

"So?"

"So I'm late shoveling everyone's driveways this year. It was one thing when I was thirteen and that was my part-time job. But now I'm thirty-two. It gets harder every year to keep up."

A shrug. "Can't blame 'em for trying to keep a good thing going. You and your assistants kept this block looking good." As a kid, Reno had enlisted several pint-size employees for his fledgling lawn maintenance and snow-shoveling businesses. "Sometimes I wish our condo maintenance was that effective."

Reno glanced at his dad. This was the first time in more than a week that his father had acknowledged his regular life with Reno's mom. Maybe that was a good sign. A sign his dad was ready to give up his newfound bachelorhood and go back where he belonged.

When his parents had retired, they'd moved to a new lake-front condo on the west side of Kismet—no maintenance, no lawn mowing, no shortage of weekly cribbage games for his dad or book club meetings for his mom. His parents' move had coincided with Reno's sudden return to Kismet, so he'd bought the house he'd grown up in. It had been convenient— and more important, close to Angela. She'd needed him more than ever that year.

Their neighborhood—Glenrosen to locals, named after the initial land developer—was close-knit and cozy, filled with an eclectic blend of cottages, colonials, and modest split-level ranch homes. Many of the residents had lived there for years. Others, like Reno, were second-generation homeowners.

The four square blocks that comprised Glenrosen contained a thriving neighborhood community center and a park carved out of the wooded western Michigan landscape—with brand-new playground equipment, paid for by a fund-raiser a few years earlier. Oak and maple trees bordered Glenrosen's sidewalks. A real sense of community thrived there—fostered by seasonal block parties, a neighborhood watch program, and plenty of mosquito-filled summertime barbecues.

Some people would've found it hokey. But Reno liked it.

His dad chuckled, sweaty and wheezing. "You had a good thing going with that lawn-care business. You were king-of-the-hill all right, even then. Especially to those other kids who worked for you. You had a real bossy streak."

"I come by it naturally, Dad." Reno gave his father a meaningful look. "Anyway, I keep meaning to get out there to shovel snow for Mrs. Kowalczyk and her friends one of these mornings, but with the shop so busy . . . I haven't yet. Now they seem to think I'm stonewalling them on price."

Which was why—he took another surreptitious glance outside—they were standing on their porches waving ten-dollar bills.

His dad tsk-tsked. "That's low, Reno. Pushing up your prices on little old ladies? Mrs. Bender is a widow!"

"Mrs. Bender made her roofing crew cry last year. She can handle herself." That didn't mean she wasn't—like a lot of other people in Kismet—counting on him though. Reno aimed one last suspicious glance toward Hal's house, then trooped to his dad's weight bench. He gestured for his father to start lifting. "So . . . have you heard from Mom?"

A grunt. The weights rattled as his dad prepared for a chest press. "Jesus, Reno." Up came the barbell. "Not you, too?"

With concern, Reno watched his sixty-three-year-old father push the barbell away from his chest, his back arching with the effort. Physical activity was great for people of all ages. But maybe not this much activity, this fast. Especially not when a terry cloth headband and SWEATMASTER 2000 pants came into play.

"What do you mean, 'not you, too'?" he asked.

"Your sister has been pestering me. Getting on my case about Thanksgiving." Blowing out forceful breaths, his dad completed his set. The weights clattered in place. "The two of you should just lay off. Don't take sides," he warned.

"This isn't about taking sides." Frowning, Reno surveyed the signs of his father's accelerating bachelorification. In the past twenty-four hours, motivational paperbacks had appeared. Most of them sported cheesy titles like, *Remake Your Life Now: The Macho Path* and *Nice Guys Get Thank-Yous . . . But Tough Guys Get Laid*. "You can't go on this way, Dad. It's not right."

Pausing in the midst of mopping his brow with a towel, his father swiveled on his weight bench. He fixed Reno with a look he remembered well. It was the *what the hell did you just say?* look that had struck fear in his heart when he'd been a kid.

Geez. It still did. Kind of.

How had his dad retained so much authority? He didn't pull it out very often, but apparently it was still there, coiled beneath his mild-mannered golf shirts and Sears blue jeans.

"Fine," his dad said. "I'll take care of it."

A little flummoxed by his dad's edgy tone, Reno nodded. "Good." He'd like to see his parents patch up their differences, preferably before Christmas arrived. Ever since they'd retired—his father from bartending at the Kismet tavern and his mother from her job as a receptionist at the ladies-only gym—their relationship had been fraught with snippy comments, eye rolling, and a vocabulary of extensive sighs. But there was a lot of love there, too. Reno felt convinced of it. "I'm glad to hear it."

His dad stood, slinging the towel over his shoulder before

picking up a set of dumbbells for biceps curls. His expression seemed particularly determined as he hefted the weights.

"Tomorrow, I'll visit your mother," his dad said on an exhale. "And I'll ask her for a divorce."

With her head held high, Rachel clip-clopped her way across the lobby of The Standard on Sunset, carrying her Hermès bag. She spied Mimi waiting for her, perched near a shag-carpeted wall on one of the hotel's ultrasuede sectionals.

Her friend seemed right at home there—comfortable in an effortlessly (and enviably) cool way that could only come from being a bona fide insider. Which made sense actually, because Mimi's father was an important film producer. She'd grown up in Beverly Hills and had only begun working as a stylist as an act of youthful rebellion. Not (unlike some people) as a way of escaping small-town monotony.

Doggedly, Rachel kept going. But the closer she got to her friend, the more her confidence wavered. She didn't want to tell Mimi that, after a long Monday of trying to repair her career, she'd been shut out by another client. That she hadn't even been allowed to take a meeting—or schedule one for a later date.

It was all too awful. Too surreal. Too hideously familiar, at least today. There was only one thing to do when confronted with painful reality, Rachel told herself. Deny deny deny.

Breezily, she stopped in front of Mimi's chair, doing her best to appear as though she weren't about to cry.

"I changed my mind," she said. "Instead of heading over to Cody's house next"—Cody was a former teen pop star she styled for events, lately consisting mostly of VH1 reality show guest appearances—"let's break for lunch. I'm starving!"

With her brows knit, Mimi glanced up from the *People* magazine she'd been reading. "Oh no, Rach. Not again."

At the sympathy in her friend's expression, Rachel nearly lost her composure. She'd fought hard to retain control all day long, even while butting heads with multiple handlers and agents and managers. But none of those people cared about her.

Mimi did. That made it all the worse.

"It's not a big deal." Rachel examined her cuticles, dismayed to find herself in need of a manicure. She was so far gone, she hadn't even realized it. "I'm down to the bottom-feeders anyway. It was time to let some of those clients go."

At least that was the story she intended to stick to. In reality, Rachel Porter had become persona non grata in L.A., literally overnight. Alayna had effectively blackballed her with everyone who mattered. Clients who hadn't switched immediately to other stylists were pretending to be "on vacation." Others had simply dodged her with outright lies and excuses.

The rebuffs Rachel had endured today hadn't come solely from lower-echelon clients either. People she'd worked with for years—people she'd considered long-standing friends!—had turned her away, too, all of them influenced by Alayna's horror story that Rachel was the one who'd had "a break with reality."

What other explanation could there be? Alayna had cooed, according to one insider—probably with an overly innocent blink of her eyelash extensions. Rachel's (former) number-one client had told everyone that she'd only worn that hideous mashup of a birthday ensemble "to prevent Rachel from becoming violent."

Apparently, Alayna was as expert at manufacturing believable spin as she was at dishing out danceable pop songs and acting in popularity-bolstering feature films.

"Mmmm." Mimi—curly-haired, curvy, and as lovable as a Prada-dispensing teddy bear—set aside her magazine. "Right."

"Just like it was time to let Jenn go." Her treasonous new assistant had sided with Alayna. When Rachel had phoned Jenn from Mimi's yesterday, determined to recoup her losses and move on, her assistant had informed her archly that she'd quit, "To, like, go where the, um, opportunities are. With Alayna."

So much for sterling references.

"Of course." Mimi nodded. "You're moving on."

"Right. So let's have lunch to celebrate okay?"

With Mimi following, Rachel strode to the lobby doors. The whole place was decked out in a luxe L.A. version of Christmas cheer, with lights twinkling everywhere and subtle touches of red and green offering hip holiday ambiance. The effect reminded Rachel of something as she pushed through the doors to confront the sunshine, smog, traffic, and parking attendants.

"I would *kill* for some of those Christmas Oreos right now," she said. "You know, the ones with the red and green filling?"

Mimi gazed worriedly at her. "*You're* craving cookies? You've lived on protein bars and naked salad for so long, I thought you'd forgotten what real food tasted like."

"I have. But I've been dying for something sweet all day." Rachel caught Mimi's increasingly alarmed look and laughed. "Don't worry. I'm not crazy enough to go for it."

Technically, she could. It was after Alayna's birthday, so all things holiday-related were okay now. But—whether out of a misguided sense of loyalty or just simple desperation— Rachel had decided it would be better to hold off on the holiday stuff. For now. Just until she got her issues with Alayna settled.

Out of the corner of her eye, Rachel glimpsed a familiar face. Dustin Park, one of her favorite local designers, emerged from a gleaming Bentley. He stood nearby, chatting with his companion while they waited for the valet.

Beside Rachel, Mimi handed over their ticket. Stripped of her car, Rachel had been obliged to ask her friend for help chauffeuring her around today. After all, she couldn't exactly piece her life together while on foot. In L.A., that really *was* crazy.

Feeling a sense of eagerness overtake her, Rachel glanced at Dustin Park again. With his rock-star looks, angular frame, and wicked knack for intricate boning, he was a favorite with red-carpet stars. His gowns were genius. She'd worked with

Dustin many times in the past—and with award-show season about to kick off, seeing him now felt like a golden opportunity.

Opportunity was practically Rachel's middle name. After all, she'd made a career out of seizing it. With a wink at Mimi, Rachel held up her index finger to indicate that she'd be back in a minute, then strode confidently in Dustin's direction.

"Dustin! Hi!" Beaming as if in surprise, Rachel held open both arms, ready to embrace him. "How are you?"

At her loud exclamation, the hotel's fashionable guests and visitors turned to see what was going on. But Rachel was not the kind of woman to be intimidated by an audience. In hug position, she crossed the few short feet separating her from the designer.

Dustin glanced up, startled. Recognition crossed his face. Just as quickly, it vanished.

He glanced at his friend, then at her. Without a word, he took his companion's arm and steered them both inside the hotel.

"Who was *that*?" his friend murmured, ducking his head.

"Nobody." Dustin practically pole-vaulted himself through the lobby doors. "Nobody important."

His words floated back to Rachel on a chilly breeze.

Nobody. Nobody important. Without her fabulous job and super successful life, that's exactly who she was. Nobody.

A few yards away, Mimi waited beside her sensible Prius, doors open as she tipped the valet. She glanced up, then smiled across the busy area at Rachel. "Come on. Let's go!"

Numbly, Rachel turned. She didn't know where she was going, but one thing was clear—she couldn't stay here.

Ordinarily on a Monday night, Rachel would have been supervising a dress fitting or scouring trendy boutiques for the latest and greatest "It" clothes. She would have been hitting a hot new club with one of her clients or hobnobbing at an industry party. But tonight, none of those things were in the cards for her. It looked as if they might never be again either.

Morosely, she broke off a piece of strawberry-flavored protein bar, then nibbled halfheartedly at it. It tasted kind of chalky and not really fruity, but it was fast and easy and dependable—virtues she'd come to value more than ever today.

Across the apartment's living room-slash-dining room, Mimi spooned up the minestrone soup she'd heated, making occasional "yum" noises and tapping away on her laptop.

Unlike Rachel, Mimi didn't particularly enjoy the social aspects of being a stylist. She was personable—very sweet actually. But sometimes Rachel thought that if Mimi could perform her entire job from the comfort of her sofa, she would.

No matter what else happened though, Mimi always seemed at peace. Not in a weird, overdone Zen way either, but in a normal, loving and happy way. Rachel envied her that. Despite the primo advantages Mimi had been born with, she'd made her own way in life. She never took anything she didn't earn.

Rachel, on the other hand, had taken everything she'd been able to get her hands on. Now most of those things were gone. The rest she'd been forced to lug to Mimi's place in boxes.

Mimi glanced up. "There's still more soup, if you want some." She gave an encouraging smile. "It's really good."

"No thanks."

"Suit yourself." A grin. "Enjoy your fake food."

"Har-har." Fondly, Rachel returned her smile.

She was grateful to Mimi for taking her in this way, but the truth was that she didn't want to hang around for long.

Taking help from someone meant being indebted to them. When you didn't know what the payback might be, it was better to stand on your own two feet as much as possible.

Which meant getting back to the job at hand.

Through force of habit, Rachel stuck her protein bar in her mouth, then used both hands to rummage through the box she'd brought from storage into the living room with her. Sitting on the floor with the box between her out-stretched legs, she removed items one by one, then divided them into piles.

"I want to get all this stuff sorted," she told Mimi. "Alayna's security guys did a pretty haphazard job of packing everything. I never put client contact info down on paper, but if I could find my old cell phone . . ."

"You know, you don't have to do all that today."

Rachel didn't even glance up. She did have to do it today. How else was she going to put her life back together again?

The piles around her grew, but she still didn't find anything seriously useful. Old photos, magazines she didn't remember keeping, an assortment of jewelry and handbags, business receipts, paperwork . . . the buildup of minutia continued as she reached the middle of the box. She kept going.

"Rachel, I think you're in denial," Mimi said gently. "Why don't you leave that stuff alone for now and come over here?" Her friend patted the sofa cushion, nodding toward her laptop. "I started working on your résumé for you, but there are a few gaps we should go over. I don't know *everything* about you."

Thank God, Rachel couldn't help thinking.

"Aww, Mimi. That's sweet, really," she said. "But I know that phone must be in here somewhere," More digging. "Hey, here's a clipping from the People's Choice Awards last year!"

She held it up for Mimi to see, then gazed at it herself, filled with pride. She'd styled a record number of stars last year, Rachel remembered, outfitting them all in fabulous looks.

"Who would have thought it could all vanish, literally overnight?" Wistfully, Rachel ran her fingertips over the glossy magazine image she'd pulled out. "Twenty-four hours after catching Alayna and Tyson together, I'm boyfriendless, jobless, homeless, *and* phoneless! It's like a bad Lifetime cable movie."

"Down and Out in Beverly Hills?"

"I think that one's taken."

"Too bad." With a sigh, Mimi typed something—more résumé filler probably. "How long did you work on that sitcom? With your experience, I can probably get you a job on *Sweetwater*."

Involuntarily, Rachel made a face. She didn't want to go backward—and that's what taking a regular job would mean.

"I doubt it will come to that," Rachel said. "If I give Alayna a little time, I know she'll take back all those things she said." Unwilling to meet Mimi's eyes, Rachel searched through the box again. "She's passionate. She's Greek! But I've never known her to hold a grudge." Something shiny caught her eye. "Hey! At last, here it is!" She pulled out a clunky-looking cell phone, probably five years old. She caressed it, hope springing to life inside her. "Hello, baby. How've you been?"

"Do you two want to be alone?"

Rachel laughed. "I'm just glad it's still here. It probably needs a charge"—she fished around one-handed for the unit's plug-in charger, her fingers brushing papers—"but after one quick trip to renew my old calling plan, I'll be in business."

Mimi squinted. "It doesn't even have a camera."

"I know. It's totally ancient. But all of my best clients are listed in here." Rachel leaned over, peering inside the box. She didn't see the charger, but she did see . . . "Oh my God."

Curious, Mimi hung over the sofa back. "What is it?"

Rachel pried out the item she'd spied—a peach-colored greeting card envelope, splashed with glued-on confetti. It smelled vaguely of potpourri and drugstore perfume.

"It's a birthday card. From my mom." Unbidden, tears sprang to her eyes. Rachel hugged the card to her chest, her fingers trembling. "It must have gotten mixed up with my other mail."

"But . . ." Mimi frowned. "Your birthday was four months ago."

"I know. But the way I go through personal assistants, it's a wonder I get any mail at all." She had managed—*did manage*—her stylist's business from an office inside her

Malibu home. Jenn was far from the first assistant to disappoint her, despite the extra effort Rachel took to ensure that whoever she hired would be efficient and trustworthy. "I can't believe I missed this!"

Sniffling back tears, Rachel carefully slipped her thumb under the envelope flap. While Mimi looked on, she withdrew the greeting card. The front depicted a cartoon bunny in high heels and lipstick, sporting a va-va-voom dress.

TWENTY-NINE **AGAIN**? BETTER WORK IT, GIRL!
HAPPY BIRTHDAY!

Rachel laughed. That was just like her parents. Christine and Gerry Porter always embraced pop culture at least a decade too late. Along with the printed message came a few lines of elegant script, a pasted-in photo (years old now) of Rachel and her mom, affixed with some elaborate scrapbook borders, and a scrawled note from her dad. Awww. Then, at the end . . .

Hope we see you at Christmas this year!
Love and miss you, Mom and Dad

She couldn't believe she'd missed this. How out of whack had her life gotten anyway?

"Awww, your parents are so sentimental!" Mimi gushed.

Embarrassed, Rachel stuffed the handmade card back in the box. Hastily, she dashed away her tears with the backs of her hands. Nobody in L.A. knew about her background, not even Mimi.

But that didn't change the facts—or the decision Rachel made next. Somebody still wanted her. That was all she needed.

"I'm going home for the holidays," Rachel told Mimi. "By the time I get back, this whole debacle will be over with."

Look out, Kismet, Michigan! Here I come!

Chapter Eight

When his kindhearted neighbor, Christine Porter, had asked Reno to please, please, *please* pick up her daughter at Gerald R. Ford International Airport in Grand Rapids for a surprise Christmas visit, he hadn't expected the errand to bring him fifty miles away from home. During a snowstorm. At midnight.

But since the frequent flyer in question was Rachel Porter—former Kismet High School cheerleader and instigator of several of that school's most renowned rebellious incidents—Reno guessed he should have been quicker on the uptake. Of *course* Rachel Porter would come back to town in the most unconventional way possible—including full-on snow flurries. It was only natural.

He'd been two years ahead of Rachel in school, already an inveterate jock, so he hadn't known her well. At all really. But it didn't take more than a passing familiarity with Rachel Porter to understand she was . . . unique. Especially for Kismet.

Squinting as he paced along the concourse, Reno tried to conjure up an image of her face. All he got were short skirts, flashing grins, and masses of brown hair streaked with different colors. Dark-rimmed Elvis Costello eyeglasses and unexpected hats, and headphones with trailing cords tucked beneath her shirt, leading to a contraband portable CD player that probably played loud, obscure indie music. In the days before iPods, sneaking tunes wherever you went had required extra ingenuity. Rachel Porter had always had ingenuity to spare.

Reno recalled seeing Rachel pass by in the hall at school once or twice, chewing a wad of gum and talking a blue streak with a posse of girlfriends. Grunge rock princess pretty much summed up the Rachel Porter he remembered, so he figured it would be easy to spot her now. People didn't change as much as they thought. He, for instance, had hardly changed at all.

Wolfing down a big bite of the Cinnabon he'd bought, Reno jangled his keys, then paced some more. Being in airports always reminded him of his days in the NFL. Then, jetting to games had blurred with practices, media appearances, and matchups on the gridiron. Now the only games he saw were on TV, and the only media appearances he made happened every few years as part of the annual Kismet Christmas parade.

In front of him, the airport security check stood silent, mostly unused at this hour. A few travelers straggled by, wheeling luggage and yawning as they spoke into cell phones. Several of the eateries had shuttered for the night, along with the kiosks selling souvenirs. Only people with emergencies and cheapskates like Nate—traveled at this hour. Idly, Reno wondered which category Rachel fell into.

Emergency, he decided, and steeled himself for the inevitable tears. He was pretty good at offering a shoulder to cry on. He'd had some practice over the years.

Soon, the trickle of travelers turned into something like, well, a bigger trickle. They emerged from a faraway gate—the one assigned to flights from California—wearing weary expressions and toting carry-on bags, moving in singles and groups.

Chomping the last of his cinnamon roll, Reno wiped off his fingers, then held aloft the homemade sign he'd fashioned with a fast-food tray liner and a borrowed Sharpie: RACHEL PORTER.

Most of the women glanced his way. A few smiled flirta-tiously, but none of them had punk rock hair of many colors or even chewed bubblegum. Reno double-checked his sign. Christine Porter wouldn't have sent him on a wild goose chase, especially at midnight. Although she *had* once asked him if he wanted to buy "scented scrapbook paper." Whatever the hell that was. He still thought she'd been joking with that one. Come on.

On the other hand, maybe Christine was in cahoots with Hal. Maybe they'd plotted to get Reno out of town for a few hours to unload a "carpet-cleaning van" full of stand-up yard displays, industrial LEDs, and a complete set of Santa and his reindeer (with sleigh) to finish off his neighbor's rooftop display.

If that sneaky bastard tried to pass off so much as one ille-gally installed C9 string as his own, Reno was going to—

"Hey. You have the handwriting of a six-year-old."

Startled, he glanced to the left.

The woman standing there wielded a bodacious figure, a head full of shiny, wild dark hair, and a mouth that could stop traffic—a mouth Reno couldn't seem to quit looking at.

She also sported big black sunglasses and a malformed sense of what time of year it was. Because she couldn't pos-sibly expect to stay warm while outfitted in a fur-trimmed, fluffy hoodie thing, a miniskirt with jet-black tights, and im-practical high-heeled boots. Even Reno—a guy who hadn't seen a real, live, L.A.-style diva in a long time—could iden-tify her in a flash.

"Rachel, right?"

She nodded, tucking away a tissue in her hoodie pocket. He could have sworn he glimpsed tear tracks on her cheek. But then she tossed her hair and delivered him a brilliant smile, and his initial impression—*damsel in distress*—vanished.

"Rachel Porter, guilty as charged." She shook his hand. "You must be Reno. My mom said you'd be here. Thanks."

"No problem."

"Still, I appreciate it." With a total lack of the feminine flirtatiousness Reno was used to (she *must* be having an emergency), Rachel looked him up and down. "Now that we've got the introductions out of the way, I guess you won't be needing this anymore." She snatched his RACHEL PORTER sign. With surprising vigor, she crumpled it. It hit the nearest bin. "Let's keep my arrival between ourselves, okay?"

"Ooh. Here on a secret mission, huh?" Sugar-buzzing on the cinnamon rolls and extra-large coffee he'd downed earlier, Reno followed as Rachel blazed a trail to baggage claim. He couldn't miss the curious gazes snapping toward her. "What is it?"

"For starters? To avoid questions like that one." She glanced sideways to get her bearings, exhaled, then moved faster, as though reluctant to be seen anywhere near the GRF ARRIVALS zone. "Look, Reno. I know you're probably a really nice guy and all. But it was a long flight and I'm wiped out. So if you don't mind, can we just get to the baggage claim?"

"Sure. No problem."

That prompted a genuine smile. "You keep saying that."

He shrugged. "It's true if you're me."

"Must be nice. I've had nothing *but* problems lately."

Instantly, Rachel's face snapped to meet his. Because of her sunglasses, Reno couldn't see her eyes. But her obvious *did I just say that out loud?* expression was easy to spot.

It was all over the O of her mouth. Her soft, luscious . . .

Determined to get a hold of himself, Reno wrenched his attention upward. His eyes met Rachel's—at least as directly as was possible through a pair of Ray-Bans. For an instant, it seemed she was going to spill the whole story of whatever emergency had brought her here. Halfway across the country. In the middle of the night. In a snowstorm.

Bracing himself—and his shoulder to cry on—Reno waited.

But rather than break down and ask for help the way most women he knew would have, Rachel only pursed her lips. She glanced up at the airport signs, located the path she wanted, then powered forward, her divalicious attitude firmly in place.

"Let's get moving. I've got lots of luggage."

"You should take that escalator." Reno pointed as they neared it, jogging to catch up with her. Even if he couldn't provide his usual sympathetic ear, he could still offer some good advice. "You'll get to the baggage claim faster."

Incredibly, she sashayed past the escalator.

"Hold on, you missed it." Reno touched her arm. "It's that one right there." He jutted his chin in the proper direction.

Rachel lifted her face to his. "I saw it. I'm going this way. Thanks anyway, but despite how it might have looked back there—" She stopped, shook off his grasp, then walked onward. "I don't need any help. I've got this covered."

She had to be kidding. She might have her nose in the air right now, but Rachel Porter had *help me* written all over her.

"Look, you don't know me, so I'm going to let that slide." Reno spread his arms in a patient gesture, his feet rooted in place while he waited for her to correct her course. "But folks around here usually take my advice about things."

Still moving forward, Rachel glanced over her shoulder. One eyebrow arched. "How ego-bolstering for you."

Flummoxed, Reno stared. "You're going the wrong way."

"Listen, I've been here before—on my way *out* of town."

"Then you didn't have to deal with baggage claim did you?" Reno trotted beside her, now headed in the wrong direction also, just like she was. He hoped that wasn't prophetic. "Exactly how long has it been since you've been home?"

She ignored his question. "There's more than one way to get to baggage claim." Looking far more energetic past midnight than any of his small-town neighbors would have dreamed of being, Rachel came to a halt. "But if you want to find out whose way is best—and fastest—be my guest. I'll meet you there."

"Is that a challenge?"

"Call it what you want, He-Man."

"Fine. You up for losing?"

"That's what you ought to be asking yourself. See ya."

With a surprisingly sassy grin, Rachel turned on her high-heeled boots, then strode away. Again, in the wrong direction.

Not that she appeared daunted by that fact.

Reno watched her go, feeling broadsided—and revved up by the challenge they'd struck, too. He wasn't proud of it, but competition tended to have that effect on him. With a shake of his head, he decided to assess his opposition . . . and got caught up in an admiring analysis of her sexy walk instead.

Man, that skirt was short. Almost indecently short. Half of Kismet would be scandalized. The leggy tights beneath it didn't conceal anything either. Really they only compelled a man to look harder, Reno decided. To look . . . and imagine. Long, long legs like those were his favorite. And with those boots . . . damn.

As impractical and kooky as that getup was, he hoped Rachel Porter had several more just like it in her luggage. After all, *he* liked short skirts just fine—and he was looking forward to finding out exactly how she planned to shock Kismet this time, too. She'd probably brought suitcases full of skimpy skirts and kick-ass stiletto boots, Reno decided. She'd probably packed fuzzy hoodies in every color, and—

Aww hell. He'd never find out what she was up to—or what was in her luggage—if he didn't make it to the baggage claim. Rachel Porter had gotten the jump on him.

That hadn't happened in a while. Maybe never.

Hmmm. This was one neighborly favor, Reno decided with a grin as he doubled back to the appropriate escalator, that might turn out to be way more interesting than he'd expected.

Digging in her Hermès, Rachel plucked out a few dollars to tip the skycap who'd spotted her—lost and rushing the wrong way—and given her a warp-speed ride on one of those airport golf cart things. "Thanks a million. I really appreciate it."

"No problem, ma'am. No problem at all."

Ha. I wish. Rachel waved away the skycap with a smile. *I wish I had no problems to worry about. Wish this was just a friendly visit home, instead of a last-ditch hideout attempt.*

Most of all, right at this instant, she wished she'd been strong enough not to nearly crumple—unreasonably—at the sight of the big, tough guy wielding the RACHEL PORTER sign when she'd wobbled off the plane. Because even though her mom had warned her that she and her dad *might* not be able to pick her up, had warned her that their neighbor, Reno Wright, *might* be the one to meet her at the airport, Rachel had spent the last tearful half hour of the flight eagerly anticipating a hug from her mom.

Because sometimes, no matter how chic and grown-up a girl was, that's what she really needed. A hug from her mom.

That hug was going to have to wait, it turned out. Because instead, Rachel had gotten a big hunk of heartland-style beefcake—along with a challenge. A challenge that was doing an excellent job (so far) of distracting her from her smeared mascara.

Competition tended to have that effect on her. Making any kind of bet—no matter how crazy—instantly motivated and energized her. Rachel wasn't proud of it, but it was true. Which was probably why she'd never been able to pass up a contest.

Spurred onward, trying to seem as if she hadn't just been exiled from her life (and okay, dumped by her boyfriend and betrayed by a friend to boot), Rachel eyed the mostly deserted, vaguely spooky baggage claim area. She hurried to the correct carousel for her flight, spotted a few familiar people who'd been on the plane with her, then leaned against a support post.

She had just enough time to strike a bored, manicure-examining pose—one she hoped would restore some of her typical L.A. cool—before she spied Reno Wright. He bolted down a distant escalator, taking the moving stairs two at a time.

At the sight of him, Rachel smiled. She just couldn't help herself. She liked a man who was motivated.

Even if he *was* a little bossy. And way too helpful.

Because the plain truth was, the more helpful Reno had tried to be when they'd met, the harder it had been for Rachel to maintain her distance from him. And she *needed* that distance right now. That invisible wall between her and everyone else—especially everyone in Kismet, whom she desperately wanted to *still* be fabulous for—was all that was holding her together.

Well, that . . . and the bet she'd made with Reno. Thank God he'd taken her up on it. Because she hadn't wanted to explain why she just needed to keep *moving* instead of talking. Or why the airport felt like one big danger zone where someone might recognize her at any second—and call her on why, if she were so incredibly brokenhearted, she was currently ogling Reno Wright?

Sobering instantly, Rachel straightened her sunglasses. She was *not* in the market for a man. No no no. The last thing she needed was to get caught up in a relationship. She was only here in Podunkville to recoup. To get herself together in a place where nobody knew about her disastrous career flameout.

Including Reno Wright. And his all-too-perceptive eyes.

Just when she'd decided *for sure* to avoid ogling him in the future, Reno arrived beside her—looking gorgeously hurried but not the least bit out of breath after his sprint across the airport—and it was impossible not to stare at him. A little.

Apparently, that athletic aura he sported was for real. It was hard to discern much detail about his physique beneath his flannel shirt (yes, honest-to-God flannel!), jeans, boots, and heavy winter coat, but that didn't stop her from . . . *not* trying.

No *way* was she trying to figure out what he might look like with fewer wintery layers covering him, Rachel assured herself. Definitely not. But a girl *had* to wonder . . . was that quilting and padding that bulked him up that way? Or muscles?

Muscles, she decided. There were lots of lovely muscles beneath that big woolen coat of his. Her practiced eye told her so. Also, looking at that coat, it belatedly occurred to Rachel that she might not be appropriately outfitted for the Kismet weather. Nevertheless, this wasn't the time to go all soft.

"I win," she announced.

He pointed one blunt-tipped finger at her. "You cheated."

"So what?" Rachel arched her eyebrow, grateful that her sunglasses hid most of her expression. They made her feel safe. And of course, chic. They also hid the effects of the six-hour crying jag her flight had morphed into once the impact of all she'd lost had finally sunk in . . . someplace above Omaha. She raised her chin. "I never promised not to cheat."

Reno appeared nonplussed. "You don't have to promise not to cheat. Everyone takes it on faith that you won't."

"Around here, maybe. Where I come from, it's different."

He paused, giving her the uncomfortable sensation that his dark-eyed gaze could penetrate straight through her Gucci lenses and see into her betrayed, turned-down, humiliated soul. *Again.*

There was definitely something about Reno Wright that got to her. That turned her usual defenses inside out and made her work twice as hard to seem unaffected. Beneath his scrutiny, Rachel nearly caved in all over again. What was *wrong* with her?

Despite his X-ray vision, Reno didn't ask her any more questions. He merely turned his attention to the baggage carousel, then quirked his mouth. "I'll get your luggage."

"Wait!" Rachel called as he strode across the short distance dividing them from the thumping, bumping, merry-go-round of suitcases. "You don't even know what they look like."

With a mighty yank of his arm, Reno lugged a Vuitton bag from the carousel. He set it at his feet, then glanced at her.

Damn it. He'd guessed right.

Rachel *hated* being predictable. When she'd been a teenager here, stuck in small-town Midwestern purgatory, she'd done all she could to stand out. To feel unique. To make it plain to everyone that Rachel Porter was better than Kismet—that great things were in store for her, just as soon as she made it out.

Somehow, the fact that Reno could read her like a book seemed to threaten her ultracool image. The image she so prided herself on. The image that reminded her that she really *had* come a long way from her dinky small town. Surely no temporary career derailment could erase that—despite Reno's lucky luggage guess.

Irked, she tapped her toe. "Hold on. There's more to—"

Deftly, Reno plucked the remaining three of her over-stuffed bags from the carousel without waiting for her to complete her sentence. It was galling. Not that watching him work was all that arduous. The way he hefted her heavy luggage made her imagine all kinds of gallant tough-guy gestures, like opening doors for ladies and sweeping them off their feet and into cozy, flannel-sheeted beds with warm quilts and lots of pillows.

Whoa. She was ogling a burly guy and imagining *bedding*? In detail? Tyson and Alayna had really done a number on her.

Reno appeared at her side. Somehow, he'd tucked a suitcase beneath each arm and one in each fist—and made the feat seem easy. She guessed there was something to be said about corn-fed, down-home men. Especially when a girl needed help.

Not that *she* needed help. Just a little downtime.

"Okay. Let's get out of here." Rachel turned, clutching her Hermès and her carry-on bag, leading the way with her chin held high. "Before you guess any *more* details about me."

"Details?" Reno's voice followed her. "Like . . . ?"

Like my bra size. My spider phobia. My single ignoble appearance on the CNN crawl.

Rachel hoped people in Kismet still kept their TV sets faithfully tuned to Fox News, where her little fashion revenge story wouldn't even register. She was counting on it.

And, to increase her odds, she was planning not to leave her parents' house until New Year's Day, too.

"Nothing." She waved. "Let's go. Mush, He-Man."

He didn't cooperate. She stopped, swiveling to see what the problem was. At least ten paces behind her, Reno waited.

"You're going the wrong way again," he said.

God. Could she do *nothing* right lately? "I am not."

"Wanna bet? I parked that way." He angled his head left.

"Oh." She paused. "Of course you did."

Embarrassed, Rachel lifted her chin a notch higher. She swerved left and sailed past him, gathering her unraveling cool.

"Would it be too much for us to walk together?" he asked.

Breezily, Rachel waved. "Keep up, why don't you?"

Reno laughed. "When we hit the parking garage, I bet you ten bucks you can't pick out what I'm driving."

Perfect. "You're on, sucker."

Newly determined, Rachel bolted for the nearest exit. If she could just handle the hour-long drive between here and Kismet, she might survive this night after all. Especially since Reno was being so obliging with the bets. After all, as she always said, there was nothing like a little competition to add spice to life.

Chapter Nine

Reno stood beside Rachel, watching as she peered across the multiple rows of vehicles in short-term parking. There was no way she'd pick out his truck. Not around here. Chevys, Fords, even Toyotas . . . to most women, all trucks blended together.

"Nothing like a little competition to add spice to life." He put down her bags, then mimicked a bored stretch, as if setting up camp for the night in Section A12. "You might have an easier time of it if you took off your sunglasses."

She didn't so much as slide them down her nose. But she did give him a long, thoughtful once-over, starting at his boots and rising—with disconcerting directness gradually higher. Beneath her scrutiny, Reno felt naked. Not in the fun way either.

Defensively, he stuck out his chin. "Well?"

"Well . . . hmmm. You're not the elaborate-truck-mural type." Rachel dismissed a nearby king cab with a sunset decorating its tailgate. "You're not the Hummer type." A nod toward his jeans. "No apparent need to overcompensate. Good for you."

He nodded. "Thanks. But if you're planning to go the elimination route, I've got to warn you. We'll freeze first."

"I know. What is it, twelve degrees out here? Brrr. I forgot how cold it is in the boondocks."

Rachel shivered, wrapping her fuzzy hoodie more closely around her—and offering him an unprecedented view at the same time. Wow. That fluffy knit really hugged her—

Reno cleared his throat, deliberately shifting his gaze to her face. Then to her fingers, as she absentmindedly plucked at the trim on her sweater . . . thing. In this light, it looked pink.

"What is that?" he asked. "Care Bear fur?"

Rachel recoiled, looking appalled as she crossed her arms. "Of course not. What kind of person are you?"

"For starters, a person who wouldn't run around with Cheer Bear wrapped around my neck."

A pause. "You're just trying to throw me off my game."

"Is it working?"

"Of course not."

"Then that's not what I'm doing." He gave her fur collar another skeptical squint. "That can't be very warm though."

"It's not, actually." Rachel snuggled inside it anyway. "So be quiet and let me guess which truck is yours already."

Wearing a determined expression, she strode up the nearest lane, examining the vehicles on either side. Stuck waiting with her pile of luggage, Reno had nothing to do but examine her.

"What happened to your punk rock hair?" he asked.

Rachel touched a now-silky hank. "My what?"

"In high school you had crazy hair." He wiggled his fingers around his ears to indicate as much. "And glasses."

"I wear contact lenses now." With brisk strides, she went from a Ford pickup to a Chevy, glancing inside their cabs and beds. She pursed her lips, then kept going. "And I grew up."

"Hmmm. Kismet will be disappointed."

Rachel aimed her sunglasses-shuttered gaze at the row where Reno's truck was parked. Remarkably, she veered toward it.

"Yeah? Well I don't care what Kismet thinks of me." With a flourish, she whacked the edge of his battered old truck bed. Striking a pose, she grinned. "This one. This is it."

For one insane minute, Reno considered bluffing his way out of their bet. That's how crazy meeting her had made him.

"It's one step up from a tractor." Rachel sized him up again, this time peering intently at his face. "But it's yours."

He stood there for another few seconds, deliberating whether to disown his reliable old truck. Nope. No way.

"It's a good truck." He hoisted her bags, then strode to his pickup truck, his breath forming puffs in the wintery air. He made ready to plop all four of her suitcases in the bed.

"Nooo!" She flung out both arms to stop him, then wrinkled her nose at his truck bed. "Can't you put those in front?"

"Only if *you're* willing to ride in the bed instead."

For a heartbeat, she seemed to consider it. "I'll scrunch up really tightly next to you. Then everything will fit right?"

"With this much luggage?" Reno made a doubtful face. "No."

"Then I'll call a cab." She fished in her purse. "If there's even one to be found out here in the boonies, that is."

"You're going to take a cab fifty miles?"

"If necessary." She whipped out a cell phone. Surprisingly, it looked like the same inexpensive, outdated model Reno had. It was probably the only thing they had in common.

"That's ridiculous," he said.

Rachel eyed his truck. "So is driving around in something that looks like it's glued together with rust and dirt. You know that kid Pigpen? In the Peanuts comics? You've got his truck."

Stubbornly, Reno gritted his teeth. Had he thought of her as a diva? She was a diva supreme. A diva grande.

A diva who plundered Care Bear fur, dissed Christmas cheer, and—worst of all—insulted his truck.

"No service. It figures." She clicked shut her phone in disgust, then stared at him expectantly, hands on hips—as if it were *his* fault her wireless carrier couldn't handle parking garage interference. "Any other ideas? I can't just put my luggage on top of"—making a face, she gestured—"*that*."

That was ordinary wear and tear. But he guessed Miss L.A. Diva hadn't had much experience with *ordinary* lately.

A few yards away, someone left the airport parking, tires squealing against the asphalt. Lucky SOB. He was getting away.

"Fine." With rough movements, Reno shrugged out of his heavy winter coat. He flung it in his truck bed to cover the dried pine needles, built-up dust, and slushy snowmelt. Then he arranged the diva supreme's luggage on top, secured it with a couple of wiped-clean bungee ties, and covered the whole assembly with his stripped-off flannel shirt. "Happy now?"

After a long moment, Rachel only shook her head, not even bothering to ogle him in his T-shirt. "I thought I was. You know what? Over these past few years, I honestly thought I was."

Something in her forlorn expression tugged at him.

Resolutely, Reno pushed it back. She was probably just upset because he hadn't given her a damn curtsy, too.

Nevertheless . . .

"Whatever's gone wrong, it'll work out," he heard himself say in a gruff tone. Apparently, he couldn't stand seeing a grown woman get sniffly. Even if she was a citified glamazon with entitlement issues. "It always does. Just give it time."

Rachel chewed her lower lip. Her sunglasses-covered face turned toward him. "You really think so?"

"I know so."

"Aww. That's sweet." She sounded doubtful though.

"We'd better get moving before the snow gets worse."

She looked alarmed. "Snow?"

"It's what happens here in the boonies. In December."

"Oh my God."

Laughing, Reno shooed her toward the other side of his truck. He followed and opened the passenger side door for her.

Hypnotized by the sweet curve of her derrière as she slid onto the frigid leatherette seat, it took him a second to realize he was standing there with the door open, gawking.

You know where to go, right?" she asked as she climbed inside. "How to get this thing between here and Kismet? Or," she asked, "are you only licensed to drive a plow?"

Reno snapped out of it. Rachel Porter was attractive. She was sexy. She was even pretty likable, despite everything. But for a person who'd grown up in the heartland, she was seriously misinformed about the Midwest.

"I'm licensed for both. But I'm better at the plow." He nodded. "You'd better buckle up."

While she scrambled for the seat belt, Reno walked around to climb in the driver's seat himself. "Ready?"

"Ready or not, Kismet. Here I come!"

They made it twenty miles down the highway—roughly thirty miles outside Kismet—before everything fell apart. Stuck in the dark night with his truck wipers working double-time against the snowstorm, Reno braked for a traffic slow-down. It appeared to go on for some distance, possibly to the next turnoff. It was hard to tell with the snow flurries going on.

Beside him, Rachel peered through the windshield, her face illuminated by flares and brake lights. "What happened?"

"Probably someone skidded off the road." Reno drummed his palms on the steering wheel, considering the problem. "It happens in weather like this. Traffic backs up until it's cleared." He gazed at her. "We might be here awhile."

"A while?" She wrinkled her nose. "How long is that?"

"I dunno. Maybe a half hour. Maybe hours. Maybe all night."

"All night? Great." Rachel groaned. "That's the middle of nowhere for you." Sighing, she scrutinized the stopped cars ahead. "It's only one A.M. What are we supposed to do now?"

"Not much to do except wait until it's cleared." Thinking things over, Reno glanced at the spangled Christmas ornament—a gift from Kayla—dangling from his rearview mirror. Next he aimed his gaze at Rachel, unable to hold back a grin. "But I can think of at least one good way to pass the time . . ."

Chapter Ten

The thing nobody had warned Angela Wright about when she'd decided on a career as a high school English teacher was that she'd be surrounded by teenagers. All. The. Time. Unavoidably.

Not that that was entirely problematic. The truth was, she loved kids. Especially the kids who wound up in A.P. Sophomore English—her favorite class—and actually learned to laugh at all the right lines of Shakespeare's plays, spontaneously and without coaching beforehand about the racy bits. She loved seeing kids connect the dots between characters in books and people in their own lives—and themselves. She didn't even mind grading papers, reading essays, and writing lesson plans.

What Angela minded, with increasing fervency, was the fact that, because of her job, she never met any new *adults*. Or more precisely, any hot, dateable, studly-or-not, quality *men*. Those were in short supply among the staff and faculty at Kismet High School, and all indications were that the situation wouldn't improve anytime soon. Especially today. Monday morning.

Why couldn't she have gone to work as an agent specializing in gorgeous male models? Angela wondered as she poured herself a cup of fresh Christmas-blend coffee from the communal pot. Or a construction coordinator, supervising scads of macho, shirtless workers? Or a business executive, in charge of a whole cadre of tie-wearing, eager-to-please, smarty-pants middle managers?

No. *She'd* had to choose a sensible, nunlike job instead. She'd had to choose teaching, her passion, and deny herself all the opportunities for adult interaction afforded by other jobs.

Well, it was never too late to take action, Angela decided as she smiled at a passing coworker, then added a dollop of gingerbread-flavored creamer (a seasonal item she'd brought in to share with everyone) to her coffee. Today was the first day of the rest of her dating life, wasn't it? She'd just have to go out there and, as Horace had urged in the *Odes*, seize the day.

Of course, all that seizing might take awhile. As a single mother, Angela had to be even more efficient—and patient— than most women were. She'd accepted that a long time ago. She'd simply have to multitask her way back into the dating scene during the time she had available between going to work, taking care of Kayla, and enjoying five-minute showers. Piece of cake.

With that resolved, Angela paused in the teachers' lounge before heading off to her first class. This was the one oasis in the Kismet High School hustle and bustle, the sole place where relative quiet reigned while students chattered and streamed past outside, occasionally whooping, hollering, or running.

The teachers' lounge wasn't outfitted with anything more glamorous than a contraband cafeteria table, a coffeemaker and minifridge, a wall of teachers' cubbies, and a bulletin board covered with notices and memos (and this week, colorful invitations to holiday parties), but it was her home away from home. Now that Kayla had reached first grade, it was about to become Angela's first-date-in-years' hunting grounds, too.

After all, she'd just turned thirty. Time was wasting.

While ostensibly blowing on the spicy coffee steaming

from her *Teachers Make All Other Professions Possible* travel mug, she studied her prospects. After excluding the married, the female, and the insufferable, she wound up with three potential dates.

First up, Jerome Dodd. He was single, appeared healthy and sane, and (obviously) held a steady job. Those were all pluses. She watched carefully as he packed up his Dungeons and Dragons figurines in their custom padded to-go kit before tackling another tough day of supervising JV Symphonic Band. Hmmm.

Moving on . . .

Next she spotted Zion Jones, this year's new art teacher. He was appealingly eclectic, very fit (in good weather, he rode his skateboard to work), and probably well-versed in the technology Angela needed to bone up on, since he was part of the MySpace generation. That made him a potential boyfriend with work-related bonuses. On the other hand, she preferred a man who could carry on a conversation. Zion's standard greeting was a "rock on" sign.

Moving on . . .

Patrick Goodger nudged his way past her, nodding hello as he zeroed in on the coffeemaker. His sleepy eyes, tousled hair, and generally charming demeanor made him the front-runner in her nouveau dating experiment. Just being near him made Angela feel all giggly and womanly—and she was definitely *not* a giggler under ordinary circumstances. However, Patrick's presence had a way of making *all* the female staffers feel like schoolgirls.

Literally. *All* of them. Angela wasn't convinced she had the feminine wiles to stand out in the crowd.

Nurturing, hard-working single mother? Of course.

Bodacious faculty femme fatale? Not a chance.

Moving on . . .

Except there was no one to move on *to*. Thwarted, Angela shouldered her big, cozy, handmade purse, then headed to class.

"Well, off to the salt mines. Have a good day, everyone."

"Whoa, Angela. Hold up." Chivalrously, Patrick rushed to open the door to the teachers' lounge for her. He offered a suggestive smile. "You do the same. Have a good day, I mean."

Curious, she stopped. Hmmm. That was new. Could it be that Perfect Patrick Goodger was actually *flirting* with her?

He'd never looked twice at her before. Maybe she was emitting *I'm available* pheromones without realizing it. It was possible, now that she'd officially decided to try dating again.

Turning to face Patrick, Angela inhaled his cologne, admired his deft hand with hair gel . . . and felt her face flame into a million shades of red. "You, too. Have a good day."

"You already said that."

"Umm. I know."

"You're cute when you're flustered." He leaned against the doorjamb, idly toying with her purse strap. He leaned his movie-idol face toward her, then lowered his voice an octave. "You look all pink-cheeked and flustery. I like that in a woman."

Hold on. Full stop. *Flustery*? That wasn't even a word. She ought to know. Also, Patrick liked *flustered* in a woman? As in, he preferred ditzy, rattled, and/or disconcerted dates?

Alarm bells jangled in her head. Unfortunately, they were overridden by the unprecedented thrill of realizing that a man saw her as something besides an erudite, five-foot-six, brown-haired dispenser of handy synonyms, useful literary references, and Band-Aids (she kept a box in her purse at all times).

"Um. I'm getting a jump on tomorrow," she explained. She hoped her excuse sounded wittier to him—the man who enjoyed, as he'd probably put it, *flusteriness*. "Now I'm a whole day ahead."

"That's admirable." Patrick gazed into her eyes. "As it turns out, there's something *I'd* like to get a jump on, too."

Ewww. Obvious *and* a faulty metaphor at the same time.

On the other hand . . . wow! Patrick had noticed her! Her, among all the other teachers. He was worldly, too. It was rumored that he'd left his former school in Connecticut amid reports of a scandalous affair with a married, well-connected colleague.

"If you're not busy over winter break," he said, leaning even nearer, "maybe we could get together sometime and—"

"Step aside," someone said. "Out of the way. Let's go. People coming through. Move along." A pause. "Bell's rung."

"The bell's rung?" Panic at the thought of being late finally wrested Angela's attention from Patrick's baby blues.

Automatically, she moved toward the door—and almost bounced off the brawny chest and gigantic, sneaker-clad feet belonging to Nate Kelly, industrial arts (and home economics) teacher extraordinaire (at least in his own mind) and her brother Reno's best friend. Nate was hard to miss, given the way he filled out the door frame, almost edging aside Patrick altogether.

Clearly, being flirted with (especially by Perfect Patrick) was completely outside Angela's realm of experience, if she'd become clumsy enough to try to bulldoze past Nate Kelly.

"Whoops! Sorry." Angela reached out to steady herself.

She was too late—Nate already had his hand on her arm. After assuring himself she was steady, he released her. Then his gaze sharpened on Patrick, who'd watched their interaction with an impatient expression. "Hey, Goodger. How's it hanging?"

"Fine, fine. How's the pie baking coming along?"

Nate's lips compressed. "It's excellent."

"Good. I was just about to get Angela's phone number, then I'll be out of your way."

Both men shifted their attention to her, Patrick's making Angela feel warm all over—kind of the way she felt when slipping into a hot bubble bath. She'd have to ease herself into this experience, too. She didn't want to get burned . . . again.

"Um. Right." Angela gestured beyond the doorway at the students moving past. "Some other time though, okay, Patrick? If the bell's already rung, I don't want to be late. Bye!"

With an alacrity that surprised even her, she slipped between

Nate and Patrick, then made a safe getaway down the hall toward room 224, her heart and mind both galloping ahead.

Perfect Patrick had asked for *her* phone number. Hers! Angela thought in amazement. This was going to be easy! Just like diagramming sentences! She might have been out of the game for a while, but clearly Angela Wright was on her way again.

Damn, Angela was fast. Probably because she was small— at least compared with him—Nate reasoned as he pursued her down the hallway, carving a path amid the student body. He ducked his head and went faster, inhaling the high school's characteristic smells of wet backpacks, teenaged attempts at cologne, and the peppermint candy canes currently being sold by the DECA club.

Mmmm. Candy canes. He'd totally have to hit Reno's store on the way home today and scam on more of that candy bonanza.

Reminded of his friend and the question he wanted to ask his sister, Nate picked up the pace. Angela's dark-haired figure bobbed into view as she moved with warmth and authority among the students, exchanging greetings with them. As always, he felt in awe of her ability to connect with the kids she taught. Sure, he'd come to teaching late. He did cut himself some slack there. But even after several years at Kismet High School, Nate didn't have the same aura of serenity and patience that Angela did.

God knows, he tried. But then some knucklehead would cram an educational DVD into a toaster oven or try to drill-press a nerdy kid's euphonium, and he'd lose it. Plain and simple.

"Hey, wait up." Finally reaching her, Nate positioned himself between little Angela Wright and the raucous student body. He straightened his shoulders. "I'll walk you to class."

Angela rolled her eyes, scarcely breaking stride. She obviously wasn't surprised to find him there beside her.

She gestured ahead. "I'm halfway there already."

"You wouldn't have been, if I hadn't come along. Too busy making goo-goo eyes at Patrick the Prick to hear the bell?"

"Nate! Be nice."

He grinned. "That's what everybody calls him, you know."

They didn't. But a little white lie could be forgiven in this instance. Angela was too gullible to protect herself.

She shook her head. "Not the female faculty members."

"Only because they're swayed by his big dumb cow eyes." Nudging Angela with his elbow, Nate gave his best lovesick Guernsey impression. She hooted. *Yes!* It made his day to crack her up like that. "I thought you were smarter than that."

A few more measured strides. "Look, just forget you saw any of that between me and Patrick Goodger, okay?" Angela darted a hesitant glance at him. "It was nothing."

"What, are you kidding me?" Nate stopped them both at the corner, touching her elbow to keep her nearby. She smelled delicious, like gingerbread, but beneath all that spiciness he felt fragility, too. "It was something, all right. I saw it." The first bell hadn't rung yet either. He'd been bluffing to break them up. "A woman like you is easy pickings for a guy like him."

Angela shrugged off his hold. Her green eyes narrowed as she looked at him. "I beg your pardon?"

Her lips tightened, too. Normally, her mouth looked soft and inviting and sweet. Whoops. This was more serious than he'd thought. Regrouping, Nate decided to hold off on his original question for her and proceed with some friendly advice. The way Reno would have wanted him to, in his absence.

"Okay, first lesson. Whatever you do, don't talk that way to Patrick the Prick. He'll just get off on your outrage."

"What?" Her eyes widened. "That's crazy."

"He'll probably convince himself it's unleashed passion, or

some bullshit. And *don't* give him those innocent eyes either, whatever you do. He'll interpret that look as an invitation."

After all, it *did* appear pretty inviting.

Angela scoffed. "That's nonsense."

"The more riled up you get, the more he'll like it," Nate said earnestly. "That's part of the prickishness about him."

"Prickishness isn't a word, and I'm not riled up!"

"Uhh . . . yes, you are. You're definitely . . . different, that's for sure." Stricken by that realization, all of a sudden, Nate scrutinized her. He'd never seen Angela look quite so . . . ripe before. So glowing and eager. In a heartbeat, the unbelievable truth occurred to him. "Oh shit. I've got it. You've entered the horny stage of motherhood, haven't you? I should have guessed!"

Her mouth flattened. "That's it. I'm going to class."

She pushed away from the wall they'd been standing beside, then easily reentered the flow of student traffic. The warning bell rang, alerting Nate to the fact that only a few minutes remained until the start of classes. Until Angela got away.

"Wait." Concerned, he loped after her. After a few strides, he caught up. "Don't be embarrassed. Once my nieces and nephews started school and got more independent, my sisters all went through this stage, too. I'll never forget it. It was horrible."

Angela slowed down. Her face paled. "Horrible?"

Soberly, Nate nodded. "Horrible for me! They wouldn't shut up about jumping their husbands in the laundry room, buying sex toys online, and test-driving phone sex." He shuddered. "Eww."

Angela gave him a curious look. "You don't like phone sex?"

For one taut moment, all he could do was stare at her.

Unbidden, his libido offered up a wholehearted endorsement of phone sex—and conjured up a likely scenario featuring him and Angela, too. Him, her, a pair of phones, and his own overactive imagination . . . mmm. That could be really, really hot.

No, it couldn't. Jesus. What was the matter with him?

Whatever it was, he refused to discuss S-E-X with his best friend's little sister. Even if she appeared to want him to.

Instead, Nate did the manly thing. He changed the subject.

"Have you seen Reno?" he asked, reverting to his original purpose for tracking down Angela this morning. "I stopped by the store on my way to work today, but he wasn't there."

"Hmmm." Thinking it over—and blessedly letting the whole fantasy phone sex scenario drop—Angela trod the last few yards to her classroom with Nate on her heels. "Well, he went to pick up someone at the airport last night. Late though, really late—the flight came in from L.A. at midnight or so. At least that's what Reno told me. But he ought to be back by now." Looking concerned, she bit her lip. "Maybe I should call him."

"I already tried. I got voice mail, which means he probably turned off his phone. Or ran out of juice." Stepping aside to let a few straggling students enter snug, poster-filled room 224, Nate scratched his head. "Who'd he go pick up, anyway?"

Maybe if he knew who it was, he could call them. Almost everybody knew everybody in Kismet. It was a nice small town.

"Um, Rachel Porter?" Angela searched for her cell phone, probably planning to pull one of her full-on mother-hen routines with Reno. She turned out her purse to reveal peanut-butter-cracker snacks—undoubtedly for her cutie-pie daughter, Kayla—vitamins, tissues . . . "You probably don't remember her—"

Nate blinked. Had Angela actually said . . . *"Rachel Porter?"*

"Yeah. She went to KHS, too, but in my class. The Porters live down the street from Reno, so they asked him to pick her up. And you know Reno. If someone needs help, of course he—"

"Rachel Porter was my dream girl," Nate blurted.

An incredible sense of excitement gripped him. Rachel Porter was coming here. Coming to Kismet. Coming *home*. He could hardly believe it. Automatically, he reached up to smooth his close-cropped haircut. This time, when Rachel Porter got a look at him, he wouldn't be sporting that dorky curly hairstyle and stupid Boyz II Men T-shirt he'd worn all through senior year. This time, she'd see him as he really was—Nate Kelly, Macho Man.

"Really? Your dream girl, huh? Another one?"

Indignantly, Nate set Angela straight. "Rachel Porter is the *only* one. The original and the best."

"Hmmm. I seem to recall your saying the same thing about Melanie, Anna, Renee . . . and that German teacher from last year."

"Ingrid!" Remembering her, Nate sighed. He glanced dreamily at Angela . . . whose know-it-all expression sucked him straight out of his happy daze. Was it his damn fault all his dream girls turned out to be wrong for him in the end? "This time it's different. Rachel Porter is different. You'll see."

"Mmm-hmmm. You're cute when you're delusional." Smiling hugely, Angela patted his biceps. "I want the whole dream girl scoop while we're on lunchroom monitoring duty today, you hear?"

She ducked inside her room, offered him a final cheesy grin through the window in the door, then waved good-bye.

That grin of hers nagged at him. Sure, he'd had his share of misguided crushes, Nate told himself. But that didn't mean he was wrong about Rachel Porter . . . or that Angela wouldn't realize it. He still wished he'd kept his mouth shut though.

It was one thing to advise Angela on her rampant horniness problem. That was only charitable, especially since they'd known one another since his peewee soccer days, when Angela had hung out on the sidelines with all their parents and her pink plastic My Little Pony and cheered on him and Reno. It was something else to admit (yet another) crush on the girl who'd gotten away.

But this time . . . this time Nate Kelly would have a second chance. With plans already coursing through him, Nate pumped out a few adrenaline-fueled pushups against a nearby drinking fountain, then hotfooted it to his own first-period class.

Dork no more, he was on the prowl!

Chapter Eleven

"So . . . thanks for the ride. And . . . everything." Standing beside her four suitcases and carry-on bag, Rachel kicked her boots at the snowy landing of her parents' front porch. It wasn't much more than a concrete slab with a minuscule roof and decorative wrought-iron supports (nothing like the palatial entryway to her Malibu beach house), but it was a relief finally to reach it. Even hours late. "I really appreciate it."

"You're welcome." Reno grinned, hunched against the bite in the early morning air. After unloading her luggage and chivalrously transporting it to the porch, he'd tossed his coat and flannel shirt back in his truck's cab, then escorted her in his T-shirt—his perfectly fitted, pectoral-muscle-outlining, James Dean-worthy, plain white T-shirt. "The trip turned out to be a little more than we bargained for though, didn't it?"

"Um, yeah." Feeling herself flush at the unexpected rapport between them—and everything else, too—Rachel wound her fingers around the wrought-iron porch support. "About that . . ."

She stopped, hardly able to articulate her feelings about the time they'd spent together. Their initial introduction might have been a bit rocky, it was true, but afterward . . .

Well, all she could say about *afterward* was that everything felt *different* between them now—now that she'd allowed herself to relax and enjoy it. Him. *Them*. Hot on the heels of the rough week she'd had, Reno's kindness had felt amazing. Especially coming packaged, as it had, along with twinkling green eyes, a killer smile, and a definite knack for filling out a pair of jeans—jeans she insisted on thinking of *not* as ordinary old-as-rocks Levis but as ultradistressed vintage denim.

Not that she intended to go all goo-goo eyed over it.

"Well, let's admit it. We were *stranded*," Rachel continued in her own defense, wrenching her gaze upward. "In the snow! We can't be held responsible for . . . you know."

Reno gave her a dubious look. She stared back at him, filled with assurance now that they were about to part. She'd spent the night in an actual pickup truck! That had to count as some kind of penance for her momentary slipup. And she'd been tied in knots for weeks, ever since Alayna's annual no-Christmas ban had kicked off. She deserved a little R & R, didn't she?

In fact, considering everything that had happened to her during the past week, she was lucky she hadn't lunged for Reno (and grabbed for his R & R) even sooner.

As though reading her mind, Reno stepped nearer.

Involuntarily—and aggravatingly—Rachel stepped back. Apparently Hollywood-style wariness died hard.

But all Reno did was zip up her hoodie with nimble fingers, then gently brush her chin with his knuckles. "I hope the whole experience taught you an important lesson."

"I doubt it." She smiled. "But for curiosity's sake . . . ?"

"Don't come to Michigan in wintertime," Reno said, "when you're not prepared."

As if she could *ever* be prepared for the likes of him.

"You're lucky you didn't freeze to death," he went on. "Next time I see you, you'd better be wearing something warmer."

His teasing, bossy tone made her want to salute him. Or kiss him. After . . . everything . . . Rachel wasn't sure which.

"You probably won't see me. I plan to just hole up here"— she gestured to the house she'd grown up in, a three-bedroom ranch currently decked out in Christmas lights and a front-door wreath—"and enjoy a nice, laid-back Christmas getaway."

"Oh. Okay. You're going to the Christmas parade though?"

"Nope."

"The municipal tree-lighting ceremony downtown?"

"Uh-uh."

"The Glenrosen block party?" At her head shake, Reno winced as if wounded. "You've *got* to go to that. It's tradition."

"Not for me." Feeling awkward—yet weirdly reluctant to part with him—Rachel hugged her Hermès. "Not anymore. I can do without the Midwestern holiday hoedown, believe me."

Reno raised his chin. He was, she'd noticed, kind of sensitive about any trash-talking she did about Kismet. But she just couldn't help it. The force of habit was too strong. Also, how else would anyone realize she'd moved beyond this burg?

"Besides," Rachel said, driven to make amends in a way that would have shocked the proprietors of any trendy boutique she frequented (and haggled at) on Melrose, "by the time the Glenrosen block party rolls around, my mom will probably have stuffed me so full of eggnog, Christmas cookies, and ranch dip—"

"Ranch dip?"

"Don't ask. It's a family tradition."

"Ah." Reno nodded. In the daylight sparkling off the snow in the yard, his eyes were flecked with gold. "Our family tradition is pizza on Christmas Eve, presents on Christmas morning, and complete bedlam on Christmas day. All day long. My niece, Kayla, goes totally nuts. Pretty boring, but—"

"No, that's nice!" Smiling, Rachel squeezed his arm in assurance. Then she realized she was touching him—again—and made herself quit. Forcing a light tone, she added, "Anyway, I probably won't be able to squish myself into a decent outfit and waddle down to the block party, so don't hold out for me."

Not fitting into appropriate garb was totally an ironclad excuse. Nobody in L.A. would have argued with it.

"If you say so. I'll save you a cup of hot spiced cider all

the same." After a quick check to make sure she had her things, Reno jogged down the ice-crusted porch steps. He winked from the sidewalk below. "It's spiked. It makes all the girls easy."

Ha. She already *was* easy when it came to him. Hadn't last night proven that?

"Oh yeah? What does it do to the boys?" Rachel asked.

His grin made her weak in the knees. Or maybe that was the effect of standing on six inches of uneven snow on numb toes encased in superchic alligator-skin stiletto boots. Whatever.

"It makes them look twice as good to the girls." Another grin. "I plan on having a few extra cups."

As if he needed them.

Before Rachel could muster up a sassy response, Reno's cell phone rang. He plucked it out of his pocket, glanced at it, then held it up to show her.

"Sorry, I've got to get this. It's my sister."

At her nod, he trod a few more steps across the snow-covered lawn, past her mother's traditional sidewalk border of plastic reindeer. His square-jawed, cheerfully stubbled face made him seem like a prototype for macho men everywhere.

Too bad his natural habitat was (ugh) the boonies.

He turned, then held up his palm in farewell. "Nice to see you again, Rachel. Catch you in another ten years or so."

Raising the phone to his ear, Reno crossed the yard, then stopped beside his battered pickup. His voice carried in the stillness. "Hey, Sis. Yeah, sorry. I got kind of stranded."

There was a pause as he listened, fishing for his keys.

Oh God. He was talking to his sister about last night!

Frantically, Rachel waved her arms—a desperate signal for him *not* to spill the beans about their impromptu night together. What they'd done hadn't been all *that* scandalous. Not really. But still—she was trying to be fabulous, not fodder for gossip.

Unfortunately, Reno turned away before he saw her.

"Yeah. Somebody skidded off the highway into a snowbank."
Reno opened his driver's side door. It squealed into the post-dawn morning, echoing down the street—kind of like a secret being blurted down the phone line. "Nobody got hurt though."

On the porch, Rachel jumped up and down, waving her arms. How did you pantomime *Shut up! Shut up!* anyway? Those white-faced French guys probably never faced this problem.

But Rachel did. Because Reno merely got in his truck and fired up the engine, then chugged down the street. Damn it.

She'd *warned* him about this. She knew how gossip worked. Before she had even gotten out of his truck this morning, Rachel had exacted a solemn promise from him.

"You can't breathe a word about this to anyone," she'd warned. "Not a soul can know what happened between us last night. No matter what. Okay?"

Reno had only given her one of those half smiles of his. Then he'd shrugged. "Come on. Who am I going to tell?"

At the time, bewitched by his *you can trust me* smile and his freak country-style machismo, she'd figured that was close enough to a vow of silence to suit her. Now Rachel realized the truth. Who was he going to tell? The whole world, apparently.

By lunchtime, the news would be all over Kismet.

Marooned on the snowy porch, Rachel sighed. Then she picked up her carry-on luggage and faced the bow-bedecked wreath on the door. At this point, there was nothing to do but slip inside her parents' house, then do her best to stay there until the eggnog, sugar-sprinkled spritz cookies, and ranch dip had worked their magic, and she felt safe enough to return to L.A. to resume her usual fabulous life . . . fortified, Christmasified—and (she hoped) entirely forgiven.

Chapter Twelve

"Ooh, Rachel! Will you get the door please, hon?"

At the sound of her mother's voice coming down the hall-way, Rachel started. She glanced up from the rerun episode of MTV's *Made* she'd been watching on the den TV. Wow, it was getting dark outside already—when had that happened? Sniffling, she swiped a tissue under her tear-filled eyes, then blew her nose.

Those damn life-changing teenagers on *Made*, with their efforts to achieve impossible goals. (Seriously, galumphing two-left-footed emo kid to dazzling Broadway dancer? Be real!) With their goofy optimism and their inevitable disap-pointment and/or triumph, they were irresistible. They got to her every time.

Also, watching them had been better than what she'd been doing—dialing up her celebrity stylist clients, one by one, on her antique cell phone. And getting sent straight to voice mail over and over again. If no one would even talk to her, how was she supposed to move forward?

"Rachel Contessa Tiffany Porter!"

Uh-oh. Her whole name. This was serious.

Thanks to Christine Porter's love of all things upscale and Hollywood, Rachel had been saddled with two middle names. Contessa, because of that old movie, *The Barefoot Contessa*, with Humphrey Bogart and Ava Gardner, and Tiffany, because of the jewelry store. Obviously. If not for her dad's insistence that Rachel was "a good family name" (and his threat to dub her Gertie, after his great-great-grandmother), she'd have greeted the world as Tiffany Contessa Mercedes Audrey Hepburn Porter.

"Just a minute, Mom!" They were on the part where the *Made* kid's dream came true—or not. "I'll be right there."

"There's no time to wait." Her mother appeared in the doorway, clutching a wooden spoon in one hand and wearing an apron. Yes, an authentic apron. She'd adopted the habit after a marathon of retro *I Love Lucy* reruns on TV Land and had never quit. "Everyone is here." She squinted at the TV. "Can't you at least put that on something more seasonally appropriate? Please. Someone somewhere must be playing *The Santa Clause*. I love that movie. That Tim Allen is so cute, isn't he? Try TBS."

But Rachel's attention had skidded to a stop on the words *everyone is here*. She muted the TV. "What are you talking about? Who's everyone? And why are they here?"

She'd only been in town for a day and a half. That couldn't possibly involve *everyone*, in any shape or form.

"To see *you*, silly! The guest of honor!"

"Oh no, Mom, no. I came here to relax—"

"And that's exactly what you'll be doing at the party. Didn't I mention it?" Unfazed, her mother made shooing gestures with her wooden spoon. "Get going, young lady, and answer the door. I've got cheese balls to finish, you know."

Right on cue, the doorbell chimed again.

Listening, Rachel tilted her head. "'Jingle Bells?'"

"I had your father rewire it." Briskly, her mother turned, then headed back to the kitchen. Her voice floated to Rachel. "It's got six different chimes for all the holidays. You should hear Thanksgiving. It sounds like a real turkey gobbling!"

If only Rachel's chichi fashion-industry friends could see

her now. An authentic-sounding turkey gobble doorbell? Fabulous.

"A party, huh?" Resigned, Rachel sneaked a final glance at the TV. Awww. The emo kid was a pretty good dancer. Lots of heart. "What's with the guest of honor stuff?" She gathered her tissues, then stuffed them in the pocket of her pilled, droopy cashmere cardigan (aka, security blanket) as she followed her mom into the hallway. "You didn't tell me you were having a party."

"Just a small get-together. People in town want to see you, you know. My returning superstar." Her mom beamed at her as she grabbed her mixing bowl from the counter. "It wouldn't be right for your father and me to keep you all to ourselves."

"But you're the only ones I want to see!"

They were the only ones who wouldn't spot her secret shame from a mile away. Her parents thought Rachel hung the moon. Which could only be good for her battered psyche, right?

Her mother tsk-tsked. "Door!" she singsonged.

Reluctantly, Rachel raked her fingers through her hair, then headed through the dining room to the foyer. In the corner of the living room, a naked Christmas tree stood awaiting trimming. That was the only evidence of restraint in the place.

Everywhere else it looked as if the Target Christmas section had exploded. Lights blinked, discoing Santa gyrated, and garland wound around every surface. Holiday tchotchkes decorated the coffee table and side tables; a mistletoe-and-holly patterned fleece throw adorned the sofa. Even the foyer had earned its own Christmas treatment with a riotous display of greeting cards.

Jingle Bells, Jingle Bells came the electronic chime.

At the last instant, Rachel remembered to wriggle out of her comfy cardigan, leaving her dressed in a knit skirt, fuchsia tights, boots, and a blousy Stella McCartney original. It wasn't the ensemble she'd have chosen to wow Kismet with, but it would have to do. Sucking in a deep breath, she opened the door.

At The Big Foot, one of the few places in Kismet's cutesy, touristy, lakefront downtown that still catered to locals, Reno dragged his beer across the bar. He took a swig, then looked around, his whole body vibrating with the guitar music.

The band on the tiny stage was loud and homegrown. The patrons were boisterous and kind of crude. The ambiance was strictly beer-stained concrete, pitted wood tables, and liquor-company "stained glass" gimme lamps featuring logos of current and long-forgotten brands, but he liked it here. The Big Foot was the kind of place a man could go and just be himself.

"Hey, Reno." Next to him at the dimly lit bar—its only nod to the season a red and white felt Santa hat propped atop a bottle of Jim Beam—one of his neighbors nudged him. "How's it going, football star?"

"Can't complain. How 'bout you, Jimmy?"

"All right." In a cheerful salute, Jimmy lifted his mug of cheap draft. He clinked it against Reno's beer, then sipped.

Slowly. Jimmy Gurche had been nursing that beer for the past hour at least, Reno realized. Times were tough in parts of the state, with layoffs running rampant and—in Kismet at least, hardly a skiing mecca—tourism temporarily in hibernation.

"Hey, you didn't get your other beer." Reno motioned to the bartender. "Let's have another one over here for Jimmy."

"No, no, Reno. Thanks, but I'm fine with this one."

Reno had been afraid of that. Smiling, he slapped Jimmy on the shoulder. "Screw that, you SOB. I bought a round for the damned house," he lied, "and you're getting yours."

"Oh. Well." A smile slipped over Jimmy's face, reminding Reno of the way he'd looked when they'd been in high school together—and Jimmy had been dangling biology class frogs in front of the squealing girls. "In that case . . . thanks!"

"No problem. I've been meaning to talk to you anyway." Reno edged closer as inspiration struck him. "I could really use some part-time help down at The Wright Stuff, if you can see your way clear to doing me a favor over Christmas. Why don't you come down to the store tomorrow?"

Jimmy looked interested. "Hey, thanks, Reno. I just might do that. Marsha's been worrying about getting Christmas presents for the kids this year. Some extra work might set her mind at ease." He shook Reno's hand. "You're a lifesaver."

"Nah. I'm just a guy who's late delivering these beers."

Grinning, Reno raised the three drinks he'd bought. After working out the details of Jimmy's new job at The Wright Stuff and spending a few minutes analyzing the current football season, Reno actually *did* order another round for the house—just to make good his initial fib to Jimmy. Then, ducking his head against the roar of approval from The Big Foot's patrons, he headed back to his usual table.

There, he set a root beer on the paper coaster in front of Angela. He slid one Budweiser to Nate, then dropped in his chair, ready for some Tuesday night relaxation.

"Listen up." Nate nodded at Angela's root beer. "That's what you should drink on your date with Patrick the Prick. Root beer. So you'll be alert if he gets all handsy with you."

"He won't get handsy. We're just having coffee."

"Make it decaf," Nate warned with solemn eyes. "And don't get any goodies, like a donut or one of those scones. You want to be able to bolt fast if anything skeevy starts going down."

"Nate—"

"In fact, I should go with you. I'll be your muscle."

"Whoa, whoa." Reno glanced from his friend to his sister. He had the feeling he'd missed something important. "What's going on?"

Primly, Nate raised his chin. He pointed his beer bottle at Angela. "Your sister has decided to sleep around."

"What?"

"With Patrick the Prick," Nate elaborated.

"Hold on." In her own defense, Angela raised both hands. "Nate's getting three steps ahead of himself as usual."

"Hey! I resent that. Next you'll be spreading rumors about me and getting me kicked off the Kismet High School faculty."

"I have *not* decided to sleep around. Or eat donuts with random men." With her usual warmth and earnestness, Angela met Reno's gaze. "I just think it's time to start dating again."

Then she picked up her root beer and chugged.

Reno boggled. "No. This is a bad idea."

Nate nodded. *"Especially* if it involves Patrick the—"

"Wait." Reno turned to him. *"Who* again?"

"Patrick Goodger." Angela sighed, then wiped her mouth. "From the high school. Remember? He's the one with dreamy eyes."

Nate snorted. Reno squinted, trying to recall. Dreamy eyes weren't high on his priority list. He came up with zip.

"You met him at the organizational meeting for Kayla's Christmas pageant. He's helping with the A/V equipment. Patrick is a real genius when it comes to handling equipment."

"I'll just *bet* he is," Nate said darkly. "If he whips out a camcorder, asks you to take off your shirt, then promises the video is 'just for him,' here's what you do—knee him in the nuts, then run like hell."

He nodded for emphasis, his blond brows drawn together.

Angela ignored him. "I gave him my phone number yesterday, and we might get together over Christmas break. That's all. It's perfectly innocent. Just a way to get my feet wet."

"Are you sure that's a good idea?" Frowning, Reno gripped his beer. The raucous music poured over him, but it no longer felt cheerful or even normal. This was big. Really big. "Getting your feet wet was how you wound up with Kayla."

"And that turned out terrifically, didn't it?" Angela stared him down. "I have a beautiful daughter. So don't worry."

More worried than ever, Reno and Nate frowned at her. Her mulish expression dared them to disagree. Reno would have sooner licked the grungy floor of The Big Foot than say another word.

Nate wasn't so smart. "Sure, Kayla's great and all. But you're not ready for this, Angela. You haven't been out there."

"Oh. And I suppose you have?"

Stonily, Nate peered at his Budweiser. "I could have, if I wanted to. With Melanie, Anna, *or* Renee." After a tense minute, he shifted his gaze to Reno. "And starting now, I want to."

Reno glanced up, still stuck on figuring out who Melanie, Anna, and Renee were. Oh yeah. Nate's former "dream girls."

"I heard Rachel Porter is back in town," his buddy was saying urgently. "And I also heard you two are tight, on account of your picking her up at the airport yesterday—"

Unbidden, an image of Rachel whooshed into Reno's brain, amplified by those crazy sexy boots, her frankly endearing smile . . . and all the ways they'd passed the time while stuck on the freeway waiting for traffic to clear. If he hadn't experienced it himself, he would never have believed it.

Him and Rachel Porter. Together . . .

Stifling a grin, Reno checked back into the conversation just in time to catch Nate twisting his high school class ring on his finger. It was his buddy's primary nervous tic, the tell that would have allowed Reno to clean house when they played five-card stud, if he hadn't been such an upright guy. Almost unconsciously, Reno touched his own Super Bowl ring.

"—because if *you* fixed us up together, it would really mean something," Nate was insisting. "You're a big man in this town, Reno. You know that. Rachel must know that, too."

It's one step up from a tractor, but it's yours.

You know that kid Pigpen? You've got his truck.

"Actually, she wasn't very impressed with me."

"So if you could, you know, put in a good word for me," Nate pressed onward, "it would really mean a lot."

Lost in remembering that outrageous miniskirt of Rachel's, Reno nodded absently. It was a shame she wasn't going to any of the Kismet Christmas events. There was no chance of her scandalizing the town while holed up at the Porters' house.

"Or even, I don't know . . ." Nate gulped, now peeling off the condensation-dampened label on his half-empty beer. "Invite her to some event so we can meet? Just give me some warning okay? Because I'm going to want to get mentally prepared."

Silence descended. Well, the crashing music kept playing, and the balls on the pool tables kept clinking, and people around them kept talking and laughing, but otherwise . . . nada.

Reno snapped out of it. He found his sister and his best friend both staring expectantly at him.

An ominous feeling settled over him. Trying to dispel it, he swigged more beer. "What? What's the matter?"

"So will you do it?" Nate prodded. "Come on, Reno."

"Yeah, Reno." Angela grinned. "Will you do it?"

He had no idea what they were talking about. Something about Nate, the airport, and Reno's reputation in town. But it was all mixed up with meanderings about Rachel Porter's sexy (and snow-inappropriate) miniskirt, her long, long legs . . . and everything that had happened between them a day and a half ago.

There was only one thing to do. The thing Reno always did.

"Yeah, of course I'll do it," he said.

"You will?" Nate's entire face brightened, from his square jaw to his blond buzz cut. He slapped Reno on the shoulder— a left tackle-size blow that would have toppled a lesser man. "That's awesome! Oh, sweet! You're the best, I swear."

He crossed his fingers over his heart, then kissed his fingertips and blew the kiss away. It was, quite possibly, the cheesiest, lamest gesture anyone in The Big Foot had ever made.

But Reno was glad to see his friend happy. He and Nate had been through a lot together, from high school football to NFL training camp to girlfriends, business troubles, and more. There wasn't much he wouldn't do for Nate.

"Glad to help." Whatever it was, he could handle it.

"I can't wait!" Grinning from ear to ear, Nate stood. His height and musculature incited people at nearby tables to lean out of the way. "This calls for another round. On me!"

Gleefully, he lumbered away, head bobbing to the music.

"Wow." Smiling, Reno leaned toward Angela. Later he'd deal with her reentry into the dating world—and what a huge mistake it might be. Right now . . . "Okay. What did I just agree to do?"

Trapped on the sofa between Bidie Niedermeyer and Susanne Fowler, Rachel took another gulp of her mother's favorite home-style holiday punch: rainbow sherbet floating in 7-Up. She shuddered. Maybe if she poured some Stoli in it?

"Tell us, tell us, dear! What's J-Load really like?"

Who? Oh. Right. "Um, I don't work with Jennifer Lopez."

"Then who's that foreign girl they're always talking about in *Us Weekly*?" Bidie asked. "The one with the big bazongas?"

Alayna would have loved to hear herself described that way.

"That's Alayna Panagakos, Mrs. Niedermeyer. From the group Goddess?" Rachel glanced around. The usual nods of instant recognition did not hit her. That's right. She was in the heartland, surrounded by people who took *The View* seriously. To elaborate, she added, "She's Greek. Oh, and a man-stealing, backstabbing devil whore, too, but in Hollywood these days—"

All conversation stopped. The only sounds were the crooning melodies of her mother's Perry Como Christmas CD on the stereo and the hilariously oblivious crunching of Mr. Fowler eating cheese balls spread on the "fancy" kind of Ritz crackers.

"Kidding!" Rachel forced a laugh, trying not to meet her father's appalled gaze. "Alayna's wonderful. She's one of my best friends in fact. Almost like a sister." At least she had been. "We live next door to each other in Malibu. On the beach."

Or at least they had. Until Alayna's latest tantrum.

"Oh, like Barbie's Malibu beach house!" Mrs. Fowler said.

"Tell us more!" Mrs. Niedermeyer urged, her eyes bright above her sequined patchwork holiday sweater with working mini Christmas lights on the shoulders. "We're all so proud of you."

"We always knew you'd make something of yourself."

"Something wonderful! With those sewing skills of yours—"

"Well, I don't sew much these days." *Unless I'm making an impromptu revenge outfit.* Rachel faced the Hendricksons, longtime friends of her parents who'd leaned forward to hear more. "But I am intimately involved in the fashion industry."

"No sewing?" Mrs. Fowler looked sad. "That's a shame."

"Rachel sets trends!" her mother piped up. "You know those stovepipe pants? My little girl got people wearing those again."

Well. Rachel could hardly take *all* the credit for the resurgence of skinny jeans. But with everyone who mattered to her parents gathered in the same room, waiting to hear about her incredible, successful life in Hollywood, she couldn't bear to disappoint. But she couldn't bring herself to lie either.

Right now, pretending to be the same person she'd always been would be the hugest whopper of all.

All she'd wanted was to escape reality for a while. How had it followed her all the way to her dinky, touristy hometown?

"Oh, come on. That's work talk, and this is a holiday party!" Rachel exclaimed. Brightly, she put her hands on her thighs, then pushed upward, cutting a swath among her parents' friends. "This is supposed to be a tree-trimming party, right?" For some reason, when her parents had learned she was coming, they'd waited for her to help with the tree. As if she were eleven again. "Who wants to decorate a Christmas tree?"

"Ooh!"

"Why, that sounds like fun."

"Where are the ornaments?"

Everyone scattered, ready to create some Christmas cheer.

In the midst of the hubbub, Rachel released a sigh. Party guests milled around her, momentarily—and purposefully—distracted from all talk of L.A., fashion, or even sewing.

She hadn't lost her touch for *everything* useful. Apparently she was still pretty good at L.A.-style razzle-dazzle—at useful misdirection. Satisfied, she grabbed her punch cup, trying to appear as if she were dying for a refill of Candyland punch.

Halfway across the living room, she glimpsed her father. Before everyone had arrived, he'd lugged a cardboard box full of ornaments from the closet in her old bedroom—which had basically been converted into a sewing room/guest room/giant junk drawer. Now Gerry Porter stood surrounded by middle-aged couples, all of them oohing and ahing over the decorations as they lifted each gaudy, careworn, or kitschy item from the box.

Catching her eye, her dad nodded at her.

Rachel's stomach clenched. Just like that, she realized the truth. Her father knew! He might not know everything (honestly, how could he?), but he knew *something*. He knew something was wrong, and he'd probably spotted her misdirection, too. Damn it.

With a gulp, Rachel escaped to the kitchen. She glanced at the clutter, at the spare cheese balls with their "elegant" coating of chopped walnuts and parsley, at the empty two-liter 7-Up bottles, at the shopping bag full of reindeer-themed wrapping paper in the corner, and the countertop with its lined-up bottles of decorator sprinkles ready for Christmas cookies.

"Rachel, honey? Hurry up," her mother called from the

living room. "We're unpacking the ornaments you made in grade school."

With a groan, Rachel leaned against the refrigerator.

"Rachel?" her father called. "Bring in more punch, please."

She'd come home to Kismet to escape. Instead it felt as if everything was coming at her at warp speed here—wrapped in Christmas paper and covered in bright blinking lights. Ho-ho-ho.

"I'll bet she's making an important phone call," came Mrs. Fowler's gossipy voice. "To someone in Hollywood!"

Instantly, chatter overtook the room and flowed to Rachel. They were off again, talking about her celebrity clients and her "Barbie house" in Malibu. Mrs. Hendrickson offered the opinion that everyone was "too naked" in L.A., while Mr. Hendrickson countered that they could afford to be "with that nice weather."

"Oh look!" her mother exclaimed. "Here's the souvenir ornament Rachel sent us when she first went away to become a famous designer. It's a tiny star, like on the Walk of Fame!"

"Come see this, Rachel," her father demanded.

"Umm, I'll be right there," Rachel called.

Then she set down her punch cup, grabbed a scarf from the hook by the kitchen door, and (for the second time in four days) made her getaway. To anyplace but here . . . in Christmas Town.

Chapter Thirteen

In the dim light of The Big Foot, Reno fixed his sister with an unswerving look. "I mean it. What did I agree to do?"

All Angela did was keep laughing, shaking her head.

"Hurry up!" Glancing over his shoulder, Reno spotted Nate on his way back to their table with more root beer and Budweisers. And a big smile. "He's almost here. Come on."

"This is just like you. Agreeing to help before you even know what's going on. Seriously, Reno. When are you going to realize that you don't have to take care of everyone?"

"What a ridiculous question. What did I agree to do?"

For a minute, his sister gazed at him with an almost regretful expression. Or maybe she was just contemplating her upcoming date with that dreamy-eyed prick guy. Who knew?

"Angela!"

"Okay, fine." She scooted her chair closer and leaned in. "You just agreed to set up Nate with Rachel Porter."

Reno frowned. "On a date?"

"No, on a fishing trip." After a deadpan look, Angela rolled her eyes. "Yes, a date! At school today, Nate told me that Rachel Porter was his dream girl." She fluttered her eyelashes girlishly, then grinned. "He's crazy about her."

"No."

"Yes."

Uh-oh. Not again. Nate was as prone to falling in and out of love—often without the object of his affection even knowing about it—as most men were to sniffing their dirty laundry in case they could eke out another wearing. It was one of his quirks, lovable but potentially problematic. Like brewing his coffee beans twice, reusing razor blades, or buying auto parts for his beat-up old Chevette from a secondhand supplier.

"But Rachel Porter is all wrong for him. She hates small towns, especially Kismet. She doesn't like trucks. Or Care Bears. Or Christmas. She's a diva with a capital D."

"Care Bears?"

"Never mind. It's . . . complicated. See, the other night when I went to pick up Rachel at the airport, we got stranded. Remember? We were stuck for hours. There wasn't much to do, so—"

Angela gasped. "Reno, no. You didn't!"

Uncomfortably, he squirmed. "It's not what you—"

"Hey, the conquering hero returns with the brewskis!"

With a jovial smile, Nate arrived at their table, thunking down new drinks, and bringing Reno's confession to an immediate halt. Which was probably good. Trying to ignore his sister's accusatory expression, he turned to his friend.

"Listen. About that Rachel Porter thing. I'm not the best guy to fix you up with her."

At Nate's crestfallen expression, Reno felt worse than ever. "I mean, matchmaking? That's for wusses right? Guys who go to spas and run teddy bear factories." He mustered up a grin. "I'm no Christmas cupid. You're better off without her."

"Yeah," Angela put in. "Maybe Reno is right. After all, you haven't seen her for a while. Who knows where she's been?"

Angela's knowing look suggested that *who* she'd been *with* was a more important question. But, true to form, his sister was going to make Reno come clean himself. Before he could . . .

"She's been in L.A." Indignantly, Nate squared off against both of them. "I Googled her. She's a famous celebrity stylist now." Eagerly, he nodded. "And she looks better than ever."

"A celebrity stylist? Wow, that sounds really glamorous!" Angela aimed a curious glance at Reno. "I wonder why she left a life like *that* to come back to Kismet?"

"We'll probably never know. And looks aren't everything."

At Reno's blunt pronouncement, Nate shook his head. "I don't want Rachel Porter because she's a smoking hottie. There's more to it than that. I've dreamed about her since high school."

"All the more reason for you not to be disappointed now."

With that said, Reno slugged back more beer. There was no way he could fix up Nate with Rachel Porter. She'd take one look at poor hapless home ec/industrial arts teacher Nate and break his heart. He couldn't do it. Nate meant more to him than that.

The woman didn't even like Christmas. Come on.

Nate looked puzzled. "Are you saying you won't do it?"

Angela smirked. "But you *promised*, Reno."

The hell? They were ganging up on him now?

"But you *always* help out." Nate sounded utterly baffled. He stared at Reno, then his eyes narrowed. "Unless . . . I know what it is. You want her for yourself! You saw her at the airport and drove her home, and she was amazing and sweet and wonderful and smart and talented, and you want her for yourself. Admit it!"

Oh, man. This just got worse and worse. With another guilty slug of his beer, Reno glanced at his friend. He should admit what had happened between him and Rachel and be done with it. It wasn't a crime. It wasn't even that scandalous. He wasn't sure why she'd sworn him to secrecy, but . . .

Hell. He couldn't do it. He couldn't let down Nate, but he also couldn't let him be hurt. He couldn't blurt out the secret of what he and Rachel had done, but he also couldn't stay silent. At least not for much longer. He'd almost told Angela. . . .

"I don't want Rachel for myself." It was a harmless lie, Reno figured. What were the odds it would come back to bite him? "And she wasn't all that sweet either." Except sometimes. "The truth is, she's not the right kind of woman for you, Nate."

"Says you." Nate scoffed, lifting his Budweiser. "You always think you know what's best for people."

"Amen." Angela nodded. The traitor.

"You're the one who wants my help!" Reno protested.

"I'm perfectly capable of impressing Rachel Porter on my own." Nate leaned back, a grin spreading over his face. "I've changed a lot over the years. All I need is a boost from you, the resident big shot. Just to get me started, that's all."

Ugh. *Resident big shot*. Nate had had to go and bring that up, hadn't he? It wasn't as though he and Nate hadn't *both* been town heroes when they'd been drafted into the NFL. The trouble was, Nate had come back to Kismet three weeks into Scorpions training camp, after being booted from the team. Reno had come back years later . . . a Super Bowl superstud in the eyes of everyone.

Trapped, Reno gazed at Nate. The truth was, he'd already agreed. He was not a guy who went back on his word.

"All right. The first time I see Rachel Porter around town," Reno promised, "I'll make sure the two of you have a chance to meet and spend some time together."

Since the odds of him seeing Rachel Porter again—by her own admission—were exactly zero, what was the harm in that?

In the end, Rachel chose her ultimate destination because it was the least Christmassy looking place on Main Street.

Also because her nose was getting numb. She seriously thought frostbite might be setting in. Despite her artistically wrapped scarf, she still wore only a cute skirt, top, and tights—hardly thermalwear.

In hindsight, she realized she probably should have had a few more qualms about stepping into The Big Foot.

It wasn't the loud local music. That couldn't compare to a

club on Sunset, where her teeth felt pried from their sockets after ten minutes. It wasn't even the patrons. They weren't any scarier—despite their obvious love of flannel—than some of the edgier artistic folks she encountered every day. Nope. It wasn't even the preponderance of country-style décor—deer heads and stuffed fish mounted on the walls—that alarmed her.

It was her reaction to seeing Reno Wright that did her in.

But first . . .

"Ohmigod! Rachel Porter! Is that you?"

At the sound of that excited feminine voice, Rachel turned from her place at the bar, where she'd been waiting for the bartender to figure out her request for a nice, body- and soul-warming saketini—evidently a drink that went beyond exotic out here in Nowheresville. Coming straight toward her was a woman her own age, dressed in wide wale corduroy pants and a turtleneck sweater, with shoulder-length brown hair and a smile.

Well, when in doubt, friendliness was always best.

"Um, hi! Yes! It's me, Rachel!" Plastering an answering smile on her face, Rachel went in for an automatic air kiss. One side. Two sides. A whiff of . . . crayons? There. "How *are* you?"

Appearing somewhat baffled—whoops, probably because of the L.A.-style air kiss—the woman put her hand to her cheek. "Um, I'm fine. You look *great*. Wow. I heard you were back in town."

"Yep. Here I am!"

"I can't believe it. Look at you!" Shaking her head—then glancing over her shoulder into the depths of The Big Foot with an unreadable expression—the woman gave a tsk-tsk. "I should have known you would wind up looking amazing."

"And you! So . . . um, comfortable." Rachel smiled, racking her brain for a name to go with the face. "That's great."

An awkward silence descended. Except for the ear-bleeding music. And the rowdy laughter. And the clanking billiard balls.

"I'm Angela Wright. Third-period geometry. Remember?"

Relief coursed through Rachel. "Of course. I'm sorry, Angela. It's been a crazy week." Contrite, she hugged her. "Let me buy you a drink! What would you like?"

"Oh, I can't stay. I was just on my way out." Looking genuinely sorry, Angela sorted through her purse. "I'm a mom now. I have a daughter, Kayla. She's with her grandma right now, but tomorrow's a school day, so I can't stay out late."

A daughter. Wow. Angela had really settled down and made something of her life. Despite her corduroys and turtleneck, she seemed truly happy. Also down-to-earth and approachable. Warm.

Genuineness had been a quality Angela had always possessed, Rachel remembered. That, and a knack for getting library passes from their KHS teachers—all of whom had loved her.

Wait a minute. *That's* where she knew Angela from! She'd been Rachel's source for get-out-of-class passes so she could smoke in the girls' bathroom (a habit she'd since kicked), get in trouble, and hang out with her latest boyfriend. Filled with nostalgia for her younger, rebellious self, Rachel smiled.

"I'm so glad I ran into you," she said.

"Me, too." Angela wrote something on a slip of Santa Claus themed notepaper, then pressed it in Rachel's hand. "Here's my phone number. We should get together sometime soon."

"Of course. Sure!"

Angela smiled. "I really mean it. It would be fun."

"Oh." Flummoxed by the sincerity in Angela's voice, Rachel gazed at her. "You *do* mean it. Okay. I'll call you."

It was going to take awhile to get her bearings here in Kismet. The mounted fish heads weren't the only things she'd forgotten about when she'd left town for L.A.

"But first, there's someone here I want you to meet."

Grabbing her hand, Angela towed her into the depths of The Big Foot. Scrambling along in the semidarkness on her stiletto boots, Rachel ducked between crowded tables, glimpsing faces lit by neon liquor signs. People turned her way. Murmuring started.

Oh no. This wasn't what she'd planned. All she'd wanted was to dodge the incessant questioning—and the Christmas decorating—at her parents' house. She wasn't ready for either one.

Self-consciously, Rachel smoothed her skirt. With her heart pounding in rhythm with the screeching guitar music and her nostrils twitching at the skunky odor of spilled beer, she followed Angela all the way to a corner table. Really, Angela ought to consider a finer wale corduroy. And maybe a more feminine top. Because while polyester knit was practical . . .

A man glanced up questioningly. Her breath stopped.

Reno Wright. Here. Again.

He looked even better than he had a day and a half ago. She guessed a shower and shave did that for a man. Also, not having just come from an hours-long layover in a cramped pickup truck. His face was strong and handsome, his hair a little mussed, his expression . . . horrified. Barely stopping on Angela, he sent his gaze straight to Rachel. Which was rude. Honestly. If he—

Wright. Angela Wright. And Reno Wright. Oh. Aha.

"Where's Nate?" Angela demanded in an accusatory voice.

For an instant, Reno simply couldn't tear his gaze away from Rachel. She was wearing one of those short skirts again. And those crazy-colored tights that made a man feel imaginative. And those boots. Ah, those boots. You just didn't see boots like those around Kismet. Maybe she was a hallucination. A sexy fantasy his brain had conjured up due to the stress of becoming an unwilling matchmaker for his best friend.

"Reno!" Angela barked. "Where's Nate?"

Startled, Reno glanced up. Keeping his voice purposefully low, he angled his chin toward the other side of the bar. "Nate recognized Rachel and developed a sudden need to shoot pool."

"What? Oh, please . . ."

"Seriously, he turned white as a ghost."

At this revelation, Angela glanced around. Her gaze finally came to rest on a big-eyed, cue-nibbling Nate, hiding behind a fat square pillar near the pool tables. She sighed.

She and Reno looked at Rachel.

Who appeared puzzled. And sexy. And sweet.

Damn it. Why sweet? Why now? She was making a liar of him.

"I thought you were staying home all week," he said.

"I couldn't take the run up to Christmas with my parents and all their gung-ho friends. I'm hiding out here."

He remembered Rachel ripping up his impromptu sign at the airport. *Let's keep my arrival between ourselves, okay?*

"You seem to do that a lot. Hiding out I mean."

"When I'm not trapped in the grimemobile."

"Hey, it's a good truck."

"With inadequate room for luggage."

"I fixed that." Reno scanned her up and down. "But you still haven't figured out that it's wintertime."

He got up and yanked off his Scorpions sweatshirt, then handed it to her. "Here. Next time, bring a coat."

Rachel recoiled. "No thanks! That thing has a cartoon football on it. And it's made of cotton." She shuddered.

So much for chivalry. Reno balled up his sweatshirt, a little miffed on behalf of his former championship team.

"Wait a minute," Angela interrupted, glancing wide-eyed between them. "You don't like football?"

"I like the tight pants," Rachel mused. "And a nice Super Bowl party is fun. Things are *so* dead until award-show season."

In patent disbelief, Reno and Angela both gawked at her.

"You don't know who Reno is then," Angela said. "Wow."

"That doesn't matter." Reno didn't want to get into it.

"No." Glancing between them, Rachel frowned. "Who is he?"

"Only the most in-demand, highest ranked, most popular—"

"Angela, aren't you late to pick up Kayla?"

"—rookie kicker drafted in the NFL in the last ten years," his sister finished proudly. "Reno was a superstar. Huge."

"Hmmm." Rachel nodded. "That explains the attitude."

Angela burst out laughing. "That clinches it. You're officially not from Kismet anymore. Most of the women around here swoon when Reno and his football fortune swagger by."

"Really?" Rachel arched her eyebrow. "Go figure."

Kind of affronted, Reno slugged more beer.

"Uh-oh. Look," Angela said. "He's pouting now."

"Aww. Would it help if I waved some pom-poms around?"

Intrigued by the idea of Rachel with pom-poms—but too annoyed to admit it—Reno zeroed in on both of them.

He offered a bland look. "Are you two having fun?"

"Actually, yeah." They exchanged glances. "We are."

"A lot of fun." Rachel smiled at her new pal.

Great. They'd already bonded. That could only mean trouble. Deliberately, Reno focused on Angela. "See you later. Give Kayla a hug for me. And while you're at Mom's, tell her to quit dragging her feet on the divorce. Dad's not changing his mind."

At least that's the way it looked right now. Reno wanted his mom to be prepared for that, so she wouldn't get hurt.

His sister merely stared at him, looking deflated. "Geez, Reno. She only asked him if they were still going to work on the Kismet Christmas decorating committee together this year."

"If there's any way they can get out of it . . . My guess would be no."

Angela put her hand on her hip. "You don't have to be all hardcore macho about this, Reno."

"I'm being realistic." If he were lucky, he was also being irritating enough to scare his dad out of the born-again bachelorhood Tom Wright seemed determined to turn his golden years into. But he didn't want to get Angela's hopes up. It was a big brother's job to protect his sister. "You should be, too."

"That's not realistic, it's lame. Have you forgotten the whole story, or what? Geez, Reno. It's almost Christmas!"

"What story?" Rachel piped up, looking interested.

"My genius dad," Angela confided in disgusted tones, "ate a delicious Thanksgiving dinner this year, cooked by my mom, then whipped out his checkbook and handed her a blank check."

"What for?" Rachel asked.

"He told her, and I quote"—she paused for emphasis—"it would 'save all the trouble' of buying each other gifts."

"No. He didn't!"

"Yes, he did." Angela nodded. "And after forty years of marriage, too. It's a crying shame. They've been split ever since, and all because of one stupid blank check."

"It all made sense," Reno felt compelled to point out. He'd already discussed this issue with his dad. "It would have saved a *lot* of trouble. Mom is hard to find gifts for."

"Making sense isn't the point. Dad hurt Mom's feelings. If he'd just get off his high horse and apologize for once—"

"Seriously." Reno stopped her with his palm in the air. He shafted a sideways glance at Rachel. "This isn't the best time."

Angela frowned. "You're right. I'm sorry, Rachel. I just hate all this family conflict. Especially at Christmastime."

She had that right. Angela typically went out of her way to smooth things over. She was even nice to telemarketers.

Now she was being nice to Rachel, the unwitting focus of Reno's unwanted matchmaking assignment. While he debated the likelihood that she and her boots would conveniently vanish to L.A. before Nate reappeared from the pool tables, his sister turned to Rachel, gave her a hug, then said her good-byes.

"Reno's going out to cut down a Christmas tree tomorrow night," Angela told Rachel eagerly. "You should go with him."

What was she, nuts? "No, I don't think—" Reno began.

"It would be a good chance for you *and Nate* to spend some time with Rachel," Angela persisted. "Don't you think so, Reno?"

Oh, yeah. That damn matchmaking mission.

"Good idea. I'll go make sure we're on with Nate."

Scraping back his chair, Reno headed for the pool tables. Partway there, he glanced back to find Rachel settling in—at his sister's urging—at his table, crossing her legs and tossing her mass of dark glossy hair, looking wildly out of place but also looking outrageously good while doing it. Damn. How was he supposed to *not* have a continuation of what they'd done together if Angela kept pushing Rachel at him at every opportunity?

On the other side of the bar, patrons leaned against the wall beside The Big Foot's two pool tables, watching the action. The jukebox was here, for use when there wasn't a live band. So was the cue rack, extra chalk, and a whole lot of wood paneling.

Nate, however, was nowhere in sight.

Persistently, Reno circled the tables. He gazed across the smoky bar and even checked out the stage (Nate had once played drums in middle school band). In the end, he found his buddy, flushed and panicky, holed up in the alcove near the pay phone.

Reno tapped his shoulder. "Hey, what's with the running away? Rachel's right over there, waiting to meet you."

Nate balked. "No. No, I can't meet her right now! Are you crazy?" He ran his hand through his cropped hair. "I need some hair gel. Maybe a new shirt. And *definitely* a better opening line than *uhhhhh*. Which is all I've come up with so far."

Reno quirked his mouth. "Some girls find a perfect dial tone imitation charming."

"Not her. Not Rachel." Penned in the alcove, Nate still managed to pace, consuming the space with his broad shoulders. "She's special. Look, just make some excuse for me, okay?

I wasn't prepared this time. But with a little more warning, things between me and Rachel will be killer. You'll see."

Reno stepped sideways, far enough to see beyond the corner of the alcove and get a view of the rest of The Big Foot. Now Rachel was chatting with the people at the next table, all of whom were smiling and laughing. Two eager-looking men arrived with drinks for her, then slid into the unoccupied seats.

"You'd better hurry," Reno warned. "She's popular."

Appearing stricken, Nate glanced out. "Oh God."

That decided it. Unwanted mission or not, Reno couldn't dick around. Nate's happiness—however temporary—depended on it. He had to make this "dream girl" thing happen. He had to cook up the perfect dating game plan for Nate . . . and keep his friend from getting crushed when Rachel left, besides.

"She's going Christmas tree-cutting with us tomorrow."

Nate turned puppy-dog grateful eyes on him. "She is?"

A nod. Reno gave Nate the details, then exacted a promise from his friend to show up. "Angela arranged it. Thank her."

"I can't thank her right now." Nate grabbed his throat, shoving at his shirt collar. "I think I'm hyperventilating."

"Relax. Everything will be fine."

Reno glanced at their table again. Drinks cluttered the surface, piling up for Rachel. Local lotharios swarmed along with smiling, gossipy women. Everyone appeared to love her.

Following his gaze, Nate grabbed Reno's arm. "Jesus, they're on her like coconut on a German chocolate cake!"

Perplexed, Reno raised his eyebrows.

Impatiently, Nate waggled his fingers. "We're on a layer cake unit. That sticky coconut icing is one mean motherfu—"

"You've got to find a new teaching gig next year."

"Just promise me one thing." With urgency blazing from his eyes, Nate stared Reno down. "Promise me you'll keep an eye on Rachel for me okay? Just until I get my shit together."

Oh no. N-O. Running interference was one thing. Taking

over the play himself was stepping over the line. Reno didn't know what might happen. "Nate, come on. You don't need me to—"

"You're the only one I trust!" His buddy shook his arm. "Promise, Reno! Make sure she doesn't get with one of those smart-talking, drink-buying assclowns before I make my move."

Awww, hell. Given the way Reno was starting to feel about Rachel Porter, *he* might qualify as one of those assclowns himself. But looking at the desperation in Nate's eyes, Reno knew he had no other choice. He was going to regret this, but . . .

"I won't let Rachel get with an assclown. I promise."

His friend—his *best* friend—sagged with relief. "Thanks."

"No problem." He'd make sure it wasn't, Reno promised himself. Whatever it took. He had self-discipline, right?

He was famous for self-discipline. Even when faced with a smile like the one Rachel wore right now, dazzling and warm and flirtatious and kind, all at once.

Appalled at himself, Reno jerked back into the alcove.

Operation Nate and Rachel was officially on. How hard could it possibly be, Reno asked himself, to get a romance going between the Incredible Hulk and Tight Pants L.A. Barbie?

Beside him, Nate stuck his head around the corner again. He gazed out for a minute. Then he propped his chin in his hand, an enraptured expression on his big, former lineman's mug.

"Just look at her, Reno." Wistfully, Nate sighed. "All I want in the world right now—all I want for Christmas this year— is Rachel Porter. That girl right there."

Reno didn't have to look. Because all of a sudden, he feared, he wanted exactly the same thing.

Chapter Fourteen

The knock on the bedroom door came when Rachel's hair was still wet from her shower. Caught in the midst of texting Cody—her former pop star client—to see if she could outfit him for the Teen Choice Awards viewing party he usually went to at Lance Bass's house, she jerked her head around.

"It's open. Come in."

Her mom pushed open the door, stepping into the weak December sunlight from the nearby window and bringing in two mugs of coffee. In Christmas cups. Naturally. The fragrance of freshly brewed beans competed with the Holly Jolly air freshener plug-in and the Holiday Alpine potpourri beside the bed.

Canceling her text message, Rachel shoved her cell phone beneath her pillow. Then, not waiting to see if her mom had noticed what she'd been doing, she accepted her coffee.

"Thanks." She turned to the bureau, resting place for her handbag, her jewelry, and her vitamins. She popped three supplements, swallowed a dose of omega-3 oil, then ripped open a chocolate fudge protein bar. Her stash was getting low, but she wouldn't be here long anyway. "Breakfast time. Cheers."

As they clinked mugs, her mother's gaze landed on her vitamins and protein bar. "I've got a nice fruit salad in the fridge—red and green apples. Christmas colors! It's very pretty. And there must be four boxes of your father's high-fiber cereal in the kitchen. You go ahead and help yourself, honey."

"I'm fine, Mom. I've got everything I need right here."

"Wouldn't you like some eggs? I only have egg substitute these days, because I'm watching my cholesterol, but it's pretty good. I could scramble you up a plate of eggs and toast."

"No thanks. Don't go to any trouble for me."

A pause. "Would you rather go out for breakfast? I know you're probably used to the Hollywood Denny's or something—"

"Mom." Smiling, Rachel gave her mother a hug. In her nubbly sweater and elastic-waist jeans, she felt exactly as lovable as she always had. Rachel added another squeeze for extra measure. "I like my protein bars. I always know what I'm getting."

"Artificial flavors and chemicals from New Jersey?"

"No, ten grams of soy protein and some fiber."

"*This* you choose over apples?"

"Yum." Feeling her smile broaden for the first time since she'd arrived, Rachel leaned back, coffee still in hand. She took a sip as she gazed at her mom. From this close, her mother's freckles were visible. So were a few more wrinkles.

Beneath both, though, was the same woman who'd talked Rachel through her first heartrending breakup in seventh grade. The same woman who'd helped her sew her first prom dress (not knowing that Rachel intended to flash the bikini she'd worn beneath it just as soon as Alanis Morissette came on—Go Girl Power!) The same woman who'd tearfully waved her off on the road to California with a rented U-Haul and a suitcase full of Pepto-Bismol, contraceptives, and a hardware-store tool kit ("just to cover all the bases, honey.")

Rachel wasn't sure when her mother had gotten to be both a little shorter and a little stronger than she was, but she did know one thing for sure. "I love you, Mom. I'm glad to be home."

"Aww, honey. I love you, too." Another squeeze. Her mom sat on the bed, then sipped some coffee and offered a no-nonsense look. "Now tell me what's the matter, because you sure as heck didn't come home to visit this year just for giggles."

Exactly at the moment he scraped his shovel along the last uncleared section of snowy walkway, Reno heard the door behind him creak open. Then came a feminine exclamation and footsteps along the porch. Damn it. He'd almost gotten away clean.

Deftly, he flipped his shovelful of snow onto the neat pile he'd already made. His breath puffed in the air with the exertion, frosting over part of his scarf. If he turned back, he'd see the path leading from the street to his neighbor's house, cleared of snowdrifts for the first time in days.

"I *thought* that was you!" came Mrs. Kowalczyk's voice.

The door slammed. The footsteps came closer. As a car drove past on the mostly deserted morning street, Reno held up a gloved hand in hello. Then he went on working. Only a few more shovelfuls, then he'd salt the icy walk and be done.

A jangle alerted him to a nearby presence—Mrs. Kowalczyk's bichon frise, Crackers, with her dog-tagged and bell-embellished collar ringing. Wearing a doggie sweater with a Christmas ornament pattern, she trotted up, then squatted and—

"Crackers, no!" Sounding horrified, Mrs. Kowalczyk hurried over. She wore an old coat, a buffalo-checked hat with sheepskin earflaps, and mittens. Plus lipstick. Mrs. Kowalczyk never went anyplace without lipstick. "I'm so sorry, Reno. She just can't control herself first thing in the morning. Mr. Kowalczyk was the same way." She crossed herself. "God rest his soul."

"That's all right." Reno scooped away the mess, cutting deeply with the shovel edge, then moved down the row he'd made.

"Here." Beaming, Mrs. Kowalczyk followed, then thrust a maple cruller at him. "Something to keep up your strength."

The scent of sugary maple wafted to him. With a smile and a thank-you, Reno accepted the cruller. He bit off half and then chewed, momentarily resting one elbow on the shovel handle.

"I *knew* you'd come through with the shoveling."

"It's not a problem, Mrs. Kowalczyk."

"I saw that you did Mrs. Bender's driveway yesterday."

"Mrs. Bender threatened to snowmobile over to my store and boycott The Wright Stuff from now till Christmas," Reno fibbed as he chomped on the remaining half cruller. "I had to do it."

"Oh dear." A tsk-tsk. "That woman will resort to anything, won't she?"

With a shrug, Reno grabbed his shovel to clear the last few feet, watching out for a scampering Crackers. The dog was determined to get in his way.

"I'd do the shoveling myself, only my arthritis acts up in the cold weather. Would you like another maple cruller?"

"Thanks, but I have to get to the store. Jimmy Gurche is working with me now, but he's only part-time. My other part-timer is on vacation, so I can't stay away for long."

"I'm not surprised you can't keep help. People don't want to sell subpar hockey equipment." Breezily, Mrs. Kowalczyk waved to Mrs. Bender. "Hussy," she muttered. "Look at that outfit!"

"Uh . . ." Without really wanting to, Reno glanced next door. On the porch, Mrs. Bender grabbed her newspaper, then waved. She was dressed in a sheer red negligee and shortie red velvet robe that must have really thrilled Mr. Caplan, the retiree next door. Whoa. With an involuntary grimace, Reno pulled his knit cap down over his eyebrows for warmth. He grabbed the bag of rock salt. "What's wrong with my hockey equipment?"

"Those old-fashioned wooden sticks? Nothing, if you don't mind playing the game like Howie Morenz in the twenties."

Reno frowned.

"Most of the stuff you have in there is fine, Reno. Honestly." Mrs. Kowalczyk patted his shoulder as he scattered the rock salt to deice the walkway, narrowly missing Crackers. "You've got your Wilson Conform mitts like the golden glovers use, and your viscoelastic polymer football pads . . . all the usual goods. But you ought to have some quality Kevlar and carbon fiber one-piece hockey sticks. Whoever talked you into stocking those antique, bargain-basement models did a number on you."

Startled to hear words like *viscoelastic polymer* coming from his kindly elderly neighbor's lips, Reno glanced at her. "Mrs. Kowalczyk, tell me the truth. You've been living a double life as a *SportsCenter* special correspondent, haven't you?"

She only laughed. "You don't spend fifty years married to a sports fan without picking up a thing or two. Hockey was Mr. Kowalczyk's favorite." She nodded approvingly at his rock salt work. "If you keep this up, you'll be earning twenty dollars a pop someday, young man. I'll get you another maple cruller. Growing boy like you needs to keep up his strength for sure."

Mrs. Kowalczyk vanished into her house, leaving Reno on the salt-crunchy walkway, staring after her in thought. If the postcollegiate slackers he usually hired as part-time staff had half of Mrs. Kowalczyk's knowledge of sports equipment, it occurred to him, he'd have a much easier time running The Wright Stuff.

People spent a lifetime accumulating knowledge, then just when they were chock full of it, they retired. It figured.

Jangle. Jangle. Brought to attention by the familiar sound of that dog collar, Reno glanced sideways. "Crackers, no!"

Merrily, the dog squatted and peed against the bag of rock salt Reno had brought. Then the little sweater-wearing trouble-maker looked straight at Reno—he'd swear the dog actually stuck out her tongue at him—and trotted off toward the street.

"Oh no! Crackers!" Mrs. Kowalczyk emerged from inside the house with another cruller. "Come back here!"

Reno glanced from her to her bichon frise. The dog glanced up, snow and dirt caked on its white muzzle, then went on digging up Hal's front-yard Three Wise Men display.

Reno knew from the reconnaissance he'd done last night that not only did the whole gimmicky ensemble light up, but it also played "We Three Kings" in sync with its LEDs *and* emitted pseudo scents of frankincense and myrrh. Aside from being a cheater in the holiday lights competition, Hal was also a show-off.

"Reno." Mrs. Kowalczyk lowered her hands to her hips in a helpless gesture. "Please, won't you rescue Crackers?"

"I don't know, Mrs. Kowalczyk." Reno gazed at Hal's yard, sorely tempted to let the little monster dog demolish his sneaky neighbor's entire unsportsmanlike display. "From here, it looks as if the three wise men need rescuing from Crackers."

"Don't be a wiseacre. Hurry up. She's chewing it now."

"Hang tight. I'll get her." Setting aside his shovel and rock salt, Reno stepped into the calf-deep snow. He waded along the same hippy, skippy, sweatered path Crackers had taken. Snow caked his jeans and froze his ankles, but this was the way it had to be. He neared the dog. "I've almost got her."

"I knew you would!" hollered a relieved Mrs. Kowalczyk.

Reno Wright had to do what he'd always done. Help people.

No matter, he realized as an irate Hal emerged from his house and started ranting about Reno's "willful destruction" of his holiday lights display, what it cost him in the end.

After a few terse words with Hal, Reno scooped up the dog. Cradling Crackers' wriggly body against his chest, he trekked across the snow to deposit the miscreant with Mrs. Kowalczyk.

"Ooh, you little ruffian!" She ruffled Crackers' ears, then planted a lipsticked kiss on the dog's furry head. "You're lucky Reno was around to get you out of trouble." She glanced up. "Thank you. For shoveling the snow and for saving Crackers."

"No problem." It's what he did—come to the rescue. When he'd been in the NFL, Reno had especially relished the times he'd come in to save the day with a perfectly timed field goal. These days, what he did wasn't much different. It simply didn't come with applause. Now he regarded Mrs. Kowalczyk with new interest. "Mrs. Kowalczyk, I know you're busy with your bridge club and the Kismet holiday decorating committee, but . . . how would you like a part-time job at The Wright Stuff?"

After all, if he wanted to map out a plan for Nate to woo Rachel Porter, he'd need a little more spare time than usual . . .

A long, low, school's-out-for-the-day whistle brought Angela out of her predate primping. Sitting at her desk, she froze with her face dimly reflected in her turned-off computer monitor. She didn't even have time to unscrew the wand of her new lip gloss before heavy footsteps crossed from the doorway into her domain—the now-deserted snugness of room 224.

"Woo-hoo. Hot stuff!" a male voice said.

Patrick? That voice sounded rough. Tough. A little sexy.

It sounded . . . familiar. Too familiar. Darn it!

"Nate! You scared me half to death." Delivering him her best censorious glare, Angela watched her self-appointed date guardian merrily prop his hip on her desk. "I thought you were Patrick. He's supposed to meet me here any minute."

A snort. "Then he's late. The bastard."

"No, he's not. We moved up our coffee date, because Kayla's babysitter will be out of town next week during winter break."

Already dating as a single mother was turning out to be more complicated than she'd bargained for. But Angela was optimistic. Everything worth having required some work.

As she went back to primping, Nate didn't say anything. What could he say? Angela reasoned as fresh excitement shook her. He wasn't Perfect Patrick, most desirable teacher at KHS.

Feeling self-conscious under her friend's scrutiny, Angela pursed her lips. She concentrated, then guided the wand of glossy pink around her mouth. Smacking her lips together, she sealed the tube and tossed it in her catchall purse.

When she glanced up, Nate was staring at her mouth.

Uh-oh. "Did I color outside the lines?" Sheesh. She really was out of practice, if the weird look on Nate's face was any indication of her makeup prowess. "The turned-off monitor trick works in a pinch"—at least it did with old CRT monitors, like KHS had—"but it's hard to see without a real mirror."

Worriedly, she lifted her face to Nate's for examination.

"Uhhh." His gaze remained fixed on her mouth. His eyes turned heavy-lidded, his features growing indistinct as he brought his face closer for better scrutiny. "It looks . . ."

Something about his husky tone made her heart beat faster. ". . . kind of . . ."

Questioningly, Angela raised her gaze to his. His eyes were still focused on her lips . . . which suddenly felt kind of tingly. Almost as if she wanted to be kissed. By Nate! Which was alarming enough in itself, but when combined with the merest flutter of his minty breath across her mouth, a gentle precursor to the contact that might come next, Angela could scarcely—

". . . like it's getting melted. And your lips look all kinds of freaky, too." With a deft move, Nate thumbed away a bit of lip gloss from the corner of her mouth. "That's better."

Freaky lips? *Freaky*? Mortified at her own fanciful interpretation of his intentions, Angela leaned back. Tingly lips. Hmmph. She was way too practical for that. Although . . .

"Ouch. My lips are burning!"

Wide-eyed, she snatched a handful of tissues from her desk.

Nate peered closer. "It's sticking. It's not coming off."

"I know. It's a special long-wearing, lip-plumping formula." Frantically, Angela wiped her mouth again. "Ow. It's supposed to give you lush, full, kissable lips within minutes."

Nate raised his eyebrows. "What *you've* got looks like those wax lips that Kayla gets at the miniature golf place sometimes."

"Great. Thanks." She was grateful to Nate for his occasional Saturday outings with Kayla—a routine he traded on and off with Reno, to give Angela a break and provide Kayla with male role models. But she didn't need his playtime-fueled analysis of her appearance right now. "Patrick will be here any second!" After another vigorous scrub, she lifted the tissues. Warily, she leaned forward to show him. "How bad is it now?"

"Not bad."

"Really?" Hope fluttered to life inside her.

"Nah, it's pretty bad. But I'd still do you."

"What?"

"I mean, if baboon lips bother The Prick, he's not the guy for you, that's all." Cheerfully, Nate regarded her. "Don't worry. You'll probably be able to distract him. You look nice." He nodded. "I like that top. Makes your rack look fantastic."

She slapped her hand over her modest cleavage. "Nate!"

He grinned. "Gotcha. You're not worried about your lips anymore, are you?"

"You are a pig." Laughing, Angela stood and wrapped her arms around Nate's big, broad shoulders. "But I love you."

From just above her head, Nate said, "Whatever you do, *don't* do this to Patrick. That skeeve will get the wrong idea. Next thing you know, his hands will be right *here*."

Without warning, Nate's home ec/industrial arts trained palms cupped her derrière. He gave a squeeze, then a *mmm-mmm-mmm* of approval.

Shocked to her core, Angela couldn't move.

No man had *ever* grabbed her butt. She'd never been that kind of girl. Straight-A student, Honor Society member, French club geek, and an animal shelter volunteer, yes. Hot-to-trot naughty girl, no. She'd been a virgin far longer than most of her friends—until she'd met Kayla's father, Bryce, during her third year of college. If not for her infatuation with Bryce, she might never have experienced the carnal side of life at all.

But now, with Nate's hands cupping her backside, all Angela could think, through her sensation-fogged brain, was *get closer*. *Make the most of this!* After all, Nate was ridiculously fit, very sweet, and she'd known him all her life. What would be the harm in trailing her fingers from his shoulders—currently bunched manfully under her hands—and exploring the rest of him?

Nate leaned back and gazed into her eyes. "You know," he said seriously, "if you want, I can help you out with that, uh, issue you were telling me about. Nobody has to know."

Angela frowned. "What issue?"

"Your . . ." Incredibly, Nate blushed. "Horniness problem."

For a split second, she actually considered it.

"Of course not!" Indignantly, she swatted away his hands from her backside. With a thud, she landed in her chair again. "What makes you think I would even *consider* such a thing?"

Nate glanced to the classroom door. "Well, you *are* dating."

"So?"

"So if you're not going out with The Prick to get laid, what is it? Because I've got to tell you, you deserve better."

"What? I deserve a two-fisted grope and a pity proposition?" Angela lifted her chin to stare him down. "No thanks."

Now it wasn't only her lips that were hot—her whole body felt overheated, filled with emotions she hadn't dared express for . . . who knew how long? How dare Nate? How *dare* he?

"You deserve someone who doesn't need you to have fake fat lips. Someone who doesn't need you to wear a Wonderbra."

Angela gasped, crossing her arms over her chest.

Unperturbed, Nate just kept going.

"Yep, I could tell. Nobody grows a pair of D-cups in a single afternoon. But that's beside the point." His voice was unusually soft, his gaze fixed on the overflowing pencil cup on her desk. He fiddled with a pair of number twos, then glanced up at her. "You deserve someone who can see how incredible you are. When that someone comes along, they're going to have to get past me first, because I'll be running interference."

Stunned, Angela looked away. Her eyes swam with sudden tears—tears she didn't understand and was embarrassed by.

"Is . . . is that all you came to say?" she asked with dignity.

"No, I came to ask you to help me impress Rachel Porter." A grin flashed over Nate's face, then he pulled a wry expression. "But I guess that's probably out of the question now."

Of course it was. She opened her fiery mouth to say so.

What emerged was, "I'd be happy to help you. Let me call up Patrick to reschedule our date, then we'll get started."

Good grief. The Wright helpfulness gene—usually manifested in Reno's overprotective, interfering ways—was part of her, too!

Guiltily, Angela glanced up. Nate's grin made her finally understand. It felt good to come to someone's rescue. Even if that particular someone had just groped her, propositioned her, flattered her, and made her contemplate a casual, torrid, almost certainly ill-advised fling, all in the space of ten minutes.

Briskly, she hung up her phone after calling Patrick, feeling a twinge at postponing her date with the most sought-after, most eligible male on the Kismet High School faculty. What if this opportunity never came her way again? What if she was stuck drawing from a shallow pool of men who played with miniature dragons and considered a ballpark hot dog a fine meal?

"Playing hard to get, huh? Good going." Nate winked. "Now Patrick will be twice as eager to go out with you."

Hey, maybe things would work out after all, Angela decided.

On the other hand, there was still the worrisome thrill she felt when Nate winked at her. *That* had never happened before. . . .

"Okay," she said in businesslike tones. "Let's start by assessing your dating demeanor and decorum."

Chapter Fifteen

At half past-four, Rachel sat knee-deep in the ripped apart cast-off clothes she'd liberated from the guest room closet (with her mother's blessing) with one hand on the blindstitch hem-presser foot of her mother's Singer Inspiration 4220 and the other hand wiping sweat from her brow. Actual sweat. Here in Michigan, where it was colder than the coldest L.A. day.

"You look just like your mom used to."

At the sound of her dad's voice, Rachel snapped her head around. She smiled. Her father stood in the doorway, wearing one of his Detroit Lions jerseys with a white turtleneck underneath (what was it with these people and their turtlenecks?) and a pair of what appeared to be grown-up Toughskins jeans.

"This is just like old times. Your mom used to get obsessed with sewing stuff, too." Raising his eyebrows in silent query, her dad waited for her nod. He picked his way past the discarded clothing items she'd hurled on the floor after ripping their seams—all the better to repurpose their fabrics for her new creation. "Whenever something was bothering her, that is."

He sat on the bed, giving Rachel a pointed look from beneath his silvery hair. At sixty-eight, her father was still a handsome man, with a demeanor that suggested integrity and a pair of hands that could repair malfunctioning electronics as easily as they could whip up his trademark buttermilk pancakes. A die-hard computer geek, Gerry Porter had gone from Radio Shack radios to state-of-the-art PCs with the same enthusiasm most men applied to riding lawnmowers and to pricey barbecue grills.

"Working on some computers?" Knowingly, Rachel nodded at his reading glasses. "Did you get a lot of them this year?"

He nodded. "People are upgrading like crazy these days, but they don't know what to do with their old equipment. I can usually find someone who wants it though."

Throughout the year, her retired father collected broken, outdated, or unwanted personal computers and other electronics from the community. He repaired them, souped them up with new components, parts, and processors, then donated them all as Christmas presents for Kismet children and teens in need.

He'd become famous for it, down to a Gerry Porter profile in the *Kismet Comet* newspaper every December. Rachel was a little hazy on the technical details, but she was proud of her dad for his hard work and expertise.

"And you're dodging me again," he continued. "Maybe you've forgotten—I've known you your whole life. I know when you're hiding something. I'm a stubborn old cuss these days, and I'm not going to quit, so you might as well fess up."

She couldn't help but smile. "You're not so old."

"Ha. Just stubborn and a cuss, huh?"

"Well . . . somebody taught me to call a spade a spade." Her mom must have ratted her out, Rachel realized. She'd managed to sidestep her mother's questions about her return to Kismet this morning by describing her need for a warm winter coat (the one black hole in her California-based wardrobe) to go Christmas tree-cutting with Reno and his friend Nate—and asking permission to raid the closets and attic for materials. "And I've got to get back to this if I want to finish in time. I'm already taking a shortcut by taping the hem, so—"

Her dad interrupted. "Why are you avoiding Christmas?"

Gulp. Rachel hadn't seen it that way. But now that her father mentioned it . . . there was some truth there. She *had* been avoiding Christmas and everything that went with it. Just as if she were still in an Alayna-style holiday boycott time warp.

Uncomfortably, she glanced at him. Her father looked smaller and a little more grizzled around the edges, but he also looked as though he wasn't taking no for an answer. She was trapped this time. Her mother had sent in the big guns.

Caught, Rachel scoffed. *When in doubt, just deny* was her new motto. It would work as well here as it did in L.A.

"How can I avoid Christmas in here?" She gestured to the bedroom's candy-cane patterned bedding, the "holiday penguin" rug, the Frosty the Snowman lamp, and the miniature holly-wreath drawer pulls. Not to mention the Victorian carolers wall hanging and the foot-high shiny silver futuristic tree with neon-colored ornaments. "It looks like Santa's secret love shack."

"Your mother went a little overboard, I'll agree. But she was so excited to have you coming home for a visit. We both were. When we got your phone call, we spent the whole afternoon in the Christmas section at the Bargain Hut downtown, getting ready."

Shamefaced, Rachel ducked her head. The Singer's bobbin thread was in serious danger of getting tangled. It probably required all her focus for a minute. There. That was better.

"Did something happen in L.A., honey?" her father pressed.

"What could possibly happen, Dad? Life is great."

Or at least it would be, once she finessed it a little.

"You know you can talk to us about anything."

"I know. Thank you." Swamped with affection for him, Rachel blinked away a wash of tears. Her stupid tear ducts were really working overtime lately. First the *Made* kids, now this. At least her cold had vanished since leaving L.A. So had her chronic headaches and acid reflux. "But if I don't get cracking on this coat, I'm going to freeze to death tonight."

"Yeah, your mother told me you were going out tree-cutting with Reno Wright. Good man. He had everything with the NFL—gave it all up to come back home and support his sister."

Startled, Rachel glanced at her dad. "Angela?"

"That's the one. Nice girl. *Too* nice to wind up pregnant, abandoned, and heartbroken, all in the same week—but that's what happened. Some punk ditched her. There was a little gossip going around when she had her kid a few years ago—she never did find a husband, you know—but not as much as you might think. Kismet's a small town, but it's progressive these days."

With her head spinning, Rachel nodded. She'd had no idea Reno had abandoned NFL superstardom for the sake of his sister.

"We've even got one of those spray-on suntan places here in town," her dad was saying. "And the Movie Hut down by the marina carries DVDs now. Two whole rows of them."

"That's great, Dad."

"Don't patronize me, missy," her father warned with a twinkle in his eyes. "I told your mother I couldn't find the DVD of *It's a Wonderful Life* for the Christmas movie marathon she's planning with you, but it might turn up at any second."

"Eeek! Not Jimmy Stewart and Bedford Falls!"

"When you were a little girl, you watched that every year."

"I'm not a little girl anymore, Dad." And I'm not getting sucked into Christmas this year. Period.

With a sigh, her father stood. "Maybe not. But I still saved your special ornaments for you to hang on the tree."

"That old stuff? Made of glue and macaroni and glitter?" She wrinkled her nose. "That's so cornball, Dad. Come on."

"The Hendricksons wanted to have a go at them, but I said those were all yours this year. It's tradition, right?"

Squeezed by a sudden wave of nostalgia, Rachel smiled at him. "You bet. Just as soon as I finish this coat."

And bolt out the door when you're not looking.

She simply wasn't ready for Christmas yet, and that was that.

Chapter Sixteen

That night, everything changed. At least temporarily.

Denying that fact even as she realized it, Rachel flopped on her back beside Reno, feeling pleasantly exhausted and a little out of breath. Her arms and legs tingled. Her cheeks still felt warm with the flush she knew must be on her face.

Closing her eyes, she let her hand touch his. "I promised myself I wouldn't do this again. Especially not with you."

Reno wriggled, making himself more comfortable. He released a macho sigh. "What's the matter? You can't take it?"

"Well . . ."

"Because you *seemed* to be enjoying it a minute ago."

"I—"

"Don't make me do it again, just to prove it."

He didn't have to, and they both knew it. She'd been there, too, luxuriating in the sheer naughtiness of being with him . . . doing the very thing she'd been trying so hard to resist.

"You do realize," Rachel said, turning on her side so she could gaze unabashedly at his profile, "that whatever threat you're trying to make is completely undermined by the way you're smiling, right? You look like someone who just scored a home run goalpost . . . thing."

"That's a touchdown. And you *whooped* out loud." He gave

her a lazy, satisfied grin. "The sound probably carried for miles."

"I couldn't help it! You started it. I only came out here for an innocent Christmas tree-cutting expedition." Of all things. Although it *had* gotten her out of a caroling outing with Bidie Niedermeyer, the Fowlers, the Hendricksons, and her parents. "That's it. Everything else is your fault."

"That's the way you want to play it, huh?"

"Absolutely."

Sensing snow melting into the seat of her pants, Rachel squirmed. Good thing she'd whipped up that makeshift winter coat. Her extremities felt toasty warm, thanks to all the, uh, activity. But her nose was starting to get cold, which probably wasn't surprising given that they were outdoors, surrounded by snow-frosted pine trees standing shoulder to shoulder in the December evening. For a Christmas tree farm (which Reno had explained was what this was), the place was pretty nice.

It wasn't exactly the Hotel Bel-Air of course. But still.

Beside her, Reno adjusted the battery-powered camp light he'd brought, making its glow sparkle across the snowbanks. She'd forgotten snow could glitter that way. On a fallen log nearby sat the things Rachel had brought with her to amp up the ambiance—a checked woolen throw, a thermos of hot cocoa, and a backup supply of protein bars (since she'd skipped dinner). Now though, she didn't care about efficient nutrition.

She cared about sheer enjoyment, and the effect it was having on her resistance to Kismet and all things Kismet-related. If this got much worse—and she succumbed to any more schmaltzy holiday sentimentality—she wouldn't have any edgy L.A.-style armor left. Before she knew it, she'd be confessing the whole awful truth to her parents.

How she'd stumbled upon Tyson and Alayna together. How she'd lost her cool, her job, her car, and her house (in that order). How everyone had shunned her back home. Then everyone in Kismet would realize that Rachel's big success had hit a major roadblock—one she might not be able to come back from.

Which would be disastrous. Because weren't her fabulous life and famous career the most amazing things about her?

Maybe. But for now, she was holding steady. And Reno Wright was proving ideal for taking her mind off her troubles—for helping her endure the season of goodwill and bad fashions in a town that seemed jam-packed with puffy parkas, staticky hair, and cheesy Christmas overkill—all of which she'd glimpsed on the drive down Main Street, past the frozen lake, to the tree farm.

And okay, so it was true that she'd put Kismet and all its close-knit ways behind her a long time ago. But that didn't mean a girl couldn't ring a few jingle bells with a cute guy, did it?

No, it didn't. Feeling inspired and more relaxed than she had in years, Rachel levered upward on her elbow. She inhaled deeply of the scents of icy pine and distant wood smoke, then gazed at Reno. It was possible his nose had been broken and reset— probably because of football—and his five-o'clock shadow was a little more aggressive than she preferred. And he might also have been wearing actual Polarfleece (not chic) over all those muscles of his. All the same . . .

"Good thing your friend Nate isn't here," she said. "Otherwise, I might think twice about doing this."

She brought her mouth to his, feeling her toes curl at the first tentative contact. Then at the next, less tentative but remarkably moving, longer kiss that followed. Technically, Reno was at her mercy—lying there in the snow like that—and he felt warm and delicious, too, so Rachel went in for another sample.

Mmmm. This kiss was even better, possibly because Reno got over his apparent surprise and participated fully. With a growl of approval, he opened his mouth beneath hers. He drew her closer with one gloved hand, trapping her between his dizzying warmth below and the dusky sky overhead. It was all Rachel could do not to squeal with delight . . . which would have destroyed her aura of coolness altogether. That was unthinkable.

Not that gawking at him, openmouthed, when he finally ended their kiss probably made her seem all that savvy.

She felt pretty pleased with herself though. She'd clearly dazzled him, too. Reno's eyes looked dark, heavy-lidded, and sensual. His face, from this close, appeared rough and handsome and kind of moony-eyed. Yes, this could be an incredible Christmas vacation, Rachel thought as she studied his goofy grin and felt her own heart expand warmly in response. This could be the merriest, most unbelievable holiday getaway ever.

"That shouldn't have happened," he said roughly, a frown pulling down his brows. "You don't understand. I'm supposed to—"

"I understand everything I need to."

She kissed him again, this time tucking her mittened hand beneath the nape of his neck to bring him nearer. She squashed her body against his, exhilarated by the whoosh of the breeze in the darkened pine trees, the glimmer of the snow, and the utter silence that cocooned them both in a place where the CNN crawl had never heard of Rachel Porter and no one cared about Naugahyde dresses.

"You'll probably get frostbite if I do what I'm thinking of doing." Grinning, she nipped his chin, then kissed her way upward for another taste of his lips and—*God, yes!*—his swirling, authoritative tongue. Her whole body felt electrified with the shock of him invading her mouth. They were perfectly matched, caught in a rhythm that felt undeniable. Breathlessly, she confessed, "But I'm going to have to do it anyway."

Feeling liberated, Rachel peeled back Reno's snow-caked wool scarf, then grappled with the zipper on his coat. If she could just get her hands on his chest, make her way past all the polyblend and cotton, she knew the rewards would be incredible. Even now, pushing on his chest as she tried to gain some leverage, she could tell he was rock-solid everywhere. Yum.

Suddenly, Reno came upward to meet her, a wicked smile on his face. All at once, they were exactly the same, two people with an identical goal to get closer. Closer closer closer . . .

Thwack! Something hit Rachel in the back of the head.

Whatever it was shattered and fell to the ground in a shower of white. A snowball! She'd have recognized that melting sensation soaking into her knitted wool cap anywhere. She was a child of the frozen north after all, as hard as she tried to deny it with her nouveau California girl chic.

Sputtering, she grabbed her head and glanced behind her—just as another snowball smacked Reno in the chest.

"Gotcha, Uncle Reno! Ha-ha!"

Blinking away snow, Reno peered past Rachel's shoulder. His whole face enlivened as he spotted Kayla, his cute, giggly niece, scampering nearby in her hooded parka and mittens. She'd come Christmas tree-hunting with them and had—until now—been happily occupied with putting together a lopsided snowman in the glow from her own camp light while Rachel and Reno flopped on the ground making snow angels.

Yes, *snow angels*. Rachel's top-secret holiday vice, along with the corny Christmas carols she'd allowed Reno to induce her to sing (loudly!) during their long, stranded-on-the-highway wait. First they made snow angels beside the highway, then they'd sung carols, then they'd fallen asleep in each other's arms while parked on the side of the road to Kismet.

She didn't know why Reno had been able to bring out the latent Christmas spirit in her when no one else could. It was sappy and silly and embarrassing. All Rachel knew was that she didn't want anyone else to find out about it. Or to find out about the way her resistance to moving on with Christmas (and giving up on Alayna) was corroding, bit by happy-go-lucky bit, the more time she spent with Reno.

"That was a cheap shot, Kayla." Flashing a grin at Rachel, Reno scooped up some snow. With deft gloved hands, he packed it together. "You'd better look out. Here I come!"

The first snowball sailed right past the little girl's shoulder—on purpose, Rachel realized—and exploded against a nearby pine tree. Kayla laughed. Reno did, too. Apparently, he was a big old softie at heart. He was obviously crazy about his niece, devoted and protective and fun. Watching him frolic in the snow with Kayla made something inside Rachel soften, too.

By the time she got to her feet to join them, Reno had made three more snowballs—and looked as gleeful as a little boy as he threw them at his niece's impromptu hiding places. Kayla peeked out from behind her snowman's bulbous snowy torso, guffawed, then hurled another snowball of her own.

"Still remember how to make a snowball, L.A. girl?"

"I'm not sure. But I do remember how to do this."

With both hands, Rachel upended a huge pile of snow on Reno's head. She scrubbed it in the way she'd done as a kid, squirming to stay out of reach as Reno yelled in surprise. He groped blindly for her while Kayla hooted in approval.

"Hey, you're supposed to be on my side!" Reno shouted.

"We girls have to stick together. Right, Kayla?"

Laughing, Rachel ran to the little girl's snowman, her galumphing steps awkward in the winter boots she'd borrowed from her mother. They weren't fashionable, but they kept her warm and dry.

"Okay, on the count of three," Rachel told Kayla conspiratorially as they both formed snowballs. "One, two . . ."

Smash. A fluffy snowball hit Rachel right in the ear, then shattered in soppy, snowy bits. Openmouthed with surprise, she gawked across the clearing at an openly victorious Reno.

"He's not a very good sport, is he, Kayla?"

"Nope. Uncle Reno plays to win."

"Humph. We'll see about that. Come on!"

* * *

Reno propped his booted foot on the trunk of the balsam fir he'd just cut down, shaking his head. At his feet lay his chainsaw. To his left perched his nemeses, evident best friends forever, cozily drinking hot cocoa in their snow-encrusted coats and boots. "I can't believe you two ganged up on me."

"You needed to be brought down a peg," Rachel said.

"Yeah, Uncle Reno. Brought down a peg. We win!"

He didn't know how they'd worked that out. By his count, he'd splattered them with twice as many snowballs—loosely packed ones, since they were both beginners at snowball fights. But if they wanted to salvage their feminine pride, he'd let them.

"Just wait till word gets around town." Serenely, Rachel tilted the thermos to top off Kayla's cocoa, then fussed with his niece's scarf. "That Reno Wright lost a snowball fight to a couple of girls."

"I *never* won before, Rachel. You're awesome!"

Kayla exchanged a mittened high five with Rachel, then gazed at her with adoring eyes and went on chattering companionably. Apparently Kayla was the latest member of the Rachel Porter fan club, Reno realized.

The effect Rachel had on people was amazing to see. While simultaneously being forthright and a little bit guarded, Rachel also managed to draw people out—exactly the way she'd done with Kayla. And Angela. And everyone at The Big Foot.

And okay, with *him*. Damn it. He hadn't been prepared for that first kiss. Or the second. Or . . . hell. What was the matter with him? He was supposed to be figuring out a way to hook up Rachel with Nate. He was *not* supposed to be mindlessly pulling her closer in a snowbank, hungry to taste more. More more more.

Determined to get back on track, Reno picked up the

chainsaw and camp light. "We'd better get started on the next tree. Are you sure that's the one you want, Kayla?"

With the camp light, he pointed to an enormous pine tree at the edge of the clearing. Although it wasn't late—only a little after seven—it got dark early in wintertime. The tree's top branches were barely visible against the almost-starry sky.

"I'm sure. It's perfect!" Excitedly, Kayla skipped to her feet. "I thought you'd *never* get to it. Let's go, Rachel!"

"Go where?"

"To cut down that tree." His niece grabbed Rachel's hand and tugged. "The big one for the town square, where the parade is. My mom's taking me. And Uncle Reno. And probably Nate, too. Everybody, absolutely *everybody*, goes to the Christmas parade!"

Rachel blanched, looking vaguely guilty at Kayla's excited rendition of the holiday events in Kismet. Apparently their returned-to-town rebel still planned to boycott the whole thing.

"Are you sure you won't be there?" Reno asked.

Not answering, Rachel got to her feet. She brushed off the seat of her pants, then eyed him dubiously. "You provide the Kismet Christmas tree? The official tree? And you chop it down yourself? Is there anything in town you *don't* take care of?"

Reno shrugged. He toed the fallen fir beside him. "I needed a Christmas tree for my house anyway, and I like fresh-cut organic ones. The tree farm helps me out every year. Why not?"

"Because . . . well, I just don't have that much civic pride, I guess. I couldn't wait to skip this burg and hit the big city."

Kayla frowned at her. So did Reno.

Rachel noticed and changed the subject. "So . . . that's the one, huh?" Her gaze zoomed upward as she examined their target. "Shouldn't your friend Nate be helping you with that?"

"He should be."

Reno still couldn't believe Nate had freaked out and pulled a disappearing act on him at the last minute. He'd been a no-show tonight, claiming he needed to "wax his eyebrows" before allowing Rachel to see him up close. Which had to be total bullshit. Seriously. Who cared about eyebrows?

How was Reno supposed to match him up with Rachel, the way he'd promised, if the two of them never officially met?

"But Nate couldn't make it. So this time, you're helping."

"Oh no." Rachel held up both hands. "If you asked me to do some themed decorating on that tree, maybe. If you wanted that tree to look chic for an awards show, definitely. If you planned to start a pine-tree trend, I'd be your gal. But cutting it down? No way." In the glow of the camp light, her face looked quirky, rosy, and adorable—now that she'd abandoned those idiotic sunglasses. "I am not equipped to live the wilderness life."

"It's just a tree." He squinted, gauging its height and probable ferocity. "I'm not asking you to skin it and eat it."

"Very funny. Look, my Christmas tree in Malibu comes custom-delivered from a local greenhouse nursery, already in a tree stand and ready for a stylish celebrity Christmas."

"It drinks too much, then goes into rehab?"

"For all I know," she bulldozed on, "my Christmas trees never even experience the great outdoors. Kind of like me."

"Come on," Reno coaxed. "You grew up here. You know there's still a down-home Kismet girl someplace inside you."

"She moved to L.A. and became fabulous. End of story."

Kayla crossed her arms. "There's nothing fabulous about skipping the Christmas parade," she announced. "Why aren't you going, Rachel? It's really, really fun. Santa is there, too."

"I . . ."

"You've *got* to go. Come with me and my mom and Uncle Reno and Nate. Nate is super nice and funny. You'll like him, too."

Rachel patted Kayla's head, then cast a helpless glance at Reno. "I just can't, Kayla. Your uncle understands why."

"I do?"

"Play along," she said through gritted teeth. She offered his niece a beaming smile. "But I hope you'll have fun."

"You said you'd go with me, Rachel," Reno fibbed in an overloud, nagging voice, unable to resist. "You promised."

If looks could shoot icicles through a guy's heart . . .

"No, I didn't! I specifically told you—"

"Yippee! You're going, you're going," Kayla sang.

Clearly caught and unwilling to disappoint Kayla, Rachel gave in. She nodded, still looking a little hesitant.

All the same, Reno nodded at his niece approvingly. Now that Nate had bugged out on the Christmas tree-cutting, he needed another opportunity to pair up his behemoth best buddy with his dream girl. Involving Rachel in a few of the town Christmas activities would work just fine. He'd have to talk to her about volunteering for the decorating committee.

"It's one little Christmas parade," Reno told Rachel in an undertone, steering her toward their next Christmas tree target. "Maybe some decorating. That's it. You won't feel a thing."

She stomped restlessly beside him. "That's what you think."

"What's the matter? Scared of a little hometown Christmas? Worried it might sand off a few of those rough edges?"

"Don't be ridiculous. I'm tough as nails."

Ha. Right. Tell that to the woman who'd almost burst into tears at the airport when he'd told her everything was going to work out okay. "You'll like the Christmas parade. In fact—"

"Come to my Christmas pageant at school, too!" Kayla piped up, kicking up snow as she bopped along. "Please, please—"

Now Rachel appeared really trapped. She bit her lip.

"It's kind of goofy, but it's tradition," Reno told her. "And it's fun. Besides, you haven't really experienced Christmas until you've experienced a Kismet Christmas."

"I *have* experienced a Kismet Christmas," she protested,

watching as he readied his chainsaw. "I grew up here, remember?"

Reno shook his head. "You haven't experienced a real Kismet Christmas until you've experienced it as an adult. In my neighborhood, everybody pulls together to help decorate each others' houses, hanging lights and stuff, because some of the older residents aren't spry enough to do it on their own anymore. That's something you can't appreciate as a kid."

"Somebody could make good money charging for that service," Rachel said. But he could tell she was weakening.

"If you come to my Christmas pageant, you'll get to see Nate in an elf costume with curly shoes," Kayla said, obviously trying to sweeten the deal. "And Uncle Reno all dressed up with a big fat belly and a long white beard as Santa Claus!"

"Uh, Rachel doesn't care about Santa, Kayla."

"It's *hilarious*!" his traitorous niece enthused.

"Really? Santa Claus, huh?" Stifling a smile, Rachel shot Reno a knowing look. Then she bent down and hugged Kayla. "You know what? You sold me. I'm *totally* up for that. I'll be there."

Chapter Seventeen

"Okay. Concentrate this time." Near the dairy aisle of the local Shoparama grocery store, Angela levered upward on tiptoes, the better to assess Nate's hairstyle. She licked her finger, then gave his buzz cut a swipe. "There. That's better."

"Eww!" Recoiling, Nate swabbed his damp forehead. "Come on, Angela. This is stupid. I don't *want* to meet any of these women. They're not"—he paused, sighing dreamily— "Rachel Porter."

"Snap out of it, hot stuff." In her best no-nonsense manner, Angela steered her protégé past a display of molasses, cranberry sauce, and brown sugar at the end of aisle six. The store's holiday Muzak made her want to be eating cookies and drinking eggnog, not trolling the aisles for female test subjects. "The whole reason this works is *because* you don't want to meet these particular women. There's no risk involved."

"Hey, a sale on marshmallows!" Nate veered sideways. "Did you know you can make excellent fudge with these? Just add a bag of chocolate chips, some sugar, a can of condensed milk—"

"Zip it, Betty Crocker." Her stomach growled in direct defiance. "We're not here to buy fudge-making ingredients. We're here to get you a date. I'm not leaving until we do that."

Looking hurt, Nate studied the marshmallows. Held in his big, gentle hands, they appeared twice as mini and defenseless.

"Don't even think about it," she warned. "See? There's a likely looking woman right over there. Go get her."

She gave him a shove. Or at least she tried to. Moving Nate was like moving a Buick. A Buick up on blocks in someone's yard.

Defiantly, Nate stuck out his tongue at her, then tossed the bag of minimarshmallows in their cart. So far it held only a jumbo box of detergent (because, as Angela had informed him, women liked a man who knew how to do laundry) and a pint of candy cane ice cream (because there had to be a reward at the end of all this, or Angela was going to go loony). He patted down his sweater and coat, shook out his pants legs above his boots, then eyed the lone woman Angela had pointed out.

"Okay." He twisted his neck like a prizefighter. "I'm ready. I'm awesome. Dork no more, I'm on the prowl. Here I go."

"Not like that!" She grabbed his biceps. "You look like a gigantic, demonic Dennis the Menace! Look friendly!"

He showed her his teeth. "How's that?" he gritted.

This uneasiness was very unlike him. Feeling hopeless, Angela sighed. She made herself let go of his big, warm . . . surprisingly interesting to touch . . . arm. "What's the matter with you? You've talked to four different women today—"

"Five, counting that dude with the mullet. My bad."

"—and you're no further ahead than you were when we walked into this place." Crossing her arms, she stared him down. "Are you honestly trying? Do you want to impress Rachel or not?"

"Of course I do!"

"Then get with the program. Be friendly, but not overeager. Talkative, but not domineering. Smile, but not so much that you look like you want to eat the poor woman for lunch."

Incredibly, Nate's gaze slipped down Angela's torso, then came to rest somewhere in the vicinity of her thighs.

She walloped him with a pack of Christmas sprinkles.

"Sorry!" His cheeks turned a shade ruddier. "All this talk about women is making me realize . . . *you're* a woman, Angela. A beautiful woman with a horniness problem. Why did you tell me about that? Hmmm?" Nate stepped closer. "Are you sure you don't want me to help you out sometime? I might not be a sparkling conversationalist, but I can deliver when it counts."

He gave her a dazzling smile, then winked.

If she'd truly been "beautiful," Angela realized, and if she hadn't known he was deliberately baiting her to get out of the task at hand—kind of the way Kayla did, when she didn't want to take a bath—she'd almost have believed him. There was something undeniably compelling about the slow, seductive perusal Nate gave her. About the unconscious flex of his hands, as though he were preparing to cup her derrière again, then pull her to him, lower his head, bring his mouth to hers and—

"Remember the hints I gave you." Decisively, Angela spun Nate by the shoulders, then aimed him at the woman down the aisle. "No pickup lines! Just a friendly inquiry, okay?"

Nate frowned at her. All spiffed up for their mission, he looked pretty good, she decided with utter objectivity. Golden-haired and blue-eyed and packed with enough muscles to make his parka fit funny. You know, for women who were into machismo.

"Okay. Here I go." Morosely, he schlepped down the aisle. "Wait!"

He turned. Behind him, the woman glanced their way, too.

"Scrunch down!" Angela pantomimed pushing something down. "Try not to look so looming and Lurchlike. It's intimidating."

Nate rolled his eyes. Then he made a goofy face at her—one that, to her mortification, made Angela guffaw out loud. Feeling herself blush, she wheeled around and pretended an urgent interest in a row of frosting in plastic tubs. She was clueless about baking. About cooking in general actually. She and Kayla mostly subsisted on frozen chicken nuggets with barbecue sauce, bagged salad with thousand island dressing, and applesauce.

"Uh, hi." Nate's voice floated down the aisle, husky and ever-so-slightly unsteady. "Do you know where the condoms are?"

The woman recoiled. "I don't work here," she said crisply.

"Well, I'm just wondering, because, uh, you look as if you might be familiar with the Trojans section. A woman like you probably knows all about the grocery store layout—ooof!"

To Angela's horror, the woman rammed Nate with her cart. Hard. Then she fled down the aisle, shouting for security.

"Nate!" Hastily, Angela rushed to his side. "Are you okay?"

Bent over, clutching his knees, Nate wheezed. "I think so."

"Oh no! No! You're really hurt!" Concerned, she patted his back, trying to peer into his face. It looked kind of purple. "Where did she get you? I'm really good at first aid. I took a class before Kayla was born, so I can perform CPR if you need it. I was tops in my class." Angela pried open her purse, searching for one of her trusty Band-Aids. "Please, Nate. Tell me where it hurts."

Still breathing funny, he shook his head.

Worriedly, Angela massaged his back more firmly. He felt warm beneath her hand, good and solid and dependable. Unlike any other man she'd ever met. What if she'd actually *wounded* him?

"This is all my fault. I should have known you weren't ready for this." She fussed with his coat, somehow feeling that if it were straightened, everything would be okay. "Do you feel any better? Can you speak at all? Should I go get help, or—"

"She cart-butted my bait and tackle." Nate cupped his groin, groaning. "The big Natearooni will never be the same."

"The big . . . uh . . ." Angela stammered to a stop.

He meant his *penis*. His *big* penis. His *Natearooni*.

Gee. That was kind of cute, as far as penis nicknames went.

"Quit smiling like that!" he barked.

"I'm sorry. I'm so, so sorry. I just didn't expect your penis to have a nickname like a hockey player."

"Are you *staring* at it?" Nate gawked. "Because I have to tell you, it's not in the best shape for viewing right now."

"Uh. Don't be silly." Angela whipped her head upward. "I'm your friend. I don't think of you in . . . *that* way."

She couldn't help but wonder though . . . would Nate be significantly different in the, er, *equipment* department than Bryce had been? Would he *use* his equipment differently?

Better?

Nate's gaze met hers. He knew she'd been looking at *it*. The knowledge was all over his cocky, increasingly good-looking face. How could this be happening? Had her decision to try dating again turned her into some kind of penis peek-a-booer?

And yet she couldn't stop looking. Imagining . . .

"Maybe sometimes," he said, "I wish you would."

Lost in a potential comparison that made her ears feel hot, Angela didn't quite understand him. "Wish I would what?"

"Think of me in that way . . . sometimes."

Caught unaware, Angela gazed at him—half doubled over, red-faced, still in obvious discomfort. For one uncharacteristically impulsive moment, she almost blurted out that she already had thought of him in *that way*. On the day he'd cupped her rear end.

Sometimes she still fantasized about what would have happened if she'd cupped his butt, too. It was a very nice butt. It would probably feel good. He would probably like it. Maybe he would even moan a little, just to let her know he liked it.

But then she came to her senses. "You're just delirious. Come on. Let me help you back to the cart. I'll buy you some chocolate chips, and more marshmallows, and what else?"

"Condensed milk," Nate said. "Sugar. Vanilla extract, too." His gaze arrowed to hers as they limped wounded-soldier style down the aisle, sharing a true camaraderie. "And I'm not delirious. You're a real friend, Angela. I'm starting to think—"

"Excuse me," someone interrupted.

Angela glanced up, one arm slung around Nate's taut mid-section to help him down the aisle. A reedy-looking grocery manager stood there in polyester slacks and a white button-up shirt with a holly-patterned nameplate attached to his pocket.

He frowned disapprovingly. "You're going to have to leave."

Chapter Eighteen

Ensconced on the world's coziest sofa, in the butt-shaped niche he'd carved for himself through repeated visits, Nate held a pack of frozen peas to his groin and watched Angela pace.

"Ohmigod! I've been banned from the grocery store, Nate! How am I going to buy food for me and Kayla? Christmas is coming up! I promised to bring a ham to my mom's house for dinner." She shafted him a forlorn look. "My mom told me ham was foolproof, even for me. But now . . ." With a groan, she threw up her hands. "We're going to starve to death. At Christmas."

"You're not going to starve to death."

"Yes, we are! We're going to starve. There are only two grocery stores in Kismet, and I can't afford the prices at the Olde Towne Gourmet Emporium on the lakefront." She headed past the gaily decorated Christmas tree near the TV and beelined for the kitchen with a determined expression on her face. "I know. I'll inventory everything, then ration it. Maybe if my mom chips in for gas money, we can drive to Grand Rapids to stock up."

"You don't have to stock up." Something about her worried expression and frazzled hair got to him. Even though she'd made him woodenly practice meeting women and "chitchatting," Nate wanted to make Angela feel better. "You're not going to starve."

She came back around the corner with a can of vegetable soup. She turned solemn eyes toward him. "We're not?"

"Nah. I'm making you fudge, remember? Just as soon as I get some feeling back in my johnson. It might be broken."

"Broken?"

"Yep. Or at least sprained."

"Oh my God. That can happen?"

Angela rushed to the sofa, setting down her soup and bringing with her the fragrance of the soap she'd bought during their last trip to the mall with Kayla. That soap smelled like gingerbread, Nate remembered, but it hadn't smelled like this in the store. Now, on Angela's skin, it smelled different. Better. It smelled good in a way that made him think of how much he enjoyed nibbling something sweet.

Just as he was considering that, Angela's gaze fastened on his crotch. In a very attentive way. In a very attentive way that might call Nate's bluff, if she didn't knock it off.

"I'm fine," he said. "Really."

"No, you're not."

"I really am."

"I don't believe you."

She fluttered her hands a few inches above his zipper, as though itching to rearrange his frozen peas. Or examine the troubled area in more detail. Which might be nice actually.

For a fleeting instant, Nate imagined Angela's gentle, caring hands settling on his thighs. Then sliding upward, her fingers touching the edge of his zipper, teasing it downward . . .

"You just don't want me to feel bad, that's all," she said.

"You're right." With effort, he snapped out of his reverie. Angela was a good person. A kind, loving, nurturing, curvy-assed person. She didn't need his horndog thoughts smutting up her living room. "Right now, I want you to feel very, very good."

Suspiciously, she stared at him.

Had he said that out loud?

"About all you've done to help me, I mean. Not everyone would do that." With effort, Nate removed his bag of frozen peas so she wouldn't worry about him anymore. "You know, helping me get in good with my dream girl, Rachel Porter, and all."

A slight frown. "I'm happy to help."

"Angela . . ."

"Yes?"

"Stop staring at my crotch. It's distracting."

Her head snapped up. A pink glow suffused her cheeks. "I'm just *concerned*. Maybe you need medical attention."

"If I do, it's for my bruised ego." He squinted at her, remembering. "Demonic Dennis the Menace? Come on."

"Uhh . . ."

"And I'm not Lurchlike. I can't help being big, but I'm not going to squash myself down either. I just need a woman who can keep up with me in the physical sturdiness department."

Sagely, Angela nodded. He recognized that pose. She used it in class with her students, too. Which kind of galled him.

He was not a teenager, damn it.

To prove it, Nate took his time examining her. "I need a woman like you, for instance. Although, strictly speaking, you're a little too curvy"—he squinted assessingly—"and a little too lacking in outright brawn to match up with me perfectly."

"Humph. I can match up with you any day."

"Oh yeah?"

"Yeah." She looked a little panicked. "Just try me."

Her dare—because clearly that's what it was—kicked his heartbeat into overdrive. Suddenly, being on the couch with Angela felt exactly like trotting onto the gridiron, desperate to impress the coach and be on the winning team. Except Nate hadn't made the winning team. And no coach had ever wriggled beside him with quite so much preparatory jiggling.

How had he gotten himself in this situation in the first place? Oh yeah. Pride. He had that in spades.

"Fine," he said. "I *will* try you."

In stupid quantities of spades. Whatever they were.

Preparing himself, Nate cleared his throat. He eyed Angela, who sat primly and expectantly beside him with her chin in the air. He smacked his lips to check his breath surreptitiously. All clear. He raised his hand, whipped off his knit cap—which he'd been too distracted to remove until now—and then leaned in. No doubt Angela would appreciate his chivalrous gesture in removing his cap. Of all the women he'd known—

A sputter of laughter escaped her.

—Angela was the most sensitive, the most thoughtful—

"What in the world is the matter with you?" she asked.

He frowned, halted in the midst of his planned move. He wasn't the world's most suave guy—he'd be the first to admit that—but most women did not giggle at him unless he told a joke.

"What happened to your eyebrow?"

Stiffening, Nate crumpled his hat in his hand. With dignity, he raised his clean-shaven chin. "I had them waxed."

"'Them'? I'm sorry to break it to you, Boy Band, but you've only got one eyebrow there. One. *Uno. Ein. Un.* Um."

"Cut it out, United Nations." He held up his hand. "You might not be aware of this, but waxing your eyebrows *hurts.*"

"Poor baby. How do you think giving birth feels?"

"Not a consideration for me."

"Or having your, um . . ." Angela gestured vaguely toward the zipper on her jeans ". . . bikini line waxed? Hmmm?"

"You've done that?" He couldn't help but feel intrigued.

"Well, no. But I'll bet it hurts like the dickens."

They lapsed into silence, Angela staring pink-cheeked toward her Christmas tree. Its lights sparkled, its ornaments (some of them gifts from Nate over the years) shone, and its homemade construction-paper chains wound around the whole thing in a haphazard fashion that suggested (although Nate already knew) that Angela let Kayla have a strong hand in decorating.

Embarrassed, Nate looked at the knit cap dangling from his fingers. A niggling sense of disappointment poked at him, almost as though he were sorry not to have finished showing Angela what he meant about needing a good, sturdy, curvy woman.

He should have finished the stupid eyebrow waxing. He was the kind of guy who committed to something and stuck with it. But for some reason, his resolve had wavered with the first rip of that wax-coated cotton strip. He hadn't been the same since.

How was he supposed to get close to Rachel Porter if he couldn't even work up the nerve to make himself appropriately Hollywood-ready? He wanted Rachel to be impressed with him. Impressed with him in the way Angela usually was, when he wasn't showing off his freaky monobrow and accosting innocent women in the grocery store when he'd rather be making holiday fudge.

As though on the same track, Angela blinked.

"Condoms, Nate?" she blurted. "You asked that woman where the *condoms* were?" She swiveled to face him, bikini-line talk clearly over with. "What were you thinking?"

Oh, man. A minute ago, Nate would have sworn he'd rather discuss anything except his eyebrows. Anything . . . except this.

"I wanted her to know I was into safe sex. You know, that I was responsible. It seemed like a good idea at the time."

Her skeptical expression made him scramble for more.

"Look, I choked, okay? I know it sounded bad." The ornaments on the tree blurred in his vision. All he could smell was Angela's gingerbread soap. "But I was trying to impress you. After all those tries, I . . . didn't want you to think I was lame."

"Nate, you know I'd never think that."

Self-consciously, he pushed to his feet, hating his lumbering footfalls for making the Rudolph and Santa ceramic bric-a-brac on her end tables rattle. He just *knew* he was going to break something around here. Angela's place was feminine and cozy, like her.

"Please. Wait." The frozen peas in the bag rattled as Angela scooped them up, then followed him. "You can't really think—"

Shaking his head, Nate charged into the kitchen.

Angela appeared right behind him on cue. "Now you're walking out on me in midsentence?" She set down the peas. "That eyebrow scalping of yours was just the beginning, wasn't it?"

"The beginning of an awesome relationship with Rachel Porter, maybe," Nate heard himself gloat as he rubbed his eyebrow. "Which is more than I can say for you and The Prick."

Angela gasped. "That's not fair. You know I put off my dates with Patrick in order to help you."

Nate did know that. But right now he felt all mixed up. Embarrassed, irked, and kind of hot and bothered, too. Defiantly, he grabbed the chocolate chips from the bag on the counter. The store had generously let them pay for their purchases before making them leave. He stomped past her to grab a wooden spoon

"Nate, talk to me!"

"Hey, I'm not a girl. I just reached my quota for sharing." He pulled out a saucepan. "Let's make fudge instead."

A sigh. "You know I can barely boil water."

"Come on. I'll let you lick the spoon."

The idea conjured up all sorts of enticing images. Images he had no right to be considering with his best friend's sister.

On the other hand . . .

"And I'll let you kiss me." He backed her up to the refrigerator, pinning Angela between him and the magnet clips on Kayla's first-grade artwork. He held her arms. "Go ahead."

Her astonished gaze met his. Beneath his hands, she felt

soft and warm, enticing him into stroking up and down. At his touch, she shivered. He didn't want to admit it, but so did he.

"Look, I'll help you." Nate leaned closer. His breath fanned over her lips, and his gaze dropped to meet it. "See?"

"If this is one of your idiotic dares—"

"It's not." With every second that ticked past, he knew it wasn't. It might have been crazy and unexpected and sort of dangerous, but it wasn't just a dare. It wasn't *just* anything. "I want you to kiss me, Angela. I want *you*."

"I . . . ummm." She licked her lips. She gave the merest nod.

He might have imagined it. "Aren't you curious? I am."

"I'm a teacher," she said. "It's my job to be curious."

"That makes two of us." Warmth reached between them, seeming to knit them together in the close confines of the kitchen. It was dim in here, lit only by the light over the stove, but Nate would have recognized the sensation of having Angela near him even in pitch blackness. "Go ahead. Do it."

"Don't . . . you want to do it?"

He almost groaned. *Yes*. Their mouths were only a few inches apart now, Angela's face blurred in his vision because they stood so close together. He could feel her quiver in his arms. He wondered what she would do if he did take charge.

"Hell, yeah, I want to do it." He trailed his hands down her arms to her fingertips. Their hands clasped. "But more than that, I want you to *want* to do it. There's only one way to make sure that's what's happening. You have to be the one to do it."

"How did we even get here?" A puzzled smile curved her lips. "A second ago, you were mad at me. And now . . ."

"Stop procrastinating. Just do it. Kiss me. Do it."

"Well, when you put it like that . . ."

"God, Angela. You're killing me. Please?"

"Mmm. I can't refuse such a polite request, now can I? It would be setting a bad example. But this is a big step, Nate. What if—"

"In ten seconds, I'm going to forget I'm a gentleman."

Another shiver. "Okay, you asked for it. Here we go."

He heard her indrawn breath, felt her rise upward to meet him, then . . . *ohhh*. The tiniest brush of her lips against his. Her kiss felt like a gift, like something he'd treasure forever, and before Nate could quite reconcile the fact that he was actually thinking in sappy phrases like *treasure forever*, Angela kissed him again, and all thought pretty much ground to a halt.

Her hands squeezed his. Their breath met, mingled, then flew away as their mouths met again. Slowly. Gently. Nate's whole body clenched with need and longing and want, hard enough to make him gasp. He moaned against Angela's tongue, unable to stop himself from cupping her backside the way he'd dreamed.

Mmmm. That was more like it. With both hands he cradled her, tilting her away from the fridge and toward him until their hips touched. Pure pleasure bolted through him at the contact, sharp and perfect, and if he hadn't been sort of dizzy with the realization that this was *Angela* kissing him, he might have lost control right then. As it was, it was all Nate could do not to kiss her harder, to grind himself against her, to lift his hand to her sweater and experience the sweet curve of her breast.

Okay, so he *did* do that. Hell, he was only human.

But touching Angela made fireworks explode inside him, made his breath come in raspy, grateful pants and his ears ring with joy. Ring, ring, ring. It was funny how vivid the experience was. He'd have sworn he actually heard bells.

Angela jerked her head sideways. "The doorbell!"

All at once, Nate came to his senses. Evidently so did Angela. Both their gazes centered on his hand. On her breast. On her lush, perfect breast as though it had been made for the job.

Awkwardly, Nate pulled his hand away. He stared at it.

Nice job, hand. It knew what he wanted more than he did.

With a few guilty swipes, Angela straightened her clothes. She lifted her gaze to his as the doorbell chimed again, then she touched her mouth. "I'm sorry. I've got to get that."

She pattered away, leaving him in the kitchen all aching and confused. What the hell had just happened? He'd thought he'd been in control of the whole thing—thought he'd been creating a diversion from their stupid argument and his stupid eyebrow(s).

But the moment their lips had met . . .

A murmured conversation drifted to him. A male voice, then Angela's engaging, slightly husky reply. Intimate laughter.

Frowning, Nate shoved his way around the corner. Patrick the Prick stood in the living room with one arm audaciously around Angela's waist. She seemed to like it, too.

"Oh, Nate! I'm sorry, but it completely slipped my mind that Patrick and I made plans for tonight. It was his consolation prize for delaying our date earlier this week."

The smug jerk smirked at Nate. "Baked any cherry pies lately, Kelly? Or are you too busy trying on aprons?"

"I gave up on aprons. They're all too small to contain me."

"I'm not surprised, with an ass that big. You should quit eating your own cupcakes and let your students have some."

Nate gritted his teeth. They were both guests here after all. Patrick stepped glibly around Angela. With an idle gesture, he picked up her prized collectible Christmas plate—the one her grandmother had given her ten years ago—and turned it over in his smarmy, irritating, obnoxiously manicured hands.

Geez, Nate hoped Rachel Porter didn't expect men with shiny fingernails. He wasn't sure he could cope with that.

"Put that down." Nate strode across the room. "Angela doesn't like people touching her plate. It's special."

"Special?" The Prick chuckled. He turned over the plate, making holiday lights glint from the pattern of an old-fashioned Christmas tree piled with gifts. "What's so special about this?"

"It's got a lot of history behind it." Carefully, Nate reclaimed the plate. He put it back. "You wouldn't understand."

Patrick shrugged. Obviously he didn't understand and didn't care to try either. He offered Angela one of his arrogant, annoying smiles. "Ready to go?"

"Sure. Just let me get my purse."

Angela headed for the kitchen. Ignoring the rudeness of leaving Patrick on his own to potentially wreck everything of sentimental value in Angela's place, Nate followed.

"What are you doing? I thought we were making fudge!"

"I'm sorry, Nate. Really." Looking flustered and impossibly pretty, Angela sorted through her purse, looking for something. "But I knew Kayla would be with Reno at the Christmas tree farm for a few hours—and our lesson at the grocery store was kind of spur of the moment—so tonight was good for me."

He waited until she glanced up. "It was good for me, too."

A fresh blush brightened her cheeks, but Angela only came near him, squeezed his biceps, then smiled. "See you later. You can still make fudge if you want. I trust you in the kitchen."

He boggled. "But it's Wednesday! Pizza and TV show night. We always spend Wednesday nights together. Did you forget?"

"Umm. I guess I did. Whoops." With a conspiratorial air, Angela leaned toward him, her eyes sparkling. "But did you see? Did you? Playing hard to get with Patrick is totally working!"

"Yeah," Nate said peevishly. "Really good."

"I've got *you* to thank for that. So thanks!"

He frowned. "You're welcome."

Hastily, she applied some lip gloss. Not the puffy-lips kind, but another brand, one he didn't recognize as hers. He couldn't help but feel sort of bereft as shiny pink obliterated all traces of the kiss they'd shared. The magical, surprising, leaving-him-wanting-more-and-more kiss that—

"Bye, Nate. See you tomorrow." Angela patted his arm in a sisterly fashion. She winked. "Don't eat too much fudge. And don't worry—we'll get you ready for Rachel Porter yet. It never occurred to me to practice kissing though. You're a genius!"

"Yeah." He couldn't admit that he hadn't been strategizing. From the instant he'd looked at Angela's lips, the last person on his mind had been Rachel Porter. "Totally brilliant."

In fact, Nate wasn't so sure he wanted Rachel Porter now at all. Not when Angela was here, all ripe and juicy and . . . leaving.

He trailed her to the living room, where The Prick helped her on with her coat, then engineered some shady bit of business during which he pretended to have trouble putting on Angela's scarf for her—necessitating lots of up close and personal contact. Their faces nearly touched. When Angela gazed up at Patrick and dreamily smiled at him, Nate almost lost it.

"She likes it like this." Huffily, he twined her scarf securely. He patted it in place, then nodded with satisfaction. "If you do it any other way, she loses it. Always has."

They both gawked at him.

"I'm not ten years old anymore," Angela said.

"*I'll* say you're not," The Prick added. "You're all woman."

Nate wanted to take the man's head off. Especially if he didn't quit smirking like that. But with Angela right there . . . he felt equally driven to just kiss her and kiss her and kiss her.

And okay, so maybe he was making an ass of himself, but Nate didn't know how to stop. He hadn't known how to call it quits when he'd been in over his head in NFL training camp with Reno years ago, and he didn't know how to turn Angela happily into another man's arms now either.

Maybe because he didn't want to.

"Good night, Nate." She waved. "Bye."

Not that it mattered, because Angela left him behind all the same. Just him, some chocolate chips and marshmallows, and a whole lot of cheerful, empty household that felt like nothing without Angela in it alongside him.

Chapter Nineteen

For the rest of the week, Reno tried to get Nate hooked up with Rachel. For his first attempt, he invited them both to Glenrosen to string lights with the neighborhood decorating committee. Rachel trotted across the snowy street right on time, bright-eyed and outrageously dressed, wearing a sweater, a vivid smile, and hip-hugging jeans that made Reno doubt the wisdom of fixing her up with someone else in the first place.

While Reno watched, Rachel dived into the task of sorting out last year's Christmas light strings. She held up the end-to-end plug of a strand of C9s, then glanced around at the other volunteers. Most of them were grown sons and daughters of the residents, or people his own age who weren't legacy Glenroseners, but who hoped to gentrify the old tree-lined neighborhood anyway. All of them were hopped up on coffee—with (or without) peppermint schnapps—and crescent-shaped rugelach baked by the unlikely team of Kowalczyk and Bender.

"Who wants to help with this strand?" Rachel asked.

A clump of people instantly swamped her. Beaming from the middle of the pack, Rachel quickly got to know everyone she hadn't already met and got reacquainted with the people she knew. As a side effect, the lights got untangled, too.

Five fully-decorated houses and yards, several light-bedecked eaves, and one painted-and-repaired nativity scene later, Reno climbed down from his ladder, having just finished stringing lights on Mr. Caplan's house three doors down from his. He directed one of his neighbors to twine more lights around the mailbox and shrubs. Then he turned to take on the next task.

Rachel stood there, bundled up in the same hat and scarf she'd worn for their kiss at the Christmas tree farm. "If I didn't know better, I'd think you were avoiding me. But the word around here is that you're always the boss of this shindig, so I guess you're just busy."

He shrugged. "Somebody's got to take charge."

"And of course, it's you. Kismet's go-to guy."

"I like to help out." If Rachel wanted to believe he was some kind of do-gooder in town, he'd let her. He knew the truth about how lucky he'd been—about how much he owed everyone who hadn't been as fortunate. After all, he was just a regular guy. A regular guy who'd lucked out with football and come home a whole lot richer and a whole lot more grateful for everything that really mattered.

"The sooner I finish this, the sooner I can get back to decking out my house for the Glenrosen competition." He nodded toward his place. In the daylight, its eaves, roof, and lawn showed no visible signs of the 47,000 multicolored twinkling chaser lights he'd been stringing for weeks now, but Reno knew they were there. "That's the winning entry right there."

Rachel wrinkled her nose. "Doesn't look like much yet."

"You'll see." He smiled at her. "Some people like to keep their flashy sides under wraps until the right moment."

"Bor-ing. I'm all about making a statement, right from the word go." Rachel looked him up and down. "And I'd say you've got the kind of flashy side that should *never* be kept under wraps."

Reno thought he might actually be blushing. "Uh-oh. I've got that naked feeling again."

Her brows lifted. "Naked? Sounds promising. Go on."

"There are two dozen people milling around, remember?"

"So? Live a little." She snuggled closer to him, her breath sending frosty plumes in the clear December air. Nearby, someone's portable stereo blasted out Christmas carols, adding to the festive ambiance. "I only came over here in the first place because I thought you might want a little warm up."

"I do." He grinned. "What did you have in mind?"

"Hot coffee." She held up a steaming mug. "Judging by the way the ceramic is melting, it's got plenty of schnapps in it."

"Ah." Gratefully—but with no small measure of disappointment, thanks to his wild imagination—Reno swallowed some of the minty brew. It burned all the way down as he eyed her empty mittened hands. "You're not having any?"

A shrug. "It's a little too Midwestern for me."

"Peppermint schnapps and coffee?"

"Well . . . the whole thing really. Everyone pitching in, helping one another, doing good for their neighbors." Watching a volunteer hang a wreath on an elderly man's door, Rachel gave a mock shudder. "It's so damn cozy, it's giving me hives."

"That's just your latent good nature wanting to come out. Part of you wants to string popcorn and sing 'Grandma Got Run Over by a Reindeer' while giving someone a discoing Santa."

She laughed. "No way. I plan to suppress whatever's left of my Midwestern roots later tonight with a few of my own more fashionable traditions. Starting with cranberry martinis, a roaring fire, and the best of Bing Crosby on the CD player."

"Bing Crosby? That's as traditional as it gets."

"That's as *classic* as it gets. There's a difference." Rachel edged closer to him, running her fingers along his coat buttons. "Gold tinsel is traditional. Silver is classic. Stick-on bows are traditional. Red velvet ribbon is classic. Fruitcake is traditional. Iced sugar cookies are classic. Get it?"

"No. Do you have this many rules for everything?"

"Depends on what you have in mind."

What he had in mind, all of a sudden, was pinning her

against the nearest snowy tree and kissing her again—maybe because of the saucy look she gave him. Rebellious Rachel Porter would probably go for it, even if it meant shocking the neighbors. *Especially* if it meant shocking the neighbors.

Reno's head swam with minty schnapps and his body throbbed with remembering how kissing her had felt last time.

Hot, urgent, and surprisingly affecting.

No. He was here to do reconnaissance for Nate, not enjoy his own R-rated Rachel flashbacks.

"I had in mind ringing in the season," he lied.

"Predictable." Rachel made a face. "Kismet-style, I guess?"

"Damn straight. It's better than L.A.-style."

"Is not and never will be. Wanna make a bet?"

He couldn't help but grin. "You have a problem with betting. You still haven't learned your lesson, have you?" Reno touched her cheek, smoothing away a wayward hank of hair. He doubted anyone noticed. "I always win. End of story."

At her answering smile, his heart expanded. He didn't bother to contemplate why. He figured it was the season, the smiling camaraderie, and the peppermint schnapps. He never had time for anything more elaborate. Not with his entire family needing him, his neighbors depending on him, and the whole town constantly expecting great things from him. It had been that way ever since he'd come home from the NFL. Maybe before.

"You don't win with me. Not unless I say so. Besides, I'm not just making this up. I can prove an L.A. Christmas is better than a Kismet Christmas any day." Rachel nodded for him to finish his liquored-up coffee, then took his cup with a naughty-French-maid's curtsy. Apparently she'd signed on for unofficial hostess duty. "Come over for cranberry martinis and Bing Crosby later, and I'll show you what I mean."

"You're on," Reno said. Impulsively and instantly. Because that's the kind of effect Rachel Porter had on him.

And that's how he wound up spending a long, intimate,

classic night by the fire with the absentee style-queen of California . . . without thinking about Nate once the entire time.

Oops.

Still determined to keep his promise to Nate, Reno arranged for his best friend and Rachel to run into each other at The Wright Stuff the next day—ostensibly so she could help one of his "buddies" with a shopping problem.

"It's Nate," Reno explained when she stopped in, glancing curiously around his crowded, holiday-decorated sports equipment store. "He needs help finding gifts for his mom."

"Is this the same Nate who was supposed to go Christmas tree-cutting with you and me and Kayla at the tree farm?"

Reno nodded.

"The same Nate who couldn't make it to the Glenrosen decorating party last night?"

Another nod. Nate had claimed that he needed to let his eyebrows grow before meeting Rachel. Reno had convinced him—he thought—to address that problem by wearing a hat pulled down really low today.

Now, fifteen minutes after the meeting time he thought they'd agreed upon (and four phone calls later), Reno was having second thoughts about his renowned persuasive ability.

"I'm beginning to think," Rachel mused, "that your friend Nate is dodging me on purpose. What's up with that?"

"Nothing! He's a great guy. Really." Torn with guilt about how much he'd enjoyed those froufrou cranberry martinis—and the hot-hot-hot kisses they'd shared in front of the fire before Rachel's parents had accidentally barged in and they'd all wound up playing a game of Pictionary instead—Reno busied himself by rearranging a rack of replica hockey jerseys. "Nate's a teacher, so he has a good job. He works out, so he's in good shape. He's incredibly frugal, so he's dependable. Nate's a real bargain for the right woman."

Not you not you not you. Damn it.

Rachel shifted her gaze to him. "Um, you might as well know—I'm not up for a fix-up, if that's what you're angling at."

Helplessly—stupidly—Reno remained mum.

"Dating is a lost cause for me, I'm afraid." Reaching out to touch the jerseys, she recoiled as her fingers encountered one hundred percent polyblend. "I just got over a bad breakup. That's part of the reason I'm here in Kismet."

"Somebody broke your heart?" He wanted to break their nose.

"Nothing that drastic. The breakup wasn't pretty, but it was a long time coming. When it came down to it, Tyson just—"

"'Tyson'?" He flapped his arms. "Like the chicken?"

She guffawed. "Yeah. Like the chicken." Her smile made her lips look luscious—and her whole attitude seem twice as light. "I think I'm going to call him that from now on. Tyson-Like-The-Chicken. Anyway, he obviously wasn't the right guy for me. He was just . . . there. He was good-looking, and he fit the part—"

"Were you casting him or falling for him?"

"Honestly? A little of both, I guess." Rachel leaned against the checkout counter, elbows flaring toward the Christmas cards he'd pinned up—greetings from other Main Street business owners. "I didn't have time for a relationship, but I did need an escort to events. I needed someone to wake up with. I needed sex."

"Yeah," Reno rasped in a casual tone. "Who doesn't?"

He could barely speak for the sexual image that flared to life in his mind though—him, Rachel, and yards and yards of *classic* red velvet Christmas ribbon.

A gentle knot here, a gentle knot there, and he'd be able to satisfy all his holiday fantasies. He'd unwrap her slowly, bit by bit, kissing every inch of bare skin he revealed until Rachel begged him to let her touch him, too . . . until they both wound up so tangled they would never get enough of each other.

"You're wrinkling that shirt pretty bad," she said.

Startled, Reno glanced down. He'd fisted a Red Wings jersey so hard, it had a permanent crinkle across the numbers.

"Want to share what you were thinking about?" she asked.

Her playful tone almost enticed him to do it. He looked at her expectant face—stripped today of some of the glamazon makeup she'd worn when they'd met—and felt an almost palpable sense of longing. Longing . . . for his best friend's dream girl.

"Boring stuff. Gift wrap bondage. Making you beg for—"

Her eyes widened . . . with unmistakable interest.

"—another shot at meeting Nate." Briskly, Reno moved behind the counter and fiddled with the cash register. Where the hell were his customers? Sure, it was early, but he could really use some distraction. "He's meeting me tomorrow morning at my place to get geared up in our costumes for Kayla's Christmas pageant. Kayla and Angela will be there. You should come, too."

Rachel crossed her arms, examining him. She wasn't buying it, he could tell. "As curious as I am about the sight of you in a full-on Santa suit, I've got to ask . . . gift wrap bondage?"

"Red velvet ribbons. Nothing major." Carelessly, Reno waved. "The usual small-town Kismet Christmas shenanigans."

"Hmmm." Her eyes sparkled. "I've been away for too long."

"I thought you might think so." Damn, he was making an idiot of himself. Why couldn't Rachel be like most of the women in town? They were so awed by his superstar football past that they didn't do much except nod, smile, and occasionally flash their bras at him. "So . . . costumes. You should help with them."

"Do you need expert advice?"

Advice about wedging him into a hideous red velour Santa

suit and a scratchy fake beard? Not really. Reno couldn't quite remember why he'd invited her to view the spectacle.

Oh, yeah. Nate. Another chance for her to get with Nate.

"Yes," he said with conviction. "Yes, I do need advice."

And that was how he wound up with yet another date with Rachel Porter. A date that included a "jolly" pillow stomach, a big pointy hat, and a frequent directive to say ho-ho-ho a lot.

She wouldn't be able to resist him.

Which was probably for the best. Because then Rachel would be twice as interested in meeting her biggest Kismet fan . . . if Nate could only get a grip on his damn eyebrows and get himself to the right place at the right time for a change.

Standing in her bedroom at her parents' house, Rachel pinned a gold-fringed Victorian ornament to her inspiration board. She added a stripe of metallic sixties-style tinsel, rearranged a scrap of gleaming snowflake-embossed paper she'd snatched while wrapping gifts for faraway relatives with her mom (she was caving in to Christmas at warp speed now), then stood back to survey the total effect.

It looked good. Almost right.

If she could just get the color scheme to match the tantalizing picture in her imagination . . .

"I liked that Reno Wright. He was a nice young man."

At the sound of her mother's voice, Rachel wheeled around.

"You two had some amazing Pictionary chemistry," her mom went on blithely. "Almost as good as your father and me. Hey, I recognize that!" Her gaze skated to Rachel's inspiration board, even as she rebalanced her armful of silk garland for the crafty Christmas decorating project she'd launched in the kitchen. "What's that? Do you have a new collection in the works?"

Caught, Rachel fisted her pins. She had to plant both feet in her boots—her own L.A. stilettos—to keep from flinging herself across her telltale board. She should have known her mother would recognize this for what it was and call her on it.

"Collection? Mom, I'm a celebrity stylist now, remember? I don't do collections anymore. Those are for designers."

"Which *you* really are at heart. A designer."

Rachel demurred. Despite her design school awards, her dreams of *creating* actual garments for people, and her long-ago hopes of expressing herself with fabric and tailoring, right now her ideas felt too fragile to discuss. What if they vanished?

"You've got talent, honey." As usual, her mother seemed undeterred by Rachel's silence—and utterly convinced of her specialness. "You've got too much talent to be happy as a glorified shopper for those spoiled stars you work for."

"Work *with*, Mom. I'm a partner, not an employee."

Wearing a strange expression, her mother closed her mouth.

"Anyway, I'm on vacation from all that, right?" Rachel spied a scrap of seam-ripped fabric atop one of the patterns she'd cut. She kicked both incriminating items under the bed. Her fledgling hopes felt way too new to reveal. "I was just heading down to the Elks Club to help the Kismet decorating committee with the Christmas parade floats. Do you want to come?"

"Mother-daughter time?" A broad smile crossed her mother's face. "I thought you'd never ask. I'll get my coat."

Chapter Twenty

Stepping over the snowy concrete steps into the Kismet Elks Club was like stepping back in time. Housed in a clapboard building a few blocks from the riverfront, the place still smelled like cigars (now outlawed indoors by a civic code), pancake breakfasts (with local maple syrup), and men wearing pants pulled up to their armpits (eau de Old Spice). There was even an I LIKE IKE campaign pin on the chalkboard near the door.

Also written on the chalkboard were an array of Christmas parade-related assignments. In the center of the room amid the volunteers were bits and pieces of two floats being repaired, along with the flotsam and jetsam of costumes, giant balloons, and tinsel. A heap of old lights lay abandoned in the corner (a sight that would have broken Reno's heart). Plates of Christmas cookies stood on a table near two popular coffee urns.

Regulars milled around, busily working to prepare for the Christmas parade and the unveiling of the town Christmas tree.

A man and a woman presided over the whole affair—working, it appeared, from two distinctly separate bases of operation. The woman, a fiftyish brunette wearing a pantsuit and a smile, manned a table full of paperwork, duct tape, and electrical cords. The man, about the same age but dressed in sweatpants, a Detroit Lions jersey, and a weight lifter's belt, supervised the float rebuilding with a coffee-stained clipboard in hand.

They spotted Rachel and her mother simultaneously. Both leaders abandoned what they were doing and veered toward them.

The woman arrived first. "Christine, hi! It's so good to see you. We can really use a talent like yours on the committee for the town Christmas tree. Are you still scrapbooking?"

Rachel's mother nodded, immediately launching into genial chitchat with her old friend. Before Rachel could get much further than reading the name JUDY WRIGHT on the cheerful woman's handwritten name tag, the male leader reached her.

"Hello!" he boomed, enveloping her hand in a fast and certain handshake that left her wobbly. "Tom Wright here. You must be wanting to volunteer. Excellent! What's your name, hon?"

Startled by his take-charge demeanor, Rachel didn't reply at first. He seemed familiar somehow, and charming in a rough kind of way, but she couldn't quite place him. Big smile, green eyes, salt-and-pepper hair, firm grip on his clipboard . . .

"Don't pester her, Tom." Judy Wright rolled her eyes. "That's Rachel Porter. Don't you remember her? The Porters *only* lived down the street from us for thirty years."

"I know, Judy. I'm not blind." He straightened his weight belt self-consciously. "I can see a pretty girl just fine."

"Humph. I'll just bet you can."

"*Some* people know how to appreciate a good thing when it's standing right in front of them." He puffed out his chest.

"Well, some *other* people know how to be thoughtful. Like me." With a sniff and a lift of her chin, Judy took Rachel and her mother by the elbows. "Come on, ladies. I'll bet you're starving! We've got cookies and coffee right over here."

While Rachel belatedly registered the fact that she'd just

met Reno's and Angela's feuding parents, Tom and Judy Wright, they sailed toward the refreshment table, dodging groups of hardworking volunteers—some untangling Christmas lights, some painting holiday signs and banners, some making repairs to what appeared to be the official Kismet Christmas decorations. The whole place felt like Santa's workshop—time-warped to 1952.

Murmured conversations followed their progress across the room. So did several smiles, along with greetings for Rachel's mother. Waves and shouts of "Hi, Christine!" echoed all around. Their movement slowed as conversations lengthened. Several people waved at Rachel, too, smiling as they recognized her.

The coziness of it all enveloped her. She felt glad to be here, glad for her mom, glad to have this experience to share with her—despite the awkwardness of coming face-to-face with the unraveling marriage of two people whom she'd liked on sight.

Remembering what Angela had revealed about her parents' quarrel—brought on by Tom Wright's post-Thanksgiving "blank check" Christmas gift and Judy Wright's predictably hurt reaction to his plan to save them "all the trouble" of buying each other gifts—Rachel felt truly sorry for the pair. Clearly they'd lost the knack for communicating with each other. More than likely, *both* of the Wrights felt misunderstood right now.

"Hey!" Someone grabbed Rachel's arm and tugged. "You can't just steal my volunteers. I found this one."

Rachel turned to find herself in Tom Wright's grasp—and in Judy Wright's grasp, too. Unbelievably, they both gave a pull.

"Well, she'd rather work with me, wouldn't you, Rachel?"

"I, uhh . . ."

"Nonsense! She's got vision. She's a world-famous celebrity stylist from Los Angeles!" Tom leaned closer, speaking to Rachel in a conspiratorial whisper. "Your folks made sure we saw you on those red-carpet TV shows and in the magazines." Then louder to Judy: "She should work on the *cool* side of things—my side. The floats are bigger and better than the decorations."

"Cool? You don't know what you're talking about." Judy spoke past Rachel's nose, her voice quivering. "I'm the one who recognized Rachel. She used to pal around with Angela, but I doubt *you* remember that. You were too wrapped up in your own little world all the time to notice anyone else, weren't you?"

"No, I wasn't!" Tom stiffened. "I never am. Or I wouldn't have given my Christmas gifts to everyone *early* this year."

"Early? Early! Of course you're early when you're just cracking open your checkbook. I hope you didn't strain anything. Or is that what that girdle around your waist is for?"

"This," Tom sniffed, "is a weight lifter's support belt."

"Ha! Do you use it to support your gigantic ego?"

Wincing, Rachel exchanged an uncertain glance with her mom. Sensing their opening, they disentangled themselves in synchronized silence, then ducked to the side of the room as Judy and Tom continued to debate. The other volunteers watched with avid interest while Rachel and her mom went for coffee.

"This is the first time they've spoken in days," confided a gray-haired woman—MABEL FENSTER, according to her official volunteer name tag—as she poured some weak Folgers. She winked, then smiled at the bickering couple. "I think it's a good sign."

"A good sign?" Rachel's mom shook her head apprehensively. "Tom and Judy aren't even being civil to one another. I've known the Wrights for a long time. This is a real shame."

Rachel chanced another glance at the couple. They stood nearly nose to nose now, anguish plain in their weary, good-looking faces. It was evident that this wasn't what either of them had hoped for from their day at the Elks Club—which only made their argument now all the more heartrending.

On the other hand . . .

"They want to make up," Rachel declared as she accepted a black coffee and a Christmas cookie. "They want to put their whole argument behind them. Can't you tell?"

"Honey, this isn't L.A." Mabel tsk-tsked. "We don't buy into all that Hollywood-style feuding and making up. It's not on-again, off-again like Elizabeth Taylor and Richard Burton."

Both older women sighed dreamily.

"It's just on . . . then off," her mother agreed. "At least with regular folks. We see it happen all the time, especially once people hit retirement age. They get in each other's way, find out they don't have much in common anymore, then . . . *pfft*."

"No, I mean it! They came here hoping for a reconciliation." Rachel gestured with her cookie. Mmm. Not only did it taste delicious, but it looked pretty, too, frosted with white and blue icing and topped with silver dragées. She snatched another one. "Look at them. Look *closely*. You'll see what I mean."

"I see arguing. Tom almost snapped his clipboard just now."

"No, really *look*." Rachel turned her mom more squarely to face the couple. Mabel followed suit. "Tom is wearing that weight belt to draw attention to his physique—which is actually pretty terrific for an older guy. And he's got on a gold chain, which—however tacky—probably passes for dressy around here, right?"

"Yes, but that's just a midlife crisis in action, not a reconciliation waiting to happen." Her mother tugged her arm. "Come on. Let's go join that table. They're making those adorable little reindeer out of clothespins and googly eyes."

"No, I mean it!" Rachel insisted. "This is part of why I'm good at my job. I understand people. I know what their innermost desires are. I help them fulfill them through their clothes."

"Really? That's a lot to infer from a weight lifter's belt and a gold chain," Mabel said. "Maybe that's just what Tom had handy this morning. It doesn't necessarily have any deeper meaning. I just grab what's in my closet that's not too tight or too pilled or too moth-eaten or too stained and go."

Her mother—God help her—nodded in agreement. Didn't anyone around here realize how much fun and purpose clothes could have?

Rachel did. Because of that, a sense of purposefulness kicked to life inside her—along with a burgeoning sense of hope that she hadn't experienced in weeks. Maybe even longer.

"Look at Judy," she urged. Mmm. Now that she'd started, she couldn't get enough cookies. It felt like *ages* since she'd experienced a flavor that didn't come packaged with soy protein and extra vitamins. "See what she's wearing? That clinches it."

"A pantsuit?" her mother asked.

"A pantsuit *and* a pair of earrings *and* high-heeled shoes."

"I didn't notice those shoes." Absently, Mabel peered at Judy Wright. "They're very skimpy shoes. And very high. Her toes must be freezing."

"She wore them to catch her husband's eye, I guarantee it. People speak volumes through their clothing," Rachel said. "Plus that pantsuit is at least twenty years old. She's clearly using a nostalgia clothing item to evoke good memories."

Her mother frowned. "You get all that from old blue wool?"

"All that and more," Rachel confirmed. Her heart melted toward the Wrights as she gazed across the room at the squabbling couple. "The only trouble is, they're both amateurs. Someone needs to help them get their messages across, so they can get to the making up they both want."

"Uh-oh," her mother said. "I recognize that look."

"It's the same look you probably had back in Hollywood," Mabel added, "when you put Alayna in that dress with the—"

But Rachel didn't want to hear any more about Alayna and

her former life in L.A. Right now, she had a more important mission. A mission of goodwill. A *Christmas mission*.

"And that someone," she announced, "is going to be me."

Sucking in a deep breath, Rachel put on her most engaging smile. Then she headed purposefully past the red and green floats, the mistletoe banners, and the gigantic faux-holiday candles (colorfully wrought in ye olde plastic) to help two clueless people say what they *really* meant—without the dubious assistance of one gold necklace, one vinyl belt, and one pantsuit that might have been filched from Murphy Brown's Closet of Enormous Shoulder Pads (circa 1989).

It was the holiday season after all. Helping those less fortunate was the very least she could do.

Chapter Twenty-One

Belly-crawling in his attic, Reno wedged himself in near the eaves, then flung out his arm. With his fingertips, he snagged the edge of a cardboard box—the last of his arsenal for enacting total domination of the holiday lights competition—and pried it loose from the rafters. After one mighty shove, it skated across the unfinished floor, then landed near his elbow.

Satisfied, he gave the box another push. It came to rest a few feet away from the exit—a floor-to-ceiling pass-through to the hallway, reached via foldout ladder. From the pass-through, the sounds of Christmas music and conversation wafted upward.

The smells of bacon and eggs drifted upward, too, making his mouth water and encouraging him to hurry up with the box. He'd been so busy getting everything ready for the Kismet municipal Christmas celebrations that he'd fallen behind with his own personal decorating scheme. At this point his supplies—and a few new items—still littered the house and garage, piled in various stages of organization.

If he really hauled ass, he could still crank out his usual holiday lights extravaganza—say, something capable of taking out the Kismet power grid for an hour or two—and put that sneaky bastard Hal in his place. Reno had the know-how, the brawn, and the experience. Now all he needed was time—

time to win that Bronze Extension Cord award and bring it
home where it belonged.

Some thumping and bumping drew his attention to the
pass-through. His dad appeared in the opening. "Scrambled
or over easy?"

"Scrambled."

"Right-o." Whistling, his dad went back down the ladder.

Angling his head, Reno listened. Ever since last night, his dad
had seemed unusually cheerful. Reno didn't know what was
behind the change. Maybe he'd finally bench-pressed one eighty.
Or he'd gotten the new Ab Roller he'd ordered and was high on
exercise endorphins. Whatever the cause, Reno was glad.

Down from the attic, he spotted Kayla hunched at the
kitchen table, making homemade pipe-cleaner garlands for
his Christmas tree. She'd arrived this morning with her mom,
toting supplies in a reusable grocery bag and brimming with
plans.

He ruffled her hair, glancing down at the results of her
work. "Hey, thanks for the help, kiddo. How's it going?"

"Pretty good, Uncle Reno."

"That looks like a tricky maneuver."

"It's not so tough. See?" Sticking out her tongue, Kayla
showed him how to attach a short piece of green pipe cleaner
to the growing chain of red, white, and green she'd already
made. She twisted the ends to close the loop. "You try now."

Reno did. His niece beamed at him, giving him that silly,
mushy feeling he always had whenever she was around.

Someday he figured he'd have kids of his own. But right
now, nobody could measure up to Kayla. He cared about
her, had fun with her, even worried about her. Speaking of
which . . .

"Hey, Kayla." Casually, Reno formed a few more loops to
lengthen the garland. It pooled across the table and onto a
chair. "Whatever happened at school with Madison and
Olivia?"

"Nothing. We're fine now."

"Oh yeah? You sound pretty blasé about it."

At the other end of the dining room table, Angela fussed with the place settings. She arranged some breakfast plates atop the set of holiday-themed placemats she'd brought, then added cutlery *really* slowly. Reno could tell she was dying to hear about Kayla's friends—the brats who'd voted her off the lunch table.

"That's because it's all over with. I did what Rachel said to do, and Madison and Olivia wanted to be friends again."

"You told Rachel about what happened at school?"

His niece nodded. "At the Christmas tree farm, when we had hot cocoa together. Remember? We had a heart-to-heart."

At Kayla's breezy, mature tone—doubtless an imitation of Rachel's—Reno stifled a grin. Soberly, he nodded. "That's good."

"Yeah." Kayla fisted more pipe cleaners, then set to work twisting and looping. "Rachel told me that sometimes people are mean to other people because they feel bad about themselves. That's kind of sad, right? Rachel said if Madison and Olivia couldn't be nice to me, they weren't real friends anyway."

Reno's gaze shifted to Angela. "That's what *I* said."

Kayla shrugged. "I guess Rachel said it better."

"I guess she did." Smiling, Angela added juice glasses to the place settings. "So everything's okay now?"

"Yup." The garland grew longer. And longer.

"What did you do?" Reno asked. "Did you go back to the store and get the Junior Pussycat Dolls outfit?"

That solution sounded about Rachel's speed to him. A die-hard California girl like her would probably tackle every problem with a fashion strategy. Or with rebelliousness. Or both. Rachel wouldn't see a thing wrong with tiny hoochie clothes—the kind his niece inexplicably adored. Getting them for her would explain Kayla's unending devotion, too.

Who wouldn't like a woman who could fulfill a person's unspoken wishes just by dressing them in different clothes?

A woman who could identify what someone wanted and needed, then give it to them? That was Rachel Porter's job description.

"Nope. No pint-size Pussycat Dolls here," Rachel said.

At the sound of her voice, Reno turned.

Rachel stood in the dining room doorway beside his father. Curiously, the two of them appeared as close as old friends. He didn't think they'd met since Rachel's return to Kismet—or at least his dad hadn't mentioned it—but it wouldn't be surprising if Rachel had added one more member to her fan club. People in Kismet were one step away from propping her up on one of the sparkly Christmas floats and naming her queen of the season.

Of course if they did, Rachel would probably moon them all, flash the crowd her fists of rock, then laugh the way she'd done as a goth caddie at the Kismet Country Club during high school.

"Hey," he heard himself say. Dreamily.

That was the best he could do?

"Hey," she replied, unwinding her scarf.

A beat passed while Reno searched for wit. Eventually, dazzled by her presence, he settled on, "You made it."

"I wouldn't miss it."

"Right. Me either."

"I hope not. You live here."

Her smile made his heart lurch. Just like in a cheesy movie, Reno felt himself grinning at her bundled-up form as the whole room narrowed to only the two of them, lit by a romantic (okay, a compact fluorescent) glow, and soundtracked with "A Charlie Brown Christmas" music from the Vince Guaraldi Trio. There wasn't any Care Bear fur in sight, and Rachel wasn't wearing those crazy-making tights of hers, but he couldn't seem to drag his attention away. He didn't know what to make of it.

His father snapped his shoulder with his kitchen towel, startling Reno into alertness. Looking exasperated, Tom waved his towel toward the living room. "Nobody heard the doorbell except the guy who's slaving away in the kitchen? Sheesh."

"Sorry, Dad," Angela said. "I was busy setting the table."

"I was engrossed in Kayla's story," Reno added.

He couldn't quit looking at Rachel. Somehow she seemed different today. Softer. Calmer. But still sort of punked out, with that wild dark hair of hers and those sexy boots. He'd never again, it occurred to him, look at another pair of black stiletto boots without remembering her.

But since stiletto boots were about as common as aardvarks in Kismet, that probably wouldn't be an issue past this Christmas. The realization left him inexplicably disappointed.

"It's not a problem, really." Companionably, Rachel patted his father on the shoulder. "Don't worry about it, Tom. I wasn't ringing the doorbell for long. I'm probably early anyway. I guess I've finally readjusted to eastern standard time. Go figure." She slung a sewing bag from her shoulder. It landed with a thump in a nearby chair. "Where are the costumes?"

Ready to work, she glanced around brightly. Angela, his dad, and Kayla only continued to gaze at her adoringly. They couldn't have appeared more smitten if they'd tried. Reno had only seen expressions like theirs a few times before. Mostly they'd involved Nate staring at a box of Christmas candy.

Reno recognized the feeling though. Rachel awakened a certain hunger in him, too. But the craving he had would not be satisfied with candy canes or rum balls.

"Nate brought the costumes with him," he managed to say. "They're in the living room, ready for fitting."

"Nate?" Rachel lifted her eyebrows. "Your legendary friend Nate? You mean I'll actually get to meet him this time?"

"He's •in the kitchen right now." Angela nodded, her cheeks turning pink. "He's supposed to be making toast. Knowing him he's baked a fresh loaf of bread and churned some butter, too."

Puzzled, Reno stared at her. Why was his little sister blushing over Nate? "Why are you blushing over Nate?"

"I'm not!"

"Yes, you are. You're as red as these pipe cleaners." Reno narrowed his eyes, focusing on the "curling iron burn" on Angela's neck. "Is Nate responsible for that hickey?"

"No!" Eyes wide, Angela slapped her hand on her neck.

"Hmmm. Frisky." Rachel gave her high-school friend a grin. "I guess if Nate's busy giving Angela hickeys, then I don't have to worry about you setting me up with him, Reno."

Oh yeah. He was supposed to be getting on with that.

"Actually, Nate is dying to meet you," Reno gritted out. Ever loyal, he glanced suspiciously at his sister's neck, then pushed away from the table. "I'll go tell him you're here."

At that moment, pounding footsteps could be heard in the kitchen. Hinges squeaked. The back door slammed.

"Nate!" His dad bolted. "Damn it, don't burn my eggs!"

An instant later, a flash of brown parka, blond hair, and left-tackle-style speed whisked past the big picture window at the front of the house. Reno pointed. "There he goes."

Rachel squinted over her shoulder. Just visible through the snow-frosted panes was Nate, sprinting toward his Chevette.

"That's Nate?" She wrinkled her nose. "Where's he going?"

Angela folded her arms. "Not the Shoparama grocery store, that's for sure. They probably have Wanted posters up by now."

Outside, Nate's old clunker of a car whined to life. It veered toward a snowbank, straightened, then headed downtown.

"Wow," Rachel said. "Nate really doesn't want to meet me."

Reno frowned. "I wouldn't say that—"

"I found this." His dad appeared in the kitchen doorway, Nate's knit cap in one hand and a skillet of scrambled eggs in the other. "He left a note, too. Says here he went to buy more eggs. Weird thing is, I've got another dozen right in the fridge. I thought I'd practice up on that goat cheese omelet your mother's always raving about. You know, the one she gets down at the B & B by the lake every year on Mother's Day?"

Angela rubbed her neck. "This looks *exactly* like a curling iron burn. I don't know what you're talking about, Reno."

Now her flush had traveled all the way to her scoop-neck sweater. Looking flustered (and redder than his Santa suit), she flung napkins on the place settings, then fled.

"I should have told Nate to get more goat cheese, too," his dad muttered, obviously preoccupied as he frowned into his skillet. "Judy likes goat cheese. Chèvre, she calls it. God only knows why, but she does. Goat cheese omelets would make a good Christmas morning breakfast, don't you think so, Reno?"

"I . . ." He'd thought their usual Christmas morning breakfast had been canceled due to his parents ongoing feud. "You bet."

"Doesn't anybody want to hear about Madison and Olivia?" Kayla demanded, throwing up her arms in exasperation. She shook her head at the adults. "What happened to *my* story?"

"You tell it, Kayla." Dismissing the runaway Nate, Rachel shrugged out of her coat, then went to sit beside the little girl. She glanced at the array of pipe cleaners and the garland in progress, then picked up a fuzzy length of green and set to work with an immediate grasp of the project. "We're all dying to know what you did after Madison and Olivia were silly enough to boot you off their lunch table. Aren't we, Reno?"

"Absolutely." Still kind of pissed at Nate for escaping—again—Reno took the chair opposite Rachel. He focused on his niece. "What did you do, Kayla? Did you wow them with some other outfit? One that wasn't a Pussycat Dolls clone?" He hoped.

"No, Uncle Reno." Kayla rolled her eyes. "Not everything is about fashion. Geez." She shared a glance with Rachel. "All I did was start my *own* lunch table. I made sure it was fun, too. Pretty soon, Madison and Olivia were begging to sit with me!"

Surprised, Reno tilted his head. That was pretty sensible advice. So sensible, he couldn't believe it had come from the same woman who'd refused to put her luggage in his naked truck bed. "That's what your mom told you to do, right? Not Rachel."

Rachel was a superficial L.A. girl. A diva supreme.

She wasn't down-to-earth and sensible like Angela.

"No, that's what *Rachel* told me to do. She's awesome."

Impressed, Reno glanced at her. Rachel didn't notice. She was too busy adding another loop to Kayla's wobbly garland. The two of them compared pipe cleaners, seemed to become inspired at the same moment, then animated their pipe cleaners like tiny fuzzy people, marching them across the kitchen table in a miniature pipe-cleaner boogie. They laughed uproariously.

Reno only shook his head, feeling himself slide ever deeper. Ever faster. Ever harder and more unstoppably.

It was a good thing Rachel Porter wouldn't be in Kismet for long. Because the only thing worse than agreeing to set up his best friend with his dream girl, Reno realized at that instant, was falling for that dream girl himself. All too quickly, that's exactly what was happening.

Chapter Twenty-Two

Dreamily, Rachel wound up her tape measure, twisting the yellow length of it round and around her fist. She'd finished taking measurements and assessing the costumes for Kayla's Christmas pageant almost half an hour ago, but she still couldn't get the experience out of her head.

How had an ordinary man actually made a Santa suit look *sexy*?

It was baffling, but there was no denying it. When Reno had come out from the bedroom after changing, looking chagrined but macho in his red velour getup, he'd made something inside her melt. Just looking at him had made her sigh. And when he'd actually smiled directly at her . . .

Whew. If her hands had trembled any more, she wouldn't have been able to take his measurements at all. As it was, she'd nearly swallowed a ball-headed pin when she'd glanced up at him after marking the hem (still on her hands and knees on the living room floor) and caught an eye-level look at his . . .

Well, let's just say that following an inseam upward had never been more scintillating. Plus now she knew that when Reno played Santa, he did it wearing boxer briefs under his baggy britches. Boxer briefs, a tight round butt, taut abs . . .

"So how long have you been crazy about my brother?"

Startled, Rachel glanced up. "What?"

Angela merely went on wrapping the gift she'd brought with her, spreading shiny gold paper beside the scissors, tape, and ribbon already arrayed on the coffee table. She'd confided to Rachel that the present in front of her was something for her mother. Rachel hoped it was a new pantsuit.

"Did your crush on Reno start in high school?" Angela asked. "Because some girls tried to be friends with me just to get close to my brother. I never thought you were one of them—"

"No! I wasn't. I—" Rachel stuffed her measuring tape in her sewing bag, stashing it between a pack of pins and the sketchbook she'd taken to carrying with her, just in case inspiration struck for one of those repurposed designs she'd been fiddling around with—cool clothes made out of bits and pieces of other garments, like her new winter coat. "I'm not crazy about Reno!" She tried to laugh. "That's silly."

"Please." Angela flipped up a neatly folded end of wrapping paper. Apparently, she wrapped gifts the way she did everything else—carefully and serenely. "It's all over your face when you look at him. Your eyes kind of glow, your cheeks flush—"

"Look who's talking. What's the story behind that hickey?"

"—and you bite your lip a lot. Like this." Angela gave her lower lip a coy nibble, moaned, then sighed elaborately. "It's like Nate staring down a batch of iced gingerbread men."

"I do not do that! Besides, I never eat gingerbread men."

"You probably don't have room." Angela's mouth quirked as she tied on a shiny piece of ribbon, then fussed with the edges. "You really plowed through Dad's bacon and eggs this morning."

"I couldn't help it. They were *so* delicious!" Momentarily distracted, Rachel cast her gaze heavenward. She'd really been depriving herself on her L.A. diet regimen. She might never eat another protein bar again. "That toast was like ambrosia!"

"That was probably the Parkay. It's addictive. Anyway, what's the deal with you and Reno? Because he keeps talking about you meeting Nate, but the way you act around Reno—"

"Is Nate really the one who gave you that hickey?"

Angela slapped her hand over it again. She fixed Rachel with a serious look. "We're talking about you and Reno."

Dreamily, Rachel sighed. "I'd let Reno give me a hickey."

Another solemn look. Angela was not a frivolous person.

"You're right. I sound like a seventh-grader. I don't want a hickey." *I want to explore what's under Reno's Santa pants.* "I like Reno. I guess I wouldn't mind getting to know him better."

"That's it?"

"That's enough! I didn't exactly come to Kismet to spark up a hot holiday romance." *As if* she'd thought that might be a possibility. Even a remote possibility. Who knew they made men so appealing out here in the boonies? "Besides, my judgment isn't that great. I've been wrong about people before."

Like I was with Alayna, Tyson, Jenn . . . the list went on.

Angela added a sticky-back bow. "Haven't we all?"

Something in her demeanor tugged at Rachel. Someone, she realized, had disappointed goody-two-shoes Angela Wright. Someone had . . . oh yeah. Someone had loved her, made baby Kayla with her, then abandoned her. All of a sudden, finding your not-that-serious boyfriend in flagrante delicto with your biggest client (and friend) didn't seem all that earth-shattering.

But Angela would probably understand what she'd been through, Rachel realized. Kind, thoughtful, corduroy-wearing Angela would probably even have some good advice for her.

Looking at her friend now, Rachel felt a bizarre compulsion to come clean. To finally admit that her life in L.A. hadn't been all sunshine and glitzy premiere parties. It had also been smog and traffic and taking abuse from spoiled celebrities who didn't care if she spent part of her time on her knees just so long as the hems on their red-carpet gowns were perfectly tailored. It had been living on Diet Cokes and undressed salads and Pepcid. It had been BlackBerry thumb and cell phone tinnitus. It had been setting aside her dreams to chase success.

It had been lonely.

"Look. Pretty, right?" Cheerfully, Angela showed Rachel her wrapped package. It even sported an old-fashioned gift tag, written by Angela herself—not a shopgirl or delivery service.

"Very pretty. But you forgot this." Setting aside her sewing bag, Rachel snatched a receipt from the coffee table.

"Why would I want that?"

"To put with the gift package. For easy returns."

"Returns?" Angela laughed. "If my mom returns this gift, I'll kill her. I spent *hours* scouring the stores to find it."

Baffled, Rachel waggled the receipt. "At least keep it to give to her afterward. It's what people do."

"People who don't appreciate the spirit of the season maybe." Angela gave her a curious look. "Does everyone you know return their Christmas gifts?"

"Not *everyone*." Staring at the receipt, Rachel felt a weird sense of disconnectedness from her usual glam self. "Okay, yes. Everyone does it. Or they have their assistants do it. Or they regift things. I don't think I've given a gift in eight years that's been kept by its intended recipient."

"Oh, that's sad. You probably put a lot of thought into the gifts you give people, too." Angela gathered up wrapping paper scraps with placid, steady efficiency. "You always were really good at knowing what people liked—what they truly wanted. Even back in high school. It was as if you could peer straight into people's heart of hearts or something."

Right. Straight into people's hearts. Except her own.

Otherwise how could she explain being with Tyson-Like-The-Chicken? How could she explain giving up her dreams of designing and creating beautiful things to become a glorified gofer?

No. What was she *thinking*? She loved her job! It was fabulous and glamorous, and the minute one (just one) of her former big-shot clients actually accepted a call from her antiquated cell phone, Rachel would be right back at it.

Gratefully.

Briskly, she glanced up. "That's right. And I can still do it, too. For instance, I can tell that what *you* really want is an excuse to get all dressed up and come to an amazing party."

"A party?"

"I'm throwing an L.A.-style Christmas party tomorrow night. It's kind of a bet I have with Reno. You should come."

"I don't know. I don't have much to wear . . ."

"*Psst*—you have a surefire 'in' with a famous stylist." Rachel smiled at Angela, feeling glad to have reconnected with her old friend. With Angela, she didn't have to be dazzling or trendy or gossipy. She only had to be herself. It was really nice. "I'll help you find something awesome to wear."

"Reno said you were boycotting Christmas."

"I was. But ever since I got back to Kismet . . ."

A burble of laughter came from the other room, catching Rachel's attention. Reno's hearty chuckle drifted down the hallway, followed by Kayla's giggle. They must be packing up the Christmas pageant costumes. "I don't know," she told Angela. "I can't put my finger on it, but something's changed."

"You're just not used to the Christmas music blasting from the speakers all over downtown, that's all." Angela made a face. "It makes everyone a little crazy this time of year."

"Hmmm. Maybe. They *did* play 'Rockin' Around the Christmas Tree' four times when I was hitting the boutiques and gift shops yesterday." She'd had some gift-buying to do, too.

"Or maybe you're just crazy in looooove with my big brother. I think the two of you make a wonderful couple. Reno needs someone like you. Someone who doesn't worship his every move. Someone who *doesn't* need rescuing." She grinned. "Someone who doesn't flash him her—"

"Stop it." Laughing, Rachel held up her palm. The very idea was ridiculous. Wasn't it? Especially for her. "People don't just fall in love within weeks, even at Christmastime."

"Even if those people are perfect for each other?" Angela, busying herself with more gift wrap, looked pensive. "Because if those people are perfect for each other, why should it matter how much time passes before they realize it?"

For a long moment, Rachel studied her friend. It occurred to her that Angela was a lot like Mimi. Both of them were quiet, gentle, and unconcerned with impressing people. Both of them were also a little too shy to say what they meant sometimes.

"'Perfect for each other'? Are we still talking about me?" Rachel asked. "Or you and hickey-boy?"

Angela pressed her fingertips to the telltale spot. If touching it had the power to make it disappear, it would have vanished faster than the first strip of bacon this morning.

And that was saying something.

"I didn't mean for this to happen." Angela cast a furtive glance down the hall, then leaned closer to Rachel. Her eyes sparkled. "But I've never made out in a car in my life! I couldn't resist. It was *really* exciting."

"I'll bet. There's nothing wrong with just going for it, believe me. I recommend doing it all the time."

"Really?"

"Yes. And I recommend bringing hickey-boy to the party."

"Mmm. Maybe I will." Angela smiled. "And maybe I won't. I've got another date tonight. For the first time in my life, I've got options. I intend to try out *all* of them."

In his bedroom, Reno finished tucking the Santa suit into its vinyl carrying case. He pulled up the zipper, stowing away all the red velour and white fake fur until Rachel could apply her expertise to making sure his costume pants didn't fall down.

Although given the way she'd been eyeing him . . . maybe catching him with his pants down was exactly what she had in mind. When Rachel had been there on her knees, adroitly measuring his inseam with her tape measure and talented fingers, it had been all he could do not to haul her upward and kiss her hard and fast, right there in front of his family and everyone.

Everyone except Nate. The weenie. He still hadn't come back "with the eggs" as promised in his bogus note.

But that was just as well, given how tricky it had been for Reno to spend time with Rachel today . . . without revealing that every smile, every joke, every brush of her skin against his made him want her. He'd stood as still as a statue while she'd taken his measurements, calculating football statistics in his head, and trying not to do something stupid like caress her hair. Or hold her hand. Or gaze inanely, sighing at her.

Because Rachel was his best friend's dream girl, and a loyal, trustworthy guy like Reno did not poach his best friend's dream girl. No matter how funny, naughty, or ridiculously hungry for bacon and eggs she happened to be.

Remembering that, Reno grinned. Rachel had really packed away the breakfast this morning. They'd practically had to arm wrestle for possession of the last piece of toast. And she'd claimed during their drive from the airport that all she ever ate were power bars and salad. Now he knew the truth.

Rachel Porter could eat like a defensive lineman. Albeit with better table manners and a *much* more appealing "Mmmm."

But all that had come before the measuring, the touching, the running of Rachel's hands over his chest and down his arms, lightly zeroing in on his midsection and down to his ass, where Rachel had appeared to have some sort of issue with getting the fit exactly appropriate for a Christmas pageant Santa who'd wouldn't exactly be backing into rooms butt-first.

Remembering that too, Reno grinned more widely. Rachel might have no trouble rebelling against Kismet's more strait-laced elements (past and present), but she did have a hard time bluffing her way through touching him.

He liked that about her. He wanted to know how far he could push her. If he brushed against her, would she shiver? If he kissed her again, would she moan? If he peeled away that tight sweater of hers, got both of them naked, then teased her with the faintest of touches, would she make a move herself?

He imagined Rachel straddling him, bringing new life to the now-deserted chairs around the dining room table. He pictured himself, gripping her hips as she rode him, her hair whipping around her shoulders, sweat beading on her neck, trickling down, her breasts puckering and swaying as the two of them—

"So," Kayla said. "How much do you love Rachel?"

Startled, Reno glanced at his niece, who was bouncing on his bed. He had to get a grip on himself. This Rachel fixation of his was getting out of control. No wonder Nate had been obsessed with her for a decade. Reno had only spent part of December with Rachel, and already he was literally speechless.

"I'd say you *totally* got your Christmas wish this year," Kayla continued, looking smug. "So how much? You love her, right? You love Rachel? Because she's perfect."

"I—"

"Rachel likes Barbies just like me," his niece recited breathlessly. "She likes puppies and Nickelodeon and pink sparkle lip gloss. You've got to get her, Uncle Reno!"

"I—"

"I can tell she likes you, too. She watches you with her eyes wherever you go. But not in a creepy way. In a pretty way. Rachel is really pretty, don't you think so?"

"I—"

"I'd like some of those boots like hers, but Mom already said no. 'You can get boots like those the minute *I* do,' is what she said, but that's what she said about the cute stick-on unicorn tattoo I wanted to get, and she *still* doesn't have one, so I think it's hopeless." Kayla shook her head, hilariously perturbed. "I think Rachel is perfect for you! Don't you?"

"I—"

"The important thing is that you're different around her."
His niece put her hand to her chin, examining him. "Your
smile is bigger and so are your muscles. Plus your hair looks
good."

Self-consciously, Reno put his hand to his head. He refused to
own up to the extra pushups and teensy bit of hair product that
had made those things happen. As far as the smile went . . .

Well, he was helpless to prevent that. Period.

"Hey, Reno. What do you think?" his dad asked from the
door.

He glanced over, expecting the worst. So far, every time his
father had trotted out that doomsday phrase it had heralded
some new midlife-bachelor atrocity. Like temporary glue-in
hair plugs. Trendy sneakers. Or so much drugstore cologne it
could have decongested a hay fever-ridden blow monkey.

This time though . . . "Wow, Dad. You look really nice."

"Very handsome, Grandpa!" Kayla chimed in.

Beaming proudly, his father rotated, showing off his simple
dark sport coat, white shirt, and upscale jeans. His gray hair
was combed (but not shellacked with gel), his beard was
shaved, and for the first time in weeks, his eyes actually
sparkled. Even his shoes were nice—not too gangsta rapper,
not too geezer mall-walker, but something in between. Reno
didn't usually notice footwear unless he was trotting onto the
gridiron to score a field goal and wanted taller cleats, but this
time—

"Check out my kicks!" his dad exclaimed. "Nice, right?"

At the joy in his voice, Reno couldn't help but smile. He
nodded, inexplicably moved by the sight of his old man looking eager about his life again—for reasons that seemed to have
nothing to do with the *Men Only* special double issue starring
the Barely Legal Cage-Fighting Beauties in their underwear.

"Rachel got 'em for me! She's a wonder, that girl. Took me
all over town until we found the right pair of shoes at Dirk's
Footwear in that new strip mall out by the Costco."

Reno boggled. "You and Rachel went shopping together?"

"Well, she's kind of a personal shopper, right? She's on the Kismet Christmas decorating committee now, and we got to talking yesterday. Well, one thing led to another, and before I knew it, shazam! I was getting all these fancy new duds."

"Shazam?"

"You should snap her up, Reno. Rachel is smart as a whip, and she had some good advice for me, too. She's a keeper. I know she might look all sophisticated and whatnot, and she talks kind of tough—bit of a potty mouth, truth be told, but you didn't hear it from me!—but on the inside, she's mush."

"Yeah, mush!" Kayla chimed. "Snap her up, Uncle Reno!"

Helpless against the two of them, Reno shrugged. "The thing is, Nate's got a big crush on Rachel, and I promised—"

The phone rang, cutting him off.

"I've gotta get that," his dad announced, hustling away with the barest hint of aftershave—one that *didn't* smell like eau de musk-that-makes-your-eyes-water. "It could be your mom. We're having lunch together today. Fingers crossed!"

Left behind, Reno and Kayla traded surprised glances. Reno could scarcely wrap his head around the news that his parents appeared to be speaking to one another again without bullhorns and lawyers and an extra helping of dirty looks.

Was there hope for a civil Christmas after all? Or was this just another gambit in his dad's ongoing march toward divorce?

Rolling her eyes, Kayla whirled her finger near her temple. "Grandpa seems love crazy."

"He's not the only one, kiddo." Reno ruffled her hair, lost in thought. "Maybe you're right. Maybe I am, too."

The only question now was . . . what to do about it?

Chapter Twenty-Three

"Oh dear, Rachel. Are you sure this is going to work?"

For the fourteenth time, Rachel smiled at her mother, even as workers hustled to complete the final touchups to her L.A.-style Christmas party and the promptest of the partygoers (they didn't "do" *fashionably late* here in Kismet) mingled nearby. The DJ booth was set up. The beach sand was underfoot. Even the spray-tan booth was ready to fake-bake all the inhabitants of Kismet who wanted to look like holiday Oompa-Loompas.

"Yes. I've done this before. Don't worry." She squeezed her mom's shoulder, automatically adjusting the shoulder seam of the cocktail dress they'd chosen together. "And quit trying to sneak those Swedish meatballs in with the rest of the food! Please. That Crock-Pot is going to melt all the ice for my raw bar."

"These things are cool to the touch. Didn't you ever use the one your father and I gave you for your birthday years ago?"

Rachel didn't have the heart to tell her mother that the Crock-Pot was still in the original box, waiting for her to have a *Desperate Housewives* moment . . . or start using it as a foot spa.

"Mom, you're the culinary expert, not me."

"That's right. That's how I know people are going to want *something* to eat besides raw fish—"

"That's sashimi, Mom. It's delicious."

"—and seaweed wraps—"

"Sushi. They have it at the Olde Towne Gourmet Emporium now. Cool, right?"

"—and oysters and vegetables and artistic fruit!" With evident dismay, her mother studied the table. "It's Christmas. It's *wintertime*. Your guests are going to want something hot."

"Mmm." Catching a glimpse of a tall, hard-bodied man standing in the dim lighting near the lounging pillows she'd set up, Rachel smiled. "I think something hot has just arrived."

Her mother scoffed. "That's Reno, dear! Unless he's packing soup in his pockets, I don't think *he's* the answer."

"All the same, I'd better double check." Trying to ignore the tingle in her middle (which surely didn't mean she was experiencing *Christmastime love*, as Angela had suggested), Rachel veered in Reno's direction. "Make yourself at home, Mom." Cheerily, she waved. "Have a candy cane margarita."

"Ask Reno if he brought a casserole!" her mom called.

But Rachel didn't care if Reno had a hot dish to share. He *was* a hot dish. And if he shared himself with anyone but her, she'd have a very blue Christmas after all.

Wait. That was pretty sappy. Wondering if saying such a thing aloud would be too over the top (even for her), Rachel flung back her hair. She sashayed over, still debating.

Hot dish? Blue Christmas? Should she actually admit that she'd changed her dress four times, had sampled not one or two but *three* preparatory cocktails, and had spent twenty minutes in front of the mirror rehearsing what she'd say to Reno tonight?

At the last instant, she decided not to. "Nice tie. Going to your second job as a used-car salesman later?"

Reno tilted his head, his brows lowering in obvious puzzlement. He fingered his necktie. "No."

Oh God. Oh God. See? She was awful at romance. She

couldn't truly be *in love* with Reno already, like Angela had said. Otherwise, how could she possibly hear herself say . . .

"Too bad. It made sense with those clown shoes."

He gazed at his feet. "These are perfectly fine shoes."

They were. Arrgh. What was the matter with her?

"If you believe that, I've got a spray-tan machine you've got to guinea pig for me, Mr. Gullible." Rachel's panic rose, threatening to cut off oxygen to her brain. Or maybe it already had. "You might find out that orange is your color."

Reno frowned at her. "What's the matter with you?"

"Nothing!" Rachel gave a glib laugh. She was, after all, a glib L.A. girl, right? This whole party was about proving that her L.A.-ness was vastly superior to Reno's supposedly wonderful Podunk-Kismet-ness. Kismet, with all its do-gooding and kindness and delicious breakfasts. "What's the matter with *you*?"

"I thought I was here for a party."

"I know you are, but what am I?"

That did it. With a strong grasp, Reno shepherded her past the DJ booth—which was kicking into gear with Gwen Stefani singing a very danceable ska "Oi to the World!"—past the raw bar, all the way to the corner. It took awhile though. The imported beach sand (and occasional beach umbrella stuck into it) seriously impeded their progress. It was atmospheric though.

"Like the party?" Rachel babbled. "It's a pity-party really. My friend Mimi footed the whole bill, now that I'm out of a—" Whoops. Moving on. "Anyway, I called to tell her about the party, and she decided we had to stick together for L.A.'s sake. Homegirls, holla!" She waved her arm in the air.

Reno grimaced. "There's sand in my shoes."

"You're supposed to take them off, silly." She nudged him, encountering rugged shoulder, a swath of rigid male chest, and a whole new batch of tingly, nervous butterflies that swooped in her stomach with redoubled vigor. "Take it *all* off. Woo-woo!"

Reno halted her impromptu bump-and-grind routine—

"Spoilsport."

—with his palms on her hips. That felt pretty good.

"On the other hand . . ." Unwisely luxuriating in the sensation of having his hands on her, Rachel faced him. She trailed her fingers up his shirtfront. "I see you wore a nice shirt for the occasion of your ass-whupping. Good for you."

Reno looked perplexed. "The only ass-whupping that will be happening around here will be happening to you."

"That's what they all say." She gripped his necktie and tugged him closer. Somehow she had to find out if Angela's *true love* theory was correct. "How about a kissing test?"

"Whew! What are we testing for? Your blood alcohol level?" He waved his hand in front of his face, then steadied her shoulder as she wavered. "How much have you had to drink?"

"Not nearly enough."

Reno frowned more deeply. She could tell he definitely wasn't from L.A., because his next question was . . .

"*Why* did you have so much to drink?"

"That's easy. Because I just realized that I love—" Rachel whirled her hand in the air, preparing to punctuate her statement with a poke to Reno's manly chest. "I love—"

"Reno!" someone called. "Hey, buddy! I'm glad you're here. The beer keg won't tap. We need someone mechanical to fix it."

Rachel's finger swerved sideways. So did her baleful gaze. She glowered at the chubby, cheerful man who'd interrupted her moving declaration of love with a crass complaint about beer.

"There's not supposed to be beer!" she cried. "This is a stylish party, not a tailgate brewski fiesta."

The man shrugged. "Somebody rolled in a keg. It's not a party without a keg. Right, Reno?" He nudged Reno, winking.

"I'll see what I can do to help." Reno shucked his jacket and rolled up his shirtsleeves, then paused to give Rachel a

stunningly handsome warning look. "Ease up on the cocktails. And keep an eye out for Nate—he should be here any
minute."

"I've heard that one before."

"It's true this time." His smile wowed her. "If you see a
dreamy-eyed guy wielding a cupcake pan and a jigsaw, that's
him. We'll talk later."

"Aye-aye, Skipper." Rachel saluted smartly.

But she had no intention of waiting around to declare her
love (now that she'd realized it)—or of obediently forgoing
candy cane margaritas at her own *très*-fashionable L.A.-style
party. Thanks to the Christmas season, all the drama she'd
been through lately, or simply Reno's refusal to share his incredible lips with her, Rachel's rebellious side had just
nudged itself to the fore. There was no telling what she might
do next. . . .

Despite Reno's urgings that he absolutely had to be there
(or face dire consequences), Nate was a little bit sorry he
went to Rachel Porter's L.A. Christmas beach bash. It started
the minute he stepped into the noisy, crowded Kismet tavern
she'd taken over for the occasion . . . and got sand in his
shoes.

While he shook them out, that little-bit-sorry feeling of his
only intensified as he glanced around the dimly lit room with
its flashing lights and music, his whole body pulsing with some
kind of reggae Christmas tune, and spotted Tom and Judy
Wright in a clinch on a low-slung sofa. Angela's and Reno's
parents didn't look much like a couple on the verge of divorce,
it occurred to him. In fact, judging by the way they nuzzled
noses, then cooed, then mashed their faces together to—

Whoa. That was *way* too much insight into their relationship. Swerving away, Nate scanned the rest of the room.

It looked pretty kooky to him. Beach umbrellas? *Sand*?
Only one keg? Obviously, as awesome as she was in most

ways, Rachel Porter did not know much about throwing a good party. That was disillusioning. Tamping down his disappointment, Nate headed for the food table—his favorite place at any get-together.

Except this one. Sure, the hamburger and noodle casserole someone had plunked atop the trays of slimy fishy stuff looked tasty. So did the marshmallow-sweet potato side dish and the Swedish meatballs someone had wedged beside a platter of artistically arranged peeled shrimp. But the ice underneath the Crock-Pot was a major mistake. Who wanted cold food in December?

Adding his box of homemade fudge (a bonus culled from the special batch he'd made for Angela and Kayla), Nate stepped back to survey the table. His mother had always taught him never to show up at a party empty-handed. So Rachel Porter would probably be impressed with his manners. If they still "did" manners in L.A. He wasn't sure. For a second, the idea gave him pause.

If Rachel Porter couldn't throw a good party, didn't know enough not to serve iced food at Christmastime, and didn't even value decent manners, was she still his dream girl?

"Hey, Nate! Over here."

He glanced sideways. Reno stood beside the tavern's open electrical panel, wiping his smudged hands with a paper towel. He wadded it up, threw it away, then elbowed shut the panel.

Relieved to see his friend, Nate hustled over. "Dude, what's going on? Is something wrong with the power?"

"Blown fuse from the spray-tan machine. No biggie. I was already over here fixing one of the jammed bar nozzles."

Nate nodded. Reno was always coming to the rescue. Sometimes it seemed there was nothing he couldn't do. The bastard. If Nate could have just one ounce of Reno's mojo—

"Rachel's here somewhere. You can't miss her. She's wearing this red dress that's cut to here"—his buddy indicated an area halfway down his chest—"and back to here"—he lowered his hand to an inch above his butt—"and it's shiny and clingy."

At the naked appreciation on Reno's face, Nate eyed him suspiciously. It was possible that resisting Rachel Porter, Dream Girl, was too much even for the most stalwart guy in Kismet. But then Reno craned his neck, trying to see over the crowd of barefoot, fake-tanned revelers, and put Nate's mind at ease with a hearty back slap. "And *you're* not ducking out this time! She's starting to think you're about as real as Bigfoot."

Inanely, Nate stared at his feet.

Oh yeah. Bigfoot. Big furry guy in the woods. He frowned.

"Very funny. And I would've met her sooner. I just had to do a little prep work first. Rachel Porter took everyone by surprise when she came home for the holidays this year. Speaking of which . . . How are my eyebrows?" He angled his forehead toward the light.

"The left one's growing back nicely."

"That's the one I *didn't* get waxed."

"Oh." Reno shifted his gaze to the right. He recoiled. "I could probably make you an eye patch out of this leftover PVC."

"Har-har."

"I think that's 'yar-yar, maties.'"

"Bite me." Cheerfully, Nate flipped him the finger. "You're just jealous because I'm about to meet my dream girl"—his stomach somersaulted, then plummeted, kind of the way it had on the Top Thrill Dragster when he'd visited Cedar Point with Angela and Kayla last summer—"and you're not."

"Hey." Reno waved away someone else who wanted him to fix something. "Who's been babysitting her for you all this time?"

"Yeah, well . . ." Self-consciously, Nate ran his hand through his buzz cut. Touching those close-clipped strands comforted him. They reminded him that he wasn't that same dork with the stupid curly hairstyle and the Vanilla Ice T-shirt whom Rachel had known in high school—aka, the years when he'd been invisible to her. "That's what friends are for, right? Helping each other?"

"That's what I hear." Reno's face stiffened. "Uh-oh."

"Uh-oh what?" Swiveling to see, Nate gazed through the crowd. They were really getting wild now, doing impromptu Jell-O shots and playing horseshoes in the corner. How had someone gotten a hold of horseshoes and pins to stick in the sand? That didn't seem very L.A. Christmas to him. "I don't see anything."

Then he did.

The partygoers parted just enough for Nate to glimpse a woman dressed all in creamy white, from her knit skirt to her body-hugging sweater. Her beaming smile beckoned everyone within viewing distance. Her sexy hair toss made sure most of those noticing her would be men like him. Men who liked gorgeous brunettes with long legs and an air of mystery. Men who liked—

Angela.

Disbelieving, Nate stared. Even as he boggled at her changed appearance, he recognized all the familiar things about her. Beneath Angela's wild dark hair was her lovable, expressive face. Behind her alluring smile was her wonderful, generous laugh. And her long, lithe legs weren't flashing around beneath a short cocktail dress (like some of the fake-tanned women cavorting on the lounge pillows); instead they were sheathed in that soft-looking knit skirt, which moved when Angela did in a way that made a man imagine he was seeing more than he actually saw.

And made him want to see even more than that.

Angela's sweater was modest, but it made Nate's fingers clench all the same, because (he realized in a disbelieving haze) he could see the curvy, wonderful shape of her breasts through that thing! They were completely covered, it was true. But they were still *right there*, occasionally bouncing as she moved, issuing an invitation Angela probably wasn't even aware of. An invitation that said, "Hey, touch me! Touch me right *here*!"

Sort of hypnotized, Nate angled his head to the right. That horniness problem of Angela's must be pretty rampant if she was running around all luscious and sexy like that. If she was all but saying "Come and get me" to every man in the room. As her friend, he should have seen this coming. He should have realized how dire her need was and offered another kiss (at least). Maybe a friendly caress, something that would let him experience what she felt like beneath that sweater. And of course, something that would make Angela feel better. Because she clearly needed—

The man next to her leaned closer, then whispered something. Angela's smile broadened. She blushed prettily.

The hell? Now that man had his hands on her, too, slipping one arm around her waist as he guided Angela through the crowd! He bobbed his head to the Christmas music, looking even dopier.

What was she doing with that jerk? And who did he think he was, slobbering all over her like that?

Anyone could tell he wanted to rip off all that virginal white she had on and take advantage of her. And not in a friendly, helpful way either. Not in a way that would mean something. Something affectionate and sweet and significant.

"I was afraid something like this might happen," Reno said in a dire tone, breaking into Nate's aggrieved thoughts.

"I know!" Frowning, Nate gestured toward Angela. "Can you believe that asshat, with his hands all over your sister?"

Reno looked. Blandly. "Not that, dumbass. That's just Billy Pendelton, Angela's date for the night. He's a single parent, too. His son goes to Kayla's school."

"Billy Pendelton? Little Bobby Pendelton's dad?" Nate gawked. "That kid wipes boogers on the playground equipment!"

"Let's hope his dad has kicked the habit."

"That's not funny." Tightening his fists, Nate watched as

Booger Billy nuzzled Angela's neck. "Somebody ought to put that guy in his place. Angela doesn't like too much PDA."

"She doesn't seem to mind."

"That's because he's getting her drunk!" In disbelief, Nate watched as Booger Billy pressed a margarita (with a candy cane stuck in the glass) in Angela's hand. She smiled at him, pulled out the candy cane, then took a sip . . . and followed it up with a suggestive lick. "A real man does not need to get his dates plowed in order to kiss them."

For an instant, all he could do was stare in bafflement. Beside him, Reno appeared to do the same thing. Nate didn't know how he could stand seeing his little sister mauled like that. On the verge of saying so, he decided he had to prioritize.

"I'd better go take care of this," Nate said.

"I'd better do something," Reno said at the same time.

They separated. Indignantly, Nate stomped toward Angela and her obnoxious date. It was only at the last instant that he glanced around and realized Reno hadn't followed him after all.

Chapter Twenty-Four

"Woo! Shake it, baby, shake it!" Rachel yelled.

From beside the table she was dancing on, Reno pulled on his discarded coat, then shook his head. From this vantage point, he had an excellent view of Rachel's long, bare legs and that scandalous dress she was wearing. He also had an intimate knowledge of her underwear habits. So did everyone else in the vicinity—a fact some people were already whispering, nudging each other, and pointing about.

"Aww, yeah. That's right," she crowed, oblivious to the thong-spotting onlookers as she waggled her fingers, chasing down one of her three male dancing partners. She squeezed the nearest man's butt and squealed. "Shake it some more!"

He obliged, making his flannel shirttails swing to the music. Next to him, her other two homegrown partners did the same, one stomping his work boots and the other swirling his Day-Glo orange hunter's cap overhead like a rodeo cowboy.

All three men looked ridiculous. But Reno figured that Rachel could have persuaded them to do a lot worse, simply by flashing one of her incredible smiles. God knew, Rachel had nearly persuaded him to throw over his allegiance to his best friend already, just to get closer to her himself. If that wasn't dangerous, Reno didn't know what was.

Well, dancing on a tabletop was. Rachel was likely to sprain an ankle doing that. Especially if she kept on shimmying.

"Rachel!" he called. "Get down from there."

"Reno! Hey!" Vividly, she smiled at him, beckoning him upward with her bottle of Jose Cuervo. "Come on up and dance!"

He shook his head. "You come down here."

"No way. That's no fun!" Rachel shook her head, making her red and white Santa hat slant sideways. Tipsily, she righted it, then kept boogying. "Come on! It's better up here. You can see the whole place! And they can see you!"

A roar of approval went up from the crowd. Candy cane margaritas (and beers) were hoisted. The nearest men stomped their feet and hooted. Exasperated, Reno glanced at them.

Then he looked back at Rachel and realized why all the men were so interested. Rachel's dress was veering dangerously close to total exposure on top, thanks to the exuberant table-top dancing she'd been doing. All that slinky red fabric just couldn't contain Rachel's curvaceous figure, especially now that she'd begun kicking off her shoes and could really move.

One of her high-heeled sandals sailed past his head. It nailed the karaoke machine someone had brought in (which Reno had subsequently had to repair), then plunked to the ground.

"Woo! Woo!" Rachel yelled as the music kept thumping.

Reno had never heard Christmas tunes like these before. They had familiar lyrics about gingerbread, Rudolph, and sleigh rides, but the music behind them rattled the rafters with its deep bass, and the overall volume would have deafened Santa.

"Yeah, baby!" Gyrating, Rachel got in line behind one of her dancing partners. The other two men filed in behind her, then they all did a salacious bump-and-grind routine across the tavern's thick wooden table. "Merry Christmas, everybody!"

The whole spectacle was like watching Shakira try to belly dance while sandwiched between two auto mechanics and a member of the Best Buy Geek Squad. Sexy in the middle, uncoordinated dweebville on the ends. Reno had to close his eyes for a second.

When he opened them, a crazy-haired, slightly panting, sexily askew Rachel was saluting the crowd with her tequila bottle. "Woo-hoo! Is everybody having fun?"

"Yeah!" the crowd roared.

She beamed with approval. "Is an L.A. Christmas better than a Kismet Christmas?" She put her hand to her ear, waiting.

"Yeah!" came the boisterous reply. Beers sloshed.

The crowd's approval didn't mean much. These people would have agreed to strip down and bunny hop, they were so tanked up on liquor, Swedish meatballs, and fake suntans. It was a good thing the Porters had made an early night of it, so they weren't here to witness their daughter's tabletop cha-cha.

Frowning, Reno stepped closer to the table. He put up both arms, then gestured for Rachel to come to him. "You win. Come on down."

Beneath her metallic gray eye shadow, Rachel's eyes widened. Her grin broadened. "You hear that, everybody? Reno says I win. Woo-hoo!" She swallowed a mouthful of tequila. "I win!"

He took away her bottle. "I'll catch you. Let's go."

The Christmas music boomed. The partygoers danced. Rachel's backup trio busted out new and ridiculous moves to try to catch her eye. But through all the mayhem, Rachel only gazed at Reno, an unexpectedly tender expression on her face.

She sighed, then crouched in a fairly indelicate position so she could hold up his upraised hand. *And in this corner, the winner!* Reno thought absurdly. *Reno Wright by total knockout.*

"Everybody!" she called. "I love this guy! You hear that? I'm in love with Reno Wright! I just realized it today, and I—"

Riveted, Reno could only stand there. *Rachel loved him?*

"—want everyone to know it. I love, love, love him!" Waving her free hand, she pointed. "Woo! I love Reno Wright!"

The music crashed to a stop between songs. The resulting

near-silence only lasted an instant, but it was long enough for Rachel's announcement to carry far and wide across the tavern with its holiday lights, beach sand, and umbrellas—long enough for everyone within Christmas caroling distance to hear.

Even Nate. No. Reno couldn't let Nate hear this.

Even if it was just the tequila talking.

In one swift movement, Reno reached up while the music kicked in again, grabbed Rachel around the knees, then tipped her over his shoulder in an impromptu firefighter's carry.

"See? He loves me, too!" she blurted joyously, shouting to be heard over the tunes, oblivious to her Santa hat falling to the floor. "This is *so An Officer and a Gentleman!*"

Clenching his teeth in a near approximation of a smile, Reno wrapped his arm around Rachel's wriggling backside.

Carrying her to the exit was like hoisting a very compact (and busty) defensive lineman during a punt return play—except no football player would have cooed at him lovingly, then started swearing at him in a startled, high-pitched voice for him to wait a minute! And put her down! Right now!

"Reno! Reno!" someone shouted nearby. "Hey, wait up."

Oh, man. Not now. Reno shook his head and kept going, headed for the table where Rachel had left her coat and purse and trying not to make eye contact with whoever needed his help now. For the rest of the night they would just have to repair the jukebox, unplug the toilet, or set someone's broken arm without him.

"Dude. This is serious." Nate grabbed his biceps. His anxious face loomed in Reno's field of vision, crazy eyebrows and all. "I need some advice."

"I'm kind of busy right now." Grunting, Reno rearranged his sexily dressed burden, hoping he wasn't treating Rachel's partygoers to another view of her red thong undies. She appeared to have settled down and was currently stroking his back. Her hands veered toward his ass. She giggled. "Can't it wait?"

Nate didn't so much as glance at the woman slung over Reno's shoulder—which he apparently accepted as a matter of course, probably because Reno was a repeat rescuer. Instead he gazed to the party throng, wrung his hands, then shook his head. "Just tell me one thing: Is it too late for me and Angela? Is she serious about Booger Billy or Patrick the Prick?"

"Serious? Nah. I don't think so." Peering at his friend, Reno tried to figure out why Nate was so interested in his little sister's love life. But he couldn't think of a reason, and he didn't want to hang around long enough for Nate to recognize Rachel Porter and ask why she was slung over Reno's shoulder. "Besides, come on—Angela loves you, dude! Always has."

Nate stared at him for a second. Then he took a deep breath. "Okay. That's all I needed to know."

Nate turned to leave. Relieved, Reno grabbed his keys.

"Hey, chug along, Mr. Tank Engine. Let's get a move on." Rachel pulled Reno's jacket as if it would start him walking again. When that didn't work, she pinched his butt. Hard.

"Yeoch!"

At his yelp, Nate swiveled. His gaze shot from Reno to the woman draped over his shoulder. For a long minute, his attention lingered. Reno held his breath. This was a pretty compromising position. He couldn't promise that Nate would understand.

Then his longtime buddy grinned, apparently (and fortunately) not identifying Rachel Porter at all.

"Looks like you've got your hands full for the night, dude," he said. "That's what you get for rescuing everybody. Good luck with that."

Ha. If Nate only knew . . .

Chapter Twenty-Five

Nate never would have thought it would come to this.

Standing in his apartment on the west side of Kismet, still sporting the boxer shorts he typically slept in (and probably wearing a Cap'n Crunch milk mustache on his face, too), he examined the cardboard box on the table in front of him.

Caution. Fragile. Store this end up. Seriously, fragile!

The warnings were underlined three times in thick black felt-tip strokes, scrawled in his best handwriting—the penmanship he'd learned at St. Mary's elementary school all those years ago. He hadn't opened this box for almost as long.

He hadn't expected to open it now. But after trying (and failing) to break up Angela and Booger Billy at the party last night (incredibly, she had been indifferent to the possibility of his having an ongoing, obviously hereditary booger habit), he'd spent half the night agonizing over what to do about her and her endless parade of boy toys (okay, and eating a ham-and-cheese sandwich with pickles around 2 A.M. because all that hard thinking made a man hungry), and no better plan had come to him than this one. This one, borne of something Kayla had once said to him about her mom's dreams of a big white wedding and a picket-fenced cottage by the lake—a plan that Nate hadn't expected to need for a few more care-free years at least.

Now all bets were off. He had to raise or fold. Otherwise, Angela would leave him in the dust, exactly the way she had on the night they'd been kicked out of the Shoparama together, when she'd gone on that date with Patrick the Prick and left Nate standing in her kitchen like a fudge-recipe-wielding nincompoop.

But all that was about to change.

Carefully, he slit open the double layer of packing tape on the outside of the box. His heart hammered as he lifted the cardboard flaps, spreading them wide. A hint of mustiness wafted from the interior, followed by a more familiar fragrance—mothballs. They made his eyes water. Slowly, Nate peeled away the thick swath of bubble wrap that formed the topmost layer.

The mothball smell grew stronger.

So did his apprehension.

Drawing in a tentative breath, Nate looked at the items he'd revealed. They were still there, exactly as expected—exactly as he'd counted on for his future. In a sense, these things were his nest egg. For a guy like Nate, a frugal guy who planned and scrimped and made sure all eventualities were covered, a nest egg was nothing to joke about. It was a big deal. A major big deal. Something to be safeguarded and kept as long as possible in the bubble wrap and tape.

For a long while he gazed at his erstwhile nest egg, his stomach knotted in exactly the same way it had cramped up when he'd been turked out of training camp in the NFL. He'd thought he was going to hurl the whole way down to the coach's office to turn in his Scorpions playbook. That had been his lowest day for sure, and now he felt exactly the same way.

Was he that worried about taking this next step? Or was he just sad to see these things go? Nate wasn't sure. He wasn't sure he wasn't just experiencing revenge of the 2 A.M. ham-and-cheese sandwich. Either way, he'd already decided what to do.

After another lingering look, Nate nodded. He edged aside a stack of grocery store coupons, consulted the book he'd borrowed from the library, then grabbed the keys to his trusty Chevette. There was only one direction to go now, and that was forward.

He only hoped that Angela wanted to go forward with him. Because as important as these items were, as much as Nate had treasured them over the years, he knew one thing for certain.

Angela was more important to him than everything else.

Rachel awakened with a sour taste in her mouth and an unswerving certainty that Jose Cuervo was not her friend, despite the many long hours they'd spent together last night.

Smacking her lips, she put her hand to her head to assess the damage. Ugh. She encountered a rat's nest of hairsprayed hair, a spike of mascaraed eyelashes . . . and not a trace of the headache she'd fully expected. Hmmm. That was weird.

She did have vague memories of someone giving her glass after glass of water last night after she'd left her L.A. Christmas party . . . under somewhat hazy circumstances. Maybe that treatment—one Mimi swore by, she recalled—had helped.

People did say that dehydration made a hangover worse. Supposedly, it was similar to the way a pair of those hideous Crocs ruined a perfectly good outfit, or the way mascara could go from good to Tammy Faye in a single additional swipe.

Frowning, Rachel opened her eyes. Then she sat bolt upright. This was not her bedroom at her parents' house!

This was an unfamiliar bedroom with white walls, a huge wooden bed, and bits and pieces of football memorabilia. A bedroom in which Christmas lights had been strung along the doorjambs and atop the bed. A bedroom in which an old-fashioned, very Kismet bureau stood near the closed door, sporting a lamp, a curled-edge paperback book, and a framed picture. Rachel squinted at it, trying to make out the people. They were all dark-haired, smiling, and stunning, and they looked happy.

She didn't recognize them, at least not from here. Oh God. What had she done last night? Frantically, she searched her memory. She remembered her mom and the Crock-Pot. She remembered beach sand, hip-hop Christmas music, and candy cane margaritas. She remembered seeing Tom and Judy Wright making out at the party, looking ten years younger and a million times happier.

At the remembrance, Rachel smiled. If the Wrights' lip-lock was anything to go by, it looked as though Rachel's reconciliation advice—to appreciate one another, cut each other some slack, and try making wish lists for gift-giving occasions—had worked.

Yawning again, Rachel gave a languid stretch. Tom and Judy Wright. Hmmm. The Wrights. Come to think of it, the dark-haired people in the picture on the bureau had looked a lot like . . .

"You're up." A dark-haired man levered upward at the foot of the bed, then blinked sleepily at her. "Morning."

Rachel yelped, clutching the blankets.

"That's all the thanks I get . . . after last night?"

Reno. In a heartbeat, the *rest* of last night came flooding back to her. The drinking. The dancing. The insulting Reno's tie. The being carried out over his shoulder.

The heartfelt—and mortifying—declarations of her true love.

She gawked at him, embarrassed from the top of her head to her Christmas-painted toenails. (She had no excuse. She'd completely caved in to the holiday spirit, even when it came to a DIY pedicure.) Still. Reno, Reno, Reno. He looked amazing in the morning, Rachel thought in a daze. Sort of rumpled and sexy and unreasonably cheerful. He might be naked right now, too . . .

She shook her head. "What are you doing on the floor?"

"Sleeping." He lifted one burly bare shoulder in a shrug. "After you took the bed, and I left the sofa for my dad—"

"Tom lives here with you?"

A nod. "There wasn't anywhere else for me to go. This was originally a three-bedroom ranch when I grew up here—"

Rachel boggled at the idea of living in the same house for so many years. She'd never experienced that kind of continuity. Except maybe with her Bene*f*it bene*tint*, which kept her from looking like a ghost most of the time. She loved bene*tint*.

"—but one of the bedrooms bit the dust years ago to make way for my master bathroom, and my dad turned the other guest bedroom into a full-on workout room when he moved in." Reno yawned, then rubbed his head. His hair stood on end. On him, the effect looked adorable. And hot. "Did you get any sleep?"

"Uhh . . ."

"You told me you didn't want to go home to your parents' house. Not in the shape you were in last night."

"Probably a wise decision."

"You kind of begged me actually."

"Uhh . . . begged you to bring me here?" At his nod, Rachel felt a spurt of hope. She lifted the blankets and peeked at herself, then was disappointed to find herself still wearing last night's red dress. "But we didn't . . . ?"

She gestured from him to her, the possibilities of what might have happened between them running rampant in her head.

Without even meaning to, Rachel imagined Reno carrying her down onto his ridiculously comfortable bed, covering her with his big, rugged body, making her shudder and clutch him as he let his hands roam all over her, from her hair to her breasts and beyond, lavishing her with the most crazy-making strokes possible, both of them hot and writhing and moaning, the bedsprings creaking as they learned every inch of each other's skin, the room vibrating with their gasps and cries, the two of them getting wild and slick and sweaty, coming together to—

"No, we didn't. I'm not that kind of guy."

Reno propped his arms on the bed and regarded her. His broad bare shoulders led to a wide bare chest, muscular and covered with exactly the right amount of manly dark hair. All the rest of him was hidden, but that didn't stop Rachel from wondering about what might be down there.

Seriously. Did he sleep naked or what?

"And I don't think," Reno went on, oblivious to her vivid imagination, "that you're that kind of girl either."

Oh come on. "How do you know? You haven't even tried me."

He smiled. "I know a little about you by now."

"Oh yeah?" Rachel jerked up her chin, eyeing him. "Well, maybe you're missing out. Maybe I'm the wildest woman this side of the Rockies. Maybe I've got moves you've never even *heard* of yet, moves that would blow your mind."

Reno's smile broadened. "Any woman with moves *that* wild wouldn't care what her parents thought when she came home drunk from her own Christmas party."

Damn it. He had her there. Despite her renowned audacity, Rachel did have her limits. She refused to hurt anyone.

"Yeah? Well . . ." She wheeled her arm around, trying to come up with a rebuttal that would really floor him. "Any man who has time to string ten thousand Christmas lights on his house—"

"It's forty-seven thousand at last count."

"—obviously doesn't have anything *better* to do with his nights." She waggled her eyebrows, making her meaning plain.

"Except win the holiday lights competition. And I *am* going to win." From the foot of the bed, Reno gave her a speculative look. "Besides, I don't believe in wasting time with anything less than the real thing. If I don't really like a woman, I don't sleep with her just to up my scoring average."

Rachel scoffed. "And you claim you're a jock."

His eyes flashed. "I'm more jock than you can handle."

His words made that revealing tingle return to her middle, swamping her with giddiness. *True love, true love, true love*, her heartbeat seemed to pound out, even as she looked at a cocksure Reno and told herself that falling for him was impossible. She hadn't even been back in Kismet that long. She'd barely known him when she'd lived here before.

Although there was an undeniable connection between them . . .

Well, that was probably just sexual attraction, right?

"I," he went on, his expression daring her to disagree, "am just plain more *man* than you can handle."

Well. That simply wasn't true.

Rachel gazed straight at him. "Wanna bet?"

When Nate drove up to Angela's house, the whole place looked small and snug, wrapped up tight against the snow blowing up to the windows. When he got out of his Chevette though, he noticed that one of the storm windows was cracked. The icicle-covered eaves needed repainting. One of the house numbers on the front door had peeled off, leaving a ghostly number five etched in its place on the frosty wood beside the holiday wreath.

How could he have failed to notice all that stuff?

Fighting an urge to grab a tool belt, a paintbrush, and a glue gun all at the same time, Nate readjusted his burden—his nest egg box—then stomped up the sidewalk, exactly the way he'd done at least a thousand times before. Probably more often. He glimpsed the light from the TV flickering, heard the familiar strains of Kayla's favorite cartoons, then knocked on the door.

After which he turned around and headed back to his car.

Swiveled and charged back toward the porch.

Panicked and bolted for the curb.

Stopped in sheer confusion, clutching his box and breathing heavily. What was the matter with him? It wasn't as if—

"Nate?" Angela cracked open the door and peeked out. She opened the door wider. "What are you doing? Come on in."

Wearing only her nightgown—Angela was the ruffled flannel type, which should have been hideous but was actually kind of mysterious and sexy—she beckoned him closer. Frozen in place, Nate gawked at his box, then shifted his gaze to her.

"Is *he* still here?" he demanded.

"He? He who?"

Nate twisted his old KHS class ring, unable to rein in his nervousness. "Booger Billy Pendelton."

The schoolmarmish look she gave him made Nate feel ashamed for even suggesting such a thing. Despite her admitted horniness problem, Angela was not the kind of woman to host an X-rated sleepover while her daughter was in the house. He knew that.

That's why he'd already telephoned Judy Wright and brought her in on his plan before coming over this morning.

"Actually, I've got Billy Pendelton, Patrick Goodger, and Zion Jones in there. You're interrupting our ménage à trois."

Nate jerked up his head. Sometime while he'd been thinking, Angela had stuck her feet in her snow boots, thrown on a coat, and come outside to stand with him on the snowy sidewalk. Probably because she didn't want to be accused of shacking up while her daughter was within earshot. Now Angela quirked her mouth at him in that adorable smile of hers, waiting patiently.

No woman ought to look that good in snow boots with the hem of a ruffled granny gown sticking out from beneath her parka. Somehow, Nate thought that Angela did. He also thought that he'd like to snuggle up to her in that gown. Maybe slip his hands underneath it. Maybe make her smile wider. He sighed at her.

"That's a ménage à *quatre*. Four people. Ménage à *quatre*."

Angela wrinkled her brow. "Actually, that's not what I expected you to take away from that statement."

"Well, that's too bad. Because I'm learning French online," Nate heard himself babble. "Someday I want to go to cooking school at *Le Cordon Bleu* in Paris. I want to study *Art de Vivre*. That means the art of living. It would be awesome."

He clamped his mouth shut, appalled to have revealed so much. He'd had no intention of laying himself totally bare.

Not without another ham-and-cheese sandwich at least.

"Wow. Teaching home ec has really had an effect on you."

"It's not that. It's you." Nate grasped his box harder. Beneath his gloves' brown leather, his palms felt shaky and sweaty. "Every time I cook something for you, you look so happy . . . I just want to be the best in the world at it."

"At cooking? Aww, Nate." Angela touched his arm, smiling up at him. "I think you could really succeed at that. You should—"

"Not at cooking. At making you happy. I want to be the best in the whole world at making you happy, Angela."

She stilled. Her eyes widened.

Uh-oh. Nate thought he might keel over—just do a face plant in the snow beside the plastic Santa and reindeer display.

While he concentrated on not visibly hyperventilating—or running away like the reformed geek he secretly was—Angela searched his face. Her smile gradually faded, sort of like the green leaves on the old plastic Christmas garland she'd strung along her porch railing. She looked as if . . . as if she were trying to puzzle him out, and that wasn't the plan at all.

Nate's heart thudded, faster and faster. This was not the scenario he'd planned while he'd been scarfing down sandwiches last night. In his imagination, Angela had run into his arms. In his imagination, she'd known exactly what he'd meant about making her happy (and he'd been a whole lot more eloquent, too, with no babbling about French classes and cooking school). In his imagination, they'd shared the same freak harmony they always had, and things had been perfect between them.

In reality . . .

In reality, his feet were cold because he'd worn skimpy socks—not having had any clean thick ones on hand for this mission. In reality, his heart clenched with the same dork uncertainty he'd always known. In reality . . . Angela frowned at him. Oh geez. What if he'd completely ruined everything?

Chapter Twenty-Six

The next thing Rachel knew, Reno was climbing up onto the mattress, leaving her scrambling mindlessly toward the relative safety of the headboard and pillows, wondering when, exactly, she'd finally bitten off more than she could chew.

Oh yeah. With that last dare.

Realizing as much, Rachel threw off the blankets and struck her most provocative seated pose. It wasn't her style to cower under the covers. There was more than one way to win a dare, and she meant to make sure she succeeded this time. Somehow, winning with Reno felt more important than ever.

"Show me what you've got, tough guy." Shimmying in place, she crooked her finger. "I'm waiting to be impressed."

Reno laughed. "You are? Prepare to be dazzled then."

It was too late. She already was dazzled. Her racing heart and flushed skin told her that. Just looking at him crawling on all fours across the mattress toward her, wearing tight boxer briefs (one question answered; she approved) and an expression of pure challenge made Rachel's breath catch in her throat.

Of all the people she'd have expected to understand her, Reno Wright was last on the list. But with a single smile, he threatened to expose her aura of bravado for the sham it was.

That should have been reason enough to avoid him.

Instead it was all the more reason she couldn't.

"There's no reason *you'd* be the one man who can handle me," she shot back, striving for control as the mattress dipped. The warmth from Reno's skin reached her just milliseconds before the man himself did. "You don't know me. I'm pretty hard to handle. I'm demanding and bossy and unreasonably suspicious—"

"Like I said, I know you a little by now."

Wrapping his palm around her ankle, Reno gave a tug.

Squealing, Rachel found herself dragged flat on her back with her dress hiked up, sandwiched between tough, hard Reno and his soft flannel sheets. At the sudden impact, her breath whooshed from her lungs. All her thoughts fled as he gave her a wolfish smile.

Determinedly, she rallied. "—and I like sex," she boasted unsteadily. "I like sex a lot. Which is probably why I've stuck with so many unlikely guys in the past. So unless you're ready—"

"I like sex, too." Reno kissed her lightly on the lips, so lightly that she automatically levered upward, wanting more. "With you, I know I'm going to *love* it. So are you."

"—to listen to me being totally honest about what I think—"

"Shh." Settling himself above her on his elbows, Reno brought his hand to her jaw. He pinned their gazes together, his expression bold and blunt. "I'm not afraid of a little honesty."

Oh boy. This was too much. *Way* too much. Somehow she'd broken through whatever distance he'd been keeping between them since they'd met—a distance she'd sometimes thought she'd only imagined. Now Reno meant to bridge that gap. For good.

Caught between her own yearning for him and a nervousness unlike anything she'd ever encountered during her tenure as red-carpet queen of L.A., Rachel resorted to warning him away.

"Demanding," she reminded him. "You forgot demanding."

His knowing look was more terrifying than any self-absorbed

celebrity tantrum ever could have been. So was her reaction to it. Inexplicably, she wanted more. More of him. More of this.

"You don't scare me." He gave her another kiss, this one a little longer but (frustratingly) not any deeper. "I know you."

"Well, a lot of people think they know me," she blathered. "They've seen a profile in *People* magazine, or they've watched me do an interview on *Entertainment Tonight*, and it gives them a false sense of intimacy. But the truth is—"

"This feels pretty real to me." Reno's hand descended to her shoulder, then swept lower. With a wholly masculine sound of appreciation, he closed his calloused palm over her breast. "It feels intimate, too. Mmmm. You feel really, really good."

"Umm . . ." Rachel gulped, quivering in his grasp. All she wanted to do was arch herself into his hands, rub herself against him, make sure he knew how incredible this felt. Her nipples peaked, confirming that fact without a sound, but at the same time, it seemed direly important that she make herself understood. That she shield Reno from any misunderstandings.

"I won't be around Kismet for long," she warned—the last of her last-ditch efforts to protect him. Her. Both of them. "That means this can only be sex between us. That's it. Okay?"

At Nate's words, a surge of excitement rushed through Angela. *Just breathe*, she told herself. *Don't blow it now.*

Not now, after she'd tried so hard to play it cool, explore her options, and dangle, whenever possible, all potential male competition in front of her (mostly platonic) pal, Nate.

The funny thing was, he was the one who'd clued her in to the strategy she'd been using successfully for weeks now.

Playing hard to get, huh? Good going, Nate had advised her once. *Now Patrick will be twice as eager to go out with you.*

Angela only hoped the same tactics would work on the man she was *really* interested in.

"Nate, come inside." She put her hand on his arm, urging him to come with her. "It's too cold and too early to be standing outside on the front walk talking about this."

"But I—" Visibly, he gulped. "*That's* why you were frowning? Because it's cold and early? Not because . . . of anything else?"

Aww. He looked adorable to her, all bundled up and handsome and earnest. Despite the fact that he'd tried to bust up her date with Billy last night, that was one of the things Angela loved most about Nate—his sincerity. She could always depend on him to tell her the truth. To be there for her no matter what.

Even when he was (theoretically) chasing his dream girl.

"Why else would I be frowning?" she asked.

"Um . . . because I said I wanted to make you happy?"

Right. Well, technically, hearing Nate say that *had* made her heart stop for a second. In fact, her knees still felt sort of wobbly. It had been so romantic and so perfect.

I want to be the best in the whole world at making you happy, Angela.

No one had ever said such a thing to her. Not even Bryce.

Especially not Bryce, come to think of it, which probably made it just as well that he wasn't around to influence Kayla.

But that didn't matter now. Because Angela had already vowed to choose a better man next time. She'd promised herself she would *not* run into the arms of the first guy who asked her to be with him. So rather than joyously confess that *she* wanted to make Nate happy, too, that she had (in fact) waited months (if not years) for him to come around and realize how perfect they were for each other, Angela only smiled at him.

"Don't be silly, Nate." With as much nonchalance as she could, she patted his arm. "Honestly, it's freezing out here. Come inside."

Nate did, still clutching his cardboard box.

While Angela shucked her coat and changed out of her winter boots, Nate gave Kayla a hello hug and a tickle. Then he glanced warily from side to side as if expecting to see naked men sprouting from behind the sofa, the Christmas tree, the Advent calendar . . . the bedroom. Angela stifled a grin as they headed, as usual, for the kitchen. She poured them both coffee (hers with cream only, his a sugary black), then handed a cup to Nate.

Their fingers touched. Angela would have sworn sparks shot between them, jolting them both. She glanced up from their hands, met his gaze . . . and felt a fresh charge rock her all the way to the toes of her baby blue pom-pom slippers. She wanted to kiss him. Wanted to hug him. Wanted to find out what the big Natearooni was up to today. And Nate could probably tell.

With her, he always could.

She had to be strong. Deliberately, Angela shifted her gaze away, then pursed her lips. "So what's in the box?"

"Hopefully . . . the future."

That got her. Especially given some of the scenarios she'd imagined them sharing. Coolly, she asked, "Really? The future?"

"That's right. Check it out." Looking as nervous as he had just before he'd ridden the Top Thrill Dragster at Cedar Point last summer, Nate slugged down some coffee, then shed his coat. And his hat. And his right glove. And his left. "Ready?"

"Whenever you're done with the striptease, big boy."

Nate paused in the midst of yanking off his scarf. His gaze met hers again. *Striptease* floated in the air between them, making Angela imagine Nate in the midst of a holiday-themed bump-and-grind routine, grinning as he peeled off his MSU sweatshirt, shucked his plain white tee, then slowly un-zipped his fly and pulled down his jeans, inch by mesmeriz-ing inch . . . just for her.

He wore old-fashioned boxers, she knew (because of the few times his washing machine had been on the fritz and she'd let him do laundry at her place), which should have been geezerish but was actually kind of mysterious and sexy.

Unlikely but lovable. In fact, all of Nate could be categorized that way.

Unlikely but lovable. At least to her.

Nate wasn't the most brilliant guy in the world, but he was kindhearted and strong. He wasn't the most clever or the most witty, but he was fun and reliable and honorable. And if he could ever get over his Rachel Porter fixation . . .

Well, Angela knew that would happen eventually. After all, Rachel wasn't interested in Nate (a fact she'd totally given away with the dreamy way she looked at Reno). But until Nate realized the same thing, all bets were off. Darn it.

Angela could have enlightened Nate about his zero-to-zero chances of scoring with his California dream girl. But that might have hurt him, and she wasn't willing to do that. She was a patient person. She could wait a little longer.

Just . . . a little . . . longer.

"Striptease, huh?" He squinted at her as he dropped his scarf on the chair. "Something's different about you today."

"Dating changes a person." Angela waved her arm in what she hoped was a worldly fashion. "Meeting new people exposes you to new ideas. You discover things you never thought you'd like."

"New people. Right." Nate gritted his teeth. A vein throbbed in his forehead. "Back to the box. Take a look."

He flipped open the flaps. Then, appearing kind of green, he stepped back so she could see. Feeling strangely nervous herself, agog with eagerness to glimpse the future Nate had apparently envisioned for them both, Angela peered in.

Hmmm. That wasn't what she'd expected.

She didn't quite get the connection. Still, at the sight of the items in the box, she almost forgot everything else.

"Oh my God." Her disbelieving gaze flew to his. Automatically her hand went to her chest. "Are these authentic?"

"You bet your ass they're authentic."

"Nate. Language."

"Sorry." He glanced to the living room, where Kayla's cartoons still blared. "Yes, they're real."

Eyes wide, she bit her lip. "Can I touch one?"

He nodded, tiny beads of sweat on his temples.

Carefully, Angela reached into the box, easing away the archival tissue paper surrounding the items. Awed, she lifted the uppermost one—an elaborate puppet of a reindeer.

Even somewhat tattered, it was instantly familiar to her. *Rudolph, the Red-Nosed Reindeer*—The Rankin/Bass TV special—might have debuted more than a decade before she was born, but Angela had watched it religiously all the same. So had Kayla. They'd TiVoed it to watch together this year, too.

"My grandmother worked at Rankin/Bass in the seventies," Nate explained. "She bought these puppets from the company, then later she gave them to me. She said I was the only one in the family who'd really appreciate them."

Angela's questioning gaze met his.

"When I was a kid, I really, *really* loved that TV special." Nate's ears turned pink. He cleared his throat. "Anyway, my nana was a smart woman. She planned ahead—we Kellys have always been planners. See? There's even an affidavit in there to confirm the puppets' provenance as original production items."

Angela couldn't believe it. "Do you mean to tell me that you've watched *Rudolph, the Red-Nosed Reindeer* with me and Kayla every year and never said anything? *Anything*?"

Nate shrugged. "I didn't plan to unpack them. Exposure to air ruins delicate items. I learned that from a library book."

"Anything?" Angela repeated.

"I'm saying something now." He drew in a breath. "Except for my family, you're the only one who knows about these."

Setting aside the mind-boggling fact that Nate had actually kept a secret from her, Angela explored Rudolph. She turned him this way and that, then pulled. "Look, he really moves!"

In amazement, she glanced up. Nate nodded.

"That's one way you can tell that's an original production design and not just a toy or a replica." Proudly, he touched Santa's beard and red suit. "They're really elaborate. They were designed and made in Japan—by hand, if you can believe it."

"Wow," Angela marveled, stroking Rudolph's head. "I can't believe you never told me about these."

"Well, they're kind of my nest egg. In case of emergency, like Nana intended. I didn't expect to ever cash them out."

"Cash them out?" Stricken, Angela hugged Rudolph. It was like holding a piece of her childhood. Those stop-motion animations had seemed so real to her as a kid, she'd been sure Rudolph was really alive. "You're going to cash them out?"

"Yep." Nate gave a hearty nod, then knocked back more coffee. "It's the only way I can afford . . . something special."

Puzzled, she stared at him. Then realization dawned, as cold as the icicles and snow outside. *The future*. He didn't mean *the future* between him and her! He meant . . .

"You're going to buy something fancy for Rachel Porter, aren't you?"

Nate didn't say a word. But his guilty, shoulder-hunching response told her all she needed to know.

Angela couldn't believe she'd been so gullible. While she'd been swooning over Nate's speech about being the best in the whole world at making her happy, he'd been plotting to get her help in selling out—all for the sake of impressing his dream girl! Obviously, he'd just been buttering her up in order to get her help. Next he'd be asking Angela to be Rachel's stand-in to try on mink coats or something. Which was not only obnoxious, it was also ridiculous. Angela only wore "fun fur." Period.

Defensively, Nate rubbed the back of his neck. "I can't say what I'm going to buy with the money."

"You haven't even actually met her yet, Nate!"

"So?" Looking frustrated, Nate took Rudolph from her hands. With meticulous care, he returned the puppet to the box.

"Look, all I want to know is if you'll go to Grand Rapids with me. There's a big holiday crafts fair going on there right now."

Sensing what was coming, Angela frowned at him.

"I think I can get a good price from some of the collectors who'll be there." Absently, Nate straightened Santa's tiny belt. He smiled fondly. "Christmas collectors, pop culture collectors, TV collectors—a lot of people would be interested in these puppets. I could sell the pair for eight or ten thousand easy."

"That's crazy. You can't put a price on Christmas!"

Mulishly, Nate crossed his arms. "I think I just did."

"Well, I won't be a part of it. No way."

"But I already asked your mom to babysit Kayla this weekend." Nate's whole body slumped. "I already booked us a hotel room!"

"A . . . hotel room?" Angela glanced at him. Despite her indignation, a wholly imprudent sense of excitement unfurled inside her. It made her feel even more reckless than the night she'd allowed Perfect Patrick to give her that hickey in the backseat of his Aspire. She figured she might as well cut to the chase—fearlessly, the way Rachel Porter would have done. "How many beds does it have?"

"How many . . . ?" Nate's expression made her heartbeat thud even more wildly. "It has one bed. One king-size bed."

One king-size bed. One! At the implications of that hotel reservation, Angela thought she might *squee!* like Kayla's little pals did when they played together. *Squee! Squee!*

"That was all they had available," Nate explained, twisting his class ring. "Because of the crafts fair being in town. But I can sleep on the floor or something, so don't worry about it."

Angela wasn't worried about it. It was just like Nate to offer her an out . . . even if she didn't want one.

"You know, you don't technically need a hotel reservation to visit Grand Rapids." Ruthlessly, she tamped down the thrills coursing up her spine. "It's less than an hour away."

"I know, but the crafts fair might take awhile. There'll be haggling, visiting other booths, probably having dinner—"

"And I don't know what you need me there for. After all, I don't know anything about the vintage collectibles market."

"Maybe not, but you're smart, Angela." Nate's gaze pleaded with her. "You're the smartest person I know. I need you there."

Something about his overly wide-eyed expression made her doubt the veracity of his story. She had a very strong feeling that Nate was hiding something—probably his big plans to woo Rachel Porter with a gaudy, ten-thousand-dollar Christmas gift. The jerk. And where did he get off calling her "smart" anyway?

Just for an instant, Angela didn't want to be smart. She wanted to be hot-to-trot, like Rachel Porter. She wanted to make men dance on tabletops and shake their bonbons on her command. She wanted to inspire men to buy her drinks and compete to sit next to her. She wanted . . . oh, who was she kidding?

She just wanted Nate.

"You really need me?" she asked.

Somberly, he nodded. "More than you know."

"In that case . . . all right," Angela replied. "I'll go."

Because after all, time was running out. She had to make her move soon—this weekend—before Nate actually met Rachel Porter, dream girl, in person . . . and realized that next to Rachel, Angela looked about as sexy as Mary Poppins, Eleanor Roosevelt, and Betty Crocker, all rolled into one.

On second thought, Nate would probably go for Betty Crocker, it occurred to her. They'd make chocolate fondue together or something. But Angela knew better than to push her luck. Now more than ever, she had to stick with her plan.

She only hoped it had a snowball's chance of succeeding.

Chapter Twenty-Seven

Reno paused. "Just sex, huh?"

For at least ten seconds, Rachel felt sure he was going to bring up her (very public) declaration of undying love at her Christmas party last night. As much as she'd truly felt it at that moment, and as much as she might feel the same things right now, Rachel didn't want to complicate matters.

"Mmmm." Reno nodded as though considering her "just sex" stipulation, absorbed in watching his fingers sweep aside her dress to pluck at her beaded nipple. "Okay. Just sex. It's probably better that way, given the circumstances."

He probably meant given the fact that she'd be leaving Kismet soon. Rachel could do nothing but nod, then gasp as his thumb nudged her in another sweet caress. "Good," she managed, writhing helplessly beneath him. "I'm glad we agree."

"Right. Only sex." More kisses. "That's it."

"Absolutely."

Despite her stout nod and stated belief in her "just sex" philosophy, Rachel couldn't prevent a surge of sheer joy as she finally gave herself permission to bring her hands to Reno's shoulders. Heat touched her as she trailed her fingertips over his naked chest. Wow. He felt even better than he looked.

The intense butterflies in her stomach didn't mean anything.

She didn't have to be scared of this at all. Because this was really just quasi-vacation sex, Rachel assured herself—enjoyed beneath the multicolored glow of several strands of Christmas lights and sweetened with a little extra affection, sure, but straightforward vacation sex all the same. Everyone liked vacation sex. It was better than ordinary sex any day.

Which didn't fully explain why, when she cradled Reno's face in her hands and brought his mouth to hers, it seemed as if she'd waited years for them to come together . . . years to feel this way. So free and complete and perfect all at once.

But that was probably just leftover sentimentality, Rachel reasoned as she gazed in wonder at his face. A remnant of the holiday season. It didn't have to mean anything that she'd already confessed her love for him. In public. From a tabletop.

Even if—to her—it secretly did.

Hiding that fact, she arched her hips upward, teasing her and Reno both as she savored the (increasingly) tight fit of his boxer briefs. "Mmmm. You feel amazing. But wouldn't you be more comfortable if you got a little more . . . I don't know. Naked?"

Reno grinned. "Ladies first."

"I don't need to be invited twice." Squirming upward, Rachel helped him peel off her dress, leaving her clad in her red thong underwear and her cute Christmas pedicure. She bit her lip, waiting as Reno's heated gaze swept over her.

His groan was gratifying. "Even better than I imagined."

"You imagined? Me? Naked?" She grinned, pretending to be shocked. "Scandalous."

"I imagined." Intently, Reno stretched out beside her, all the better to caress his way from her shoulders to her toes in long, languid, exasperatingly slow strokes. "Reality is better."

"Then you should share the fun. Come here." Rachel turned over, pushed him onto his back, then straddled him. With a triumphant smile, she thumbed the waistband of his strained boxer briefs. "I'll just help you off with these."

"Good idea."

"I know. I've got just the strategy, too."

Filled with excitement, Rachel gave him another kiss, followed by a teeny-tiny tug. The movement bared a quarter inch of beautiful male skin from hipbone to hipbone, tantalizing her with the merest promise of everything still to come.

Knee-walking her way carefully down the mattress, she held her breath and pulled a little farther.

Below her, Reno moaned. Rachel stopped.

She arched her brow. "Hmm? Is something wrong?"

"Give . . . come . . ." His hooded gaze met hers, his mouth drawn with tension. "I want . . ." His hands rose to her. "You."

"Nope. This time it's my turn."

"Not like this." A low, guttural groan. "I need—"

"Forget it." Tantalizingly, Rachel revealed another quarter inch. His body throbbed in response. "I'm in charge now."

Reno laughed. An instant later, he closed his hands on her hips and flipped them both around, making the blankets billow.

"Damn it! Do you always settle disagreements this way?"

He made a face. "My accountant thinks it's kind of weird when I jump him over a misappropriated tax credit, but—"

"Very funny." Panting, Rachel surveyed her (now ruined) progress in undressing him. "Obviously I've given you too much leeway. You clearly can't stand waiting for anything."

"Ah, that's where you're wrong." With a single heady movement, Reno captured her in his arms, kissed her into blind needfulness, then made her forget her complaint altogether. He gazed deeply, soulfully into her eyes. "It feels as if I've waited a *very* long time for you."

"Lucky for you, that wait is about to be over."

"You think so?" Reno rasped, sliding his fingers toward her thong. For several long minutes, all conversation stopped. Blissfully. "Are you sure about that? This might take awhile."

The only reply she could manage was a lingering shudder as a stealthy, mind-boggling climax shook her.

"Whoops." Reno's hoarse chuckle washed over her, filled

with satisfaction. "You're finished. I guess we'll have to do that two or three times more . . . just so you can really enjoy it."

Panting, Rachel stared up at him in disbelief. She still wasn't sure how he'd done that. There should have been more foreplay necessary, more mechanical gyrations involved . . . more *something* besides a soul-deep connection and an avid interest.

"I'll give you four seconds to get those boxer briefs off," she said. "Otherwise I can't be held responsible for damage."

Eagerly, Reno complied.

"Ooh!" At her first glimpse of him—*all* of him—Rachel couldn't help but smile more widely, despite the fact that she was pretty sure her ears were still ringing. "You've got *just* what I wanted. It looks as if Christmas came early this year."

"Season's greetings," Reno said with a grin.

Then, for the space of at least four or five *classic* Best of Bing Crosby albums, he made Rachel feel very, very merry indeed.

Right up until the phone rang.

Chapter Twenty-Eight

Reno hung up the phone, his body still thrumming with the aftereffects of being with Rachel. After spending this morning with her, he felt sated and giddy in equal measure, an un-macho admission he'd never make public in a million years.

He didn't know if this was love—especially the kind of love to be shouted about from tabletops, a memory that still got to him—but he did know he felt powerless against it.

He rolled over to face her again, his most apologetic expression in full view. "That was Mrs. Bender. She needs help digging her car out of a snowbank downtown. It sounds as though the tires are ground in pretty deeply, so it might take awhile."

"Bummer. So where were we?" Smiling, Rachel ran her hand down his chest, then trailed a suggestive path over his abs, making him clench. "Oh, I remember. We were right about *here*."

Her fist closed over him, skillfully stroking. Awash in pleasure, Reno gritted his teeth. This was how he'd gotten in trouble in the first place. Well, this . . . and that dare of hers.

Of all the reasons to crack, to betray his promise to a friend, buckling under to a dare had to be the most ridiculous and inexcusable. Reno had done his best not to think about it, but now—as he tried to withstand Rachel's touch without begging for more—the truth smacked him in the face.

Because of his stupid jock ego, he hadn't been able to resist a wild romp in the sheets with his best friend's dream girl. Even if it was just sex—and they'd both assured each other that's all it was—he ought to be ashamed of himself. Was ashamed of himself. Really. Almost ashamed enough to . . . mmm. Ah.

Yes. God yes. Just like that. Never stop, never ever—

Where was he again? Oh yeah. With Rachel.

Murmuring something sexy and riveting about what she'd like to do to him next, Rachel stroked him again. Up. Down. More.

Yes. Ah. Reno shuddered and faced reality at last. He was a bad, bad man. He was going straight to hell for this.

"Mmmm." He grabbed the sheets, helplessly arching upward. "Oh God. Don't stop doing that. Whatever you do, don't stop—"

The phone trilled, breaking into his low, panted moans.

Reno stilled. No. *Not now not now not now*. He groaned, then closed his eyes in disappointment and reached for the phone.

"Yeah?" he barked into the receiver.

"Reno? Don't forget a shovel. And rock salt!"

"I won't, Mrs. Bender. Hang tight. Keep warm."

He hung up, then lifted his gaze to meet Rachel's disbelieving expression. "I'm really sorry, Rachel, but—"

"You're going?"

To his regret, he was already disentangling himself from her. He sighed, then swiveled uncomfortably to sit upright in bed. What first? Clothes? A shovel? Truck keys?

Desperately needing to move some blood from his groin to his brain, Reno raked his fingers through his hair. Maybe that would make him look a little less as though he'd just had his brains screwed out by the most incredible woman he'd ever met in an airport.

Who was he kidding? The most incredible woman he'd ever met. Period. Rachel was funny, sexy, sweet . . . and surprisingly shy when it came to certain things. He liked that about her. He liked that he could astonish her, move her . . . love her?

"That's ridiculous." Propping herself on her elbow, Rachel gawked at him. "You're going to help your neighbor *now*?"

He didn't understand the question. Nevertheless, he did his best to answer it. "It's what I do. I help people."

"But you're *busy*! We're right in the middle of—"

"We can pick up where we left off later."

Her sigh—and a muffled expletive (he guessed his dad was right about her language)—reached all the way across the bed.

"Is there *nothing* you won't do? You know . . . except me?"

"Very funny." Frustrated, Reno scraped around with his fingertips, looking for a shirt and some pants. He found the pants first and pulled them on commando-style. "I'll make it up to you tonight, I promise. After all, it's just sex, right?"

Inexplicable silence met his question. Reno glanced over his shoulder to see Rachel wearing an unexpectedly wounded expression . . . and nothing else. *Amazingly* nothing else.

But it wasn't her nudity that gripped him so fiercely. It was her forlorn expression. It tugged at him in ways he hadn't counted on and couldn't explain.

"Hey . . ." He touched her chin. "What's the matter?"

"Not a thing." She jerked away, her hair skimming over his wrist with the motion. "I should have seen this coming."

"Seen what coming?" Determined not to get sucked back into that bed (where he really wanted to be), he made himself grab a shirt and pull it on. Socks next. One. Two. Boots . . .

"You're overcompensating, that's all." Rachel spoke in an airy tone, her gaze following him around the bedroom. "I see it all the time with the celebrity clients I work with. They achieve sudden success in whatever field they're in, then spend the rest of their professional lives trying to make up for it."

Reno scoffed. "I'm not one of your hard-luck head cases from the land of sunshine and surfing." He moved away from the bed to search for a sweater. He might be outside for a while. He needed to stay warm. "Save the fashion therapy for someone who needs it." He stopped. "Where the hell is my sweater?"

Rachel threw it, smacking him full in the face with it.

Reno plucked it off his head. "Hey. What's that for?"

"For denigrating my professional expertise."

"Hey, I call 'em like I see 'em."

"So do I." Rachel tossed aside the covers and got out of bed, a series of movements that bared a few of her best assets and made him regret his neighbor-saving mission with twice as much ferocity. "And what I see is a man who feels a little guilty about being superlative at what he does."

"Running a sports equipment store?"

"And fixing things. And cutting down Christmas trees. And being an exceptional athlete. I might not be a football fan, Reno, but even I know how competitive it is in the NFL. If it weren't super hard to succeed, they wouldn't pay players those outrageous signing bonuses. Everyone's looking to start a buzz and grab a big opening day. It's just like Hollywood."

Reno made a face. "The day the NFL is like Hollywood is the day quarterbacks do blocking drills in training camp."

"Whatever. Maybe I've got it all wrong. Just tell me one thing: Have you ever bought a loved one an expensive gift?"

He didn't have time for this. "Define expensive."

"New car. Vacation. Fishing boat." Rachel paused. "House. Hummer. Yacht." She ticked them off on her fingers. "Jewelry—"

Damn it. She had him there. He'd bought his parents their retirement condo, Nate a fishing boat, Angela a new car, Kayla just about every pink sparkly thing Toys "R" Us had to offer. And he'd taken several buddies on vacation to Hawaii a few years ago. But was that so wrong? The fishing was really good there!

"It's not a crime to be generous," Reno said.

Her knowing gaze followed him as he strapped on his watch, then stuffed his pockets full of his wallet, change, and keys.

"Have you ever downplayed your accomplishments?"

"I don't know." Reno gave her a sarcastic look, irked that she thought she knew him so well. "I'm terrible at remembering things. You're probably much better at total recall than I am."

"Har-har." Doggedly, Rachel continued as she wiggled into her red thong underwear, nearly giving him heart palpitations that had nothing to do with the interrogation currently underway. "Do you think you have to do everything yourself, or it won't be done right?"

"That's just common sense."

"Have you ever refused to accept help? With anything?"

In his mind's eye, Reno saw Nate stringing Christmas lights at The Wright Stuff—and himself giving his friend painstaking step-by-step instructions the whole time. Every damn year. Regularly enough that Nate always threatened not to come back and put up with Reno's "Nazi Christmas commando routine."

That didn't prove anything though, Reno assured himself. Nate sucked at doing unpaid work. The fact that Reno was forced to supervise didn't mean he had a problem with accepting help from people. Only an idiot would have relied on Nate Kelly to see a project through to the end. And Reno wasn't an idiot.

But then he saw his dad volunteering to assist with his big holiday lights display—and himself turning down the offer. He saw the eager-to-please face of Derek Detweiler, the Multicorp franchising rep whose deal had sounded pretty good (except for the idea of giving up control of The Wright Stuff)—and himself giving the man the boot not once but three times.

He wasn't an idiot, but maybe he was a little stubborn.

He grunted. "A real man *gives* help. He doesn't take it."

"Riiight." Now Rachel had slipped back into her sexy red dress. It appeared a little wrinkly and worse for the wear, but she still looked totally hot in it. "Have you ever lost at something on purpose, just to make someone else feel better?"

Finally she was wrong.

Triumphantly, Reno said, "Hell, no. Screw that."

"Then you're a healthy adult male." Wearing an irritatingly shrewd expression, Rachel ducked into the bathroom, still talking as she brushed her long dark hair. "But that doesn't change the fact that you've got to get over feeling that you owe the world something because of the good fortune you've had."

Reno scoffed. "I like being generous. End of story." He gave a curt wave. "There's nothing wrong with that."

A pause. "No, there isn't," Rachel said softly, watching him from the bathroom doorway. "But there is something wrong with feeling that you *have* to be generous twenty-four-seven."

"I don't." He swore, feeling antsy and out of place. He'd liked it better when they'd both been naked. "Look, we had a good time together. I'll be the first to admit that. But that doesn't mean you know me. You don't know anything about me."

Rachel swished, spit, hung up his toothbrush, then gave him a playful look. "I know a little about you by now."

Damn it. Where had he heard that annoying phrase before?

Oh yeah. From himself. And he'd meant the hell out of it, too. He did know about her. Good and bad. He liked all of it.

Could it be possible Rachel felt the same way about him?

Stricken, Reno put down his head and focused on getting his cell phone, a flashlight, and all the things he'd need to dig out poor Mrs. Bender. Despite that fact, Rachel came to him.

"I know a little about you," she said again, "by now."

She put both hands on his 11-A.M. stubble-shadowed face and made him look at her. Grudgingly, Reno did.

What he saw there scared the bejeezus out of him.

Rachel could see right into his soul. She could see his guilt, his pride, his knowledge that nothing but a freak spin of the wheel had separated him and Nate—who'd enjoyed all the same practice and training that Reno had—and had made Reno excel in the NFL while his best friend washed out in week three. She could see how self-conscious he felt to have a ridiculously fat bank account while people he'd grown up with and cared about struggled to get by. She could see that he felt he did—and didn't—deserve all of it, both at the same time.

He didn't know why Rachel was able to understand him so easily, especially when no one else in town could. Maybe she had special insight because of her job. Or maybe there was some other reason. Either way, it was sappy and embarrassing, and Reno didn't want anyone else to find out about it. Or to find out how his resistance to his best friend's dream girl had eroded, bit by sexy bit, with every day he spent with her.

The plain truth was, Rachel could see *him*, Reno realized, in a way those giggly, bra-flashing fangirls never had and never would. Somehow, Rachel knew him, inside and out. And instead of scaring her away or making her think he was weak or unfairly blessed or selfish, that knowledge made her want to stick around. With him. Not so he could rescue her—because she sure as hell didn't need that—but so he could love her.

"You know I'm right," Rachel said, sure and strong.

Barely realizing he was doing it, Reno nodded.

"I was good. The best," he admitted. "But I was just one man. I didn't deserve to be so much luckier than everyone else."

"Lucky is in the eye of the beholder. Don't you know that?"

He made an incredulous sound. "Most people can behold a multimillion-dollar contract or a spot on the starting lineup, season after season. Those things set the world straight pretty quickly about who's on top and who's not."

"Depends on who's keeping track." Smiling to herself, Rachel stepped away to put on her shoes. "Maybe no one is."

Impossible. Reno's football fame had made him a legend

in Kismet—known along the shores of Lake Michigan and in several of the towns and cities between the Great Lakes. He was a hometown boy who'd made good. No one was likely to forget that.

Especially him.

"People around here respect you. Anyone can see that." Rachel wrapped a scarf around her neck, twining it in some artsy L.A. style. "All I'm saying is, you don't have to keep earning that respect over and over again. You don't have to be the go-to guy for everyone all the time. Give yourself a break."

A break. Ha. As if he could ever do that.

"Is that what you're doing here? Taking a break?"

She looked surprised. "Maybe. I guess."

To Reno's matching surprise, the idea felt tempting. He liked helping people. But already he'd opened his house to his dad, his weekends to his sister for babysitting duties, his wallet to his friends and neighbors, his Santa-suited self to his niece for her Christmas pageant, his expertise to his customers at The Wright Stuff, his brawn to Mrs. Kowalczyk and Mrs. Bender for shoveling their driveways, and his supposed match-making services to his best friend.

If he stepped back, he might have time to relax. To go on a few more dates. To finish the damn book he'd been reading for weeks. To really go all out with his holiday lights extravaganza, wow everyone, and win the competition.

To find out if he ever *could* know what love felt like.

Nah. Taking a break was sissy stuff. He could do it all.

"Mrs. Bender is waiting for me. I've got to go."

Rachel emerged from the bathroom for a final time, looking fresh faced and pretty. "Okay. Let me grab my purse."

"You're going with me?" Frowning, he watched Rachel hustle to the bureau, where he'd stashed her handbag last night.

"Unless you think you can simultaneously entertain Mrs. Bender with some sparkling conversation *and* dig out her car."

She gazed at him expectantly. Flummoxed, Reno stared back.

He hadn't expected this. Usually he helped people on his own. Having Rachel along for the ride might be . . . kind of fun. At least for today, he could be part of a team again. A team of two. That was something he missed about football. Teamwork.

Letting Rachel tag along was tantamount to surrendering, to admitting that maybe he didn't want to do everything himself anymore. All the same, Reno shrugged. "You have a point."

"I have several, and don't you forget it." Smiling more broadly now, a minty-smelling Rachel raised herself on tiptoes to kiss him. She gave him a fond look. "So . . . How's it feel to be completely transparent to someone?"

"Hell, I wouldn't know," Reno lied, feeling weirdly relieved. He grabbed Rachel's backside and squeezed, holding her close enough to inhale the fragrance of her skin. For an instant, he indulged in sentimental memories of this morning in a shameless way that probably lowered his testosterone levels on the spot. "But you ought to. Because you're completely transparent to me."

"Oh, yeah?"

"Yeah." He paused, then scrutinized her. He grabbed a Scorpions sweatshirt from his bureau and tossed it to her. "You're going to have to wear more than that. Try this."

Too late, Reno remembered Rachel's reaction the last time he'd tried to offer her something warmer to wear. She'd acted as though licensed NFL gear would give her monkey pox.

But this time, she only wriggled into his sweatshirt, then struck a seductive pose. "Thanks. What do you think?"

"I think I'd rather have you naked."

"You and every other man for miles." Rolling her eyes in pretend boredom, Rachel grinned. She smacked him on the ass. "Quit lollygagging, hero. You've got a little old lady to save."

"Bossy."

"You know it."

In perfect synchronicity, they headed for the living room. Reno had never felt less like doing his go-to guy routine. Especially when he had to follow Rachel's side-to-side sashay all the way from the bed to the sofa, where . . . Reno stopped.

He pointed. "Nobody slept out here."

Rachel was putting on her makeshift coat, adding it to her scarf, sweatshirt, and dress combo. "Hmmm?"

"The blankets and pillows haven't been touched. My dad didn't come home last night. He wasn't here when we got here, but I thought he was just staying out late."

What the hell could have happened to his dad? Tom Wright was getting older. He'd never been very street smart to begin with. His eyesight wasn't good. And his hearing sucked, too, even though he tried to pretend all those acid rock concerts in the seventies hadn't affected him. They had. Oh God.

Chapter Twenty-Nine

All kinds of nightmare scenarios flashed through Reno's head. Pacing, he reached for his cell phone. He'd call his dad's number first, then Angela, then 911.

Or the hospital? Damn it, he wasn't sure.

"He probably spent the night with your mom," Rachel said.

In mid-dial, Reno froze. "What?"

"Didn't you see Tom and Judy at my party last night?"

"Uh . . ." Reno was still getting over the realization that this panic—this utter freak-out—must have been what he'd put his parents through all during high school. He'd done his share of sneaking out past curfew. He ought to be shot. Concentrating hard, he said, "I saw them, I guess. For a second."

Truthfully, he'd started blotting out any thoughts of his parents together. Thanks to their lame-ass divorce talk, it was too painful to remember how happy they'd once been. Not that he'd admit as much. Trying to seem tough, Reno jerked up his chin.

"Did *you* see them?" he asked.

"Of course! I'm the one who invited them. And, you know, helped them end their feud. I guess you could say my advice worked, judging by the hot and heavy make-out session I saw them indulging in." Looking pleased with herself, Rachel squinted at the blankets folded on the sofa. "Ugh. These are polyester, Reno. And *plaid*. Show some respect. Your father is a great guy."

Ugh. *Make-out session*. Reno shuddered. That wasn't something he wanted to associate with his parents. Ever.

In a mighty effort to turn his thoughts toward something less parentally X-rated, Reno finally realized what Rachel had just said: *And, you know, helped them end their feud.*

Could it be true? Sure, Rachel's advice to Kayla had helped her patch things up with her Kismet Elementary School posse. But it wasn't as if his very own L.A. diva was some kind of miracle worker. On the other hand, Rachel *had* taken his father shopping for new shazaam!-style clothes. She'd bought him cool shoes.

Check out my kicks! Nice, right?

She'd restored his hope and his excitement for life.

But that didn't explain all this. That didn't explain . . .

"Did you take my mom shopping, too?" he demanded.

"Of course! Right after we finished crafting about six dozen of those reindeer ornaments with the wooden clothespins and the glue-on googly eyes. She just needed a few new things—"

"So you *are* responsible!"

"Um." Rachel backed up, looking alarmed—probably at the sudden intensity Reno felt. "Maybe. Responsible for . . . ?"

"Bringing my parents back together." He didn't know how, and he couldn't begin to fathom all the details, but all of a sudden Reno believed it was true. It made sense.

It made a weird kind of sense, but it made sense.

"Do you know what this means?" Overflowing with relief, Reno pulled Rachel into his arms. He didn't want her to see the stupid, gullible tears that sprang to his eyes. Even though she could probably hear him sniffle all the same. "We can have Christmas together again this year!"

"Mmm-hmmm." Rachel's voice was muffled, squashed against his chest. "Behold the power of fashion." Apparently her solutions weren't always as pragmatic as the one she'd dished out to Kayla. She patted him. "Just one big happy family, right?"

"Right." Another sniffle. Manfully, Reno got a grip on himself. He set Rachel apart from him, but he couldn't distance himself from the beaming smile on his face. He realized it was happening and tried to suppress it with a tough-guy grimace.

"Are you okay?" Rachel asked, looking concerned.

"I'm fine." Gruffly, he cleared his throat. "Let's go."

He hustled her toward the door—the better to prevent her from witnessing him swabbing at his eyes. His chest felt light, though, his shoulders loose, his whole body free. The little-boy part of him had apparently been terrified of that divorce all this time, but the grown-man part of him had ruthlessly quashed all those fears. Now Reno felt seriously at risk of breaking out with some sort of shake-your-groove-thing celebratory dance.

Rachel pivoted. Instantly, Reno sobered as he opened the door for them both. He ushered her toward the snowy porch.

No dice. "Are you sure you're all right?" she asked.

"I'm fine. Look, there's my neighbor." Right now, Reno felt prepared to grasp at any distraction. "Hey, Gerry!"

Rachel gasped. "That's my dad! Ohmigod!"

"Oh yeah. That's right." Too damned cheerful to ask why she was bolting behind him, using his body as cover, Reno waved.

Rachel's father, busily walking up the drive, waved, too.

"Hide me. Hide me!" Rachel said in a harsh whisper.

"Hide you? Why? Everything is *awesome*!" Reno's head swam with remembrances of happy, close-knit Christmases past—and with anticipation of the bright and cozy holiday that now lay ahead for him and his family. "What's up, Gerry?"

Boisterously, Reno stepped onto the frosty porch to greet the man. They shook hands, Gerry Porter looking exactly as happy-go-lucky as he always did. The icicles on the eaves glistened in the sunlight. The holiday yard decorations Reno had already put out stood at the ready. The lights on the porch railing lay on the snow like jewels. Everything really *was* awesome.

"I just came to see if I can borrow your ladder."

"Sure," Reno said. "I'll open the garage for you."

"Thanks. Appreciate it."

On cue, Reno stepped toward his garage.

A muffled squeal came from behind him.

He glanced back to see Rachel, frozen in an awkward position with her eyes wide and her gaze directed straight at her father. Without her shield—aka Reno—to hide behind, she looked utterly conspicuous. Especially in that sexy red dress of hers, with her bare legs and strappy shoes plainly visible beneath her Scorpions sweatshirt, coat, and scarf.

"Rachel?" Gerry Porter breathed. "Is that you?"

Doh. That was when Reno realized what all the whispering had been about. Rachel didn't want her dad to see her doing the morning walk of shame. In last night's dress. With—it suddenly seemed to him—Reno's handprints glowing in neon relief against her skin in all the most indecent, erotic places. The two of them couldn't have appeared more naughty if they'd tried.

Stricken, Reno gawked at Gerry Porter.

Rachel continued to do the same.

"So, uh, Rachel. Thanks for dropping off Kayla for me to babysit," Reno improvised quickly. "That must have been one crazy and totally innocent slumber party you and Angela and Kayla had last night."

"Err . . ." Rachel's perplexed gaze met his. She caught on quickly. "It was! Cra-azy slumber party. Pillow fights, pink nighties, curlers, sing-alongs . . . the whole nine yards!"

United in their completely improbable lie, they nodded vigorously and faced her father. Gerry crossed his arms.

"Now you're a cast member of the musical *Grease*?"

For an instant, the only sounds were a distant snowplow a

few streets over and the strains of "We Three Kings" wafting from that bastard Hal's garish yard display.

"Yes." Rachel nodded. "Yes, I am."

"Rachel—"

"No. Dad, I'm sorry. Just hang on. I can explain!"

"So can I, Mr. Porter," Reno offered.

Instantly, they were teenagers again, hands clasped behind their backs in contrite poses. Reno hoped like hell that he hadn't accidentally given Rachel an Angela-style hickey as a souvenir of their night together. Just in case, he nudged his shoulder sideways, gesturing for Rachel to cover her neck with her hair. Hastily, she complied.

"This isn't what it looks like," Rachel said.

"It's all perfectly innocent," Reno added. "We were just leaving to help shovel Mrs. Bender's car out of a snowbank."

"That's not all you're shoveling this morning. Don't try to sidetrack me." Gerry Wright frowned. "It's daytime, and my daughter is dressed like one of those hoochie girls on MTV."

More silence. Then . . .

"What are you doing watching MTV, Dad?"

"Uh . . ." Gerry stamped his feet, staring at his boots.

"Does Mom know about this?"

Now Gerry found an intent interest in Reno's eaves. "Er . . ."

"Come on, Rachel." Sensing an opening, Reno helped out. "What's a little *Pants-Off Dance-Off* to a fully grown man?"

Gerry Porter blanched.

Rachel tsk-tsked. "That show is on Fuse.tv, not MTV, Reno. My dad probably doesn't even know *Pants-Off Dance-Off* exists."

They both crossed their arms and raised their eyebrows.

Gerry spread his arms wide. He beamed, his smile rather shaky but nonetheless earnest. "*Grease*, huh? Congratulations!"

Rachel stepped into her father's embrace, blushing furiously but appearing grateful all the same. Reno stood by, awkwardly examining the snowbank for signs of a Crackers invasion. If those were tiny bichon frise footprints—

"Come here, son!" Gerry Porter blustered. "Don't be shy!"

Suddenly, Reno found himself enveloped in a Porter-style embrace himself, pounded by his neighbor's hearty back slaps and nearly muffled by the fluffy wad of Rachel's scarf that got in his mouth. Helpless against the onslaught, Reno gave in.

He hugged them back.

Mashed against Rachel, welcomed by her father, Reno had the strangest feeling he would never be the same again . . . even if he wasn't really part of a touring musical road company in the midst of a Christmastime *Grease* revival.

Chapter Thirty

Walking down Kismet's Main Street at Christmastime was like being transported into one of those vintage 1970s TV specials—colorful, overeager, and a little bit cheesy, but ultimately lovable. Holiday music blared from hidden speakers, red and green banners fluttered over the snow-covered, brick-paved streets, and everything had been wrapped in shining holiday lights—from the old-fashioned power poles to the mailboxes and the bare-limbed oak trees growing at the edge of the sidewalk.

Small businesses strung lights and painted their windows with festive holiday scenes. Vendors on street corners peddled candy canes, hot cider, and actual roasted chestnuts in small paper sacks. People milled around with smiles on their faces, coming together in groups of three or four or more as they lined up to wait for the annual Kismet Christmas parade to kick off.

Wending her way through the throng at dusk, nose twitching with the scents of evergreen and peppermint, Rachel munched through the bag of authentic (and delicious) caramel corn she'd bought from a local vendor, her gaze sharp for signs of Reno. She hadn't seen him for a few days—since their excursion to rescue Mrs. Bender from her snowbound car—but he hadn't been far from her thoughts. Now (she'd just decided) she had something to tell him. Something momentous. Something she hoped he'd like.

Shivering against the chill in the air, Rachel kept moving, striding past a wooden cutout of two elves bearing a gigantic bow-bedecked gift—an advertisement for homemade Kismet Christmas fudge. People passed by wearing jingle bells strung on their boots, long striped-and-pom-pommed stocking caps, and pretend reindeer antlers on their heads. In public. Non-ironically.

But Rachel only nodded and smiled at them, for the first time appreciating the joy in doing what felt right instead of what was chic or trendsetting or likely to land a feature spot in *Us Weekly* for one of her celebrity clients.

The truth was, these days she felt like a changed person. Her guardedness seemed to have vanished for good, swept away by her unexpected vacation and a traditional dose of Christmas cookies and ranch dip (courtesy of her mom). Thanks to Reno and his ability to see (and appreciate) the real woman behind the celebrity stylist aura, Rachel had started to feel the magic inherent in the whole Kismet shtick.

So instead of finding the local "joyful community" thing unlikely or kitschy, she thought it was kind of sweet. Instead of feeling too cool for Christmas tree decorating and floats depicting decades-old mascots for local businesses, she actually felt eager to see some of the things she'd helped work on down at the Elks Club. And instead of ducking her head and striding briskly past all the people on the street, the way she typically did to get around in L.A., she found herself greeting friends and neighbors warmly, with real gladness to see them.

It was kind of remarkable how thoroughly Kismet had changed her. Today Rachel had arrived unstressed, unhurried, and totally unwired. She'd actually left her cell phone at home—*without* dutifully working her way through her call list of former (and potential) clients first. That was just how at peace she felt.

Maybe she hadn't given Kismet a fair shake before . . .

"Rachel!" Mrs. Hendrickson waved. "I *love* your coat. I just realized it today. I absolutely *love* your coat."

"Thanks, Mrs. Hendrickson. All set for the parade?"

"Yes, we are, dear." She nestled closer to her husband, both of them positively brimming with good cheer. "We *love* parades."

Wow. That was kind of an extreme reaction to a simple parade, even here in Kismet. But Rachel only waved back at them and then moved on, still chomping her caramel corn. Yum.

She was seriously never eating another protein bar again.

"Rachel! How's the caramel corn?" Bidie Niedermeyer asked.

"It's really good. You should try it."

"Yes, but do you *love* it?" Bidie persisted, wearing a sly grin. "Do you love, love, *love* it?"

"Um." Maybe Bidie was friends with the caramel corn vendor. Just in case, Rachel nodded. "Yes, I think it's delicious."

Tittering with approval, Bidie waved and vanished into the crowd. Rachel watched her go, feeling momentarily perplexed.

That feeling ebbed as she moved farther down the sidewalk, enjoying the cheerful sounds of "Joy to the World" and watching Kismet's youngest generation get geared up for the parade by climbing onto their fathers' shoulders for better views and talking animatedly about Santa Claus. Reminded of Kayla, Rachel smiled. That little girl was a real sweetie.

"Rachel!" Mrs. Fowler stopped her, a curious expression on her face. She glanced over her shoulder at someone, giggled, then quickly scanned Rachel's outfit of jeans, a sweater, and the (slightly more utilitarian but still awesomely chic) boots she'd bought herself at Dirk's Footwear. "I *love* your hat!"

"Thanks, Mrs. Fowler. It's only practical—"

"I just realized it today. I absolutely *love* it."

Perplexed by the woman's enthusiasm, Rachel tilted her head. Maybe she was a knitter? A crafter like her mom, with a special appreciation for handiwork? "Um, thanks. It's my mom's actually. I don't have much need for a hat in California."

"Love, love, *love* it!" Mrs. Fowler chortled, then left.

Baffled, Rachel stood on the corner as warmly dressed Kismet residents surged past her, chatting about the parade's likely start time and the official town-square Christmas tree lighting ceremony to take place afterward. She glanced up at the huge holiday bows affixed to the street signs, then shrugged.

Probably everyone was just being friendly.

But where was Reno? He ought to be here by now.

"Rachel!" Mr. Caplan, whom she recognized from the Glenrosen decorating party, hailed her from his prime spot beside a mailbox. "How are you? All set for the parade?"

This time she was ready. "Let me guess. You *love* my boots."

He looked. "No. They're kind of flashy, if you ask me."

"Then you love, love, *love* my sweater. My purse?"

"I'm not a fashion maven. You are, is what I hear. In fact, I hear you took some of the folks from the Elks Club on a shopping expedition to give them your expert advice."

She had, just yesterday. It had been fun acting as a personal holiday shopper for regular people—people who didn't constantly wear sunglasses, demand fresh bottles of vitamin water, and let their teensy lapdogs slobber on the designers' sample clothes. Rachel had decided she could get used to being treated like a real friend instead of a peon-slash-confidant.

Not that all her celebrity clients had acted that way.

But still.

"I did. And I know someone who's getting a *very* special secret Santa gift this year . . ." Rachel hinted.

"Don't tell me!" Grinning, Mr. Caplan put his wrinkled hands over his ears. "I want to be surprised."

Rachel smiled, then pantomimed zipping her lips. "The secret's safe with me. Merry Christmas, Mr. Caplan."

"Merry Christmas to you, too. Enjoy the parade."

"Thanks, I will." Happily, Rachel headed on her way, feeling more a part of the community than ever. She had secrets to share with folks in Kismet, a happy Christmas morning to anticipate . . . and a few more unusual comments to puzzle over.

Everyone she recognized—and a few people she didn't— had something to say. Something that sounded a lot like, "I *love* your . . . whatever. I just realized it today. I *love* it!" Followed by a guffaw and a quick scamper away. It was really weird.

"Rachel! Over here!" someone called.

Steeling herself for another bizarre encounter, Rachel turned. Angela and Kayla waved her over from their parade-watching position near The Wright Stuff. The store's window glowed with twice the quantity of holiday lights and Christmas cheer as any other on the block. Rachel hurried toward it.

"The strangest thing is happening," she said after she'd hugged Angela and Kayla hello. "Everyone keeps saying—"

"Rachel!" Jimmy Gurche, at the parade with his wife and kids, offered her a grin and a double-finger-gun salute. "I *love* your scarf! I just realized it today. I love, love, love it!"

His wife frowned. She swatted him, offering Rachel a contrite look. Doubled over with laugher, Jimmy vanished.

"They keep saying *that*. Did you hear that? 'I *love* your whatever. Love, love, love it!' It's driving me crazy!"

"I heard it." Angela's mouth quirked. "I hate to be the one to tell you, Rachel, but . . . you're really part of Kismet now."

"Huh?"

"You're part of the community. Kismet has embraced you." Her friend, bundled in a parka, offered a semiapologetic look. "People feel free to give you a hard time, poke a little fun—"

"Poke a little fun? At my *clothes*?" That's what everyone had mostly singled out, after all. In disbelief, Rachel glanced down at her outfit. "That *absolutely* can't be true. My clothes are fantastic. I might not have embraced elastic waistbands and comfortable shoes, but I'm still—"

"It's not your clothes. It's your party."

"My party?"

"It's . . . what happened at your L.A. Christmas party."

Angela closed her mouth on another smile, clearly unwilling to say more. Baffled, Rachel glanced around as a holiday fanfare trumpeted the start of the parade from one block away.

"What do you mean, what happened at my party?" Everyone had seemed to be having fun. "Jimmy Gurche wasn't even there."

"Yes, but Kismet is a small town, remember?" Angela said. "Your party was a big deal. Everyone's heard about it by now."

"Bobby Pendelton said you danced on a table," Kayla piped up. "How did you keep from falling off? I tried dancing on the cafeteria table, but the teacher said I'd fall off. I said, 'Nuh-uh, because Rachel didn't,' but she just laughed."

Uh-oh. Feeling her last bite of caramel corn turn tasteless in her mouth, Rachel stared at them both. Then it hit her.

I love this guy! came flooding back to her, punctuated by the sounds of ska Christmas music and hooting backup dancers. *You hear that? I'm in love with Reno Wright! I just realized it today and I want everyone to know it. I love, love, love him!*

She'd told the whole world she loved Reno.

No wonder everyone thought she was a laugh riot.

Glancing around at the milling parade-goers, Rachel wanted to dig a hole in the nearest snowbank and crawl in. She'd never felt more exposed. Except maybe the first time she'd tried on a pair of skinny jeans after years of wearing low-rise bootcuts.

Well, maybe she could still salvage the situation.

"You have got to be kidding me," she said, affecting her best air of indifference. "Everyone took that seriously?"

"You mean your love declaration?" Wearing an inscrutable expression, Angela nodded. "Yes, everyone did. Including Reno."

Whoops. Angela had her there.

"And me." Her friend gave her a solemn look. "You're not in L.A. anymore. People around here mean what they say."

"Um . . ."

"Just like I mean it when I say thanks for patching things up between my parents. They tore up their divorce papers and moved back in together a few days ago. I don't know what you did for them, but they seem to have a new appreciation for each other. They're really happy now."

Encouraged, Rachel glanced up. "I'm glad. I just did what comes naturally—made sure everything was perfectly coordinated."

All the Wrights had needed was a chance to feel heard—and a chance to remember the good things they'd shared during their marriage. Angela and Reno, as *very* involved onlookers, probably hadn't been able to help with that quite as much as they'd wanted to. When it came down to it, Judy had just wanted to feel special. Tom had just wanted to feel appreciated. Now they did.

And they also had some ultraflattering, feel-good outfits to go with their newfound sensitivity toward each other, too. Plus some actual holiday *gifts*, not blank checks, to share.

"And just like I mean it," Angela continued steadfastly, breaking into Rachel's remembrance of her time with the Wrights, "when I say that if you really *don't* love Reno—"

"Rachel loves Uncle Reno?" Kayla interrupted. "Really?"

"—then you'd better make that clear to him right now. Because I've never seen my brother look happier. Not even when he got drafted into the NFL, then went to the Super Bowl."

"I knew it! I knew it!" Kayla whooped, dancing around.

"So if you break his heart, you'll have *me* to answer to."

Rachel scoffed as the parade began. "Come on, Angela. You're about as fierce as a basketful of kittens."

Her friend only pursed her lips. "I have untapped reserves of ferocity. Especially when someone I love is at risk."

"Okay." Rachel gave a titter, suddenly believing it. "Make that 'as fierce as a crateful of PMSing ninjas.'"

Angela nodded. "That's right. Look, here comes the parade!"

But Kayla still wasn't finished. "Didn't I tell you, Mom?" The little girl nudged Angela, crowing with evident glee as she continued dancing in her snow boots. "Uncle Reno loves Rachel, too! That's why he's been doing pushups when he thinks I'm not looking. That's why his hair looks especially shiny these days."

Reno had been doing pushups? To impress her?

Gee, that was kind of endearing, Rachel mused. Silly, when Reno had a totally hard-bodied physique to begin with, but sweet all the same. On the other hand . . .

"So *everyone* in town knows about me and Reno?" she asked.

Angela's expression turned enigmatic. "Almost everyone."

But Rachel didn't have time to wonder what all the mystery was about. She was too busy imagining the spread of gossip via the same local grapevine that—if given the chance—would plaster the news of her L.A. job meltdown all over town. Worried, she said, "I don't usually lower my guard like that. But something about Kismet just makes me feel all"—*careless!* her brain volunteered—"*trusting.*" Mimi would have boggled to hear her admit such a thing. "As if nothing bad can happen here."

She made a face, realizing the improbability of that even as she admitted it.

"It'll be all right. Kismet has that effect on people sometimes." With her usual warmth and steadiness, Angela patted her shoulder. "Don't worry. Everyone around here loves their gossip, but they'll move on to something else soon enough."

Rachel bit her lip. "I hope you're right."

Otherwise she didn't know how she'd forgive herself for

having yet *another* lapse of judgment and blurting out the truth about her feelings for Reno. Especially after the Tyson and Alayna debacle and all the disastrous developments that had followed. Losing her clients. Her friends. Her house. Her car and phones. Her trust in the people she'd thought she'd known—people whom she'd truly believed cared about her as a person.

Now she could see how wrong she'd been about them.

About herself.

Everything could change in an instant, Rachel knew. But now, just when she'd been getting her mojo back, feeling her good judgment and faith in human nature restored . . .

"I am right," Angela assured her. "If you're lucky, Judge Boswell will get tipsy again and drive the Kismet Historical Society float straight into the marina."

"That *would* be distracting."

"It happens three years out of five," Angela assured her.

Feeling a little better, Rachel nodded. But then . . .

"Hey, Rachel!" came a boisterous male voice. "I'd *love*—"

"Okay, that's it." Maybe everyone in Podunk trusted in their fellow man's fundamental kindness—or in the diversionary value of serial drunken float navigating—but Rachel was different. "Knock it off, pal. It's not funny anymore."

She wheeled around . . . and Reno was there.

He looked handsome. He looked smitten. He looked—it occurred to her—very much like everything she'd ever wanted in a man and hadn't believed truly existed. Apparently it did. Here in Kismet, in the last place she'd ever have thought to look.

"I'd *love*," Reno finished with a grin as he moved through the crowd and wrapped his arms familiarly around her hips, "to officially welcome you to the Christmas parade. You game?"

Judging by his tone, he'd received his share of ribbing from the folks in Kismet today, too. It appeared he didn't care.

"Me?" She didn't know what he had in mind, but her

gullible, hopeful heart soared all the same. She barely managed to keep her cool. "You know me. I'm always up for anything."

"Good. So am I."

Just like that, Reno lowered his gaze to her lips. Before Rachel could do so much as catch her breath, he followed with his mouth, losing them both in a kiss that left her woozy. And hot. And kind of unsteady. And hot. And . . . whew! Was it December or what? It felt pretty hot out here. Rachel fanned herself.

Boy, Reno really knew how to greet a girl. Apparently when he knocked down a few barriers, they stayed down. Whatever had been keeping him at arm's length from her seemed totally gone.

He lifted his head, looking dazed. "Mmm. Sweet."

Merrily, Rachel nodded. "You betcha."

"Sticky."

She smirked. "Just try to get away."

"Caramel corn-y."

"Oh." He actually made her blush. Rachel felt her cheeks heat, and knew that Reno Wright packed an amazing amount of charm if he could make a woman who'd once worn a backless gown to a straitlaced country club fund-raiser feel exposed and giddy "Yeah. It looked good. I couldn't resist."

"There's a lot of that going around." His smile could have made solid stone turn gooey. "I can't resist you either."

Another kiss, this one gentler and even more dizzying, lasting long enough that the Christmas parade enveloped them as it marched past with all its riotous music and colors, parade watchers cheering as floats passed and Shriners threw candy.

"Wow." Rachel smiled. "That was—"

"Unforgettable." Reno cupped her face in his hand and gazed at her for a long while, oblivious to the Christmas music, shouted greetings, and boisterous passersby all around them.

Just like that, Rachel didn't care about the gossip, the teasing, or the very real possibility that she might have to ride in Reno's pickup truck again. Maybe on a regular basis.

This was it. She was falling. Falling—

"You know," she said with all the nonchalance she could muster, "I think I might stay in Kismet for a while. Work on a new project I've got going." Her designs were progressing well, but she wasn't ready to share them yet. Not even with Reno. "Given time, I think I could come up with something great." Her heart pounded at the gravity of her admission, but she managed to go on. Bravely, she said, "I'm pretty proud of what I've done so far. In fact, this coat I'm wearing is kind of a sample—"

Incredibly, Reno's gaze wandered over her shoulder.

Rachel frowned. She couldn't believe he was tuning her out now—now when she was baring her innermost dreams to him.

"—and it's kind of edible," she said, testing him, "if you put enough ketchup on it first. Although—"

"Mmm." Clearly distracted, Reno shifted his feet.

"—the wool might stick in your teeth, and the buttons are kind of crunchy. But that's the price you pay for high fashion."

"Right." Reno edged behind the nearest lighted tree, taking her with him. His gaze darted sideways. "Mmm-hmmm."

Rachel frowned. What was the matter with him?

Thoroughly exasperated, she poked him. "Hey! I just told you I might be staying here in Kismet for a while to start up a new venture. Don't you have any reaction to that?"

"Uh . . ."

"Don't you have anything else to say?"

"Uh . . ."

Great. She'd finally fallen for a man—for real this time, she felt sure—and he turned out to be phobic over the idea of her hanging around for a while.

Deeply disappointed, Rachel tapped her toe, waiting for an explanation. She wanted to think the best of Reno, she really did. Which was probably why she barely blinked when he suddenly grabbed her arm and hustled her sideways.

"Let's watch the parade from over here. The view's better."

"But—wait!" Wheeling her arm, Rachel glanced back to see a big blond man approach Angela and Kayla. He looked familiar. Nate maybe? "I promised Kayla I'd watch the parade with her!"

"She'll understand." Determinedly, Reno kept moving.

"Hang on. Where are we going?" Rachel tripped as they hurried between clumps of people. Incongruously jolly Christmas music accompanied every step. Reno's broad back and shoulders filled her vision as he towed her farther away from The Wright Stuff. "I was fine over there. And what about my announcement? Don't you have anything to say about my announcement?"

He stopped suddenly. "That you're staying in town?"

With her teeth chattering, Rachel stared at him, feeling annoyed. "Yes. That I *might* be staying in town."

"I say I'm screwed." For an instant, Reno appeared absolutely miserable. Then he took her hand. "Come on."

Chapter Thirty-One

I'd say I'm screwed.

Reno knew it was the wrong thing to say the minute the words left his mouth. But by then it was too late—too late to take it back and too late to pretend he didn't mean it.

Mostly because it was true. He *was* screwed.

Being in the same town with Rachel Porter during the holidays was one thing. Living there with her 24/7 was another. Reno could scarcely rationalize what he was doing to Nate to begin with. Now he was supposed to be okay with pushing it past Christmas? With seeing Rachel behind Nate's back indefinitely?

He wasn't okay with that. No man with a conscience would have been, and Reno definitely had a conscience. He was supposed to be keeping an eye on his best friend's dream girl. Finding out how to make her want to date Nate. So far, he'd done exactly . . . none of that. Unless you counted savoring her naked body just before kissing her all over as keeping an eye on her.

Reno didn't. Despite how much he'd enjoyed it.

He didn't understand what was wrong with him. One minute he was his usual dependable self. The next he was kissing Rachel like there was no tomorrow—right on the sidewalk in full view of everyone! Everyone including Nate, whom Reno had spotted lumbering cheerfully in their direction a few minutes later, carrying a fistful of candy canes and one of those ELF CROSSING! signs the holiday craft fair vendors sold.

Reno had no explanation for any of it. He'd just seen Rachel standing there and . . . whoosh. His heart had made the decision for him. The next thing he knew, she'd been in his arms, as if no one else existed except her.

He should have left right then.

He should have shoved Rachel at Nate, made the damned introductions, and been done with the whole thing. Instead he'd bolted with Rachel at his side, and although they'd made it safely away before Nate had spotted him and Rachel together, Reno knew he'd taken a stupid and unnecessary chance. Was *still* taking stupid and unnecessary chances . . . all for the sake of one more minute with the woman beside him. Rachel, who currently stared in anticipation at the darkened Kismet municipal Christmas tree as the annual countdown commenced.

"Four," thundered the mayor over his loudspeaker. Hundreds of other voices joined in. "Three. Two. One. Merry Christmas!"

The huge fir tree in the town square blazed forth, lit in multicolored lights, thirty feet high and decorated from tip to trunk. Beside Reno, Rachel gasped. She squeezed his arm, staring wide-eyed at the glittering, flashing town Christmas tree.

"It's just like when I was a little girl! It's beautiful!"

The awe on her face—the sheer enjoyment in her expression—held Reno spellbound. At her side, he felt ten feet tall. Not because he'd protected her, saved her, or rescued her cat from a storm drain. Just because he'd helped bring that sense of wonder to her face. He was hopeless. No wonder he'd been acting like an idiot for the past . . . well, every day since he'd met her.

He cleared his throat and shifted his feet, on the lookout for Nate. "It's probably not much next to the L.A. tree."

She shook her head. "You don't understand. I'd forgotten all about this." She caught his hand, their gloved fingers touching. "I'd forgotten the part of *me* that likes this."

Rachel gazed fully at him, and for an instant, Reno couldn't even continue monitoring the crowd for signs of Nate. He was pretty sure he'd found a spot for Rachel and him on the far side of the town square, away from the usual position Nate and Angela occupied to watch the tree lighting with Kayla every year, but he . . . he couldn't remember anything except his sheer gladness at being with Rachel. Here, just like this.

"And you gave it back to me," she said. "Thanks."

She leaned sideways and kissed him, the fingers of her other gloved hand turning his cheek to face her, holding him in place, her breath warming his skin as her lips gently met his.

"So . . ." When she raised her head, her mischievous grin caught him off guard. "Still feel as though you're screwed?"

Reno couldn't stand it. There was only one way out. "I already told you. I only said that because I thought someone else had snagged this prime spot by the Christmas tree."

"Uh-huh." Her skeptical squint made her disbelief plain. "Right. And next year I plan to march in the parade nude."

"Nude? Mmm. Sounds good to me." So did getting out of here. It was the least he owed Nate. Wrapping his arm around Rachel's waist, Reno pulled her to him with his best caveman-style move. He loved the way she met him toe to toe, with no reservations. "Had enough of the Kismet Christmas tree? Because I have a party for two in mind, and it's starting right now."

"Well, I think that's everything," Nate said.

At the sound of the trunk slamming, Angela glanced up from beside Nate's car, where she'd been daydreaming in the frosty, starlit night. After the big finale of the Kismet town

Christmas tree lighting, she'd entrusted Kayla to her (now reunited) mom and dad, handed over her own sensibly sized overnight bag to Nate, and gotten herself prepared for the trip ahead.

Featuring a hotel reservation with one king bed. *One!*

"Great." Staunching her smile, she watched with deliberate insouciance as Nate trekked from the rear of his Chevette to the passenger side. "I guess we'd better get going then."

"Hold your horses. I have one more thing to give you."

His grin made her giddy. "Oh? What's that?"

"A proper sendoff, of course."

Nate stopped at her side of the car, close enough that she could catch a whiff of the holly berry soap she'd bought him at the mall. Close enough that she could reach out and touch him. Close enough that she really, really wanted to.

No. She had to play it cool. That was her plan, and Angela was definitely the kind of person who stuck to a plan.

"What did you have in mind?" she asked. "As a sendoff?"

He angled his head as if she'd asked him how many ice cubes he'd like in his beer. "Opening the door for you. Duh."

"Oh. Of course." Disappointment assailed her.

With a flourish, Nate crunched down two more footsteps worth of snow, then opened the car door with a squeal. In the light from her parents' condo, his face appeared familiar and exotic all at once—probably because she was still getting used to imagining it on top of his fully naked body, a fantasy Angela had been entertaining more and more often lately.

Including just a few minutes ago.

He gestured gallantly with one gloved hand. "After you."

A hot flush climbed beneath her turtleneck. "Um, thanks."

Angela slid onto the cold vinyl seat, fastened her seat belt, then waited for Nate to join her on the driver's side. He passed along the front of the car, his profile and his familiar way of moving suddenly seeming rough and tough and dangerous.

She was going away on an overnight trip with a man! Angela realized all at once. She was embarking on a journey where *one* king-size bed awaited them at the end. At the thought, her whole body tingled. It had been a long time since she'd felt a man's hands on her . . . a long time since she'd wanted that. With Nate, she wanted more than a simple touch. She wanted everything.

Too bad she was being so adept at playing it cool.

"Ready?" He clasped the steering wheel, having started the engine. It chugged in that way it had—that coughing, sputtering, my-parts-are-from-the-junkyard kind of way. "Here we go."

With his customary caution, Nate backed them out of their parking space, then sent them zooming along at two miles below the legal speed limit toward the freeway. His hands mesmerized her. So did his face. And his legs. With the help of the streetlights flashing overhead, she could see the muscle tighten in his thigh when he pressed the accelerator. That tiny motion was enough to make Angela feel a little bit exhilarated.

Too bad playing it cool was *definitely* the way to go.

She inhaled and squirmed, making the vinyl seat squeak.

Nate glanced her way. "Everything okay?"

Just the way he said it—so solicitously, so manfully, so *respectfully*—made her feel breathless. For a long time now, Nate had been her best friend. He'd been there hours after Kayla had been born. He'd been there when she'd cried at the bus stop after seeing her daughter off for her first day of kindergarten. He'd been there when Angela had been hired at KHS, when she'd struggled with the school bureaucracy, when she'd dated other men in an effort to find out what she'd been missing.

It turned out that what she'd been missing was Nate. No other man was like him. No other man even came close.

"Pull over," Angela said in a tiny voice.

"What?" His startled gaze met hers. "Why?"

"Pull over," she repeated, more firmly this time. "Please."

He did. He was just that kind of guy. He didn't need a

reason—he only needed to know that she wanted him to do it. For a standup guy like Nate, that was enough.

Looking worried, he steered his Chevette to the bus station parking lot, right at the edge of the highway. When Angela spotted the big lighted Greyhound sign outside, she almost laughed out loud at the serendipity of it all.

"What's wrong?" Nate asked. "Did you forget something?"

She looked at him. Sweet, sweet Nate. How had she waited so long to get here? How had she waited so long for him?

Angela nodded, feeling more certain with every heartbeat. "I did forget something. I forgot to tell you something."

"What?"

She unbuckled. "Playing it cool is overrated."

Nate stared. "You're going to have to buckle that again when we get going. You know I don't move the car if everyone isn't safely buckled up."

"I know." With a sense of destiny, Angela glanced at the bus station sign. "This is the last place I saw you before you left for Scorpions' training camp. Did you know that?"

"Are you sure you're feeling all right? Maybe you had too many candy canes. Maybe I should take you back."

"I sat right in my car, parked way back by the Dumpsters, and watched you get on the bus. Then I cried my eyes out."

"You cried?" Nate looked stricken. "Why? I mean, I don't even get what you were doing here, really, but . . . why?"

She looked straight at him. "Because I was afraid you'd never come back. I was afraid you'd go away and become a football star, and you'd forget all about everyone in Kismet."

Nate scoffed. "Fat chance. I wasn't good enough."

"You *are* good enough! Don't ever say that."

"Okay, okay!" Sheepishly, he held up his hands. He gazed through the windshield into the night, toward the taillights whizzing past on the freeway beyond the overpass. "Sorry."

For a minute, they lapsed into silence, Angela caught up in memories of the girl she'd been (and lost) and of the man she'd watched leave (and then found). Most people weren't as lucky as they were. Which was why she felt brave enough to go on.

"If you still want Rachel Porter," Angela said, "if she's still your dream girl, then you'd better just let me out right here. Right now. Because I don't think I can stand watching you walk away again, knowing that you might forget me."

Wearing an astonished look, Nate stopped her. "Angela—"

"Wait. Let me finish. Please." She sucked in a deep breath, feeling herself quake with the immensity of everything she'd left unsaid all these years. "I've waited and waited, and I've tried to move on, but all I ever really wanted was you, Nate. I love you. It's silly and it's crazy, but it's true. All true."

"Angela. Oh Angela." Nate shook his head. "I—"

He was turning her down! Panicking, Angela scooted sideways across her bucket seat. Waaay sideways, so that her shoulder bunched against the door and frosted-over window.

"But you know, if you don't return those feelings," she said hastily, "I completely understand. It's only natural that we would enjoy a certain closeness after all this time, but if you don't feel anything more than that—if you'd, say, rather get frisky with Betty Crocker or Eleanor Roosevelt—"

"Huh?"

"—then there's nothing I can or should or want to do to get in the way of that. Honestly. As they say, the course of true love never did run smooth, right?" She gave a choked laugh. "I can hardly expect to compete with an actual California glamazon, can I? I mean, I wear granny nightgowns, for Pete's sake!"

"I love your granny nightgowns. They're sexy."

"And I say things like 'for Pete's sake,' too! No, I understand where you're coming from, Nate." Distraught, Angela took off her hat and kneaded it in her hands. "My only excuse is that I let the sentimentality of the season get to me. My imagination ran wild, that's all. Everyone has an ideal, and I'm not yours. I'm not one of those girls. I don't wear miniskirts and I do understand grammar. I actually like it. Believe me, sometimes I *want* to get utterly wanton. I *want* to add random quotation marks to phrases that don't need them. But I can't, Nate. I'm just not that girl. I'm not one of your dream girls."

"I know." His voice sounded indescribably sincere. "And you never, ever will be one of my dream girls either."

Angela straightened. "You don't have to rub it in!"

"No!" Nate's face beamed at hers, bright with what appeared to be . . . hope? Joy? *Love*? "Will you quit talking for a second? You're confusing me. That's not what I mean. Don't you get it?" He leaned toward her, earnest and intent. "Those dream girls were all just stand-ins. Until I found you."

"Wha . . . ?" Oh no. He'd reduced her to incoherence.

"They weren't real. *You* were! You are. I was just too bone-headed to realize it. Until you left me there to make fudge all alone and went out with Patrick the Prick. On a Wednesday! Then the light finally went on." Nate hung his head, his crazy eyebrows briefly catching her eye. "I wanted to prove to myself that I was really over my nerdy past. I thought that snagging a girl like Rachel Porter would help me do that. But it can't."

Angela hardly dared to breathe. "It . . . can't?"

"No. Well, maybe it could. For a while . . ." Dreamily, he stared at the dashboard, apparently lost in macho reveries.

"Nate!"

"But that wouldn't really be a solution, because I'm the only one who's bugged by my geek past. *You* aren't."

"Of course I'm not." Angela scooted the merest millimeter closer to him. "I joined the Calculus Club with you, remember?"

"I remember." He gave her a goofy grin. "So I guess what I mean is . . ." Nate paused, darting a glance at her as he drew in a deep breath. "If you think you could be happy with a guy who wants to dedicate all the rest of his days to making you smile"—he broke off, gleefully pointing at her—"yeah, just like that! Then I'm your man. I mean I *want* to be your man. Please?"

"Nate, I—"

"Angela, I love you. From now on, you're *it* for me."

Sniffling, Angela scooted the final few inches to meet him. She bumped her head on the Chevette's rearview mirror, but it was worth it to see the unabashed joy in Nate's face—and feel that joy reflected in her own unstoppable smile. "Yes. I feel very sure that I would like that. I'd like that very much."

"Oh, Angela—"

Their first official kiss (as a real official couple) was silly, jubilant, and tender . . . all at the same time. It felt to Angela as though she'd waited a very long while to feel Nate's mouth against hers this way—to feel free enough to kiss him with all the passion she'd been holding back thanks to her plan. Her ridiculous, misguided, abandoned plan.

Nate lifted his head. "Wow. Where did you learn to—"

"You can't learn passion like this." She pressed her lips to his again, straining across the Chevette's console to meet him. Blissfulness soared through her. "Not even with a very good teacher. It has to come straight from the heart."

"I dunno. I know some pretty good teachers."

"Be quiet, please, and kiss me some more."

"Yes, ma'am. My pleasure."

After a few long minutes, while the windows fogged up and the little clunky car rocked and traffic zoomed by outside, Nate and Angela lost themselves in another amazing kiss. It wasn't innovative, and it wasn't inventive, but it was heartfelt. It was perfect. Perfect for the two of them . . . together.

At last their mouths popped apart. Nate appeared dazzled. Angela knew she must look the same way—disheveled, crazy-haired, and breathing hard. Her sweater was hiked up to her rib cage, her body felt tingly again, and both of them breathed rapidly.

"So . . ." Nate grinned at her. "I'm not sure if I still need to go to the crafts fair to sell my nest egg or not—"

"That was for *me*? Oh Nate! Please don't sell Rudolph."

"But do you still want to go to Grand Rapids with me?"

"Go to where the king-size bed is? Where we'll be all alone?" Angela swiveled to buckle her seat belt. "While the babysitting is already booked for two whole days?"

Eagerly, Nate nodded.

"Yes I do," Angela told him. "Floor it, baby!"

Chapter Thirty-Two

Sprawled on the floor of Reno's living room, bathed in weak but cheery midmorning Michigan sunlight, Rachel gazed up at the Christmas tree she and Reno had decorated together two days ago. It was considerably smaller than the official Kismet tree that had inspired them, but it was prettier and (even better) it was located in a much more private, more enjoyable spot.

Yawning, Rachel stretched. She and Reno had spent the whole weekend holed up together—now that Tom Wright had decamped for his retirement condo with his happy wife, Judy—subsisting on hot cocoa, the neighbors' gifts of Christmas goodies, and delivery pizza, going gaga for each other in a way that she had never experienced before and likely would never experience again.

Now it was Sunday morning, and Rachel could feel the rest of the world about to intrude. Resisting the idea, she snuggled more deeply into the double sleeping bag Reno had spread on the floor. She hadn't expected it to be comfortable but it had been, cocooning them together with the scents of fir tree and cinnamon sticks, with twinkling lights glowing above them on the tree.

With a smile, Rachel sent an angel ornament swinging on a low-hanging branch. She watched as it sparkled. "You know, I have the weirdest feeling something wonderful just happened."

"Something wonderful *did* just happen." Lazily, Reno smiled as he trailed his hand up her naked thigh. "You were on top of me, and I was touching you"—he moved his hand a languid few inches—"right here, and then you did that twisty maneuver—"

"I don't mean—oh!—*that*." Giggling, Rachel squirmed.

"I do. And I intend to mean it again and again and again."

With a sigh, Rachel watched Reno as he levered himself on his elbow and gazed into her face, looking happier than she could remember seeing him. Coming here, getting away from everyone else, had done something to him—it had loosened him up in a way that no amount of bourbon-laced eggnog could have done.

Although they'd tried that, too. Last night, while snuggling on the sofa to watch *A Christmas Story* together, both of them laughing over Ralphie's adventures and indulging in holiday sentimentality in a way neither of them would have admitted, they'd tried eggnog laced with bourbon. And rum balls made with Captain Morgan's best. And fruitcake that must have been soaked in eighty-proof brandy. None of those tipsy treats had made Rachel feel as drunk with contentment as she did right now.

"I love Christmas," she said, hugging him. "I don't think I'll ever look at the holidays the same way again."

"Me either." Reno lowered his head to kiss her. His mouth felt wonderful, his jawline raspy with unshaven beard stubble. His body felt taut above hers. They fit together like the heirloom nesting ornaments he'd shown her—collectibles from a Wright relative whose passion had been traveling. "For one thing, I've never gotten lucky beneath a Christmas tree before."

"You're kidding. Poor baby."

"*You* have?"

"Well . . ." Rachel hadn't. Although now that she had, she could verify that making love in the glow of shimmering lights and vivid ornaments had a romantic charm that was hard to beat. Admitting as much would have put a serious crimp in her rebellious image though. So all she said was, "Not until you."

Whoops. With Reno, it seemed she couldn't hold anything back. Except for one very crucial part of her recent past—her encounter with Tyson and Alayna and her subsequent job meltdown.

She couldn't tell Reno about that though. What would he think of her? Stripped of her fabulous job and super-cool L.A. life, Rachel was just another girl. Just another girl with nothing to make her special except a knack for creativity and an apparent skill at helping out people with their problems. But that was something she liked to do. That wasn't a quality that people tended to brag about on their dating-site profiles.

Busty brunette single woman, overflowing with helpfulness and a talent for seam-ripping, seeks sensitive, 25-40-year-old man for long walks in the snow and occasional tree-trimming.

"Rachel, there's something I want you to do for me."

At Reno's serious tone, Rachel started from her reverie. She gazed up at him, then ran her hands reassuringly over his shoulders. It was hard not to be distracted by the yummy muscles she found there, but she did her best. "Sure, what is it?"

He glanced away, his throat working with effort. Whatever it was that Reno needed, it was hard for him to ask for it.

"Really," she urged. "Whatever it is—"

"Help me finish decorating for the Glenrosen holiday lights contest." Reno blurted the words, appearing startled to hear them come from his lips. "I'm way behind this year—"

"Because of me?" She felt (a little bit) delighted.

"—and if I'm going to have any shot at winning again, I need to get cracking. I . . ." He hesitated once more. "I don't think I can do it all by myself and still finish in time."

Rachel grinned. "Does this mean I can use your big ladder?"

"You've got a danger fixation."

"I'll take that as a yes."

"It might be fun to do it together." Unexpected vulnerability softened Reno's chiseled, athletic features. "You know, as a team, like when we dug out Mrs. Bender."

"I heard you the first time." She kissed him. "Let's go."

Giving Reno a playful shove, Rachel rolled out from beside him and got off the sleeping bag. She caught him watching her as she stood, bare and freewheeling, to reach for her clothes.

"If you keep doing that, we'll never make it," she said.

"I was just thinking . . . if you tell anybody I asked you for help, I'll permanently boycott that special maneuver you like."

"Threats now?" Rachel raised her eyebrow. "Nice try, pal. But I know you like that maneuver as much as I do."

"Guilty." Reno got to his feet to give her another kiss—a deep, slow, thorough kiss that told Rachel she wasn't the only one who could be set off-kilter by a vulnerable look or a special request. He broke off, eager as a little boy. "You'll never guess what I have planned for the rooftop display!"

"Oh yeah? You wanna bet?"

At her words, that familiar competitive spark flared between them. Rachel felt enlivened by it . . . connected by it. Reno did, too, if his answering grin was anything to judge by.

"First one dressed gets to hang the new LED lights."

"You're on!"

They had never dressed faster—at least not while in each other's company. Rachel scrambled into her jeans and sweater and boots, doing her best not to be distracted by Reno's cheating tactics of parading around in all his perfect-rear-view glory while he pretended to search for his pants and flannel shirt.

A few minutes later . . . "I win!" they both shouted.

Rachel looked at Reno. Adorably bundled up, he gazed back at her. And in that instant, as in so many others, she knew the whole truth. As long as she and Reno were together, they both won. That was the sweetest victory of all.

Chapter Thirty-Three

It snowed the day of Kayla's Christmas pageant. Big, fluffy flakes drifted down to coat Kismet's trees and buildings and houses, creating a winter wonderland that was a million times more authentic than anything Rachel had ever created for Alayna at her beachfront house. Despite the extravagant resources she'd had at her disposal then, Rachel figured some things just couldn't be faked. Like pre–Christmas snowfall. Authentic love. And triple-ply cashmere, knit into a sweater as soft as a dream.

Hey, a girl had to stay warm somehow.

Fortunately, the blustery weather didn't keep away audience members for the Kismet Elementary School holiday pageant that night. When Rachel arrived, shivering with cold but excited, the hallway leading to the school gymnasium was packed with people. In L.A., she'd seen less well-attended nightclub openings.

Unwinding her scarf, she craned her neck for a glimpse of Reno in his Santa costume but saw only familiar friends and neighbors, all of them eager to witness the holiday spectacle Kayla's classmates had planned. Evidently, connections ran deep in Kismet. Nobody wanted to miss this annual event.

Rachel spotted Angela waiting by the gym door. Row upon row of folding chairs and bleachers stood visible in the room behind her as she nervously twisted a program in her hands, gazing out over the noisy crowd. People made their way to their seats, passing by her with nods and smiles and comments, but Angela only fanned herself with her program and kept searching.

Rachel hurried to her. "Hi! Sorry I'm late." She hugged her friend. "You look worried. Is Kayla okay? Is she nervous?"

"No, not a bit nervous! Kayla practiced her part with Nate, so she's got it down cold." Laughing, Angela squeezed Rachel's arm, then leaned in. "I'm the one who's a wreck. I'm a bona fide stage mother, Rachel! What if I scar Kayla for life somehow?"

"You won't. You love her too much for that."

"Easy for you to say."

"Not really. Love is a new revelation for me. Come on."

Beneath Angela's curious gaze, Rachel led the way into the gym. The whole place buzzed with anticipation and laughter, along with a lineup of parents-turned-amateur photographers and a squeaky rendition of "Santa Claus Is Coming to Town" performed by the Kismet Middle School band. It was, quite possibly, the least sophisticated holiday event Rachel had ever attended.

She loved it. She loved the kids, dressed in pint-size costumes and waving to their camcorder-wielding parents as they shuffled self-consciously onstage wearing crooked grins. She loved the music, piped out with vigor by the KMS band. She loved the storyline, performed in fits and starts by the adorable first-grade players. She loved Reno, yukking it up as Santa Claus beside Nate the Elf. She loved the curtain calls when the show was over and the whole place exploded into applause.

There was so much love here, Rachel realized. Nobody was perfect—as evidenced by the little boy portraying a Christmas camel, who'd forgotten his lines and decided to improvise. But nobody minded. Nobody expected flawlessness. Looking around at the whooping, foot-stomping, down-home audience, Rachel realized that as far as she could tell, everyone here just wanted to see their loved ones have their moments in the spotlight. They just wanted a chance to applaud the people they cared about so much.

Rachel did, too. That was why, when Reno lumbered out in full red-hat-wearing Santa Claus regalia, still playing his part to the utmost ho-ho-ho for the students and parents, she was the most exuberant applauder of all. And that was why, when Reno finally made his fake-bellied way over to her corner of the gym, where Rachel had been noshing on Christmas cookies and punch with the other audience members, she had the courage to do what she should have done from the very start.

"Reno. You were amazing!" Smiling at him, she touched the red velour arm of his Santa suit, wanting to hold his hand but not prepared to act as a stand-in for Mrs. Claus just yet. "There's something I've got to tell you. Something about me."

"Uh-oh." Above his snowy faux-whiskers, Reno's green eyes sparkled. "You have a thing for Santa. I *knew* it! Kinky."

"No, it's not that." Although he did look really cute. Maybe because he'd been so darned sweet with all the kids, letting the first-graders and their smaller siblings whisper Christmas wishes in his ear, maul his outfit while climbing on his lap, and douse him with sticky spilled punch. "It's . . . something I've been meaning to tell you for a while now."

With no warning at all, her throat closed up. Feeling a panic to match the sensation, Rachel glanced at the treat she'd been nibbling. She tossed it away. For a moment this vital, she could not be sugar-buzzing on red- and green-iced Christmas cookies.

"It's about my life in L.A.," she began . . . but couldn't go on. She shifted in her boots, glancing from one clump of eager audience members to the next, feeling overheated and nervous in the midst of the boisterous crowd. "It's . . . well, nobody here in Kismet knows this about me yet, but—"

"It's okay." Reno caught her hand, looking concerned. He

angled his body sideways, keeping their conversation private amid the chattering people. "You can tell me anything."

Ha. That's what her dad had said. And her mom, too, several times. Rachel still hadn't had the strength to admit the truth to either of them. But Reno . . . well, maybe he would understand.

Maybe he would still want her . . . afterward.

"Okay. I had this big important stylist job in L.A., right? I worked with all kinds of celebrities, from Alayna Panagakos to that big blond rocker who won the last *American Idol* competition to—well, you name them, I probably dressed them. I had a big house and a fancy car, and invitations to everything that mattered. I was *major* in L.A. I mean seriously—nothing opened in town if I wasn't there for the red carpet. Ask anyone."

She glanced at him, feeling her heart pound crazily as she gauged his reaction to her former fabulousness.

Looking perplexed, Reno nodded. "I know. Nate told me—he Googled you. Ever since you made it big in Hollywood, you've been a local legend around here. Kind of like me."

Reassuringly, he rubbed her back, probably sensing her anxiety. Smiling at him, praying the good times between them wouldn't come to an end once Reno realized what a gigantic washed-up failure she was, Rachel sucked in a deep breath.

She might as well just lay it on the line.

"Well, now I'm nobody. Most of my clients fired me, and the ones who didn't have been dodging my phone calls for weeks."

There. She'd said it. Feeling weirdly light-headed, Rachel glanced at Reno. He didn't appear shocked or appalled, so she went on. "Now nobody will hire me. Nobody will take a meeting with me. Nobody will even return my calls! And it's all because of the stupid lapse of judgment I made when I found my biggest client—Alayna—in bed with my boyfriend."

Ooh, you're a wild one, Pookie. Yeah, oh yeah . . .

Shamefaced, Rachel bit her lip. She'd put off this moment

for so long. It wasn't easy confessing that she was both unemployable and unlovable . . . at least to some people.

But Reno only stared, then gritted his teeth in a menacing manner that seemed wholly unfit for a jolly guy like Santa Claus. "Your boyfriend? You mean Tyson-Like-The-Chicken?"

Rachel nodded. "I was hurt! I was upset. That's my only excuse. I obviously wasn't thinking straight after I found them together, and I wanted to get back at them both for hurting me. They were really, really mean. That's why I did . . . what I did."

Reno angled his head in interest—almost in admiration. He didn't seem the least bit horrified at the prospect of her wanting to exact a little revenge. "What did you do?"

Could it be possible that Reno *didn't* think she was a total loser? Emboldened by his indignation on her behalf and his curiosity, Rachel continued. "I outfitted Alayna and Tyson in a horrible pair of revenge outfits for her big birthday bash."

She bit her lip, waiting for Reno's response.

Nada. Maybe he didn't grasp the true awfulness of it.

"I mean, they were wearing Naugahyde," she elaborated, wanting to make sure he understood the enormity of her actions. "Lace. Pleather. Man-capris and a bustle. All at the same time!"

"That doesn't sound so bad."

"It was on TV! And the Internet. And magazines, too. Because of that outfit, people thought Alayna was headed for rehab."

"She probably *was* headed for rehab."

"Still." Rachel bit her lip. She wasn't exactly proud of this but . . . "The incident made the CNN crawl. My first time."

Reno's mouth quirked. "Congratulations."

"You don't understand! I'm ruined in L.A. I screwed up in a major way. I'm trying to fix it, but I don't know if I can. I haven't so far." Drawing in another deep breath, Rachel faced him squarely, ready to admit the worst part. "I might," she said solemnly, "be just a regular woman for the rest of my life."

For a minute, the only sounds were conversations nearby, the intermittent tooting of one of the trumpet players showing off his mastery of "Jingle Bells," and shouting children.

Then Reno stepped closer, his jawline obscured by his fluffy Santa beard and his forehead covered by his red Santa hat. He cupped her cheek in his hand, then shook his head.

"*You* could never be just a regular woman."

"I am! It's already happened!" As proof, Rachel frantically offered up her sleeve. "Look. I wore this for *comfort* instead of style. Yes, it's cashmere, but it's a slippery slope. What if—"

"You could never be just a regular woman . . . to me."

Hardly daring to breathe, Rachel quit plucking at her sleeve. The soft knit slipped from her fingers as rapidly as her rising hopes soared. Maybe foolishly. "Really?"

"Really."

"Then you're not . . . disappointed?"

"In you?"

Wordlessly, Rachel nodded. The people around them were a blur, as inconsequential now as a bikini in December.

Reno gave her a sturdy look. Even (or especially) dressed as Old Saint Nick, he appeared rock solid. Trustworthy. She knew that whatever he said to her would be absolutely reliable.

"The only way I could be disappointed in you is if you caved and went back to Tyson-Like-The-Chicken."

"Reno! I'm serious."

"So am I. I want—"

"Hey, Santa Claus!" someone shouted from nearby, waving to catch Reno's attention. "Can we get some pictures over here?"

Rachel and Reno turned. One of the camera-wielding parents gestured to "Santa," an entreating grin on his face. He pointed to the children he'd arrayed in a holiday pose. "You game?"

"Sure." Glancing back at Rachel, Reno squeezed her hands. He gave her a wink. "Duty calls. I'll be back in a minute."

And he would have been. Except that one photo op turned into two, which morphed into a camcorder vignette. Before long, Rachel's erstwhile Santa had been fully commandeered for a series of photos, holiday wishes, and jolly conversations.

Leaving him to it, Rachel gazed around the gym. The PTSO had decorated the place with green and red streamers, with joyful holiday pictures pinned up beside the cartoon posters exhorting kids to exercise and eat enough fruits and vegetables. The basketball hoops contained Christmas balls of plastic holly. It was a very ordinary room, but Kismet had made it special.

Just like Reno had made her feel special.

He *wasn't* appalled at what she'd done, Rachel realized. Or at what she'd lost. He *hadn't* run the other way when she'd admitted the Naugahyde and pleather. He'd heard her confession and then stood by her. To Rachel, that meant the world.

Especially coming from someone as honest as Reno.

Feeling lighter than she'd ever imagined—now that she'd unloaded her secret at last—she hugged herself. A grin broke over her face, goofy and relieved. She was helpless to stop it, no matter how ridiculous it made her seem. Reno still cared about her! If that didn't merit a smile, nothing did.

A familiar-looking blond man near the refreshments table caught her eye. Still wearing her grin, Rachel headed toward him.

She touched his arm, then stuck out her hand. "You must be Nate. I think it's about time we met. I'm Rachel Porter."

He turned. "Rachel Porter!" His grin was infectious, his handshake firm and a bit awed. "How did you know it was me?"

"The other elf was much smaller. You stood out."

"Oh that." Laughing, Nate gestured at his costume. He wiggled the curly toes of his elf shoes, not looking at all like a man who would repeatedly ditch her or their opportunities to meet each other. "You did work on this, didn't you? Thanks."

"Angela's measurements helped. We kept missing each other."

"I know. My bad." Beneath his green felt hat, Nate's earnest gaze softened. "Rachel Porter. I can't believe it."

"Did we go to school together? I think I remember you."

"Oh, you don't have to say that." He blushed, waving off her comment. "I know Reno probably coached you, but it's okay."

"No, I . . ." Squinting, Rachel recalled a burly student with a penchant for jokes. "Do you still have that Boyz II Men T-shirt? You could probably get a fortune for it on eBay now."

Nate shook his head, still seeming fascinated. "Nah. I figure memories ought to stay with their original owners."

"A sentimentalist, huh?" Liking him immediately, Rachel noticed a volunteer unwrapping a platter of treats behind him. "Oh look! Mini pecan tartlets. Would you like one?"

"Ugh." He made a face. "You *like* those?"

"Yes! They're my favorite. You don't?"

"Can't stand them."

Speculatively, Nate watched as Rachel selected a tart, bit into it, then moaned rapturously.

He winced, appearing horrified. "That gooey filling is like supersweet boogers studded with nuts. Yuck."

"Ha. You're not scaring me away." Rachel finished her first tiny tart, then snatched another one. "These are the *best*."

Dubiously, Nate wrinkled his nose. "I can't believe you like those. You like pecan pie filling, don't like beer, don't like pickup trucks, and you serve cold food in December. Plus you like guys with shiny fingernails, and I'm not going there." He shook his head. "Dude, it's a good thing Reno's efforts to fix us up with each other were so sucktastic, right? Because we are clearly not meant for each other."

Holding her free hand beneath her chin in an indelicate maneuver designed to catch wayward pecan tart crumbs,

Rachel stared at him. Hastily, she chewed and swallowed. "Reno's what?"

"You know, his mission to fix us up with each other. On dates. Romantically." With a suggestive expression, Nate waggled his eyebrows. One of them looked sort of . . . bald. "That's why you two have been spending so much time together, right? You don't have to pretend not to know. He's been dedicated to it night and day for weeks now. That's Reno—once he promises to help someone, he's unstoppable. But now that I'm totally in love with Angela—hey, here she is!—I don't need Reno's help anymore."

Angela arrived at his side. "Need Reno's help with what?"

While Rachel boggled at Nate's revelation, Angela levered up, kissed her gigantic elf boyfriend, then beamed at him. They looked like a couple all right. A deliriously happy couple. A couple who, if Rachel's befuddled observations were correct, had just recently made their relationship, um, *intimate*, and couldn't quite keep their hands off each other now.

"Nate was just telling me how Reno has been trying to fix up me and Nate," Rachel said. "On dates. Romantically."

Angela blanched. That was when Rachel knew it was true.

Chapter Thirty-Four

In that moment, Rachel remembered warning Reno—jokingly—not to bother trying to set her up with anyone, because dating was a lost cause for her since her breakup with Tyson-Like-The-Chicken. If only she'd known *he* hadn't been joking. Not a bit.

"Well, maybe not so much *fix us up together* as babysit you for me, is how it turned out in the end," Nate said. "That's how Reno put it anyway. 'Who do you think has been babysitting Rachel Porter for you?' he asked me, and it was totally true."

"Reno said that?" Rachel asked. "He said *babysitting*?"

Angela's warning look was totally lost on Nate.

He nodded. "Because I was too afraid to meet you."

"Afraid to meet me?" Rachel wanted to get this straight. Still stuck on the uncomfortable notion of Reno *babysitting* her for Nate, she reviewed her time so far in Kismet. "So that's why you were never there!" she realized. "At the Christmas tree farm, the Glenrosen decorating party, the costume fitting—"

Nate nodded again. "Those were all the times Reno was supposed to make sure we *got it on*." He said this last in an exaggeratedly sexy voice, then laughed. "But I couldn't make it, and the whole time, I was afraid some assclown from The

Big Foot would snatch you up first"—he smiled at a worried-looking Angela, seeming oblivious to the *stop talking* look she gave him—"so Reno offered to keep tabs on my dream girl for me."

Meaningfully, Angela jabbed her elbow sideways.

"I mean my *former* dream girl. That's you, Rachel, FYI." Nate gave her an endearing, semiembarrassed look. "So I knew I didn't have to worry, because Reno is my best friend. I don't think he ever let you out of his sight, that's for sure."

Because he really was *trying to fix me up with you*, Rachel realized in a daze. *Because he was busy babysitting me . . . for another man*. Reno hadn't been with her because he'd cared about her. Or because he'd liked spending time with her. He'd done it because he'd made a commitment to his dating-challenged friend.

And everyone in Kismet knew Reno kept his promises.

With no warning at all, Rachel recalled the first time she and Reno had slept together. *This can only be sex between us, okay?* she'd asked him, trying (misguidedly as it turned out) to protect him. *Just sex*, he'd agreed almost instantly. *It's probably better that way, given the circumstances*.

At the time, Rachel had thought Reno had been referring to the fact that she'd be leaving Kismet soon. Not to the fact that he was only doing romantic research on her likes and dislikes, preparing to offer her up as a date for his happy-go-lucky friend like a trout on a lakeside B & B's special of the day.

With a queasy feeling, Rachel imagined Reno kissing her—then reporting back to Nate. *She likes soft, slow kisses*. Reno touching her. *She likes a firm, sensual grip*. Reno laughing with her. *She's completely gullible, Nate. No worries*.

Stricken, Rachel glanced at the one person who possessed no ability to lie whatsoever. "Angela, did you know about this?"

Her friend's cheeks bloomed pink. "Well, yes. But I—"

"But *you* liked the idea!" All at once, everything became

clear to Rachel. "You liked that Reno was keeping me busy, because that meant you could make your move on Nate!"

Looking at them together, it was as obvious as black pants, a white shirt, and a classic trench coat as wardrobe staples.

Guiltily, Angela hunched beside Nate. "Well . . . sort of."

"Angela!" Nate appeared elated. "You schemed to get me?"

"Um—"

"I'll never need one of Reno's idiot-proof seduction plans again," Nate crowed. "I have a woman who *really* wants me."

Idiot-proof seduction plans. Rachel guessed that's what Reno had been cooking up for Nate and her. A plan to get her away from Reno and into his best friend's arms.

All the interest he'd shown, all the admiration he'd volunteered . . . They'd all been fake. As fake as his feelings.

And Rachel, too gullible (again) to tell the difference between someone who cared about her and someone who was just using her—just laughing at her, like Tyson and Alayna!—had bought the whole scheme—hook, line, and sinker. She'd never doubted Reno's feelings for her for a second.

"I have to leave," Rachel said.

"Really? Bummer. I thought it was fun talking to you."

Helplessly, Rachel gazed at Nate, wounded by the merry tone of his words. Was she just a joke to *everyone*? The latest Kismet punch line? He and Angela turned unfocused, blurred by the tears swimming in her eyes. Rachel didn't know where they'd come from. Surely she was inured to heartbreak by now.

"Tell Reno he's off the hook." She pulled her coat closer, suddenly chilled. "I'm not interested in being set up with anyone. Especially the way you people do it in Kismet."

"Rachel, wait," Angela said. "You don't understand."

"Yeah, wait, Rachel," Nate insisted. "There's more—"

But Rachel couldn't wait. She couldn't wait to leave, couldn't wait to push through the crowd of curious, gawking onlookers . . . couldn't wait to get herself back to L.A., where at least people were up-front about breaking your heart.

And nobody pretended you mattered to them when you didn't.

Half-blinded by camera flashes, Reno emerged from his Santa-style photo session with spots dancing before his eyes. He moved across the decorated gym away from the parents and children who'd enlisted him to pose for their holiday pictures, feeling a few ho-ho-hos still left in his belly even as people began to drift toward the exits, headed into the snowy evening.

Tonight, all was right with the world. Kayla had been fantastic in her Christmas pageant, Angela and Nate were a couple (so Reno no longer had to worry about his sister dating dreamy-eyed lowlifes or about his best friend's heartbreak at being deprived of Rachel), and Reno had almost caught up on his Glenrosen holiday lights competition groundwork, thanks to Rachel's help. The only thing better than all that was knowing Rachel was here somewhere, waiting with that special smile on her lips just for him—and probably a saucy grope, too.

Dating the town rebel definitely had its advantages.

Looking for that rebel now, Reno grinned and edged his way through a clump of proud grandparents comparing snapshots on their digital cameras. All he wanted now—all he *had* wanted ever since an elf-costumed Nate had confided backstage about his "life-changing" trip to Grand Rapids with Angela—was to be with Rachel. To show her the kind of man Reno could be once he wasn't skulking in the shadows trying to hide their relationship.

She'd caught him off guard with her confession about her life in L.A., but it had seemed important to her that she get it off her chest, so he'd listened. Now that that was over with—

There was no sign of Rachel anywhere.

Reno whipped off his Santa hat and hurried onward, moving past the hallway just in time to glimpse Rachel. She slipped through the big double doors leading outside, her dark glossy hair whipping over her shoulders as she moved quickly, headed for the school parking lot.

What the . . . ?

He caught up with her just as she skirted a grungy snow-bank, highlighted against the darkness by the school's light-ing, surrounded by first-graders and their parents but clearly apart from the trailing crowd. Rapidly, she strode forward in her sexy stiletto boots with her head down.

"Hey!" He grinned, touching her arm. "Wait up."

She turned. He was shocked to see tears in her eyes.

Rachel swabbed those tears with an impatient gesture, then squared off against him. "Why? Do you have someone else in mind for your idiot-proof seduction plan now that Nate's taken?"

Darkly, hands on her hips, Rachel waited for his reply.

But all Reno could manage was a trickle of dread, trailing up his spine like a backward icicle.

He'd felt he was home-free, now that Nate knew the truth. Reno had confessed everything to his friend backstage tonight, from his feelings for Rachel to his hopes that he could make her see the magic in Kismet and want to stay longer than "a while." But it hadn't occurred to him that there was a lot Rachel didn't know—and didn't understand—about how they'd come together.

Maybe he'd misheard her. "What did you say?"

"I'm sure I'm not such a desirable conquest," Rachel bit out, her gaze as intense as her sarcastic tone, "now that you know the truth about my 'fabulous life' in L.A., but—"

"I already knew about that." Interrupting, Reno waved off what seemed to be inconsequential details. "All of it."

Rachel looked as if he'd punched her. "You couldn't have."

"I knew before you told me tonight. Rachel, we get CNN here in the heartland," Reno told her, confounded at her sur-prise. "We get the E! channel, too. Everybody knows what happened to you. Everybody knows why you left L.A. the way you did."

Her tearful gaze widened. Shaking her head, she took a step backward. Reno had only meant to make her get to the point without leaving anything unspoken between them, but he could tell he'd hurt her. He came nearer, trying to hold her hand.

"We were being kind by not mentioning it! That's why—"

"Save your 'kindness' for someone else."

Defiantly, Rachel stuffed her hands in her pockets and swiveled. Her footsteps carried her ten feet down the icy sidewalk before Reno realized what was happening.

"Wait! Rachel." Doggedly, he followed with his idiotic Santa boots flopping in the snow. Why was this happening here? Now? When he was the least prepared? "I can explain."

"Explain how you never really cared about me, just like Tyson and Alayna and all my celebrity friends?" Rachel looked at him as if they'd never laughed together, never cut down a ferocious Christmas tree together, never scaled his eaves on his tallest ladder to hang holiday lights together. "No thanks."

She turned again. Fiercely, Reno grabbed her arm. He made her face him straight on, exactly the way he'd faced her on the morning after they'd first slept together—the morning when he'd realized that she knew him, inside and out. And he knew her.

She blinked up at him, stone-faced, rebellious to the last.

"Don't make this out to be more than it is," he said, striving for patience. "Do you think this has been easy for me, lying to my best friend while I sneaked around with you? Pretending I planned to give you to Nate at all?"

"*Give* me to him?" Rachel issued a hoarse laugh. "Angela was right. You *are* full of yourself, football star. No wonder you can't stop helping people. You need the applause."

Stung, Reno stared at her. "And you don't?"

For a long moment, tension stretched between them. A family wandered out of the Christmas pageant and headed toward the Kismet Elementary School parking lot, chattering animatedly.

Reno glanced at them, frowned, then released Rachel's arm.

"What were you planning to do when you came home for the holidays?" he demanded with inexorable logic, determined to make Rachel see reason. "You said yourself that you're jobless. I took your mind off things. The way I see it, I did you a favor."

Her hands came free in a jerky motion. "A *favor*?"

"A favor with a bonus. Several . . . bonuses."

Her scathing look could have melted an igloo.

Reno only raised his eyebrows. "You'd rather have spent the last few weeks holed up at your parents' house, surrounded by Christmas tchotchkes and stuffing down cookies with ranch dip?"

"Don't you *dare* make fun of our traditions!"

She was right. That was unfair of him.

But she was also frowning tearfully at him, making him realize how much his deception had hurt her, making him face the possibility that maybe Reno Wright *couldn't* fix everything with a dose of machismo and a pair of pliers. He couldn't stand it.

"Look, Nate and Angela are happy." Reno fisted his hands, willing himself to keep talking. "It all worked out in the end."

Rachel snorted. "I see where your dad gets it from."

"Gets what from?"

"His complete wrongheaded stubbornness! *That's* your excuse? *Nate and Angela are happy*? That's *it*?"

"For now." He gritted his teeth. The L.A. diva was back in full force, and she was a bitch to deal with. He wasn't equipped for this. Not tonight. Not when he'd finally allowed himself to hope for more between them. "If you'd just be reasonable—"

Rachel shook her head. Her lips tightened.

Reno swore. "I'm trying to make you understand that—"

"I understand." Again Rachel wiped a trailing tear from her cheek, but her stance was straight. Her gaze never wavered from his face. "I understand that I trusted you. Wholeheart-edly. Stupidly, I'll admit it. Only to have my heart broken again."

Looking at her, Reno felt filled with contrition.

But he also felt wronged. Misunderstood. And angry.

"Rachel, I never meant to—" *Break your heart.* He couldn't say that. He couldn't begin to believe it was true. Not when he knew the whole story—and she still didn't. "I risked every-thing to be with you! I put my friendship with Nate on the line, over and over again. Now you're telling me—"

"I'm telling you good-bye."

Before he could finish talking—before he could reason out what was happening and why—Reno felt Rachel's gloved hand touch his. He felt the rush of warm air that came with her, dis-placing the bitter cold for one sweet instant. He felt her lips touch his and knew an amazement he'd never expected . . . not while dressed as Santa. Not while having a ridiculous battle just twenty yards from the snowed-over playground swings.

He closed his eyes to savor the moment—the moment he hoped would turn everything around. No angry woman would kiss him.

"Good-bye, Reno," Rachel whispered.

By the time he opened his eyes, she was gone, treading down the sidewalk in the falling snow, moving farther into the dark, moving farther away from him with every second. An angry woman wouldn't kiss him, Reno realized. But a heart-broken one might.

At least she might kiss him once. Once to say good-bye.

In the distant parking lot, someone started their car, sending the muffled sounds of Christmas music wafting through their rolled-up windows. The tunes were cheery and warmhearted—exactly the opposite of the way Reno felt right now.

He'd been wrong about what he'd told Rachel tonight, he knew as he looked up into the empty sky, alone with his hands propped absurdly against his black vinyl Santa Claus belt.

There was one thing more disappointing than knowing the woman he loved had gone back to her asshole ex-boyfriend.

Watching her walk away from him.

But Reno would be damned if he'd chase her down again.

Why should he? Rachel hadn't batted an eyelash when Reno had told her how he'd risked his friendship with Nate—the most enduring friendship of his life. She hadn't let him explain. She hadn't listened to anything he'd said. And if Rachel couldn't see how much his friends meant to him, then she didn't understand him at all—no matter how much Reno had fooled himself into believing she did. Rachel Porter didn't know him.

Not really. Not the way he'd hoped. Deeply. Honestly. With no holds barred. It looked now as if no one ever would. Because Reno would be damned if he'd let himself be that vulnerable again.

He should have known better right from the start. Because the hard truth was, Reno had taken the pro-football spot Nate had wanted all those years ago. Then he'd taken Nate's dream girl. Having that dream girl walk away from him—just as he'd realized how much he needed her—was the very least Reno deserved.

Chapter Thirty-Five

Rachel spent all the remaining days leading up to Christmas trying to deny its existence altogether.

Just because she'd come home for the holidays didn't mean she had to participate in the holidays, did it? No! That's why she did her best to block out Christmas carols, turn a blind eye to decorations, and ignore the bell-ringing Santas on the Kismet street corners, all of whom reminded her (painfully) of Reno.

Instead Rachel spent her days watching *Made* reruns on TV, morosely munching through her depleted stock of protein bars, washing down their sawdusty nutrition with Diet Coke, and occasionally calling Mimi for support.

She kept the curtains closed—the better to block out the colorful sight of her parents' and their neighbors' holiday yard decorations. She wore her pilled, droopy, security-blanket cardigan almost exclusively and didn't even bat an eyelash when the mail carrier saw her in all its saggy-butted glory one day.

Rachel knew things were truly dire when she received a phone call from Tiana Zane, former member of the pop group Goddess, with an offer to dress her for a charity gala, and she could barely muster the energy to discuss Tiana's offer.

"It's a tiny event, Rachel. So I can't pay you much. In fact,

I probably won't be able to give you credit—my new manager advises against it. But there will be photographers there—"

"I'll do it," Rachel croaked. Why not? There was nothing left for her in Kismet. She had to rebuild her life somehow.

"You don't sound well. Do you have another cold?"

"A cold?" That's right. She'd been plagued with constant sniffles in L.A., Rachel recalled—as if her time there had been decades ago. It was sweet that someone still cared enough to ask about her health. Buoyed by a rush of fondness for Alayna's onetime singing partner, Rachel summoned up an uneven smile. "Maybe a little one. I have been feeling sort of—"

"Just make sure you don't sneeze on my gown. I have a part in the next Shyamalan film, and I don't want to get sick."

Oh. Dispiritedly, Rachel agreed to meet Tiana in L.A. in two weeks, then made a few more calls (because those weren't Christmas-related either, she told herself in bald defiance). She managed to line up two postholiday stylist jobs—one for a *One Life to Live* guest star and one for a director's nanny.

"She's applying for citizenship," the director's assistant barked over the phone. "So she has to look *très* American."

"I'll dress her in red, white, and blue," Rachel joked.

"Excellent idea. See you in one month." *Click.*

Disconnecting her call, Rachel frowned at her ancient cell phone—which had performed pretty well, come to think of it. Then she glanced at her bedroom's inspiration board, still sporting the fabric scraps and other items she'd pinned to it in preparation for her new "collection." Everything still looked amazing. It still looked . . . It looked as if all her lost hopes had been set askew and stabbed through the heart with pushpins.

Feeling queasy, Rachel got up—and almost tripped over her dad, who was passing through the hallway.

"Rachel! You're up." His gaze met hers, skimmed over her security-blanket cardigan, then softened. "I was just coming to get you. I need some help with my train set. How about it?"

If he'd asked her at any other time, Rachel would have

refused. After all, her father's train set was arranged beneath the Christmas tree right beside her mother's mini Christmas village—the one she'd painted and fired herself in ceramics class years ago. There was no avoiding Christmas when you were hunched under a fully decorated tree beside an Olde Sweet Shoppe replica tinkering with the caboose of the SantaLand Express.

But today she didn't refuse. Maybe she was tired of feeling embarrassed that her L.A. failures were so widely known. Or maybe she just wanted a little old-fashioned paternal affection after all her setbacks. Because Rachel took one look at her turtleneck-wearing father and caved. "Okay, Dad. Let's go."

But she regretted her moment of weakness immediately, as her first step into the living room almost made her stumble. "Please Come Home for Christmas" was playing on the stereo—the same song she and Reno had danced to after decorating his Christmas tree together. *A Christmas Story* was flickering on the TV—the same movie she and Reno had laughed to together. It was almost too much to bear . . . especially when her gaze fell on the fireplace mantel, where four hand-knitted stockings hung, each with a first name embroidered on its turned-down cuff.

Stomping toward them, Rachel grabbed the nearest. *Reno* winked up at her in green embroidery floss. "What's this?"

"Oh, that's just something I made." Airily, her mother bustled in, her hands full of wrapped gifts. She added them to the mountain piled beneath the Christmas tree, then straightened with one hand to her aching back. She surveyed the tableau with pride. "We invited Reno to drop by on Christmas Day—"

"You *what*?"

"—and we needed someplace to put his gifts, didn't we?"

"No, you didn't!" Rachel fisted the *Reno* stocking, her heart aching at the thought of him. She ripped it from its holder.

"Rachel!" her dad boomed. "Put that back."

"Reno doesn't deserve a stocking," Rachel protested.

"Your mother put a lot of work into that. Put it back."

She threw it on the floor instead. With relish, Rachel stomped it. She ground it beneath her boot. "There!"

Her parents both gawked at her.

"You need a timeout," her mother announced.

"You, young lady, are going to your room," her father said.

"I hate it here. I'm leaving!" Rachel cried. Feeling a sob well inside her, she ran to her bedroom and slammed the door.

By the time she emerged, toting a suitcase and making plans to come back for her nonessential luggage later, her mom and dad were nowhere to be seen. The living room stood glittering with Christmas lights and the humble-looking tree. A new Christmas carol played for an audience of no one. The foyer waited, empty except for its avalanche of holiday cards. The dining room was silent, outfitted with special green and red placemats and a mistletoe and holly centerpiece with fat scented candles that bore the unmistakable stamp of her mother's crafty side.

Frustrated, Rachel dragged her suitcase from room to room. It was no good leaving in a dramatic huff if no one saw you.

You need the applause, she remembered telling Reno.

And you don't? he'd shot back.

It turned out that both of them were right— and more alike than they'd wanted to admit. But that didn't matter now. Nothing did. Just like her spectacular exit wouldn't matter if she couldn't track down her parents. Miserable but with her head held high, Rachel stomped through a couple more rooms.

She finally located her parents outside in the snow, making last-minute adjustments to their holiday yard display. It wasn't dark yet, so the display didn't look like much, but her mom and dad fussed over the location and angle of each object anyway.

Rachel thumped her suitcase onto the porch, then regarded the scene through jaded eyes. There wasn't anything here for her. She'd turned into a laughingstock. Even her parents hadn't been truthful with her, and they were the least duplicitous people she knew. Her father had once driven fifteen miles to pay for an item he hadn't been charged for at the Bargain Hut.

"That looks exactly the same as it does every year."

Her mother glanced up. "Of course it does!"

"Why do you think we fuss with it?" her father asked.

Momentarily deterred from her drama-queen exit, Rachel shook her head. "You're making it look boring on purpose?"

"Not boring." Her dad spoke, but it was her mom who gazed at her with sympathy. "Traditional." He gestured at the yard. "Blow-up balloon snowmen are boring. Real handmade snowmen are traditional. All white lights are boring. Multi-colored lights are traditional. Huge plastic snowflakes are boring. White paper scissor-cut snowflakes are traditional. Get it?"

"No. Do you have this many rules for everything?"

Hmmm. That sounded familiar to her . . .

Oh yeah. *Reno*. He'd asked *her* that once, when she'd explained the difference between a classical and a traditional Christmas. Apparently she'd learned to spot the dividing lines from her parents—who watched her now with distinct wariness.

Wariness because . . . she was stomping off in a huff. Right.

"Rachel." Her mom stepped forward, bundled up in her old blue coat and the boots Rachel had borrowed to cut down Christmas trees with Reno and Kayla. "I know you're hurting—"

"But don't be so hasty this time!" her dad butted in. "You're always flying off the handle, Rachel. That's probably what got you in trouble with whatshername: Alayna Panagakos."

That did it. For a second, Rachel had almost buckled.

Instead she jerked up her chin. "Well, I hope you both have a"—*Merry Christmas*, her stupid sappy heart volunteered, but she ruthlessly squashed the sentiment—"happy week. I'm leaving."

Then she hauled her suitcase off the porch and headed down the street, her satisfaction slightly punctured by the fact that in Podunk Kismet, cabs didn't operate in the off-season. She'd have to walk, then take a Greyhound bus to the airport.

At the thought, Rachel shuddered. But she strode onward relentlessly. If there was one thing she'd learned as a self-proclaimed rebel, it was never to back down. And never to admit being wrong. Even if, it occurred to her as she rounded the corner and lost sight of her perplexed parents, she had been.

She had been wrong, because she never should have come home for the holidays in the first place. Everything that had happened here had been a mistake—starting with the moment she'd fallen for Reno . . . and ending with the realization that, no matter how much she'd wanted him to, he'd never loved her back.

Chapter Thirty-Six

Just when Reno needed business to be booming at The Wright Stuff, everyone in town seemed to have deserted his store. His bins stood full of basketballs that no one bounced, bats that no one swung, and equipment that would have made ideal Christmas gifts but instead lay ignored and overlooked.

Frowning, he swiped a dust rag over the small display of out-of-season scuba gear in the farthest corner of the store, his expression doubtless as grim as his insides felt.

He didn't know what was wrong with him. He'd been this way since the night of Kayla's Christmas pageant. Bleak. Miserable. Defiant. Technically, Reno figured he'd won his showdown with Rachel, so he should have been pleased. She'd left. He'd held his ground. That counted as a victory even if no one else knew about it. And he was pretty sure no one else knew about it. But that didn't make Reno feel any better. Damn it.

Just as he reached a pinnacle of frustration and impatience—and the end of the gear that needed dusting for the fourteenth time—the bell over the shop's door jangled.

At last! Customers were here. Reno glanced up, hungry for distraction. But it was only Jimmy Gurche, his latest part-time employee, striding in with his perpetual-prankster's aura.

Reno frowned. "Go home. I'm holding down the store today."

"Today and every other day. Go on, take some time off!" Jimmy urged. "Tomorrow is Christmas Eve. I can watch over things here. You must have things to do—"

Find Rachel and beg her to come back occurred to Reno.

"—places to go—"

If Rachel was still at her parents', he could find her.

"—gifts to buy—"

He'd never get to give her her Christmas gift now.

"—parties to attend." Jimmy sauntered to the cash register and smiled at the holiday cards hung there. "You're a popular guy, right? You must have been invited to a few shindigs."

Reno had been. "Not interested. I'm busy."

"You're worn out, is what you are. Look at those bags under your eyes." Jimmy peered at his face, then shook his head. "At least go home for a while. Take a damn nap or something."

Home. Reno couldn't go there.

Everything about the place reminded him of Rachel. He stepped in his front door and remembered making love to her at the base of his Christmas tree. He picked up his Scorpions sweatshirt and pictured her wearing it, adorable and all but branded as his alone. He walked in his bedroom and yearned to find her, naked and smiling and totally unwilling to back down.

You know I'm right, Rachel had said to him, and she had been. She hadn't been afraid to call him on his bullshit. She hadn't been afraid to love him. All of him. The *real* him.

Or at least that's what he'd thought, Reno reminded himself with a final savage sweep of his dusting cloth. Now he knew better. Rachel might have figured out his issues with football and fame and money—but those were ephemeral things. Job-related things. His family and friends—and especially Nate—were *real* things. Authentic things. Things that mattered . . . things that Rachel just didn't understand about him.

She also didn't understand—although he'd bet she was learning it now—how much pride Reno placed in not backing down. That pride had gotten him through the NFL. It had gotten him through life. It would get him through heartbreak, too.

"Screw that." He scoffed. "A nap? I'm way too busy."

As though to prove it, Reno jabbed his chin toward the store's interior. It was so empty, crickets practically chirped.

Well, who cared? Not him.

Ignoring Jimmy's sympathetic look, Reno shouldered his way to the soccer balls. Some punk kids had mixed them up with the baseballs. Damn miscreants. Dourly, he sorted through them.

Jimmy hustled over. He tossed a baseball in the next bin.

Reno glared at him. "What do you think you're doing?"

"Helping you."

"Go home."

"I will if you will."

"Jerkwad."

"Dickface."

At the sight of Jimmy's mulish expression, an odd gratitude suddenly welled inside Reno. For days now, he'd been hiding out inside The Wright Stuff, avoiding everyone and refusing to do so much as turn on the Christmas lights in the windows.

He hadn't shoveled anyone's driveway. He hadn't repaired anything. He hadn't lent tools to his neighbors, dug anyone out of a snowbank, babysat, moderated a parental crisis, or acted as a date broker for his best friend. He hadn't done anything.

And everyone had left him alone. Until now.

The bell over the door jingled again. Reno glanced up.

Tom Wright sauntered in, an expression of contentment on his face. He spotted Reno and headed in his direction.

"Hey, son! How's it going?"

Reno would rather not say. "What are you doing here, Dad?"

"I'm in the market for . . . um, some new weights." His father rubbed his hands together, seeming newly energized as he examined the mostly vacant shop. "Yeah, that's it. Some new weights. I definitely need new weights. Can you help me out?"

Suspiciously, Reno squinted at his dad. "You have so many weights that I'm not sure your condo can hold them all."

"I'm, uh, helping to outfit the community rec room."

"You don't have a community rec room."

"It's new." With blustery, brisk movements, his father strode forward. He waved to Jimmy, then gave Reno a nonchalant pat as he surveyed the contents of The Wright Stuff. "This might take me all day, so get used to having me around, okay?"

Reno compressed his mouth. There was something very unlikely about this scenario. It was possible that his dad fancied himself an expert in weight training—given his experience as a late-life bachelor—but . . . all-day shopping?

In Reno's experience, Wright men would rather pluck nose hairs with rusty barbecue tongs than endure all-day shopping.

But before Reno could express his skepticism, the bell over the door dinged again. Derek Detweiler stepped inside, bearing a shiny leather jacket emblazoned with the Multicorp logo.

Great. Just when Reno was at his lowest, he was going to be pounded by another unrelenting franchising sales pitch.

"Go away, Detweiler. I'm not interested."

"Geez, Reno. Take a chill pill, will you?" The man approached him, holding the leather jacket the way a lion tamer held a chair. "I just came by with a Christmas present for you."

"Oh." Reno studied it. Goaded by Detweiler's waggling of it, he took it. Gruffly, he said, "Thanks. That's nice of you."

"Not a problem, my man. You're more than welcome."

Feeling churlish next to Detweiler's good humor, Reno fisted his new leather jacket. "Uh, why don't you help yourself to one of those jerseys over there?" Stiffly, he nodded to the hockey jerseys, his most popular items. "A gift from me to you."

"Mighty nice of you, Reno. I think I will."

Appearing delighted, Derek Detweiler made his way across The Wright Stuff. He exchanged hellos with Jimmy, then with Reno's dad. A few minutes later, all three men had huddled beside the athletic supporters, engaged in a lively discussion.

Sullenly, Reno went on sorting soccer balls. Fragments of conversation drifted toward him though, carried easily because of the lack of his usual Christmas music. *Heartbroken* fluttered past, followed by a surreptitious *betrayed* and a harshly whispered *help him*. Occasionally one of the men glanced his way.

Reno scowled. "This isn't the damn gossip hour."

"We're not talking about *you*, Reno!" his dad exclaimed—with about as much believability as he'd used to proclaim his love of gangsta rap music after his split with his mom. "Don't mind us!"

All three of them stifled guffaws. There was another muffled exchange. Then Derek Detweiler broke from the pack, holding a Redwings jersey in his fist. He approached Reno.

He spread his arms wide and enveloped him in a huge hug.

"What the . . . ?" With a startled obscenity, Reno shoved backward. "What do you think you're doing, Detweiler?"

Derek glanced over his shoulder. Jimmy and Tom Wright gave him quadruple thumbs-up signs. "Thanking you for the jersey!"

"I don't need that much gratitude."

A fond sigh. "Things will work out somehow. Don't worry."

The hell . . . ? Now *Derek Detweiler* was consoling him? "My only worry right now is turning you down for a date."

Detweiler laughed. "Oh, Reno! You're so funny."

Then he hugged him. *Again.* While murmuring comforting

platitudes about loving and losing. Utterly bewildered, Reno stared over the Multicorp rep's shoulder at his dad and Jimmy.

But they weren't there. They'd zipped across the store when he wasn't looking, and now they ambushed him, too. Feeling like a running back receiving the Malachi Crunch from three burly defenders, Reno was too surprised to move at first. The scents of Old Spice and leather assaulted his nostrils, followed by . . .

"Damn, Jimmy! What did you eat today?"

"Braunschweiger. Mrs. Gurche is German, remember?"

"Whew! Try a breath mint, will you?"

Jimmy nodded but didn't budge. Just when Reno thought he might collapse from sausage fumes, the bell over the shop's door rang again. The timing could not have been worse.

Mrs. Kowalczyk stepped nimbly inside, her arms burdened with a rectangular, boxy-looking thing. She stopped on the threshold, startled. "Hmmm. Should I come back later, boys? I don't want to interrupt a private moment."

Chapter Thirty-Seven

With her boot heels wobbling against the uneven icy side-walk, Rachel pounded her way toward downtown, passing gaily decorated yards and wide picture windows featuring various families' Christmas trees. Evidently, everyone else in Kismet was ready for the holidays to arrive. Everyone except her.

She'd tried to stay through Christmas; her parents had ruined that for her with their talk of not being "hasty" again. But her mom and dad would be sorry when she was gone, Rachel told herself with a sniffle as she adjusted her scarf and kept moving toward (she hoped) the Greyhound station. They would miss her and feel bad. *Really* bad. For . . . for what exactly?

Stymied by the thought, Rachel faltered. Her chest felt raw from sucking in big gulps of frigid air, and her feet hurt from forcing her stiletto boots actually to transport her more than a few fashionable yards. Her hair was almost certainly filled with static from her borrowed hat. All of those things made *her* feel like the one who was sorry. Sorry and mad.

Mad at herself. Mad at Reno.

Mad at Alayna and Tyson for kicking off this whole December debacle with their two-timing A.M. delight.

Frowning, Rachel swiped a few tears from her cheek and then walked on, dragging her pitiful wheelie suitcase in her wake.

All she really wanted was . . . what exactly?

For the first time, Rachel wasn't sure. As the breeze ruffled her scarf and the naked-limbed trees flashed by in her peripheral vision, she thought about it. At first she'd wanted to excel as a celebrity stylist. Then she'd wanted to get her celebrity stylist job *back*. Then she'd wanted to survive the holidays, keep her job meltdown a secret, and make sure she looked good to the people of Kismet. To everyone who knew her.

But from the instant she'd stepped into the airport, the only person she'd been fooling was herself, Rachel realized with an unwelcome sense of vulnerability. Everyone here already knew about her job-house-car-friends fiasco in L.A. They didn't care.

They didn't care because . . . they didn't care?

Or maybe because they loved her anyway?

Before she could decide, Rachel heard the purr of an engine coming closer. *Reno*, she thought with a stupid surge of hope. *Maybe he'd come to get her*. But then she realized the truth.

Reno's pickup truck sounded *way* worse than that.

Feeling disappointed, she kept moving. A car slowed beside her, crawling along the street between the gray-tinged snowbanks. Its window rolled down with an electronic whirr.

Rachel steeled herself. This wouldn't be the first time one or both of her parents had followed her. But it would be the first time they'd done so since she was approximately sixteen.

A blur of motion caught her eye as a woman stuck her elbow out the driver's side window. Steadfastly, Rachel walked on.

"Rachel, is that you?" came Judy Wright's voice.

Startled, Rachel glanced at her. Then she absolutely *had* to stop for a minute. "Judy! Your new highlights look terrific."

Her friend patted her hair. "Thanks! Good idea you had."

"I knew you'd like them," Rachel said, feeling pleased.

So shoot her. She was upset, but she wasn't an animal. Expert highlights like those deserved to be acknowledged.

With her car still idling in readiness, Judy spoke loudly enough to be heard above the "Three Tenors Christmas" music on her stereo. "Where are you going? Hop in! I'll give you a ride."

"Oh, no thanks." Somehow it seemed wrong to accept help from the mother of the man who'd broken her heart. Rachel waved her off. "That's very nice of you, but I'm fine."

Judy gave her a perceptive look, as though sizing her up.

The attention made Rachel nervous.

"You know, people use rock salt on their driveways around here," Judy said. "Do you know what salt does to leather boots?"

Perplexed, Rachel frowned at her beloved stiletto boots. "Makes them hard to stop nibbling on, once you start?"

"No." Judy shook her head. "It destroys the leather."

Oh. My. God. How could this barbaric fact have escaped her notice growing up? Stricken, Rachel hopped toward the street.

"Don't move!" she yelled, suitcase bouncing. "I'm coming."

At Mrs. Kowalczyk's entrance, the men broke apart instantly, not meeting one another's eyes.

Jimmy walloped Reno on the back, Tom Wright guffawed in a self-conscious way, and Derek Detweiler flexed his biceps.

"Amateurs. Don't be afraid of a hug!" Making her way across the shop in her usual no-nonsense manner, Mrs. Kowalczyk shook her head, then stopped in front of Reno. She got down to business right away. "I heard you broke up with that Rachel Porter. Nice girl. Good teeth. Stupid of you to let her go."

She reared back. Reno feared another hug.

She kicked him.

"Ouch!" Reno's shin smarted. "What's that for?"

"For you to remember not to be such a butthead next time." Mrs. Kowalczyk pursed her lips. "Is there any chance you can patch things up with her? I'm thinking she could probably wrangle me some designer clothes or something for Crackers."

"I don't think Rachel dresses dogs."

"Ha! You haven't been to Hollywood."

"Mrs. Kowalczyk, what are you doing here? You don't have to work today, remember?" A little concerned, Reno peered at her. "I gave you the day off and took your shift myself."

"What do you think I am, senile? I came to introduce you to . . . well, I'm calling her Peanut Butter." Mrs. Kowalczyk set down the rectangular carrier she'd brought, unzipped it, then reached inside. Carefully, she lifted out a tiny bichon frise puppy with white curly fur. "Because Peanut Butter goes with Crackers. Get it? Peanut Butter and Crackers?"

At the sight of that puppy, wriggly and big-eyed, with miniature paws and a distinct penchant for trying to get away, Reno smiled for the first time in days. Without even meaning to, he reached for it. Mrs. Kowalczyk transferred Peanut Butter into his open palms as Jimmy, Derek, and his dad crowded around.

The puppy blinked up at him. Her little tail wagged.

Something inside Reno just melted. The stony efforts he'd made to wall himself off crumbled, cratered by one warm puppy and the simple realization that nobody needed a day off spent at work, a whole day's worth of shopping for unnecessary weights, or *two* impromptu man-hugs in a row. Jimmy, his dad, and even Detweiler had all been trying to help. Trying to help *him*.

"You think she'll do?" Mrs. Kowalczyk prodded, nodding at the dog. "You committed to buying that puppy when Crackers was still preggers, so maybe you're having second thoughts by now."

"No. She'll do fine. Kayla will love her."

Rachel likes puppies and Nickelodeon and pink sparkle lip gloss, he remembered his niece saying. *You've got to get her!*

Rachel. Everything seemed connected to her now. Even

parts of his store—which was why Reno had exiled himself to the scuba zone. He hadn't spent any time with Rachel examining snorkels.

It was funny though. Even Kayla had believed that Rachel was special. Of course, it was easy to dupe a six-year-old. It should have been tougher to fool a grown man like him.

Rachel. Rachel. He had to quit thinking about her. The ironic thing was, if he hadn't been helping Nate hook up with his dream girl, Reno realized, he never would have found time to fall for Rachel in the first place. He would have been too busy—was *always* too busy to do things like date.

Wasn't his canceled dinner with Sheila proof of that?

Not that it mattered now. Grumpily, Reno transferred Peanut Butter to her pet carrier, getting ready to transport the puppy home so he could surprise Kayla with the teeny bichon frise as an early Christmas present. Just as he got the puppy securely tucked in though, the bell over the shop's door jangled again.

Now what?

Angela and Kayla crowded inside, toting shopping bags, with Nate galumphing in the rear. Warily, Reno stepped back. He could handle a few hugs from the Gossipy Mens' Club trio, but if Nate tried to hug him, all bets were off. Reno might just blubber like he'd done at the end of *Invincible*, that movie about Vince Papale getting a shot at playing for the Eagles in '76.

That guy Vince had so much damn heart.

Not that Reno intended to blab about it. Or let himself be ambushed by unwanted sentiment right now. Hoping to waylay any more surprise hug attacks, he held the pet carrier in front of him like a shield. Then he spotted Kayla again, realized what he was doing, and shoved the pet carrier behind his back to Jimmy instead, shuffling sideways to disguise the movement.

"Hide this!" he whispered. "It's for Kayla!"

"Gotcha, boss." Jimmy said. "Here, Derek. Take this!"

"No!" Reno said. "Wait—"

But it was too late. Jimmy had already handed off the pet carrier to Detweiler, who grabbed it like a hot potato and gave it to Reno's dad. Tom Wright balked, turned his back to the newcomers, then sidestepped toward Mrs. Kowalczyk.

"I don't want it!" she said. "I've got four more at home."

The men all chuckled, forming a clump of outstretched arms as they tried to shield the pet carrier. The puppy inside scrambled. Reno heard its paws skitter, then a muted whimper.

Kayla perked up. "Hey, what's that?"

"Nothing." Reno watched uneasily as Jimmy, Detweiler, and his dad shuffled to the counter where the cash register was. "Hey! How's it going? What's new? Doing some shopping?"

"Nope. Visiting Santa," Angela said. "We just got done."

"I had to change my wish list." Kayla skipped closer. She eyed the men at the counter curiously, as though guessing what they were up to. "Now that you've already *got* the perfect girlfriend, Uncle Reno, I had room for something else for me."

The perfect girlfriend. She meant Rachel. Reno remembered his conversation with Kayla while shopping for something from the Junior Pussycat Dolls Collection to wow her school friends.

"You wished for a girlfriend for me?"

Kayla grinned. "I knew *you* wouldn't do it. So *I* did."

He hadn't done it. He'd been too busy falling for Rachel.

"Huh. Like mother, like daughter, right, Sis?" Smiling despite everything, Reno greeted Angela and Kayla with hugs.

Then he turned to face Nate.

At his friend's solemn expression, Reno's grin faltered.

"Hey." Nate nodded in greeting, his forehead furrowed. "Where's Rachel? I thought she'd be here with you."

A hiss came from the shop's checkout counter.

"Psst! Hey, Nate! Don't talk about Rachel!" Reno's dad made shooing-away gestures. "Reno is brokenhearted over her!"

Jimmy and Derek Detweiler nodded gravely. Seven sympathetic gazes arrowed in on Reno. He shifted uncomfortably.

"I'm not brokenhearted, damn it!"

"He hasn't shoveled my driveway for days," Mrs. Kowalczyk volunteered. "He hasn't cleared Mrs. Bender's driveway either."

As though that were proof positive of Reno's broken heart, those seven gazes turned from sympathetic to concerned.

"He took a Christmas gift from *me*," Detweiler piped up.

Now disbelief edged out the concern.

"He let me *help him* sort out the soccer ball bin."

A gasp of shock went up from everyone.

Aggrieved, Reno glanced at his friend. "You, too, Jimmy?"

His part-time employee shrugged. "The truth's gotta come out, Reno. And the truth is, getting a job here with you boosted my confidence so much that I went after—and got—a job at the regional office of Multicorp. Full benefits and everything." He straightened his shoulders. "Detweiler and I got to talking one day, and one thing led to another. So thanks, Reno. And I quit."

Gawking at him, Reno barely registered the congratulations and jovial back pats that flowed toward Jimmy.

In the midst of the hubbub, his dad stepped up. "Reno didn't even argue when I said I'd be staying here *all day*."

Now the concern was back, buffered with empathy.

"I couldn't kick you out of the damn store!" Reno boomed.

But his argument didn't matter to anyone. They all came closer—Mrs. Kowalczyk, Jimmy, his dad, Angela, Detweiler, and Nate. Even Kayla paused in her momentary pursuit of the poorly concealed secret behind the checkout counter. Tightening his muscles into rigid knots, Reno stared defiantly back at them.

"You've got a problem, Reno," his sister said.

"I do not."

"You're giving up too easily," Angela persisted. "We can all see it. That's why we're here. For once *you* need help."

The very idea was an anathema to Reno. He shook his head.

"Real men give help," he told them. "They don't take it."

Nate—who until this point hadn't said a word—finally stepped up. "I never thought I'd see the day—Reno Wright, giving up when the going gets tough. Acting like a punter."

"A punter?" Reno glared at his friend, hands fisted. "Those are fighting words, you jerk."

"They're true words," Nate said blithely. "I was just giving you the benefit of the doubt before. I heard about you and Rachel. I thought maybe you'd patched things up already. You are kind of a miracle worker most of the time, you know."

Completely puzzled, Reno stared at him.

"But now I know the truth," Nate went on. "You're punting. Trying to keep things from getting worse. Trying to make sure that, if you can't win, at least you won't lose by as much."

He meant with Rachel. Of course he meant with Rachel.

Reno muttered an obscenity. "You, of all people . . ." Feeling sucker punched, he shook his head. "I don't believe it."

Oblivious to the tension in the air, Detweiler raised his hand. "Uh, what's wrong with punting? *You* were a kicker, Reno."

"A kicker, not a punter." All but snarling the words, Reno turned to the man. Everyone took a step back. "A kicker starts the game. Earns field goals. Saves the day when the clock's running out." Those were all things he was proud of having done. "Punters only come in when it's time to cut losses and bail out. When it's time to make sure the other team doesn't have the advantage. When *not losing* becomes more important than winning."

Detweiler shrugged. "Sounds pretty nitpicky to me."

"It's not. It's an important difference." Frustrated by all of them, Reno ran his hand through his hair. "You'd think all the booters would get along, but I hated the punters. I *hated* seeing those guys take the safe way out. Every damn time. No risks, no guts . . . nothing but giving up."

Surely everyone would see the truth now. Any idiot could.

After a weighty pause, Nate shook his head. "And that's different from the way you're acting right now . . . how, exactly?"

Settling into a booth at The Coffee Cup Diner—next door to the Kismet Greyhound station—Rachel shoved her suitcase into the far corner of the bench seat. She set down her purse beside the old-fashioned sugar shaker, then dropped her one-way bus ticket to Grand Rapids beside the chrome napkin dispenser. With a sigh, she sank onto her seat's creased vinyl to peruse the menu.

This was it. She'd done it. In exactly forty-one minutes, she'd be boarding a bus for the airport. Sayonara, Kismet!

"I guess I'm all set," she said as Judy Wright slid into the seat opposite her. With her best attitude of rebelliousness, Rachel surveyed the older woman. "From here on, it's only a few hours back to the sunshine and backstabbing of L.A." She lifted her water glass in a toast. "See you, Kismet! It's been real."

Real kitschy. Real heartwarming. Real painful.

"How about something to eat first?" Judy asked. "The pancakes are good here. So are the patty melts and the shakes."

"No thanks." Rachel patted her purse. "This baby's filled with just enough protein bars to get me back home."

Judy wrinkled her nose. "You can't live on those."

"You sound like my mother." Rachel made a face. "Sure I can. They've got protein. Vitamins. Nutrients. Everything."

"But none of it's quite real, is it?" Her new friend's penetrating look met Rachel's. "None of it can keep you going."

Just like, Rachel read in Judy's perceptive gaze, life in La-La Land couldn't keep her going—at least not without all the good things Rachel had rediscovered in Kismet. Things like friendship. Creativity. Security. Love. Well, pseudo-love at least. But she could definitely get *that* in Malibu.

"I don't need much." Rachel glanced up as their waitress

dropped by to take their orders—one patty melt with fries for Judy and one Diet Coke for Rachel. "In the can please," she told the waitress. "I don't trust those fountain machines. Sometimes they have nondiet soda in them. I refuse to be bamboozled."

The waitress rolled her eyes. Judy sighed.

Defiantly, Rachel stared back at them. Nobody was making her crack now. Not now that she'd learned the truth.

People couldn't be trusted. Not even her.

On the street behind her, cars chugged through the snow. Buses groaned past, squealing with one last stop at the corner before breaking free for other destinations. Rachel couldn't see them with her back to the diner's Christmas-decal-decorated plate glass window, but she could hear them. She could see their shadows reflected in the diner's revolving pie case, the afternoon light shifting every time someone drove by.

She concentrated on those sounds, those shadows, and the uniquely Kismet ambiance of The Coffee Cup Diner. There was nothing quite like this in L.A. Something had imbued the diner's checked linoleum, chrome fixtures, and busy grill with a special homeyness. Maybe it was the pictures on the wall—black and white historical prints of lakeside beaches, long weathered docks, and sailboats. Maybe it was the miniature poinsettias, dusky red and perfect for the holidays, stuck in milk bottles at each table. Maybe it was the people . . . including her sour-faced waitress, who set a dust-tinged can of cola in front of Rachel.

"One Diet Coke, *in the can*, your highness."

Rachel raised her eyebrows in surprise, but the waitress only flounced away. Across the table, Judy stifled a grin.

"You've got a few things to learn about dealing with people in Kismet," her friend said. She toyed with a poinsettia leaf, avoiding Rachel's eyes. Then, appearing to come to a decision, Judy spoke. "There's a lot of history here. Things you either forgot or never knew. Take Reno, for instance—"

"No thanks." Rachel cracked open her Diet Coke. "No of-fense, Judy, but what happened between me and Reno was—"

Tragic, her pitiful heart volunteered. *Excruciating, stupid, inexplicable* . . . The adjectives just kept piling up.

"Completely understandable," Judy said firmly. "Maybe even inevitable, given the circumstances."

"What?" Rachel blurted. "*Inevitable*? Why?" And if it made so much damn sense, then why couldn't she understand it?

"Well," Judy began. "There's a few things—"

On the cusp of knowing, Rachel came to her senses. She held up her hand. "Never mind. Forget I said anything. Thanks for the ride here, but let's just forget about me and Reno, okay?"

"Nope." With the blunt certainty of a woman of a certain age, Judy shook her head. "You need to hear this. Partly be-cause you helped me and Tom not too long ago when we needed it. Partly because I like you, and I doubt that if you were thinking straight you'd be sitting there with that kind of hat-head—"

Aghast, Rachel clutched her hair. It crackled. Why had she whipped off her knit hat the moment she'd gotten inside?

"—but mostly because judging by how happy my son has seemed, until recently," Judy drove on relentlessly, "you two are good for each other, and a mother never stops wanting what's best for her children. For Reno, that seems to be you."

As if. This awkward situation was exactly what Rachel had been afraid of. "I don't have to sit here and listen to this."

"No, you don't. But I think you will."

"Oh, yeah?" Rachel fired back. "You wanna bet?"

For an instant, Judy Wright's gaze sparkled with the same can't-lose spirit that her son's always had. Rachel had the awful sensation that she'd seriously underestimated her.

"Sure," Judy said. "I'll take that bet. Winner gets your plane ticket to L.A. If I win, I'm going to Disneyland."

"What if *I* win?"

"I'll drive you to the airport to catch that flight myself. No Greyhound bus ticket necessary."

Hmmm. Rachel really wasn't keen to ride the bus for an hour or more. Especially while still wearing her ratty cardigan. And toting her luggage by hand. With her red-rimmed eyes and blotchy cheeks, she was barely fit to appear in public as it was.

"What do you say?" With an audacious wink, Judy stuck out her hand. "Do we have a deal?"

Chapter Thirty-Eight

Reno stared at everyone, his gut in a knot and his mind in a whirl. *A punter*. Nate had actually called him a *punter*.

Even if there *had* been hope for him and Rachel, even if Reno *had* been somewhat at fault, that kind of name-calling wasn't necessary. Besides the situation was . . . complicated.

"I should go," he said abruptly. "As all of you pointed out"—his dark gaze slid to Mrs. Kowalczyk—"I've been slacking off lately. I have driveways to shovel. Things to repair—"

"All we need you to do," Angela said, touching his arm warmly, "is take care of *yourself* for a change."

Frowning, Reno went on, "And since Jimmy is so keen to work today, I'll let him handle things around here while I'm gone."

Jimmy shifted in his boots, appearing discomfited.

"Dad, take any weights you want. They're on me. Merry Christmas to your nonexistent community rec room." Obstinately, Reno shoved past them all. His boots rang in the silence left by his lack of Christmas carols. "Nate, bite me. I'm not a"—a swearword slipped out—"a punter. I'm just trying to get by."

"Reno, stop." Nate put out one beefy hand. "Wait. Wait!"

For an instant, Reno paused. At the sight of his friend, a

sappy, impossible, Vince Papale-style lump rose in his throat. He shook his head. "If I do, I might say something I regret. I've already got enough regrets, so . . . I'll see you around."

He made it all the way to the section of improved hockey sticks before Nate spoke again. "Regrets? What kind of regrets?"

Reno stopped. It felt as if everyone in the place held their breath. Maybe even him. He'd already said too much.

"Do you mean regrets with Rachel?" Nate asked.

That was the last straw.

"Not with Rachel, you dumbass." Although there were those, too. Reno turned to face his best friend. "With you!"

Nate jerked. His whole attitude sobered. "With me?"

"Yeah." Silently, Reno squared his shoulders. "With you."

Nate's brow furrowed. It was the same expression he wore when figuring out a new recipe for home-ec class. The effort required was mighty . . . but his desire for mastery was greater.

"Why?" he asked. "What do you have to regret about me?"

Looking at Nate's bewildered expression, Reno could tell he was on the verge of hurting the big guy's feelings. It killed him to think that Nate might be unhappy because of him . . . all over again. That's probably what made Reno keep talking.

"Oh, I dunno." Deliberately keeping his tone light, Reno stuffed his hands in his pockets. He couldn't look at Nate. Couldn't stand to see the confirmation of everything he'd feared for all these years. "Maybe I regret that I took the life you should have had. Or that I took the Scorpions contract and football spot you wanted. Or that I took the Super Bowl trip you would have loved. Or that I came home a hero"—*and you didn't,* rushed to be said, but Reno's throat closed up, and he couldn't manage it—"when you deserved it just as much."

"Reno—"

"No, I might as well finish now." Reno forced the words past the lump in his throat. "I did all that to you, Nate, and then, when you trusted me to help you, I took the woman you wanted, too. I took Rachel, and she should have been yours."

With a mighty effort, Reno swallowed. His whole body felt on edge, taut with tension the way it had before a big kick. He didn't know what Nate would say or what Nate would do, but he did know there was one more thing he had to tell his friend.

"I'm sorry, Nate. Sorry for all of it. If I could take it back, I would."

For one long moment, there was nothing but silence.

Then Nate spoke. "Well, that would be a dumb thing to do."

Startled, Reno glanced up. "What?"

"That would be the *king* of dumb things to do." Nate spread his arms in apparent exasperation. "Geez, Reno! What the hell would that prove, if you gave up everything for me?"

"Uh—"

"I can't believe all that football stuff is still bothering you." Nate came closer, his fierce left tackle's stance almost looming over Reno. "Don't you know? I only went to training camp because I thought it would be fun to hang out with you. We used to do everything together, remember? Sure, I loved playing ball, but I love being a teacher in Kismet more."

"You . . . what?" Reno frowned up at him.

"My major was education. I knew better than to count on football for my future. Duh. I'm a die-hard planner, remember?" Nate's incandescent smile beamed down on Reno. "Once you came back from the NFL, it was even better, because we could hang out together again. That's all I ever wanted. I hate traveling, and I don't care about money or fame. That stuff isn't for me."

"It's not!" Timidly but with clear excitement, Detweiler stepped forward. "I offered Nate a job with Multicorp's media division as a color commentator. With his personality, he'd be a shoo-in. Major money, too. But he turned me down."

"You what?" In astonishment, Reno gawked at Nate.

His best friend only shrugged. "I've got everything I need

right here in Kismet. And as far as you stealing away my dream girl goes . . . dude, I'm *so* over it." Nate wrapped his arm around Angela's shoulders, then pulled her closer. "I've got the only woman for me right here. So get over yourself!" He made a goofy face at Reno. "You are not the beginning and end of my life, no matter how much you like to boss me around. Everything's cool."

Reno could scarcely believe it. "Then . . . you're okay?"

"I'm better than you," Nate said, raising his good eyebrow.

Reno scoffed. "That'll be the day."

"That's what you think, punk."

"Oh yeah? Bite me, dogface."

"Not worth it. You're so little, you're just an appetizer."

"Come closer and say that, you big lummox."

"Boys, boys." Beaming, Angela stepped between them. "Let's just hug it out and quit with the name-calling, okay?"

Sheepishly, Reno and Nate looked at each other. They shuffled closer. Their one brisk hug made tears sting Reno's eyes. Nate stepped away, wiping his nose.

"All good?" Mrs. Kowalczyk asked. "Everything settled?"

"Settled," Reno and Nate croaked in unison.

"Good." Eagerly, the older woman rubbed her palms together. "Then let's get down to strategizing, Reno. There might still be time to patch up you and Rachel Porter."

He looked at her. "You really want those doggie clothes."

"Darn tootin', I do. Crackers needs a pick-me-up."

"But Rachel and me . . ." Tantalized by visions of the two of them together again, Reno frowned. He shook his head. "It's too late. She doesn't get me. She doesn't understand—"

"Did you call her a dogface, too?" his dad inquired mildly.

"There *are* a few things that could use improvement in your communication style," Angela pointed out gently. "For instance, Rachel had no idea you were really setting her up with Nate. You know, until Nate told her about it at Kayla's school pageant."

"Yeah. I kind of . . . failed to mention that."

"So it was probably a big surprise to her," his sister continued steadfastly. "A big unwelcome surprise, kind of like the one she got in L.A. with her cheating boyfriend. This might come as a shock to you guys, but unless your surprises involve flowers, candy, a trip to Acapulco, jewelry, or foot rubs—"

Nate gazed at her, practically taking notes with his eyes.

"—women don't necessarily like *all* surprises, Reno."

"Amen to that," Jimmy said fervently . . . if puzzlingly.

"Yeah. You can't give up if there's still hope, Reno," Detweiler blurted. "Sometimes you just need to be persistent."

They all stared at him.

He shrugged. "Hey, sales is my business. I don't quit."

There it was again. *Quit.* At the word, Reno scowled.

Was that really what he was doing? Quitting? Giving up? Or just protecting himself?

"Listen, Reno," Nate said in a reasonable tone. "I've known you since we were playing with Transformers in kindergarten, right? If *I* couldn't tell what you've been thinking—about me and football and all that—how the hell is Rachel supposed to know how you really feel about her?"

Stung, Reno gazed at him. Maybe Nate had a point . . .

Agreeing, everyone nodded. But rather than feeling like an ambush to Reno, suddenly their concern felt like encouragement. Hell, he might as well lay it on the line. It felt like love.

"Don't wait like I did, son," his dad said. "If you care about Rachel, tell her now. Before it's too late."

"Too late?" Reno glanced at his father. "What do you mean?"

"I mean Rachel is on her way out of town." Tom Wright held up his cell phone. "I just got a text message from your mom."

Angela raised her eyebrows. "Another one? Racy!"

Their father's cheeks reddened. "Not *that* kind of message," he said sternly—but Reno could tell there was some truth to his sister's comment. Apparently his parents had reconciled . . . and more. "She's trying to delay Rachel at The

Coffee Cup Diner, but her bus to the airport is supposed to leave in twenty minutes."

Twenty minutes. Reno needed more time than that. More time to tamp down his pride, think about his part in his split with Rachel, reconcile what Nate had said, come up with a plan . . . .

Mrs. Kowalczyk approached him, her winter hat with the earflaps pulled down low and her lipstick shining a vibrant pink.

"I'm sorry to have to do this, Reno. But it's necessary."

He blinked, distracted. "Do what?"

"This." She reared back and kicked him again. "Don't be a butthead! If you love Rachel, for God's sake, go after her!"

"Ouch!" Reno grabbed his shin.

"Apparently the other kick didn't stick. Maybe that one will."

"Maybe." Wincing, Reno gazed at his family and friends and neighbors. And also at Detweiler. No scratch that. Detweiler was a friend now, too. He wanted to go, but . . . "What will I say?"

"It'll come to you." His dad shoved him toward the door.

"Just speak from the heart!" Angela urged.

"Remember to kiss her!" Nate added. "Make it good."

"Not too much tongue," Mrs. Kowalczyk warned. "Remember, you're going to be in public. Be decent. But passionate."

"It never hurts to look your best." Jimmy dashed over, fussed with Reno's hair, then stepped back critically. "There."

Feeling mauled, Reno paused with one foot out the door.

"Just tell her you love her and you're wrong!" came the advice from Detweiler, the sixth member of their helpful troupe. "Men are always wrong in arguments. You probably misunderstood."

Smiling, Reno fisted his truck keys. He was really going to do this. He was going to get Rachel back. But first . . .

"Kayla, don't you have any advice for your Uncle Reno?"

After all, it was partly because of her that he'd found the perfect girlfriend. Maybe Christmas wishes could come true.

"Look! It's a puppy!" Kayla squealed.

Reno glanced her way. While they'd been talking, his niece had crept close enough to the checkout counter to snag her Christmas gift a little earlier than planned.

"Sorry, Reno." Jimmy shrugged. "We were trying to put a bow on the pet carrier, and the little bugger slipped away."

Kayla faced Reno, cooing as she cradled Peanut Butter. Her face shone with exhilaration. "She's for *me*, isn't she? I *know* it!" She giggled as the puppy licked her fingers. "Look! She loves me already." Gently, she hugged the puppy to her chest.

Reno smiled. "Merry Christmas, Kayla."

"This is *all* I wanted, Uncle Reno! Thank you, thank you!" Looking overjoyed, Kayla cuddled with the puppy.

Angela caught Reno's eye. *Thank you*, his sister mouthed.

He nodded at her, then shrugged into his coat, nervous and hard-faced and not at all sure that things would work out. If he was going to do this, he had to hurry. Because all Reno wanted for Christmas—always and forever—was Rachel. If he really moved, he might still be able to catch her.

Chapter Thirty-Nine

Rachel settled back in her seat at the diner, gazing at Judy Wright in surprise. "I had no idea Nate played football. Or that he and Reno went to Scorpions training camp together."

"I thought maybe you didn't." Judy nodded kindheartedly. "Everyone around here knows the story so well, it probably didn't occur to Reno or Nate or even Angela to bring it up. But in light of everything that's happened . . . it's important."

Rachel nodded. "And when Nate didn't make the team, but Reno did . . ." Wide-eyed, she considered everything she'd learned in the past few minutes as she'd stayed put to win her bet with Judy. "That must have been tough on them both."

"It was." Judy sipped her milkshake, then gave a *mmm*. "Reno and Nate were always close, but things changed after Nate came back from the NFL. They changed again when Reno quit football. He was different when he came home to Kismet. More mature."

"I was already in L.A. by then," Rachel said. "I never knew them as adults. I barely knew them growing up." She gave a rueful smile. "The rebels didn't mix with the jocks much."

Judy nodded. "I know. I was a bit of a rebel myself."

Hardly able to believe it, Rachel squinted at her. All of a sudden, there it was . . . a feisty sparkle around the eyes.

"When they were smaller, sometimes those boys gave me a

hell of a time, believe me." Cheerfully, Judy waved off Rachel's scrutiny. "But mostly Reno and Nate were best buddies—inseparable from kindergarten onward, all the way to today. Except when Reno was playing ball, they've rarely been apart."

I risked everything to be with you! Rachel remembered Reno telling her after Kayla's Christmas pageant. *I put my friendship with Nate on the line, over and over again.*

Now those words held new meaning. No wonder Reno had looked so wounded, so angry, so disbelieving when they'd stood on that snowy sidewalk together. No wonder he hadn't apologized. But Rachel had been too shocked and hurt to consider *why* he'd been talking about Nate, when all she'd wanted to talk about was the two of them. So she hadn't let Reno finish explaining.

"That's why I knew it was a disaster in the making when Angela told me how Reno planned to fix up Nate with his dream girl—you. By then, I'd already seen the effect you had on my son, Rachel. I knew he wouldn't be able to let you go—"

Rachel made a face, remembering exactly how he had.

"—but I also knew Reno wouldn't be able to hurt Nate." Ruefully, Judy twirled her straw. "It was bound to turn out badly and it did. For that, I'm sorry. Reno is a loyal man. He'd sooner lose something for himself than hurt a friend."

Ironically, that was a quality Rachel admired in him. Reno had integrity—something that seemed in short supply with everyone else she knew. How, Rachel wondered, could she be mad at Reno for one of the very characteristics she loved about him?

Feeling her understanding broaden, Rachel thought about everything Reno did for the people here—his rescue mission for Mrs. Bender, his giant Christmas tree for the citizens of Kismet, his hiring of friends and neighbors at his store, his snow-shoveling, repairing, babysitting . . . it just went on.

She'd been right. Reno really *was* the go-to guy of Kismet.

"So in the end, when it came to you, Reno couldn't back

down," Judy said, "but in all good conscience, he couldn't go forward either. Not without hurting Nate. He was stuck."

I say I'm screwed, he'd told her when Rachel had announced she might stay in Kismet awhile. It all made sense now.

Except for one inescapable thing.

The most important thing of all.

"That would make a great story," Rachel said, "*if* Reno loved me. Since he doesn't, I'd say we're done here."

Judy boggled, her straw halfway to her lips. "What?"

"I win." Rachel ripped up her Greyhound ticket. When she'd accepted Judy's bet, she'd put the stakes on the table. Now she intended to claim them. "So you're driving me to the airport. I'm going to go make a phone call and freshen up—"

"You cheated!"

"I didn't cheat. I listened." After Reno had accused her of cheating during their first bet at the airport, Rachel had learned to play it straight. "That's all I had to do to win."

Looking panicky, Judy darted a glance at her cell phone. The *incoming text* light flashed. "Our food isn't even here yet!"

"We can stay long enough to eat. I don't expect you to drive me all the way to Grand Rapids without sustenance." In the meantime, Rachel intended to call Mimi, beg her for an ordinary job on *Sweetwater* or another network show, and start over. The right way this time—without snobbery, a quest for fame, or an attitude of entitlement. "I'll be back in a minute."

Steeling herself, Rachel gazed around the diner. For an instant, she thought she heard the growling sound of Reno's pickup truck passing by on the street behind her, but she closed her ears to the rumble. She wouldn't be fooled again.

Locating the ladies' room, Rachel grabbed her purse.

"Wait!" Judy said. "Reno does love you! He does!"

Rachel shook her head. "The only one who can tell me that is Reno," she said. "And he's not here, is he?"

Judy bit her lip, glancing at her cell phone again. Sadly, Rachel stood. Thanks to Judy's explanation, at least she understood things better now. At least she knew she hadn't been entirely gullible. The situation with Reno had been complicated.

She turned . . . and almost collided with their waitress.

"Whoa!" The woman veered, giving Rachel an accusatory look.

She carried Judy's patty melt and fries. The delicious aromas wafting from the plate nearly made Rachel's knees buckle. She'd picked a heck of a time to abandon real food again.

"Watch out there, your highness," their waitress snapped. "Some of us peons have to make a living, you know."

Oblivious to Rachel's incredulous expression, she slid the plate of food in front of Judy. She inquired sweetly about the necessity for ketchup, more napkins, or a milkshake refill, pointedly ignoring Rachel while almost hip-checking her.

Annoyed, Rachel grabbed her suitcase. Her non-security-blanket cardigan was in there, and she wanted to change into it before embarking on the trip home. She yanked her bag from the seat—and almost dropped it on their waitress's toes.

"Sorry," Rachel mumbled, brushing her hair out of her eyes.

For the first time, their waitress actually seemed human. She glanced at Rachel's hat-head hair, her droopy cardigan, and her luggage. "Hmmm. What are you doing, princess? Running away?"

Mutinously, Rachel glanced down at her telltale suitcase. It was dappled with wet snowmelt. The handle was squeaky. The whole thing leaned crookedly because of the wheel she'd broken while lugging it over a frozen pothole on the way to Judy's car. But it was still a quality piece of luggage. It didn't deserve such a disparaging look from that horrid, know-it-all waitress.

Running away. Ha. As if.

Then it hit her. That's exactly what she was doing.

All over again. Just like she'd always done.

"No," Rachel decided in that moment, her eyes opened for

the first time ever. Standing straighter in her favorite kickass boots, she fixed the waitress—and a hopeful-seeming Judy—with a determined look. "This time I'm not running away. This time, I'm staying to fight."

But first . . . she was putting on some lip gloss.

Chapter Forty

The minutes Reno spent driving the slippery two miles between The Wright Stuff and the Kismet Greyhound station were the longest in his life. He gripped the steering wheel in ungloved hands, scanning the streets and sidewalks for any sign of a woman with wild dark hair, a sassy strut to her walk . . . and a pair of sunglasses that (he now knew) concealed a hurt she'd been trying to hide from everyone.

Rachel. Just thinking of her made his heart race faster as Reno rounded the corner off Main Street and searched for a parking space in front of The Coffee Cup Diner. The place looked worn but cheery, snug in a Midwestern way and fully outfitted with a set of holiday lights and Christmas window decals.

He hoped he wasn't already too late. As he wrenched his truck to a stop, Reno peered through the diner's big plate glass window. He thought he caught a glimpse of Rachel. An instant later, she was gone. He was probably hallucinating. Given the trauma he'd been through when he'd thought he'd lost her, it was no wonder. From here on out, he'd probably imagine he saw audacious women wearing miniskirts and tights and boots everywhere he went—and every instance would be torture if he didn't track down Rachel and somehow convince her to stay.

With that thought in mind, Reno jammed his parking brake into position, then yanked out his keys. He thought of what Jimmy might have done to his hair, then hastily fixed it in the rearview. Okay. Better. Damn, he was going to hyperventilate.

In. Out. In. Out. Breathing deeply, Reno jumped out of his truck and slammed the door. People on the sidewalk sent him curious glances, but he didn't care. His mind was all for Rachel—for Rachel and for making her stay in Kismet forever.

How the hell to do that though?

Skating across the icy path between his parking space and the diner's entrance, Reno racked his brain. He'd already shown Rachel the best of Kismet—the people, the parade, the town square with its holiday lights and decorations. They'd been to the surrounding wooded areas, to The Big Foot, to Kayla's Christmas pageant, and the Glenrosen neighborhood. There was nothing special enough in Kismet to hold her here.

Nothing except him. Damn it.

With no plan at all, Reno wrenched open the diner's door. Warm air rushed at him, coming from the central heating system and the busy grill alike. Heads swiveled in his direction. A few diner customers leaned together and whispered. Ignoring them, Reno squared his shoulders and looked for Rachel.

She would be easy to spot. She had a glow about her—a special way of existing that drew everyone to her. He'd probably find Rachel in the midst of another adoring crowd, Reno told himself with the faintest beginnings of a smile. He'd probably have to fight his way to her, desperate to get closer.

He squinted harder, scoured the diner's occupied tables again . . . and then caught sight of his mother, waving him over.

Waving him over to a table where she sat alone.

Rachel had already gone, Reno realized. He was too late.

Feeling flattened, he slumped where he stood. Then he inhaled deeply and headed toward his mom. She would want an explanation. Or maybe some company. Right now . . .

Right now a weird tingling was starting at the back of Reno's neck. Transfixed by the sensation, he stopped.

Slowly, he glanced to the side, past the long counter with its swiveling stools full of customers, past the cash register with its poinsettia, past the pay phone . . . all the way to Rachel.

Rachel. At the sight of her, Reno knew he'd done the right thing. There was no one like Rachel, no one who could make him feel whole again, no one who could make him smile with quite the same width and dazzle and happiness he felt right now.

She was still here. He wasn't too late.

Rachel stood riveted in place, her whole mind filled with the realization that Reno was here. He was *here*, right now, standing there with that smile she loved and those eyes she wanted to gaze into forever and those arms she wanted to hold her for a very long time (also possibly forever), and it was all she could do to let go of her suitcase handle and raise her hand to the back of her neck. Just a second ago, she'd felt the most peculiar tingling there. A little tickle, telling her to *look*.

Then she'd glanced up . . . and she'd understood why.

"I'm sorry," she said. It was the first thing that came to mind. Without so much as an order from her, Rachel's feet carried her to him, away from her forgotten suitcase and into the rest of her life. "I'm so sorry, Reno. I didn't know. About you and Nate. I didn't know, and I should have listened—"

"I'm sorry, too!" Reno said. His feet copied hers, totally in sync, and an instant later he was right there in front of her, overwhelming her with his presence and his handsomeness and his utter earnestness. "I didn't know what to do," he insisted. "I wasn't thinking. All I wanted was to be with you—"

"I wanted to be with you!"

"—and then it was so complicated. You didn't like trucks or Christmas *or* Kismet, so I didn't think it would matter—"

"I do like Kismet! And Christmas!"

"—but then I spent some time with you, and you made me crazy with those tights and those boots, and somehow I couldn't get enough." Reno gulped in a breath, taking her hands. "By the time I knew I loved you, it was too damn late, and I—"

Rachel stared. "You love me?"

Reno's whole face brightened. "You didn't know? I thought it was all over me. Every time I saw you, I couldn't quit smiling. Every time I got near you, I couldn't quit touching you. Rachel, don't you get it? You're the only person who's ever understood me! You're the only one who's ever looked past my football fortune and my fame and my store and wanted *me*. Just me. That's why it kills me that I hurt you. I'm so sorry." He squeezed her hands in his and brought them to his lips for a kiss. "If I could take it back I would, I swear. If you'll let me make it up to you, I promise I will. I'll—"

"You love me?" she asked again, feeling dumbfounded.

Reno's eyes widened. With a delicious smile, he raised his hand to her cheek. He brought his gaze directly to bear on hers, bringing their faces together, forehead to forehead.

"I love you, Rachel. I love your smile and your sexy walk and your Care Bear fur sweaters. I love your sandy L.A. Christmas and your goofy Bing Crosby CDs. I love the way you look at me. The way you touch me. The way you wrap gifts and make your own winter coats"—he glanced at her handmade creation, her only truly warm garment—"and play with Kayla and bring people together like magic. I love that you don't think I'm crazy for putting fifty thousand lights on my house for the holidays—"

"I'm pretty sure it's forty-seven thousand," Rachel said. "Officially."

"—and I love"—Reno broke off, his throat working in the same way it had when he'd asked her to help hang those lights—"that you put my mom and dad back together again. I love that you care about people even though you hardly know them. But most of all, I love *you*. Just you. With all my heart."

"Reno—" Sniffling back tears, Rachel felt her heart pound faster with every husky, genuine word he said, with every squeeze of Reno's hand in hers. "I—"

"So please, please don't leave Kismet. Not yet," Reno urged. His gaze remained fixed on hers, honest and true. "Not until I have a chance to make things right between us. Not until I have a chance to *really* love you."

"You mean this has only been the starter version?"

Reno's mouth quirked at the corners in a downright devilish way. "Baby, you haven't seen anything yet."

"Oh." Good grief, she believed him. Caught beneath Reno's gaze, beneath his firm grasp and his sincerity and his intensity, Rachel felt herself quaver for possibly the first time in her life. "Then I don't know what to tell you, Reno. Because all I have is . . . well, me. And I'm not really all that amazing or fabulous or tough. I'm just a girl."

"You're *my* girl."

"I mean, I love you. God knows, I've been a fool over you!" She waved her hand, helpless to prevent a laugh. "I can't get enough of you. When I see you coming toward me, my whole body feels like it lights up. When I see you smile, I can't help but smile back. When you touch me, all bets are off. I love you like crazy, Reno. When you let me go the other night—"

"Never again," he swore. "Never ever again."

"—it was like leaving a piece of my heart behind with you. I felt as if I'd never be whole again. But now . . . now"—Rachel broke off, unable to keep from cradling his face in her hands, reveling in the sight of his familiar angled cheekbones, his beloved crooked nose, his intense, beautiful, merry green eyes—"now you're here, and I have never felt luckier in my life. I love you, Reno. And if you don't kiss me pretty soon—"

His mouth descended on hers instantly, cutting off her words with a kiss that made Rachel almost swoon in his arms.

She clutched him and kissed him back with all the fervor, all the love her heart could muster, and it must have been a lot, because just as Reno came up for air, just as he gave her a softer kiss, then another and another, she felt his knees buckle a little, too, and they both had to hold on to each other.

"Wow." Breathlessly, she stared at him. "That was—"

"Unforgettable." Very softly, Reno kissed her again.

Rachel tugged his coat lapels. "More please."

"Later."

"Now."

"I'd be more than happy to oblige, but you might regret that." Grinning, Reno nodded to the side. "We have an audience."

With no warning at all, the whole diner erupted in cheers and applause and foot-stomping. Feeling herself blush, Rachel turned to see everyone in the place unabashedly watching them, from her revelation-causing waitress to Judy Wright. Some people crowded closer to Rachel's and Reno's position near the cash register to hear, some craned their necks to see, and a few sat on the tops of their bench seats to catch the entire show.

Only a few feet away stood a particularly conspicuous group of onlookers, all looking as though they'd just burst into the diner at the last moment. In the middle of them, Angela wiped away a joyful tear. Nate hugged her, his eyes suspiciously red-rimmed. Kayla sat on the floor with a white puppy in her lap, oblivious to the adults' goings-on. Tom Wright, Jimmy Gurche, and a broadly grinning man Rachel didn't know cheered them on. Even Mrs. Kowalczyk was there, offering a winking thumbs-up.

The older woman caught Reno looking at her. She struck a defiant pose. "What? You thought we'd miss *this*? No way, José!"

Reno laughed and hugged Rachel to him. Happily, she glanced up at him. "Is everyone always this nice in Kismet?"

"No," Reno deadpanned. "After Christmas we become zombies."

Grinning, Rachel smacked his chest. "Be serious."

"Okay." Tucking a hank of hair behind her ear, Reno eyed her very gravely. "The truth is, everyone really *is* this nice. Once a Kismet Muskrat, always a Kismet Muskrat. Nobody can stay away. Once you get sucked back in, we've got you forever."

"I am *not* a muskrat!"

" . . . said the former KHS Muskrats goth cheerleader."

"Oh yeah." Rachel wrinkled her nose. "You've got me there."

"I've got you. Period." Reno gazed into her eyes. He shook his head. "And I'm never letting you go."

"Awwww," the crowd gushed all around them.

But Rachel was too busy kissing Reno again to pay attention to the applause. She was too busy loving Reno, too busy holding him, and too busy realizing that if she never got another gift for Christmas for the rest of her life, she would feel perfectly content. Because all she really wanted was Reno.

Reno, her newly polished self-respect, and a chance at a brand-new future. Beginning right now, it looked as though all three of those things were within her grasp. Starting with Reno.

Feeling a devilish streak of her own, Rachel leaned into Reno, put her head on his shoulder . . . then made her move.

"Whoa!" Reno jerked, his surprised gaze meeting hers. "Did you just grab my butt?"

"With both hands, tough guy." She grinned. "You might as well get used to it. When you live with Kismet's number one rebel, there'll be a lot of that going on."

"I—" Grabbing his delectable backside, mouth open, Reno gawked at her. Then he grinned. "I can hardly wait. Come on."

Chapter Forty-One

As Reno was surprised to learn, there was no place on earth more Christmassy than Christine and Gerry Porter's Glenrosen home, just down the street from his, on Christmas morning.

Their decorated tree sparkled, resplendent with *almost* enough light wattage. Not a square inch of balsam fir had escaped being loaded with tinsel, homemade ornaments, old-fashioned bubble lights, garland, or all four of those things. Beneath the tree, the SantaLand Express chugged past a village of homey ceramic buildings. Mountains of wrapping paper and bows—remnants of the festive gift-opening party they'd just held—lay crumpled atop the tree's homemade quilted skirt.

On the TV, a Yule log burned—crackling and snapping in full HD clarity—with Christmas carols playing as an accompaniment. Several pots of poinsettias and blooming amaryllis bordered the Porters' living room, greeting cards overflowed from the foyer to the entertainment center, and on every horizontal surface stood candles, garland, animated Santas, and ceramic Rudolphs.

Truly, the whole thing would have been overkill . . . if not for the fact that it was finally Christmas, and if not for the unabashed joy the display had brought to Rachel's face as she'd ushered Reno, hand in hand, into the family's annual version of Christmas when he'd arrived for breakfast this morning.

He glanced at the fireplace, filled with a crafted wicker basket full of ornaments and garland. The Porters didn't want to fuss with an actual smoking Yule log on their hearth, but they had gone to some trouble to make the area Christmassy, with tall candles ringed with mistletoe and four stockings, all in a row.

The stocking that bore Reno's name appeared a little worse for the wear. There was a stiletto-shaped mended spot in the toe. The embroidered part of his name looked ragged, too. All the same, looking at it now gave Reno a warm and fuzzy feeling. He liked it here. He liked it here with Rachel. He liked being part of a family who, whatever their differences, always loved one another . . . a lot like his family did. Eventually.

On the other hand, there were a few drawbacks.

Groaning, Reno clutched his stomach. Technically, his abs still felt as taut to the touch as ever, but he couldn't shake the feeling that he'd packed on his fake Santa belly for real. "Christine, you're going to kill me with breakfast! That special holiday French toast . . . what was in that? It was amazing."

"Oh, not much." Rachel's mother looked pleased. "A little cream. Some eggs. Nutmeg, of course. Some very good brioche."

"That's it?" If only Nate were here. Nate could probably replicate a recipe like that. But Nate was spending the morning with Angela and Kayla. Reno wouldn't meet up with them until later, when he and Rachel traveled to his parents' house for the first (of many) Christmases together. "That sounds easy."

"Don't let her fool you." With his reading glasses on, Gerry Porter glanced up from the newspaper. He, an intransigent geek, was reading the *Kismet Comet* in digital form on his PDA, after having given sections of the printed newspaper to Rachel. "She'll never tell you her secret Christmas French toast recipe. She hooked me with it when we were still dating, and I've been trying to finagle it out of her for years."

" . . . a little orange zest," Christine hinted. "Butter—"

"I need a pen to write this down." Maybe Nate could still reconstruct it. Reno glanced around, caught sight of Rachel on the sofa beside him, and forgot what he was doing altogether. Even wearing her fuzzy-hooded sweater and jeans—with no miniskirt and no boots—she still looked drop-dead sexy to him. He was the luckiest man on the planet. Not only had he skipped out on being a punter, he'd scored the best woman around.

" . . . and a whole lot of love," Christine was saying in a dreamy, satisfied voice. "That's all there is to it, Reno."

Reno snapped out of his reverie just in time to see Gerry Porter gawking at his wife. "It's got *what* in it? I couldn't quite make that out, honey. Can you say that again?"

"Nope." Going back to her knitting, Christine shook her head. "It was only for Reno. Now that he's part of the family."

"But Reno didn't even hear you!" Gerry protested. "He was too busy mooning over Rachel to pay attention!"

"Hmmm." Christine gave a small smile. "That's too bad."

"Arrgh!" Gerry gave her an aggrieved look. "So close."

"And yet so far." Smiling, Rachel folded back a newspaper page, then held it up to them. "Look. We made the paper!"

Reno leaned forward. He immediately recognized the photo that accompanied the article in the *Community* section. It had been taken yesterday, at the annual Glenrosen block party. In it, Reno stood beside Rachel in front of his fully decorated and light-bedecked house and yard, beaming for the camera.

He looked like a complete goofball. A goofball in love.

"See?" Rachel waggled the newsprint. "*Kismet's Christmas Couple*, the headline says. Isn't that sweet? It's all about us. About how we met and how I helped decorate your house."

She glanced down to read aloud, but Reno lost track of everything again. Her nose was so cute, her expression so intent, her mouth so luscious as it formed the words.

He tried to catch a tidbit here and there as Rachel shared

the reporter's version of how Reno had *not* won the Glenrosen holiday lights competition (that honor had gone to Hal—who, in a controversy, had admitted hiring professionals to set up his display), how the rules for winning the Bronze Extension Cord were being fervently debated, and how Reno Wright—because of his daring and ingenuity—had been awarded a special prize.

"Ooh! A special prize sounds nice!" Christine enthused.

"It's a *plaque*," Reno muttered, but he didn't really mind not winning this year. There was always next year. Besides . . .

" . . . who won an engraved plaque," Rachel read aloud, "for signifying extraordinary creativity and exemplifying the true meaning of Christmas. Congratulations to Reno Wright!"

Beaming, she glanced up from the text. A smattering of applause came from Christine and Gerry, then Rachel's father squinted at the newsprint. "Show us the other photo, honey."

"There's another photo?" Reno didn't remember posing for another photo. All he remembered was Rachel, hot spiced cider, and not needing the hot spiced cider to make Rachel easy *or* to make himself look twice as good to her, as he'd described to her from her snowy yard on the day after they'd met. "Really?"

"Really." With relish, Rachel turned around the newsprint. Right there, below the fold, was . . .

"Oh, it's so sweet!" Christine clasped her hands.

"It'll do," Gerry muttered. But he couldn't hide a grin.

"It's *perfect*," Rachel exclaimed.

Her gaze met his, and Reno had to agree. No matter how surprised he was to see it there in blurry newsprint. No matter how embarrassed a big, tough, former football star like him should have felt to see his rooftop holiday lights display caught on film for everyone in town to see. Especially since, in vertical three-foot letters, painstakingly framed in miniature lights, that display spelled out the absolute truth:

RENO LOVES RACHEL.FOREVER.

Across the room, Christine sighed again. "So romantic."

"You can blame your daughter," Reno said. "Rachel helped—"

Suddenly, his cell phone beeped. Reno frowned at the interruption. He glanced at the text message displayed there.

flat tire. need help! Nate.

Momentarily distracted, Reno fisted his phone. He should help. He should . . . He should text Nate back right away.

call AAA. merry Xmas. Reno.

Reno put away his phone. "Rachel helped with the display."

"I didn't help do *this*!" Rachel hugged the newspaper.

"Yes, you did," Reno insisted. "When I was on the roof, what did you think you were doing up on that ladder?"

Rachel peered upward, remembering. "Handing you lights."

"Right. Lights to spell out RENO LOVES RACHEL. FOREVER."

"No way!" Blushing prettily, Rachel shook her head.

"Way." He leaned sideways and kissed her. "The whole world might as well know it. Because it will always be true."

"Oh." Happily, Rachel bumped her knees against his, awkwardly kissing him back. "For me, too. I love you, Reno."

"I love you, too. Merry Christmas."

"Merry Christmas!"

They kissed again, surrounded by holiday music and bathed in the Christmas tree's multicolored sparkling lights.

Gerry and Christine tactfully went on reading and knitting, but for Reno, there wasn't anything more important than reveling in his time with Rachel. Openly. Honestly. At least until they both turned into zombies on December 26th.

Kidding.

"Hey, you two. Your lips are going to get blistered if you don't take a break." Smiling, Christine glanced up. "Is there anything in the newspaper about your new venture, Rachel?"

With visible reluctance, Rachel disengaged from Reno. Somehow the newspaper had gotten wedged beneath her thigh during all the kissing, but she managed to extract its crumpled pages.

"Yes, there's a sidebar: 'Rachel Porter, former Los Angeles celebrity stylist, is currently offering one-on-one personal shopping expeditions to the people of Kismet and surrounding areas,'" she read. "'Those services are expected to wane as Porter's new design venture, Imagination-Squared, gets off the ground early next year. Featuring designer apparel created from deconstructed clothes, Imagination-Squared is—'"

"Does that mean you'll be ripping apart more clothes?"

"Yes, Dad." Smiling patiently, Rachel nodded. "'—expected to feature exclusive items refashioned from celebrity castoffs, including clothing worn by such stars as Tiana Zane, Cody, and the cast of the hit TV show *Sweetwater*, to be sold online and in local boutiques.'" She glanced up, clearly energized. "See, I always knew it was a shame that celebrities often wore garments only once, then didn't want to be seen in them again. This way, all those clothes will be put to good use."

"Good idea," Gerry said. "Recycling. Very hippie-dippy."

"Did I tell you?" Rachel went on. "Mimi's coming to visit after Christmas. We're going to be partners!" She squeezed Reno's knee, leaning toward him. "Mimi's going to love you!"

"Congratulations." Rachel's mother beamed at her. "I always knew you could do it. I'll be first in line for a sweater."

"I think you'll have to wait." Reno plucked at the shoulder seams of his new sweater—a Christmas gift from Rachel. He lifted his chin proudly. "I'm pretty sure I got the first one."

"You did." Rachel snuggled up to him. "You're not going to believe it, but that used to be two vintage sweaters and a pair of boots. I tore them all apart and sewed them together again."

Whatever it was, it was all right with Reno. As long as it came from Rachel . . . and as long as she'd made it with love.

"What about you, Reno?" Cutting the sentimental aura with a piercing glance, Gerry Porter looked his way.

"Will you be selling out to Multicorp? Franchising The Wright Stuff?"

"I'm sure it would be very lucrative," Christine said.

But Reno shook his head. "Nah. I turned down Derek's offer. Franchising wasn't the answer for me. I like helping people at the store. But I will be keeping Mrs. Kowalczyk on staff. She's a wonder. And I will be taking some more time off."

"Time to spend with me," Rachel announced. "We've already talked about it. After we go back to California to get all my stuff—the things that are *really* mine at least—Reno and I will have lots to do together. As soon as I tap into my nest egg—"

"Nest egg?" Her father raised his eyebrows. "That's not very fashionable is it? I heard practicality was passé."

Rachel made a face. "Not with me, Dad. I made a lot of money in my old job, but I saved a lot, too."

"See? We raised her right, Gerry," Christine said.

"I'll have to lease a workspace, draw up a business plan, start sourcing materials, hire a Web site designer—"

Gerry Porter waggled his eyebrows meaningfully.

"—and *that's* just for the wedding planning!" Rachel said.

Her parents gawked at her. Reno only smiled.

He didn't see a problem with getting married. Otherwise he *definitely* wouldn't have presented Rachel with that engagement ring last night on Christmas Eve. And she definitely wouldn't have accepted it, squealing and laughing and crying. At once.

"So." He pulled her close, getting in on the action before Rachel could regale everyone with talk of zippers, sergers, antique fabrics, and "foundation garments" (whatever those were). "Rachel, maybe you can finally settle a bet for me."

Smiling, Rachel nodded. "I'm sure I can."

"Which one's better?" Reno asked. "An L.A. Christmas or a Kismet Christmas?"

Interestedly, Gerry and Christine watched them both.

"Hmm." Looking adorably perplexed, Rachel gazed up at

the ceiling, mulling over his question. "You know, I *am* a die-hard nouveau California girl. I like sunshine and surfing and seventy-degree weather as much as the next person. So there's a lot to be said for L.A. But I have to admit," she added, "when it comes to Christmas—and the company that goes along with it—nothing can beat a Kismet Christmas. It's the very best Christmas of all."

"Mmm." Reno nodded. "I guess that means I win."

Rachel's answering smile made his heart feel twice as big.

"Nope. It means we *both* win."

She was right, Reno knew as the televised Yule log burned and the Christmas lights twinkled and the *Kismet Comet* was passed hand to hand (and then commandeered by Christine for a future scrapbooking project). Because a Kismet Christmas really was the best Christmas of all. Especially when it came wrapped up with a brand-new happily-ever-after for him and Rachel . . . and the promise of many more just like it still to come.

Dear Reader,

Thank you for reading *Home for the Holidays*! I hope you had fun. This can be a crazy time of year, but I absolutely love the holiday season. With Rachel's and Reno's story, I tried my best to bring a little of that Christmastime magic to you. As Reno would say, "Ho ho ho!"

Are you curious about how to make Nate's can't-fail fudge? Christine's top-secret Christmas French toast? As a bonus for you, I've posted the recipes for both goodies on my Web site at www.lisaplumley.com. Please stop by and try them! While you're there, you can also sign up for new-book alerts or my reader newsletter, read sneak previews of upcoming books, request special reader freebies, and more. I hope you'll visit today.

In the meantime, I'd love to hear from you! You can send e-mail to lisa@lisaplumley.com, "friend" me on MySpace at www.myspace.com/lisaplumley, or write to me c/o P.O. Box 7105, Chandler, AZ 85246-7105.

Here's wishing you the very merriest of Christmases!

Happy holidays,
Lisa Plumley